GOING
UNDER

Also by Justina Robson from Gollancz:

Keeping It Real
Selling Out

QUANTUM GRAVITY: 3

GOING UNDER

Justina Robson

GOLLANCZ
LONDON

The right of Justina Robson to be identified as the
author of this work has been asserted by her in accordance
with the Copyright, Designs and Patents Act 1988.

First published in Great Britain in 2008 by
Gollancz
An imprint of the Orion Publishing Group
Orion House, 5 Upper St Martin's Lane,
London WC2H 9EA
An Hachette Livre UK Company

A CIP catalogue record for this book is
available from the British Library

ISBN 978 0 575 07866 6 (Cased)
ISBN 978 0 575 07867 3 (Trade Paperback)

1 3 5 7 9 10 8 6 4 2

Typeset at The Spartan Press Ltd,
Lymington, Hants

Printed in Great Britain by CPI Mackays,
Chatham ME5 8TD

The Orion Publishing Group's policy is to use papers that
are natural, renewable and recyclable products and made
from wood grown in sustainable forests. The logging and
manufacturing processes are expected to conform to the
environmental regulations of the country of origin.

www.orionbooks.co.uk

CHAPTER ONE

An unkempt dawn with ragged clouds crept to daybreak in Daemonia. Fitful winds swung the gather-baskets outside the windows and made small trails of raw magic fizz and evaporate out of their tiny holes as Lila watched them move to and fro. Presently the grumbling, muttering form of the Collector appeared on Lila's balcony.

The old demon was almost petrified with age but his movements were sure. Horned, thorned, blue and knot-sided he climbed along the walls on his sticky feet and plucked the baskets from their hooks, replacing them with empties and chucking the full ones into a large sack on his back with all the expertise of a hundred years of practice. He ignored her, even though she was standing right in front of the full-height windows that overlooked her private balcony and in turn she fixed her stare beyond the western edge of the city to the lagoon. It wasn't polite to stare at old demons and they had some interesting curses to award for gawpers.

One of the Collector's feet adhered briefly to the crystal pane in a biologist's miracle of exquisitely tiny scales, hairs and magic, then was gone without leaving a mark. It was said there was no surface that those creatures (she couldn't remember the name, there were more kinds of demon than there were species in Otopia) couldn't walk on, even the face of eternity.

They said a lot of things like that in Daemonia, Lila reflected. To a human these gnarly little gnosticisms became irritating and portentous after a while. It was even more irritating later on at some point, if you stuck around, to discover that most of them were true. A frown made itself on her brow as she drew her silk dressing gown closer around her and folded her arms more tightly. The sight of the rising city was not comforting.

In the dawn's light the dirigibles and boats that never ceased to ply the air and water dimmed their enchantments and changed their signal flags from the glowing night colours to day's brilliant but ordinary hues. Blimps and zeppelins lost their resemblance to giant lightning bugs and became simple balloons. Then the giant gaudy fancy of the Théâtre des Artes suddenly blazed up from the Mousa Precinct as the sun rose high enough to catch its roof. Lila changed the filtering in her eyes to adjust for the shocking glare and continued her monitoring of the activity – demons everywhere, busy, active, full of energy as if there was no tomorrow. She felt tired with the kind of tiredness that follows frenetic activity, fear and grief once it has all passed. Pleasant, but still tired and in need of a lengthy, solitary rest.

There was a sigh and a yawn from behind her in the room. It was followed by the soft sound of silk sheets. From the voice's tone she knew it was her husband, Zal, turning over and stretching out into her part of the bed. He was a heavy sleeper, for an elf, and had a fondness for pretending to lie comatose late into the morning whilst secretly being awake the entire time and composing songs in his head. He said it was the best time of day to imagine new things, before you opened your eyes and the world grabbed your attention and tried to make it fit yesterday instead of today. So she guessed he was wide awake, and faking.

A messenger sprite, decked in house colours, flitted up over her railing and deposited yet another covered basket with a beribboned handle on to the balcony floor after a momentary struggle to find a space among all the other baskets that were already set there, covering the table, the chairs and some of the larger plant pots. It tipped its ridiculous little blue porter's cap to her when the job was done and zipped off over the roof, farting methane that ignited on contact with its sparking tail and sent it jolting into the sky. The wind made all the ribbons flutter and dance. A few minutes later the clouds disbanded entirely and the sun shone with spring heat through the windows. It was deliciously warm.

Lila heard padding sounds just behind her and turned to look. A white demon, griffonesque, dragonish, horsey, with feathers and fur and quills and the air of a big cat, had crossed the floor. It lay down in the lozenge of sunlight beside her and closed its long, silver eyes to enjoy the heat. Its lengthy tail was curled upwards in a semicircle of pleasure as it made minor adjustments to reach perfect basking posture and settled down. Its wings, with their thorny and razored edges, were furled neatly along its back. Its ribs moved under its iridescent skin as it breathed and elsewhere thin muscles like iron bands ran in ropes of efficient power that looked dynamic even though it was, she was certain, already and properly asleep again after its move. Teazle, her husband, could sleep for Daemonia.

He could fall asleep at the drop of a hat though she had always found him getting up halfway through the night. He would fall asleep in human form, out of politeness but then slide out of bed to shift to this, his natural shape. This was unsuited to humanoid beds and had a tendency to rip sheets and mattresses. He had his own nest that hung from the ceiling like a giant beehive. He said that the luxurious furs that made it up were all stripped from the bodies of his enemies but he might have been lying. Most demons just didn't have such great fur.

Husband. What a stupid word that was. Wife. That was even stupider. Both carried a vast and toxic cargo of expectations and she could only stomach the associations for an instant because Zal was an elf demon and Teazle was a demon and the marriage was Daemonian in nature and had nothing to do with her human culture's hulking great trainloads of stupidity. Some people, she understood, found marriage and its roles a pleasantly comforting drama to enact. A shudder and a vision of her parents, screaming at one another through a fog of alcoholic disappointment invariably accompanied thoughts about it. As her mother gambled away fortunes and then flung herself into torments of guilt and self-loathing her father became sweetly dutiful and the picture of noble caretaking. Then, as their finances recovered and Mom got increasingly bored and began to fuss around the house, he would quietly pickle himself with vodka until he lost his job. Mom would then solve their problems by entering various poker tournaments at which, sober and determined, she would do well, until recklessness took over and so the cycle began again . . . Lila had, by the age of fourteen, long since given up the hope that this round would be the last of its kind and something banal and comforting would take its place.

Death had brought the curtain down on that one. How curious that in death they should so quickly forget the petty occupations that had obsessed every living moment. But they had. She'd met them there, in the afterworld, and it was as though they had never struggled. Her heart stabbed her with pain as she remembered, because in their faces,

3

just before they had crossed over the final brink to Thanatopia's unknown shores, she had seen their lonely and sober knowledge that the lives that were over had mostly been wasted. And there was nothing to be done about it. Nothing at all.

And she had not saved them.

Until they were dead she hadn't even known that was her mission in life. Her firm, yet unacknowledged plan: she would make a successful career, save plenty of money, become socially impeccable and marry someone also of that mould in order to set an example and to become wealthy enough to start both parents off in detox programmes that really worked . . . gaining their undying love and gratitude and, above all, attention. No, that motive hadn't revealed its tawdry martyred glory until she was back in her own body, what was left of it, and they were gone for good.

Are you going to maunder along all day? murmured a testy voice just to the left of the middle of her head.

She shot a dart of sullen loathing at Tath, the presence in her chest.

The elf made the spiritual equivalent of a shrug as his aetheric body – the last surviving fragment of his being – circulated slowly around inside her heart where he had lived since his physical death, months ago. He sounded as precise and chilly as a mathematics professor intent on lecturing a tardy student even though – and, she thought, possibly because – he had been young and full of hopes when he died. *Demons usually vent their rage more creatively. Let us do something excessive.*

You hate demon ways.

I am beginning to find them curiously liberating. At least they do not hate themselves more than once a day.

Stop badgering.

Stop wallowing.

Trauma much? I'm allowed some wallow time.

I cannot see the point of it.

Lila flicked at her sleeve, flicking away his comment as she glared down at the sleeping white demon near her feet. She let Tath have his superiority, since it was all he'd got, but damn if he didn't test her to the limit. She wanted to scream but that would entail a conversation with the living afterwards.

Teazle didn't know about Tath's permanent residency – his *andalune* body supported by her physical one. Only Zal knew, as far as she was

4

aware, and she intended to keep it that way but Tath was unhappy and restless in a human host; anyone would be, she reasoned, if they were a helpless passenger in somebody else's body. She ought to be more compassionate towards him, but she was tired of his eternal presence too, never knowing how much of her feeling and thoughts he was privy to. It made intimacy difficult with others whilst between Tath and herself their enforced closeness was like a wound that could open at any time and must be carefully protected. Since her parents had been murdered she and Tath had entered a strange and sympathetic truce of sorts and as time passed they had naturally become more relaxed about the whole thing. She didn't like that. She wanted it to stay frosty and uncomfortable as that was the only distance possible. It ate at her that eventually casual attitudes would lead to a nasty truth as she started another round of

. . . marital bitching? He said, beating her to it.

Thank you.

Yes, marital bitching, with him.

I have not married you, human.

I wouldn't marry you, elf, if you were the last person alive.

Fortunately that situation will never arise, Tath said with sufficient frost that she had cause to stop and doubt his sincerity for a moment. But she was too anxious to think on it, instead rushing into another defence,

I hope you didn't find last night too . . . soiling. She was surprised at the stinging tone of her thought, which amply conveyed her embarrassment and anger at being perpetually spied upon, whether wilfully or not. It was a struggle not to let any memory surface for his perusal: she clearly saw one image of Zal naked.

I kept my promise. I have no idea what you are talking about. Did you all enact some dire orgy together? Who knew such an innocent little thing like yourself could be capable of that sort of debauchery?

Lila's fear and anger suddenly evaporated and she snorted with laughter.

I overdid it?

You can't carry off Puritan, she told him. *It's not your nature.*

Tath grumbled but she sensed that he was pleased. She was reasonably sure that he hadn't missed a trick either. At least he had been

5

completely discreet about it and that was about the only mercy she was going to get.

She moved to the wall and pressed her face for a moment against the cool stone of the pillar that supported the window arch. Its solidity was reassuring. Memories of other kinds: her parents walking away to the cruise liner that would take them far from Thanatopia's fragile shores into the infinite: an imagined vision of Zal's first wife, Adai, taking the same journey, forlorn aboard an airship with white wings: these visions came as they always did, accompanied by a flood of guilt and sadness. And then other visions – darker and less certain. These came later, tripping trapping across the bridge of suspicion: she was not the first person to be made over using the Bomb-fault technology. There had been others. Surely. What happened to them? The existence of remote controllers was proven, but not how many there were, or of what kind. The intentions of those who held them were also a mystery. And for how long could she attempt to embrace the demon life when she was no demon? Or an elven life, being no elf, nor anything but herself – and even that not what she had dreamed it a few scant months before.

Something moving caught the corner of her eye and she looked up to see the imp, Thingamajig, hopping over the baskets on the balcony towards the door. He pressed his small, hideous face to the glass and stared at her; the pet who could not come in. On the carpet, Teazle yawned and hooked some loops with his claws in a satisfied sort of way that seemed entirely in keeping with his leisurely pose but which signalled to Lila that he was highly alert. Teazle didn't have a lot of time for imps; possibly less than ten seconds.

Outside, Thingamajig was doing an elaborate mime. When she frowned at him he went off and shortly returned with a dead bird. He tore out the tail feathers and stuck them to his bottom and then held the loose-necked head in front of his face. Then he dropped his props and wiggled his fingers close to his eyes before stretching his arms out, indicating all directions. Satisfied from the change on her face that she had understood he returned to yanking ribbons off the baskets and licking them for traces of aether.

'He's right,' Teazle murmured without opening his eyes. His tail twitched. 'You should go and see her. It's time.'

'If it's time why is he still here?' she folded her arms and watched the imp's activities. 'Surely I'm still Hell-bound if he hasn't gone away of his own accord?'

Teazle grunted, 'Unlike most imps he seems to have an agenda that goes beyond tormenting the damned.' He sounded vaguely intrigued, but only vaguely. 'If that weren't the case I'd have eaten him already. But he hasn't been on your shoulder in a week, and that's good enough. Will you go alone?'

She knew enough about the white demon by now to know that a leading question from him was always a taunting opportunity in the making; if she said no she'd drop in his estimation and his power over her – always a factor that must be accounted for, even with demons with whom you were intimate – would rise. This was a world where yielding to fear had dire consequences.

'I'll get dressed and take a flight,' she said casually, not wishing in the slightest to make the visit.

'Zal and I will amuse ourselves,' Teazle murmured, making it sound in just those few words as though he had elaborate plans that would involve a great deal of life-threatening activity. No doubt he did. Lila wondered just how long they could survive a vacation in Daemonia. 'Don't worry your human head about it,' was added into her silence.

'I don't have a human head,' she said and turned around, heading towards the bathroom.

'Heart then,' the demon said with surprising fondness. 'I know you love him. I'll be sure and be the first to die.'

She couldn't think of an adequate reply to that, so she just went and took her bath.

CHAPTER TWO

Thingamajig rode on Lila's shoulder to the Souk. He babbled anxiously all the way about whatever caught his attention and, instead of his customary piercing of her earlobe with his sharp talon, he clutched the cloth of her padded vest in a vice-like grip.

'Can't you sit still? I don't know what *you* have to be nervous about,' she said crossly. The day was hot and humid, the roads seemingly full of lazy, torpid demons who were content to simply stare at her and mutter or else call various congratulations or deathwishes on her marriage. They oiled from their idleness into sudden huddles as she passed. She wanted to smack them, but for once nobody seemed in the mood for a duel.

Occasionally, strangers attempted to press small gifts on her, as she had been warned they would, and she directed them to the servant behind her whom Teazle had instructed to collect and check all items. The servant had already sent one full bag back to the house. Lila hoped that personalised thank you notes were not required, but reasoned that for what amounted to bribes, they were almost certainly not. The House of Ahriman had been a major demon cabal and the House of Sikarza was in a similar position before the wedding. Now their joint power was vast. Everybody who wasn't allied to one of the great families was angling for a position with them.

The imp by her ear came to the end of his babbling history of the allegiances of the House of Ceriza, which they had passed some time ago, and made an unhappy noise before piping, 'I have more business than you being damn nervous. She . . .' But he wasn't able to go on. In fact the word as he said it was so loaded with dread and the impossibility of escape, that it was quite sufficient.

'You will tell her that you want me around strictly on a retainer basis, won't you?' he asked, for the thousandth time. 'I mean you'll say it quickly. I don't want her getting the wrong idea and banishing me before you get to say it when you really intend to keep your promise and help me discover my true identity, which is your mission, you and the others, to do good things, like heroes of old, eh? Like the Maha Animae of the old days. You'd not let a small friend such as myself languish in the abysses of the infinite like just any old imp, waiting for some hopeless neurotic to walk past and pull them back into physical being with the force of their madness, would you? No. That would be a terrible thing indeed. And who knows where I might be stuck? I could be stuck halfway up the sky over the Lagoon and not even in the city, and then what would the chances be of some possessed dimwit flapping by close enough to pull me free of the miserable torment of limbo? None. Not for thousands and thousands and thousands . . .' He continued for a second as Lila's hand clamped over his head but then stopped as she closed the implacable machinery of her fist.

'I'll mention it,' Lila said in a very even voice, speeding up her tread to a pace just short of running. 'Oh, I'm sorry, I seem to be crushing your skull . . .' She let go.

The imp remained motionless for a moment, then very carefully rubbed its face against her vest. 'You have the tender mercies of a goddess. I shall say no more.' And it didn't, although it vibrated with anxiety so violently she started to feel that his talking had been a better option.

Madame Des Loupes was the greatest clairvoyant of the age. Lila had met her before, and taken tea. Nothing bad had happened. She had been given no dire prophecies or information, and the tea was good. Madame had been infallibly correct and polite about Lila's descent into Hell, Lila thought. A pity for Lila that she had imagined fiery morasses and roasting spits instead of intense emotional and mental anguish but, either way, forewarned was not forearmed.

She had not understood her personal situation until much too late. Too late she realised that when a demon talked about living in Hell it meant you were living inside the worlds of your own illusions. Demons considered this a form of victimhood – you were a victim of an inaccurate reality. This made you easy meat for anyone who could push your buttons, whatever they were. And for those who were without illusion, seeing the hotspots of other people's lies, self-deceptions, motivations and fears was simple.

Lila still wasn't sure it was *human* to live without some illusions and to see what was there as clearly as the demons claimed to see it although seeing of reality for what it was . . . that had a power she couldn't deny. But again, it wasn't a power you could wield like a sword. It was a power you could follow, like a current, or you might fight and swim against it and drown. Either way you might drown in fact. Just knowing what things were like wouldn't save you from them any more than knowing how a volcano works would save you from a fiery death if you got close to one that was going up.

Lila had once thought that all great powers of that kind, such as seeing The Truth and suchlike, were the powers of champions which would grant a kind of immunity from harm. They seemed legendary and otherworldly, supernatural abilities for the rare people who were spiritually developed enough to have gained them. But no. They were not like that at all. The only thing you had to do to acquire them was to stop fooling yourself (though that was not easy when you had spent a lifetime being bamboozled into your illusions by other bamboozled people who came from great long heritages of similarly bamboozled people who all had very good and proud reasons for wanting to believe bamboozling things).

However, the visionary gifts of the champions who saw truly – which she had thought of as so grandly elevated and conferring great privilege – showed instead the limits of one's power; what one might do, or might not, and when. She got that now. Compared to the dreams she used to cultivate about knowing everything; dreams in which everything was so obvious that it was only a matter of doing the right thing at the right moment to ensure the whole world turned in a more favourable direction – why, the realisations of her own mistakes in so believing were like repeated slaps in the face with a wet, week-old dead fish. Look at Mom and Dad, who had finally seen through their self-destructiveness in the moments of their death, but never bothered to do so in life when it could have been of use. And look at Lila, who had shored them up in their folly with her protective lies and deceptions, while despising them secretly and pretending the entire thing was loving care. The horrific and pointless waste of it made her eyes prick with tears and her throat close with pain. And to think *she* had been going to show *them* with her nice job and her superior sense of how to organise life, exactly how to be better people when she was busy blaming her sister for leaving home and bailing out and saying rude, nasty things about Mom and Dad . . .

Yes, the vision of the demons was hard to take. Because she felt she had at least managed to face most of its revelations, Lila was not as scared of Madame as she might be. But then, that was perhaps due to the limits of her vision, she thought, whereas Thingamajig was much better informed about Madame, even if he had forgotten exactly in what ways. Lila had no idea and so she was content to go and find out if Madame was prepared to, somehow, let her out of Hell, for Madame had that power at least. Lila knew, because Madame had given it to Zal.

A thought struck her as she turned through the beaded door of the Souk; its soul-guards tinkling in the wind with the sound of a thousand tiny sighs, 'Is that why you're an imp then, because you wouldn't acknowledge some truth?'

'It was not a truth,' Thingamajig snapped, emphasising the last word. 'It was a *conjecture*. An hypothesis. A notion. An idea unverified by scientific observations. A matter,' he intoned with the utmost loathing, 'of *opinion*.'

'What was?'

'I don't remember,' he said hopelessly and fell into a slump.

Lila set her eyes to tunnel vision as they began to pass the esoteric stalls. She had seen them once and once was enough. Part of her wanted to look again, to reinforce its belief that living things preserved in fluids twitched in bottles and much worse things lay dead in various ways . . . but she didn't indulge herself. The dark magics were as practised as any other skill in Daemonia; to artistic perfection, and beyond, to *zeotika* – corruption.

She was afraid she might see necromancers' vials, and if she did how could she pass, knowing what they held? Souls, or spirits, or whatever aetheric portions of beings could be detached from the gross mortal body would be imprisoned there. The bodies themselves might be in any state. No, she didn't want to see them and to know, from Tath, what they were for. She didn't want to feel his own cocktail of repulsion and desire. It felt shamefully weak, but to survive this world it didn't pay to bring your human sensibilities too close to the surface.

Lila remembered when Tath had *eaten* Teazle's brother. The glorious

11

vampirism. The thrilling jolt of power, the gluttonous, eager bite that seized the spirit and shredded it to nothing more than primal energy.

No, she didn't want to think about that. In her chest Tath was utterly silent, a suspended shimmer of presence no more intrusive than a breath of air. He and she were so closely attuned now that they rarely needed to speak, although they frequently did, to pretend that they didn't feel one another's hearts. Of their secrets, they were each other's keeper. How soon that had come about . . . how easily.

Lila's view widened as she cleared the narrow walk with its over-hanging webs of fine floating coloured gauze and came to one of the major ways that led to the Souk's ancient heart. Along this passage there were fewer items on display and they were all artworks of various kinds; sculptures, paintings, fabrics . . . every kind of designable item. In the dim interiors of the old plaster-daub warehouses demons worked to pack things into crates and to load crates on to pallets which waited for nightfall when the trade closed and the streets admitted the passage of goods carts. She saw some marked for Otopia and, without any awareness of the long machine processes involved in the research that her AI performed, she understood that their barcodes directed them to Home Depot. She wondered if the buyers had any idea what the demons were capable of doing with apparently ordinary items, but that was a Customs matter, not for her to concern herself with.

'Wait wait wait!'

A blurt from the imp shook her out of her surreptitious spying. She slowed down and then stopped. They were alone in a narrow coil where the buildings blotted out most of the sky with their overhang-ing upper storeys, their flags and hoardings and drying laundry. She saw Thingamajig's skinny arm pointing to a stand of unremarkable statues set close by the pavement. Rows of varying sized demon models were ranked on cheap wooden shelving, held in place by lengths of rough twine. They looked like they were cast in resin, or some kind of clay.

'Go closer!'

Oh. My. God.

Lila raised her eyebrows at this double jeopardy taunt and questions flicked through her mind. 'What is it?' She idled across and pretended to browse the statues. On closer inspection she realised the workman-ship was exquisite on every single one. They were models of demons in various dramatic poses, and incredibly lifelike. Every scale and hair was minutely rendered and the smallest ones were small enough to have fitted into a small pocket. Paper price tags were stuck to each one and after doing the conversion she thought they were reasonably good value, if you liked that kind of thing. They were coloured, but not as brightly as real demons, as if the trend in that particular art leaned towards a muted understatement.

The imp crawled down the front of her vest, claws clinging, and hung there, fixated. 'It's really him.'

She tracked his gaze and found him looking at one of the largest pieces, almost waist high to her – standing to the side of the shelved items.

It's really him, Tath echoed with a profound irony she didn't understand.

The statue had a lot of horns and was various hues of red and orange. Large leathery wings and a spined tail were half extended, as though it was about to do something. Its face wore an expression of annoyance and the mouth was partway open.

'Someone you know?'

'Knew,' the imp said softly. 'Yes indeed, the leader of my Precinct. A fearless hunter of the unrighteous he was, not only a mage but gifted with a shaman's powers to call on the land. Rare. His art was geomancy. He could flatten cities with a stamp of his hoof or raise towns out of living rock. Made a lot of money in building. Had a whole passel of architects and pretty much the entire business all paid a tithe to him in some way or other. No way you could put up anything if he didn't like you. He'd destabilise your foundations and make your materials fall into dust. A right bugger, he was.' It had grown thoughtful on the last few phrases and stared closely. 'Just look at the size of him. Very powerful. How much is he?'

Lila looked for a tag but there was none . . . and at that moment the shopkeeper came out. She was thin and tall and green, with beautiful fins on her head. 'May I help you?'

'I was just wondering how much this statue is,' Lila said.

The finned demon raised a membranous eyebrow. 'Indeed. He's not for sale at home. Export only. Are you perhaps a trader from Otopia?'

'No,' Lila said quickly. 'Just a tourist.'

'Mmn,' the demon looked at her, not believing a word. 'Well, if you're very keen you can make me an offer.'

'I don't even have a garden,' Lila said apologetically.

The demon nodded.

'Or a house big enough.'

'He's not a domestic size,' the demon agreed. 'Small ones for that. Lucky statues. Not a big totem. He's more a corporate kind of . . . relic.'

Lila thought it best to keep to herself that she had no idea why anybody might want such things in the house or anywhere. 'Company forum,' she agreed politely.

Lila, they are not facsimiles. They are real. These are demons who have passed into their pre-death ages.

Lila felt her social smile freeze on her face, but then suddenly the strange conversation that she had once overheard in a tea-house, where she had seen a demon shrink and ossify, clicked into place. His friends had bitched that he wouldn't fetch much money. Pre-death?

Before true death a demon separates from the physical plane and its body petrifies and reduces, depending on how much spirit it had. Inside the remains the demon itself lives on, detached from worldly proceedings. It may stay there indefinitely, seeking to influence others through the aethereal planes, or it may depart for the endless shores.

How do you tell which ones are – really dead?

Only a necromancer can know, Tath said smugly. *And I can tell you that most of these, including the big one, are fully present and listening to every word.*

Just like you, she said and regarded the rigid little forms with a new wariness.

Well, good luck to them in the human world, Tath said acidly. *They have as much chance of accurately placing a psychic influence on you dullards as they have of running a three minute mile. You would think that thousands of years of effort occupying new age jewellery would have taught them that.*

She decided not to ask for more detail, because she knew he wanted her to. 'Come on,' she said to Thingamajig, and turned back to the road. 'We've got other things to do.'

'Hey! What's he retail for?' the imp screeched from her shoulder as she walked away.

The trader made some reply and Thingamajig bristled. 'Overpriced.'

'So,' Lila said as she walked, 'demons have infiltrated the human world.'

'Everyone has infiltrated the human world,' Thingamajig asserted breezily. 'Long before you started noticing us with your fancy Bomb whatsit. I wouldn't doubt that was an arcane invention that required a lot of *influence*, if you may say, in its creation. You were a lot of innocent fun before it all became this serious diplomatic angst-fiasco and formal governmental whatnot. I often wonder who made that thing and why they wanted to spoil everything. Not only did we have you for light entertainment but before it went off we also had worlds that were stable and pleasant and not prone to breaking up and dissolving into the primal materials. Of course many say it's a con-spiracy. Don't know by whom and for what though. Can't see what anyone had to gain by ruining everything. Now we have you on the case however, I'm sure it will all soon be sorted out.'

'That was sarcasm,' Lila said.

'Allow me some benefits,' the imp replied dourly. 'I am facing my doom.'

They had arrived at Madame's house.

The door opened as they reached it, not a step too soon and not a step too late. It revealed a lofty hallway lit with golden lights and decorated with filigree of golden wire in onyx. They were greeted with a silent bow by one of Madame's potential suitors, who had now become her minion following his rejection rather than face exile from the object of his desire. This one was very tall, very thin with skin like antique paper. He was basically human in shape save for his long tattered tail and his green reptilian eyes. Lila was briefly grateful to have missed Madame's favourites, the pair of hulking monsters with dead raven heads, but regretted the thought as soon as she had had it, for at this range there was nothing she could think or remember that Madame would not know.

'Greetings Ms Ahriman Sikarza Black, Friendslayer,' the doorkeeper murmured, beckoning with a soft, slow underwater gesture of his hand. 'This way.'

Madame Des Loupes was, as Lila remembered her, hideously beauti-ful in the way of demons. Her massive carrion bird's head was angled to look out of the window where she leaned against her special backless chair, the train of her peacock tail sweeping gracefully to the wooden floor. Her woman's body was wearing a delicate white lace blouse and skirt that looked like sea foam. It covered her legs to the knee, concealing the snakelike phallus that Lila knew she also possessed. Her feet were clad in delicate silk slippers.

She adjusted the open window as Lila entered and beckoned with one of her simple human hands on its powerful arm. 'Look,' she said. 'Did you ever see so many faeries here? And for once not high on powder and spells. Their bags are full of rare artefacts and essences.' Her voice came from her beak, perfectly articulated despite the fact that neither beak nor tongue were suited for speech. Lila had no idea how she made the sound. On her shoulder Thingamajig clutched and shivered.

Lila was stuck for an answer, since she had not noticed much of anything at the Souk in her preoccupation with not noticing the things she particularly wanted not to notice. 'Is there a special occasion?'

'They are preparing for war.' Madame did not seem particularly to care if this was the case. She showed Lila to the guest couch, a slender chaise longue, and waited for her to sit down. Lila did so cautiously, keeping most of her weight on her feet in case the delicate furniture didn't want to take the weight of her machineries. The couch creaked faintly but seemed to hold firm.

'How do the Otopians care for the moths?' Madame asked then, finally turning her attentive gaze towards Lila. She left the window and brought her own chair to a more easy position for talking, slightly to Lila's side rather than opposite her.

Lila knew she was referring to the invasion of creatures that were causing havoc across the human world and which, if she had been in Otopia still, she would be tracking down and capturing, attempting to talk with, perhaps killing if things were bad. And reports said sometimes things were bad even though most of the incidents on record were of people being terrified rather than properly menaced or killed. 'Not much. Do you know where they are from?'

'But of course, they are fey,' the demon replied as if it were common knowledge. 'Hence my cause to mention it. Faeries everywhere. Most unusual to see such clusters of activity. The moths are not true faeries, merely a part of the fey world. They may take up the form of others and speak in words sometimes but they are more truly beasts than self-aware beings. A plague of them is an occasional phenomenon. It signals something important, though who can say what?'

'I'm not here about them,' Lila said, though she hoped she seemed

16

grateful for information which was already more than the secret service had managed to provide her with.

'I know,' Madame said and for the first time fixed a gleaming black eye on the imp cowering on Lila's shoulder. 'You are here to request deliverance, such as Zal must have told you he received from me but I hope it is not as a forerunner of an attempt to become demonic, because you are not capable of that.'

Lila stiffened, feeling insulted for a moment.

'You are human,' pointed out the demon with simple fairness. 'You might conceivably copy our ways or be possessed by some of our vigour, but you cannot be one of us because the humans have no true affinity to the aether. Your connection to that aspect is passive. You are materially bound. Besides, two demon partners is more than enough of a connection to our spirit. You will do well to survive them.'

'Madame,' Lila said simply. 'Can I be released now?'

'From Hell, you mean.' Madame signalled to the minion who had remained at the door and he went off. 'But at any time of course. Simply stop pretending. You don't need me.'

'But I thought . . .'

'Yes,' the demon continued, picking up on that thought, 'you thought that if I gave Zal clearsight I should have to give it to you. But for the same reason I am unable to satisfy your wish to know what it is to be demonic, I can't grant you the sight. It's not a power that is transferable. Zal already had it himself, all I did was to open it fully. I didn't make anything new.'

'And I don't have it.' Lila remained composed, though underneath she felt an impending crush of disappointment and attempted to fend it off, searching for a scrap of pride with which to feel better.

'That,' Madame said, moving her beak and somehow pointing directly at Lila's attempt to shore herself up, 'would be the wrong way.'

'Humans are pathetic. Can't see, can't know, can't do magic, can't do anything,' Lila said, realising as she did so how childish it sounded. 'I get it.'

'You don't like it, but don't pretend,' the demon agreed. 'That's just how it is. As for the seeing, well anyone can do that to the end of their own nose but most don't. My kind of sight goes much further but it is no different. You have as much sight as you need. No, you came here wanting me to fix something about you, because you think that to escape the clutches of Hell means an eternal ticket to being right. Or to

17

have the world turn the way you think it ought to. But I must emphasise that it will change nothing. Not one bit.'

'I . . .' Lila began but had nothing to say suddenly because Madame was, of course, right. 'What does it mean, for a human?'

'Two things,' Madame said gently. 'First that you are free to accept or reject the influence of others, and secondly that you are no longer prey for the devils.'

'The devils,' Lila repeated. 'I thought devils and demons . . .'

It was Madame's turn to stiffen, this time with repulsion.

'Are they different?'

'Your ignorance is that of all your kind – loathsome yet inescapable given your sorry history of misinformation, deceit and general blindness to the aether so I may overlook the remark . . .' Madame laughed at her own outrage briefly, a girlish and oddly carefree sound that, coming from her huge beak as it did, was chilling. 'My dear wretch, no. The devils and the demons are most certainly different. A demon might torment you via possession, but a demon is always passionate and vibrant and full of life, even if that is a kind of life and vigour that becomes destructive. Demons consume with fire and excess.

'A devil has no form outside the host except its ghost trace. They have no lives of their own. They are part of the undead realm, but also part of Zoomenon, a form of elemental negativity. Unlife. Where a mind is struck with self-hatred, where it would rather be moral than gentle, or right than compassionate . . . there you will find a devil at work.

'As you may see, no demon could be possessed by such a creature and function as a demon in any way. Demons are pro-life. Devils enjoy withering life where they may, and most of all they enjoy withering it when they encourage the host to spread the contagion and seed devils in the minds of others. Evangelism is their modus and moralising their watchword. Hell is the making of devils, and escape the work of demons. Elves and humans are frequently infested, and spread the infection to their descendants and associates without attempt to stem the plague. The more devilment in the world the more miserable it is. It is why we despise those races the most.'

Lila nodded, recording everything and trying not to think of whether this did or did not qualify her for escape. 'And how do you identify a devil?'

'It is simple. A voice in your mind will say that suffering leads to virtue or that virtue requires a sacrifice. It will justify misery in terms of a greater good coming later, or as the resulting karma from previous misdeeds – a deserved punishment. If the person afflicted with the devils is not religious it will explain its ways in terms of social acceptability and personal pride. Thus you may know its work.'

Lila fought an urge to squirm on her seat. Thingamajig was stock still as Madame turned to him with her bright black eye.

'Imps are able to recognise devils in others because they are themselves possessed. They are a kind of immune system for our society. But where a person is not beset by evil then imps have no use at all.'

'He keeps saying you will make him leave . . .'

'Dead useful I am!' piped the imp suddenly, leaping into life and striking a swashbuckling kind of pose beside Lila's head. 'You know full well that it's not easy to be rid of devils. They're always lurking. Always coming back in that moment of doubt, that niggling feeling . . . you can't be certain of your own mind once you've had them in. You gets in the way of them just now and then, and even if they go you carry on like they were there if you're not careful: then they comes back.'

Madame stared inscrutably. 'Wantonly consorting with an imp is unheard of. We discard them. If you wish to amuse yourself or engage his services as a prophylactic be warned it will be considered a weakness of character. Imps that do not leave once the devils are routed are generally slain on the spot. It is traditional.'

'I couldn't keep him as a . . . pet?'

'You must realise that to linger around those infected with the devils is very dangerous. They will jump across at any opportunity. And as the imp says, there are few individuals who never suffer a second of doubt into which a devil might leap.'

Thingamajig sat up eagerly in the begging position and smiled.

There was a moment of pause and in it Lila felt Madame's energy shift as clearly as though it were her own. The demon brimmed with power, ascending, because Lila had shown her a chink in her armour. Madame preened a feather on her tail with one hand and said coldly,

'We do not have *pets*, only minions or, for parties, slaves. But an imp is already both; a public variety of scum.'

'And he's an imp because he's a demon with a devil?' Lila felt quite proud of herself for figuring this out.

'Yes. Who could be freed, if he had the balls for it, although that almost never happens. But enough talk about this sad creature. Tell me, how do you like your married state?'

Lila straightened her back and flicked the long scarlet swatch of hair out of her eyes. 'Well now, I don't know if two husbands will be enough.'

The surge of Madame's power rise abated somewhat with this swagger and the demon laughed. 'Glad to hear it. Did you want something more of me?'

'Since I'm here, I don't suppose you know anything about this.' Lila held out her right arm, cued her AI and activated it. The metal and weapons flickered, and they were so fast and so perfectly liquid in their movement that they looked like a blur of soft, watery things shifting in the light for a second. After that second there was simply the stark, oily blackness of strange metal, the blade and the gun of what the AI knew as Standard Offensive Mode for the Right Arm. What remained of the shape of a human hand grasped the blade and the skin which had looked so perfectly ordinary was simply gone. There was no blood and it happened in silence.

Madame did not blink. She cocked her head with a fast, birdy movement to look more closely. Then she looked up at Lila and sat back again, 'Am I to understand, given that you anticipate my reading, that this is not how it used to be?'

'Damn straight,' Lila said. 'Used to be slower, messier, and I had to do some of the maintenance myself. There was just one mode and I had to equip it the slow way. Actually, I still have to equip it with various bits of ammunition and so on, but not like I used to. Let's say it's undergone some kind of upgrade. And the part that freaks me out the most is the skin. Watch.'

Lila wished for her ordinary arm back. There was the liquid movement, the blur of grey becoming soft beige and red, and then there was her arm, quite ordinary looking, with skin that creased in the right places, short nails and warmth.

'But no maker on the human side has touched it?'

Lila nodded. 'I get the impression that they don't *want* to touch it any more.'

Thingamajig crouched, silent and unmoving. In her chest Lila felt Tath's relief and her own surprise; he was relieved that she had finally spoken about what was going on.

In Alfheim she had been 'cured' of the medical difficulties of

20

becoming a cyborg. Where her body had been weakened and threatened to break under the strain of fusion to metal prostheses it flourished with health and strength. But lately, pain had started to return. A new kind of pain, it had at first seemed that the magical process of her restoration was reversing itself and she and Tath had both assumed grimly that without more treatments in Alfheim it must surely revert entirely. She had prepared herself to begin once again the daily treatments, drugs and practices that allowed her to survive; a wearying series of ministrations that took hours. But when she looked for the damage and let the AI analyse her blood she didn't find any sign of deterioration. But the pain was there . . . and then a trip to the Security Agency medical centre revealed the cause. The machine was growing, and so was she. They were growing into each other slowly, but surely. At some points she was stronger, at some points it was. New lines of tissue were appearing, neither human made stronger by the exposure to elfin energies, nor metal made animate by its weird fusion with metal elementals but something new. Something that was both.

Well, that's was they said and she thought. It was new. So you could say what you liked about it. It was only theory. The reality had no name and, so far, no explanation.

The demon closed her bird eyes and sighed a heavy sigh that lifted her beautiful bosom and let it drop slowly. For a moment her heartbeat was visible in the slight tremor of the skin. If she was reading Lila's thoughts Lila had no sense of it.

'You wear a talisman,' Madame said at last, in a quiet voice.

Tath tensed. Lila had forgotten it, it was so familiar. Now she touched it without thinking. There were two necklaces: one given by the faeries, which looked like it ought to fall off the chain any second but never did – a silver spiral. The other was a smooth jewel held in a wooden circle hanging from a leather cord. This was the one Lila thought of first. It had been given to her to prevent demons from detecting Tath. The spiral had been passed to her via Zal and he'd said nothing about special powers, though he did mention that Poppy seemed to think it was useful for something. The problem, as ever, was with the fey vagueness of that 'something'.

'Yes,' she said, since the matter was impossible to deny.

'This interests me as much as your strange biology.' Madame moved on her seat and her tail fanned out. A thousand eyes, all different, all alive, opened upon the pattern of the feathers. Some blinked and some did not. They all stared into distances beyond Lila's appreciation and seeing them do so made a cold shudder run down her spine. Madame clacked her beak, 'I have seen such items before, though not for a long, long time. And I have seen something like your arm before also, with my other eyes, in other minds and other places. So I am minded to say – if you tell me where one came from, I will tell you about the other.'

Lila frowned slightly, 'I thought you knew all my thoughts.'

'I know who gave you the talisman and that he placed some added charm upon it, but not how he came by it, for you do not know that either. I am sure he did not make it. If you tell me its story, I will tell you where you can find another piece of the machine. Meanwhile I can tell you that the talisman itself, however and by whom it was apparently made, is the creation of no demon, human, faery, elf or deadwalker. Their hands might have put it together, but their minds did not. It blinds me.'

Lila was momentarily nonplussed. 'Then who?'

'There are others,' the demon said. 'If I were you and I wanted to find the answers I would search out a strandloper. They are most likely to be willing to talk about these things as they feel no allegiances to those who would prefer their silence.' She brushed her hand almost carelessly against the plumage of her tail and plucked off an eye from the masses that blinked there. With a conjuror's flourish she opened her hand and held it out to Lila. A smooth stone lay there, clouded and softly coloured in shades of brown and cream. It looked like a pebble from the beach. 'Take this. When you have news for me place it on a feather.'

The imp on her shoulder went rigid but didn't speak.

Tath whispered, *She asks you to become one of her Eyes* . . . He sounded very doubtful and more than a touch frightened. By his tone of it Lila judged that becoming one of Madame's eyes might well entail a lot more than a few conversations. And now she must weigh where she stood and where the demon stood and if the deal was true and as it appeared, or was much more. Through the window Lila saw traces of sparkling lemon vapour brim momentarily and spill out of thin air. They brushed softly through the hanging veils of fabric there. Above them on the guttering a raven cawed suddenly, harshly, and there was a brief, deafening clatter of wings.

Wild aether.

There was a powerful conjunction looming here and the chance of a Game. If only Lila had any sense at all for magic. But she was human, and she had none. The only reason she could detect the aether at all was through Tath; his senses on loan to hers. But if nothing else demons were creatures of their word, she knew this for a fact. Find some information and in exchange she would be able to get her hands on another piece of technology. This path seemed easier than trying to beat Dr Williams, her boss, and others at the Agency to information that they didn't want exposed. She knew they held more pieces of the puzzle, but they also possessed systems that could directly contact and control pieces of her AI, and she'd do anything to avoid giving them more opportunities to use them. The wish she barely dared acknowledge to herself, that consumed all her energy, was that she could find a way to ensure her freedom from outside interference. She was not going to be the Agency's pet robot.

Lila looked at Madame but the bird eyes showed no trace of human emotions and the beak remained expressionless, of course. On her shoulder Thingamajig twitched and muttered a warning, making a warding sign with his free hand. Tath said,

If there is a Game bigger than the one she speaks of in the offing then I would be less than hasty to agree to it if I were you.

Lila had to admit he was right. Madame was surely deadly and her schemes potentially far more cunning than anything she herself was going to think up, but she had no illusions that she was able to outsmart the demon. Game or no Game, it was the only way she was going to get what she wanted.

She reached out and took the pebble. It was warm, and felt so much like flesh that she almost dropped it straight away.

'Put it in your pocket,' advised the demon. 'A pocket you do not much use.'

Lila found a small zip-up on her combat vest. She tried not to rush pushing the eye into it so she didn't offend the demon, but her nerves jangled with the urge to get its unctuous touch off her as fast as possible. At last the pocket was closed, the shaking of her fingers concealed as she pressed them hard against it.

'Good,' Madame said conclusively.

Lila nodded and ignored the offer of an open door from the footmen. She walked to the open balcony and stepped over the rail, igniting her jet boots as she started to fall. Beneath her the warren of the Souk spread itself flat under the heat of the midday sky. She had no desire to set foot in it again so soon. Flight was easier and, she thought with a grim smile, more fitting for someone who had agreed to become one of the crows.

CHAPTER THREE

Lila returned to their lodgings at the Ahriman house, dragging her feet as she considered whether or not doing a deal with Madame was a wise thing. Probably it was not. But she told herself she had no other leads and squashed the thought that kept springing up so eagerly – that two could tango, and if the Agency wanted to use spyware and controlware on her she might as well try to use her own technological spells on them. Only the grim boredom of entering some tit for tat security contest stalled her from trying it. That and a fear of finding information she'd rather not know right now, about herself, and Zal, and Dr Williams whose rather magnificent *coup d'état* on the Agency's last director was disturbingly well planned and executed for a nice little old lady psychologist.

She was not surprised to discover Zal and Teazle were both gone. Once conscious they rarely wasted time loitering when they could be doing something suicidal or artistic. Her human self, she found to her dismay, reacted prissily and with uptight negativity in the face of most of their suggestions for recreational fun. She felt an overbearing urge to remind them that they had important business to attend to; music for Zal and intrigue for Teazle . . . they should be getting serious and working, not loafing around all the time while their respective Romes sizzled merrily away with the smell of carbonized career. She hated that part of herself so it was a good thing they weren't here or she'd probably have said something and given them one more reason to notice she was supremely mentally and emotionally unsuited for demonic life, and probably nowhere near as fun or attractive as they had been duped into thinking so far. And wasn't that twist of self-hatred just the peach on the cake? She was grim as she looked up and found they weren't there. And relieved.

In their place she *was* surprised to see the elegant figure of Malachi reclining and reading his personal organiser as he sipped a cup of tea. The black faery got up as soon as he saw her and set the cup down without a sound. His charcoal-grey suit gave him a dashingly sinister air and his amber eyes glowed fiercely; a feature she had long grown used to. She barely noticed them, looking instead at the huge wings that were just visible behind him, like watercolours painted on the air. They were slightly ragged and butterfly shaped, veined with black and moved in their own clouds of anthracite dust. The dust sparkled and tumbled and gave the appearance of being capricious – it whirled in little eddies and seemed not to want to settle on anything. Not for the first time Lila wondered exactly what properties it had and how powerful it could be in Otopia. She had felt more confident around him before Tath, when she couldn't see this aspect of him. There was a lot she didn't know about the faeries.

You know absolutely nothing, Tath corrected her with amiable pedantry. *And if more people who attempt to deal with the fey assumed that from the outset the better it would be. Even the elves, who have vast forehouses full of collected faery knowledge, do not presume to know them.*

They're old then? Lila asked him silently, at the same time as she moved forward with a grin on her face to give Malachi a hug. She was hoping that Tath would have to admit there was somebody older and smarter than the elves. Not because it mattered to her if there was or not, but because it would make him annoyed and for reasons she didn't like to speculate on too much his being annoyed by her in small niggly ways made her happy.

Old, new, it makes no difference, the elf replied with genuine unease, giving Lila a sensation like her heart being lifted and lowered a millimetre – his equivalent of a shrug.

She frowned, unable to help it, both from the dismay of his not rising to the bait and also because she had learned that Tath's magical instincts were spot on. The idea of his being discomfited by the fey, including Malachi who was her friend, annoyed and disquieted her. Tath could sense these feelings in her, but instead of notching himself another victory in their little contest he stayed quiet. That made her feel even more peculiar, since he never missed an opportunity to score points.

'Something the matter?' Malachi asked, withdrawing gracefully from the hug and adjusting the lie of his sleeve.

'No,' Lila said. 'Just one of those days in the making, you know, where you set out with a simple objective and then everything gets so complicated before lunchtime you wish you hadn't started. What're you doing here?'

'Can't a friend come to visit without a reason?' Malachi recovered his teacup and remained standing, looking around the place with interest. He was a picture of elegant distraction though Lila was not fooled. Malachi wouldn't appear without a good reason. 'Where are the hubbies?'

'If you use that word again I will kill you,' Lila said. 'I have no idea. And seeing as it is still my honeymoon, technically speaking, I would have thought you'd call ahead instead of just appearing godmother-style in my bedroom.'

Malachi gave her a long, level look and then put the cup down. His voice became serious – as serious as it ever got. A few motes of dust scattered from his wings to the floor. 'There's a lot of what you might call Trouble At The Mill, since we started our gang. The Otopians don't much care for the idea of you having so much freedom and are scampering through their paperwork for ways to make you come to heel. Things are tough for the Doc at the top and even more so because of the moths.' He looked down for a second, and Lila wondered what was going on. In a human such a movement was a signal of guilt or dissembling but it would be rash to read this into a fey. Malachi shrugged and continued, 'They're proving more troublesome than it seemed at first. Doc was wondering if you'd return early and provide some help disposing of them. The boys too, if they're willing. Unofficially for them of course although Zal's manager is, I understand, regularly coming within inches of hospitalisation due to the lad's failure to turn up for band practice.' He hesitated. 'And I have someone you should meet. I was on my way here – halfway over – when a little bird told me you'd be looking for a strandloper.'

'A little bird?'

'Mmn, about yay big,' Malachi held up one hand over his head, about seven feet high. 'Dark stinking cape, human body, long beak, maggots for eyes.'

'She's keen,' Lila said with a sense of dismay. She hadn't even got home and Madame was pushing her on her way.

27

'That's what I thought,' the faery said, suddenly animated with interest, his casually aloof features losing their hauteur. Of course he knew all about Madame and her minions, it was only the humans who were ignorant about the 'new' races, their ways, wiles and celebrities. 'D'you know why?'

Lila shrugged. 'I invited her. She wants me to find some information for her, and then she's going to tell me about this,' Lila lifted her left hand and held it out between them. She knew that Malachi was familiar with what her hands could usually do, including growing new skin on demand, and performing a variety of interesting mechanical tasks generally reserved for laboratory precision robotics and armaments, but these all involved a degree of ordinary human activities such as adding components like blades to achieve the desired effect. Now she was wearing black leather gauntlets as part of her ever-ready duellist preparations for regular Daemonian life, which would ordinarily have got in the way of anything particularly clever. She waited until Malachi gave the hand his full attention, and then created a bottle opener out of the end of her middle finger. She then re-assembled it as a finger, before shaking the hand as though it stung. It didn't, but she felt it ought to have. A feeling of creepy satisfaction snuck through her flesh; haunted but loving it. Who wouldn't love the ability to spontaneously accessorise? Who wouldn't wonder why the hell they couldn't do it two weeks ago?

'Drinking bottled beverages is so important they made it a design priority?' Malachi asked, not really asking but covering the awkward moment with his best quip. His look was halfway between charmed and alarmed.

'Strangely enough, no. Look.' Lila made a can opener from the same finger, then a socket wrench, then a screwdriver, then set it back to a finger, blowing on it because it was suddenly hot from the changes. A silver nimbus of agitated metal elementals shone briefly around her hand and then sunk back into the matte black illusion of a leather glove. Her hip twinged with an ache, like an old athlete's joint sensing oncoming bad weather and she frowned. She'd been ignoring small pains for a month, but there was no denying they were related to her new party tricks. She kept silent about them because worrying about it privately and suspecting the worst seemed better than coming out with it and having the worst formally confirmed by medical. Her own stupidity sometimes amazed her.

'I'm thinking it didn't used to do that.' The faery stared unhappily at her hand and then his eyes narrowed in speculation. She flexed her fingers and put her hand down.

Lila gave him a slow, thoughtful nod. 'You're right. I was definitely much more like a robot with rubber gloves on a year ago. Now I don't even need to bother requisitioning gloves. Or, come to that, boots and stockings.'

Malachi raised his eyebrows, 'Does it do other colours?'

Lila imagined her hand wearing a red glove. The black became muddy brown and then mottled, as if cancerous. She went back to black quickly. 'Seems I don't have the hang of that. Or it doesn't like it. Maybe it's a goth technology.' She hesitated. 'I don't really like to dwell on why it will do some things and not others.'

They shared a glance of profound discomfort and worry and then both looked away at the same moment. Lila felt strange again, as she had with Madame when she had showed the demon the same thing, and she tried to forget that just now she had referred to parts of herself in the third person, as if they weren't really her at all. A shudder tried to get going in her back but she didn't let it show and instead it closed on her spine with a cold grip – the fear she didn't want to know about that kept on screaming silently 'What if it's alive? What if it's *not* you but something else? Was it always like this? Did they know when they remade you? Or is it something made lately, in Alfheim, because of Zal, in Daemonia . . . what is it? Whose is it? Why? Didn't Spiderman once have this kind of trouble and look what happened to him . . .'

No, she didn't want to give in to that kind of fear. That was a luxury reserved for people who feared something they could actually flee from.

Tath sighed an elfin sigh – long, soft and so eloquent you could have sent it to a debating competition as an irrefutable speech on the folly of human nature. Lila imagined herself giving him a kick in the pants and sent it as a mental image, but he was impervious to taunts.

Meanwhile, 'On the plus side I don't have to bother with two hours of medical and maintenance every night,' she said, attempting to be breezy and failing.

'You still go back for ammunition, medical gear or downloads?'

It was a good question. She didn't know the answer since she hadn't used up any supplies since her last trip back to the Agency. In one of the wardrobes a large unopened holdall contained a field-base's worth of spares. Of the duels she had fought during and since the wedding she used bare-hand and blade techniques to be on the safe side. She didn't know what rounds were fatal and nonfatal to demons, and anyway, getting out a missile or bomblet seemed unsporting and not in the spirit of ritual mortal combat. At least the demons seemed to agree with her. None of them had made an attempt on her life with anything more accurate or long range than a single-hand crossbow.

'The AI processes go up almost a hundred per cent when it happens,' she said because it was all the hard information she had.

A voice said from her ear, 'Yeah but even that's been going down lately. I keep telling ya to change into something interesting like a speedboat and give it something to worry about but do you listen?' Thingamajig crawled out of his hiding form as a ruby, jewelling Lila's ear, and stretched out on her shoulder to stare at Malachi with proprietorial interest. He was slightly hunched and stroked the backs of his own hands, eyes narrowed, like a villain in a pantomime.

'He must be an interesting third party in bed,' Malachi said. 'Unusually quiet today.'

'I've got a name, you know,' the imp said sulkily, slumping back into his recent despondent state.

'Yeah, when you know what it is give me a call,' the faery replied.

'Myeh.' Thingamajig turned his back and buried his face in Lila's hair, aiming his small rump directly at Malachi and briefly emitting a fart of yellow flame.

'Can you turn into a speedboat?' Malachi asked.

'No. When can I meet your strandloper?' Lila asked.

'Soon as,' the faery said. He returned his cup to a side table and straightened his coat. 'I have to be getting back. A few matters . . . well, you'll see.'

She guessed that his stiff formality was a signal to her that whatever was bothering them in Otopia was particularly irritating. He was usually so relaxed, this businesslike attitude was the equivalent of some other person's major anxiety attack. So she nodded agreement and gave him a reassuring smile, hoping it didn't seem to eager. On top of everything else she was fighting hard not to admit that going along with the demon code of marry-to-payback might have been a mistake. Visions of having to live with Teazle and Zal for ever danced regularly through her head like a tacky vaudeville show. But she didn't want to think about it. The Ignore file in her brain would just have to get to gigabyte sizes.

'Before you go. I wanted to ask. Do you know anything about this?' Lila reached into her neckline and pulled free the faery necklace with its spiral. The other was tangled up and came with it, but it was the spiral she held forward.

Malachi glanced at it, almost nonchalantly although his wings gave a sudden flick and discharged about a pound of coal dust into the air in a glittering black cloud. The sooty bits spun and danced, forming curious storms. They would not sink down but circulated around him, globulating as if they wanted to make forms but couldn't decide what. A tang of citrus flavoured the air suddenly. Lila recognised a local magical sink forming, her conviction boosted by Tath's sudden nudge as the aether made him alert. The spiral tingled between her fingers as if it had been attached to a small battery and a tendril of white metal energy stretched cautiously forward from her fingertips towards it, but did not make contact.

'Is that the one the *eachuisge* singer gave you?'

Lila recognised the strange sound as the official faery name for Zal's backing singers – water horse fey. 'Poppy. The annoying one. Yes, her.'

'Is it now?' Malachi had become almost somnolent, his eyes glazing with a look that was focused into the never. He stepped forwards with his usual grace but slowly and raised a hand up towards the spiral, stopping when he was inches away. 'When did she give it to you?'

'She gave it to Zal to give to me actually, before he tried to come here and ended up in Zoomenon instead. He gave it to me when he got back.'

'So he carried it while he was there . . .' This was a statement, not a question and Lila didn't say anything. Malachi's expression was serious, his gaze drifting idly, it seemed, down to the spiral though he kept his faraway stare so that he was both looking and not looking at it. 'I'm supposing she didn't say why or what it was for?'

'A good luck charm,' Lila said, repeating what Zal had said, although he'd been so casual about it she never thought it was more than a bit of decoration with some faery twirl set on it, the kind you could buy for a few pounds at any fey roadside caravan or truck stop. They were magical items, of the only kind available in Otopia under the present laws, and usually held a petit-glamour of some kind, such as adding a little brightness to the eyes or, in the case of the famous Faeryware, enhancing flavour in food.

'Aye, it was lucky for him to survive more than a few hours in Zoomenon, locate the only source of organised energy in that world, free a lot of ancient ghosts from millennia of torment and in so doing to discover the one shameful secret of elven history that would give him proof that the Shadowkin and the elves of light are blood relatives. So it was. Lucky indeed,' Malachi said quietly and let his hand drop without touching the spiral. Motes of carbon flirted with touching it and rebounded, as if repelled or frightened. He shook his head and broke his own trance. 'Have you ever tried losing it?'

'No, why would I?'

'You should ask Poppy where she found it.'

For the first time in a long time Lila thought of Zal's kidnapping – faeries had been involved in that, though it was an elven plot. She was about to mention it when Malachi said,

'And the other one? That's not a faery thing.' His gaze was fixed on the talisman, narrowed.

'Sarasilien gave it to me. Just a token,' she mumbled, knowing that it was the only thing keeping all the magical adepts in her proximity from discovering Tath. She had no idea what magic the old elf had used to make it, even though she'd seen it done. It had seemed a trivial thing, but then again, Malachi had more than once hinted that a big song and dance routine was just that when it came to the magical arts; a great spell or a small one was the work of a moment and for true adepts no props were required. She hadn't entirely believed him, mostly because faeries liked slinging grandiose claims around, but now she wondered.

'The understatement there is so low I'm starting to feel that I'm back in the old country,' Malachi said, straightening the hang of his jacket. Abruptly the clouds of scintillating black dust shot back on to his wings and skin, like iron filings to a magnet. 'Next you'll be telling me your new family are just like regular folks. I'll be on my way. See you at the Agency.' His amber gaze was direct, meaning she'd better be there soon and that he was wise to her attempts to omit important information.

'Sure,' Lila said, showing him to the door.

As he turned to go he cast a last glance over the room, lingering on the huge rumpled bed. 'A year since you first walked into Alfheim, huh? You've come a long way, baby.'

'It's not what it looks like.'

He nodded and she wished to hell he would stop being so serious, like he was her sad and wiser father or something. Her own father of course . . . no, she couldn't even imagine beginning to explain this to him – 'Hi, Dad. Here's my new husband. He's an elf. And a demon. Yes, both. I know, isn't it weird but yes, you can be both apparently. And this is my other husband. He's just a demon and we all live together, oh, and this is a dead elf I had a hand in murdering six months ago – no, he doesn't share the bed, just my body . . . and this is Thingamajig. Demon? Uh, yes, well just an imp. Like a cat but more irritating. He lives next to my head. Yes, husband in THAT sense of the word. Want some help opening that beer?' And then she wouldn't be able to say any more because she would literally have died of embarrassment.

The faery turned and looked down into her eyes for a moment. 'You don't need to defend yourself to me,' he said. 'I just want you to be safe.'

She didn't like the implication in that and before she knew it said, 'You're not responsible for me. Don't think about it.'

His gaze hardened with a flash of anger and then he laughed. 'Telling a fey to be free is like telling water it's wet.' His anger returned and hardened out into resolve, 'I am what I am. And I say you are into things deeper and stranger than you understand. You run in without a second glance, yes, like the children the faeries love the best. No hesitation. A child of the heart. Wedded to demons. But you don't—'

'I do so know about them,' she said, thinking of the Souk, the glamorous, deadly violence of every day.

'You know what they like to show you,' Malachi said, suddenly more gentle so she wished he was angry again. 'And we're the same. And the elves, and that's all.' He glanced at her forehead and hair, where they were stained scarlet by the deadly magical energy which had destroyed her limbs.

'I'm not under any illusions,' Lila insisted, angry in spite of knowing he was only being thoughtful. 'I don't need protection. I'm not a little girl.'

His look said he thought otherwise and she scowled at him.

'Sling yer hook,' Thingamajig muttered from her hair. 'I'd have thought you'd have more sense, faeryman. The lassie doesn't like to know what she knows.'

'Spoken like a pro,' Malachi retorted. He leant down and kissed the air next to Lila's cheek. 'Tell the lads I said hello.'

She closed the door after him and leant against it for a moment. It put her opposite the balcony and the huge sprawl of beribboned baskets but all she saw was Malachi's deadly seriousness. She would never have believed he could be spooked by anything if she hadn't seen it for herself.

CHAPTER FOUR

Calling short her holiday was something Lila wanted to do about as much as she wanted a hole in the head, but on top of her burning desire to get the information out of Madame was the uncomfortable feeling she'd got from Malachi. Add to that the mention of a strandloper and Zal's discoveries during and after his last visit to Zoomenon, and suddenly the idea of sitting around doing not much of anything was too annoying to bear. She decided to leave as soon as possible and went to ready her backpack so she didn't leave anything behind her which the demons could tamper with, like artillery shells, bullets or the slim vials of various biochemicals that were the precursor compounds for all the drugs and treatments she was capable of manufacturing. It was an intricate and methodical task that left her just enough time to bring her memories of the Mothkin out of storage in her AI module and into her mind. She read as she worked:

The Mothkin were a form of fey. They were suspected of crossing into Otopia in times prior to the Bomb, in ones and twos, and they were pencilled into the annals of cryptozoology as the most likely culprits in the Mothman incidents in the USA. Of course there was no USA now, only the myriad small islands and their tiny gulfs – independent states, cities and townships packed into the endless channels of the mighty river system, Fluvia, and known collectively as the Millefoss. On a good day you might attempt to crossmap the old USA and the Millefoss. As for Europe, Asia and Australia, nothing very recognisable remained of their seemingly permanent geography and even the oceans and their currents were all changed about – so much so that doubt was regularly cast on the whole Bomb story, and not only by the denizens of the other five Revealed Worlds. Lila wasn't interested in fitting history together though, she just wanted an update on how to handle human-sized fey with big wings when they weren't being ordinarily friendly like Malachi or the hundreds of other faeries who legally worked and lived in Otopia.

The Mothkin were a part of the fey world which was least human and most animal-like, including many beasts previously featured only in cryptozoological tracts. They were counted by the faeries as 'sluagh', a term they used for certain fey.

Fneh, Tath said, figuratively reading over her shoulder. *The sluagh are no faeries. Trust fey to throw names and information about carelessly. The sluagh are Death's gleaners, the souls of the restless dead.*

People who didn't cross over? Lila asked, recalling her brief visit to Thanatopia; its vast harbours and anchorages filled with ships and each ship the destination of a long line of slow marching people. That scintillating ocean of light.

Yes. They include those who cannot let go of their mortal business, but also necromancers and others who went willingly to band together and live on the shores between life and death.

What for?

The power. The elf shuddered with a strange mixture of anticipatory pleasure and revulsion. *The sluagh enjoy the company of many magicians, shamans and other crafters who have many chances to cross over from Thanatopia to other worlds to gain power and to use it for whatever ends they desire. They seek out the living in order to hurt them and suck their souls to ride.* He hesitated, *Much as I did to get us into Thanatopia.*

So these fey are like that; same power source?

It seems so, the elf admitted. *Though they do not sound particularly intelligent, unlike the sluagh.*

Lila read on. Faeries working in the Agency had insisted that Mothkin be classified as part of the Soul Traders. The key difference between sluagh fey and others was twofold. First, sluagh fey had magic that was primarily focused on the psychic and spiritual planes, and secondly they were much less ready to adopt a human form when manifesting across worlds.

Mothkin were quite low among the sluagh, according to Lila's carefully cross-referenced pointer to The Fabula, the Agency's unofficial guide to all outworlders. They were regarded on a par with animals in terms of their level of consciousness, occasionally getting up sufficient acuity to mimic humans or even become briefly human in form, but usually simply working on the basics of eating, sleeping and causing trouble. They had a purely psychic form that was considered their 'worst' manifestation, since it had no physical element and could not be trapped or bound by ordinary means. This form of the Mothkin was a secondary stage in their lives – a late development, when they shed their bodies entirely after a successful mating and/or egg laying. In addition, the dust shed by adult Mothkin wings had a mildly narcotic effect. Among the dust were spores that, if inhaled, opened the carrier's spirit to infestation by the psychic adult form.

There is a saying among the elves that the bodiless fey are the same as the devils, Tath said quietly as they both absorbed this piece of news.

'The devils?' Lila said aloud, surprised by the name. 'Shouldn't they be here then?' She meant in Daemonia, instead of Faery.

There was a sudden pull and pain on the side of her head and a voice muttered, 'You metal-headed glowwit. It ain't the same thing. Just very similar.'

Lila scowled.

The Fabula had a footnote appended with official stamps by human agents:

Note: this was a *faery* entry written by *faeries*. Faery information should be regarded with the due degree of suspicion.

That was close to one hundred per cent suspicion, Lila reflected and Tath's green became lime with laughter.

Note 2: Officially the 'psychic' form of Mothkin is to be disregarded as an hysterical fabrication by humans. It is assumed not to appear in Otopia or in human subjects, due to their demonstrated lack of magical affinity. At best it is simply a term that might be used to apply to any mental affliction. Agents encountering claims of Mothkin interference by subjects should refer the subject to ordinary medical and psychiatric care.

After skimming this part, Lila paused in a moment of consideration. She was used to the bull-headed atheistic rationalism of the Agency, which plodded grimly onwards with its revisions of magical and supernatural explanations no matter what. Everything had a scientific label and a theory. She was mostly able to shrug this off as a necessary defence for people with fragile minds who had to make everything they encountered conform to their vision of how the world was supposed to be. Otopia, prior to the Quantum Bomb, had been filled with all kinds of religions and so forth but since the Bomb the Agency and its governmental allies had become ruthlessly materialist, perhaps as a reaction to the huge influx of simply inexplicable, and untenable, things that had hurtled its way ever since. But however you chose to read the cause and effect they were pussyfooting around from this one bleak, dry note she reckoned that a plague of Mothkin meant a plague of madness.

Her hand pushed the last magazine of explosive rounds into its place in her pack and she sat back on her heels giving the whole thing a final shake to settle the contents and test its weight. No wonder Malachi had been looking hangdog at her – reporting the Mothkin was akin to reporting a covert declaration of war between his homeground and hers.

She zipped up the pack as she read on:

Exposure to Mothkin is rarely fatal. There was a link to official databases, which showed clearly the number of facts backing up this last 'statistic'.

There were none. Not simply no deaths. No data.

The last sentence read: At worst it is reported that a Mothkin assault on a human subject could result in a type of coma, therefore these creatures are not regarded as a High Alert threat.

After this there was an addition with a faery signature, underlined three times: 'Stupid human. Mothkin are soul tappers. Coma=as good as dead unless a necromancer or shaman can rebuild the soul well enough that it can recharge itself in the old form. What is it with you people and this denial business anyway? Sometimes I wonder why we bother. Anyway, you're not likely to encounter many Mothkin in Otopia. They don't have the power to cross worlds unaided so just don't do anything stupid

Stupider.'

The file ended there.

I wonder what not doing anything stupid means in this context? Lila thought, hefting the pack in one hand and setting off for the roof with a light step, glad to leave the apartment behind.

I will forgo the obvious reply and say simply that it means that you should not anger people who have the power to aid the Mothkin across. One might suspect that this is exactly what has happened in Otopia.

So, to get rid of the moths I have to find out who sent them over and what their problem is?

One would assume. But being a faery matter I doubt it will be so simple. And do not forget that the fey do not dabble in diplomacy as you know it, whatever that sly black cat might be pretending. Any human could have annoyed any faery and got this result one way or another. Will you interview your entire species?

Well, it would have to be a big annoy, Lila said. *Surely?* And then she remembered the kinds of things that annoyed Poppy and Viridia and Sand, Zal's fey backing singers, and she sighed.

Quite so, said Tath.

Lila had reached the roof and the landing deck where the sizeable number of Sikarza vehicles were parked at her disposal. She nodded to the deck officer and tucked her pack neatly into a corner of his warm little cubby where it was safe. He was used to her leaving things with him and not taking any of his craft. Stretching out her shoulders and taking a deep breath she strolled across the long flat top of the palazzo to the edge.

Thingamajig put his head out of her hair, 'Where are we going?'

'I'm looking for Zal,' she said. She initialised her jets, running through a little safety check to pass the time as she scanned the city. There were many possibilities for two demons out there but she was pretty sure she knew where Zal would have gone, whether or not Teazle was in a mood to follow.

She kicked off from the roof with a stamp of her right foot, not because it helped the jets any but because it felt good. Her arms swept back towards her sides as she let the AI and the propulsion power take care of her flight path. The warm breeze turned cold as it buffeted her face and whipped her hair around. She went up high, rolling and turning lazy circles, experimenting with moving her arms into different positions and seeing how they affected the flight. All the while she slowly moved closer to her target in the district of Muses and kept a little of her attention on radar, watching for signs of imminent attack. Her wedding had brought her a fresh list of duellists, no less than three hundred and forty-seven at the last count, and she had been crossing them off at a rate of four per day on average, excluding days spent entirely at home. She grinned at the sky as she swept a curve on her back, arms wide as a diver and pretended she wasn't dallying, her blood starting to rise with the anticipation of a fight.

Sure enough, she had been airborne only a minute before she picked up signs of pursuit. Without thinking about it she began to change course, taking herself away from her planned route and out over the waters of the lagoon. The pursuit followed, lingering over the shoreline where the warehouses of the cargo district were squashed cheek by jowl to the water's edge. It was airborne but low and she almost lost it amid the masses of boats shuffling for position at the quays, thick as autumn leaves in a forest stream. But her tracking systems were tenacious as only machines could be. A pleasing flicker of hunter/ hunted shivered through her and her mouth spontaneously formed a small grim smile. When you were good at something, no matter what it was, there was a pleasure in doing it. She preferred airborne fights. Flying demons had wings and wings were a distinct liability.

By the time she had reduced her speed almost to a loiter and was waiting testily for the attack, wondering if she could legitimately take a first strike before making a positive identification of the demon as a bone fide duellist, she was beyond the range of all the airtrade lanes except the major circular bus route and its huge, ponderous balloons. These were so stately that as far as she was concerned they were virtually stationary objects and thus were useless as anything except temporary cover, though for that they were very useful indeed as it was a capital offence to damage a public transport vehicle or its passengers in a duel.

Thingamajig put his head out of her hair and said, 'Another fight is it? Well let me tell you, Missy, you'll be paying for it with yet another devil for me to talk about if you're not careful – the one sits up late at night in your older years making you curse your stupid youth and the joy you took in the death you dealt.'

'Ah crap,' Lila said. 'I don't see any of you guys suffering from guilt.'

'Yeah, but we was born our way and you was born yours and you don't have it in the blood. A yu-man . . .' He spoke as if he was talking about something unsavoury. 'A *yu*-man *conscience* is a terrible thing.'

As is a demon one, supposing such a thing exists, Tath said icily.

Lila was brought up short. She never thought that Thingamajig's outbursts were ever related to himself. It was true, her conscience did nag her about the consequences of a demon lifestyle, particularly the death rates. But she had not asked any of them to fight her, and if it was her life or theirs then she didn't feel any guilt over what she had to do. Well, she shouldn't . . . but maybe she did feel it when her inner voice reminded her that staying in Daemonia was optional, not required. *You did*, it kept whispering just as Thingamajig had promised, *you chose.* Then again, what was she supposed to do? Never come here again? A slow burn of anger at her position started up in her belly as she turned and stood on the jets to face her assailant.

'Now is not the moment,' she said to the imp. 'You can keep your cupboard full of skeletons to yourself.'

The tiny demon shrugged and dug his claws into her shoulder armour. 'I see you lying, you know. And I'm not the only one. The devils have a sense for lies that can reach beyond time itself and let me tell you there are at least three of them stalking you right now, close as your own skin,' he said with a raspy primness. 'But I'm your friend here. You stuck by me when She Who Shall Not Be Named wanted to fling me back into limbo – quite prematurely I must say, 'cos you is far from in the clear. But she don't care if you spend eternity in Hell either way, that was only up to you, but you don't get that about us that we don't care for anyone else's business no matter what, never mind that isn't the point, point is I say this: did it ever occur to you that your conscience is wrong and that you're right not to give a damn about the demons and whatever other bozos you've killed? 'Cos trust me, they all were asking for it, just like this lot.'

Her attacker was a large humanoid demon with black and blue hide, dancing carefully among the highly populated boats below. Her senses, some of them human but most of them robot, tracked it effortlessly. Scans revealed its weapons – claws, a poisoned knife, a garrotting wire, some kind of boomerang, several grenades of various kinds plus an intricate and interesting personal display of tentacles and stinging appendages. It had a mouthful of teeth like a crocodile and a huge set of wasp wings. It was armoured. But most of all, supported by a girdle and two of its powerful arms, it was holding a very large and sophisticated gun. She could not determine what kind of gun.

As it moved, it watched her and she got the impression it was smugly biding its time from its protective cover whilst she was simply standing there in the sky. She was winning on points, but points didn't count in the end.

'Killing is wrong,' Lila said, almost on reflex, though as she said it she considered herself to be asserting a basic humanity that was inviolable. There was an absurdity to be saying it at that moment which seemed to demand a laugh, but she couldn't muster one. She was too busy studying the gun.

'Who says?' The imp dug his claws into her ear with familiar pain.

She saw a variety of rounds inside the clip and the typical twin barrel design of demon guns: one for sport and one for serious. 'Everyone.' She tried to figure out which it was going to choose – although technically she could not be penalised for murder, even if the instigator of the duel only set out with maiming weapons.

'Oh *that's* convincing,' Thingamajig hoicked up a wad of phlegm and spat down into the lagoon. 'Everyone. Of course. Everyone. Fneh. He's not alone I bet. Look at him prancing around there like some fey princess.'

'I see them.' She had picked up the two others working with the obvious demon just as the imp mentioned it, having thought of the same thing herself. One was high above her in the cloud deck, the other was on the rooftops at the water's edge. As ordinary Lila she would have missed them, but her AI was in permanent battle mode here and it had no problems locating the telltale movements of those showing too much interest in her position. It had started out with twenty-one candidates, but settled on just the two after a few picoseconds of hard thinking. To Lila it was no more than her own intuition talking. Without hesitation she shot straight up as fast as her jets would carry her.

An instant later the air shimmered where she had been and there was a loud bang.

'Matter Vaporisator,' the imp said with relish. 'Disguised as a common Letemhavit Repeater. Mmn, impressive. These guys have money behind them. That Zoomenon technology doesn't come cheap.'

Lila, who had heard of MVs, but not seen them, was suitably silent. Humans didn't know how MVs worked, only that they instantly reduced their target to its constituent atoms. There was a theory about information removal . . . but the design didn't interest her nearly as much as the sure knowledge that whatever it hit didn't survive.

'They need three for the triangulation point,' Thingamajig informed her happily. 'But the power source has to be with the one on the ground, the others will just have some crystals or shit. See, I went to this exhibition once in the Engineering District . . .'

Lila focused on the space above her. Icy air tore at her and vapour turned to water on her face, streaming down toward her temples and chin. Her skin burned and tingled but her inhuman eyes were able to stare without pain. She raised her right arm, felt the gun system assemble itself and the shot depart without having a single thought go through her head. There was only the wind, the vector, the target and the intent. Cold brilliant.

A few hundred metres above her the round detonated – shatterstar – and she darted sideways in the soft white mist as the shining fragments of coalescing and deteriorating elements burned in their characteristic sunburst yellow, white and blue. They glimmered like witch lights and then winked out, their moment of astonishing destructive power spent. A second later two dark and indistinct lumps fled past her heading downwards. There was a trail of dark smoke and the stink of burning flesh.

'Barbecue,' muttered the imp happily.

As he spoke a thin, almost invisible tendril of green leapt out through her arm.

Lila felt Tath's grab snag on something aetheric and, to her, intangible. Like a frog's tongue, the tendril snapped home again and lodged in her chest. Satisfaction spun there, slowly.

I didn't say you could eat them, she objected, but her words rang hollow because she felt the same glow of victory and there was a grin on her face, even if it was a grim one.

It never pays to be a soul short if death comes calling, Tath said. *I've left most of them alone but we all have debts to pay and things to consider. You are not my master.*

The imp, who was still ignorant of Tath's presence, said, 'Hey, did you see that?'

'See what?' she said after a second's hesitation. She didn't know what made her angrier, her revulsion at Tath, her hypocrisy or the imp's perfectly timed annoying and dangerous inquisitiveness. *What are you doing with it?* She snapped at the elf.

Storing it, came the reply. *Later I will take one for you, just in case we need to travel to Thanatopia and back again. Shall I be so kind as to insure your pet as well?* His tone left her in no doubt that he felt he had been more than generous so far in withholding his activities when she was fighting, but she couldn't help raging.

These are my *fights, you can kill your own damned . . .*

43

Spare me, Tath retorted. *We both know you need me fully capable if you are going to go haring back to Otopia on some crusade against the fey creatures. If you had any brains you would already have had me preserve the spirits of all your vanquished, so we had energy enough and to spare. I am simply performing the most basic and least cruel of the Arts. They were already dead – we are only delaying their journey a while. Perhaps you can think of other sources of the deathbound for me to collect? Maybe we can go and loiter outside a hospital for a lucky opportunity?*

They're people, she said stubbornly.

And what I do is wrong, he murmured. *I know, I have heard it all before. But you will sing another song when I can be of use to you.*

It's not . . . She was going to say it wasn't like that.

It is. It is just not to your liking. Or mine.

It was. Once upon a time she had been a saving grace, carrier of a soul; a good girl. Now they were part of a team. She felt like the agreement had been foisted on her, and maybe it had, because she could have made him leave. She chose not to. And here he was, her own private death collector.

I don't know how you live with yourself. But she could have said it to herself.

'Hey!' Thingamajig dragged on her ear as she took a zagging, randomised path downward, watching all the time for a chance at the demon below. 'I said, did you see . . .'

'Shut up, I'm trying to think,' she said. The glow in her chest was black, laughing. *You idiot, you're supposed to stay secret.*

'. . . cause I was under the distink impression you had no aetheric capabilities at all. Nada. Zilch. Even the French Bird didn't say otherwise and you know that she can tell. So if you ain't possessed by no demons and you don't have any powers, then . . .'

'I said shut up,' Lila repeated, quietly, coldly, sidling through the cloud as beneath her the bits of dead demon began raining down on the cargo boats in steaming chunks.

Now that their first attack had failed the other two demons were in retreat. She was within her rights to pursue and exterminate – no duellist had a right to leave the grounds alive if their opponent lived – but they were heading in opposite directions. It was not possible to tell if they would regroup or flee. The MV would be of no use now unless she were to foolishly stand directly between the two of them. Her first impulse was simply to leave them.

'No, no, no, you can't be serious,' the imp jumped up and down, his claws snagging and pulling threads out of her vest shoulder. 'Do you want to be hunted down like a dog by the devils from all the ages? Not to mention the demons from right now . . . KILL something!'

'But . . .' But she pitied them.

'Because . . .' The imp shook her ear violently, insisting that she finish. 'You pity them because . . .'

Lila stood in the cloud, her gun at her side slowly remoulding itself, as though bored, into a long, curving blade. 'Because they have no chance against me.'

'Is there some problem with this I'm not understanding?' Thingamajig sighed. 'Do you have any idea how many demons want to be in your position?'

'But that's just it,' she said, all the while continuing to track both of her victims.

'If you say "it's not fair" I will be forced to extreme measures,' the imp snarled. 'It ain't. But look, now you've had your identity crisis you've given them a sporting chance. If you wait much longer you'll disappoint the audience.'

She had not noticed the interest coming from elsewhere – but yes, dirigibles and boats were turning in their ways and the fast-moving craft of single demons were heading in her direction, some winking with camera lenses.

'I don't like to kill,' she objected, electing the demon she had first seen, the one with the gun.

'Liar.'

She arrowed after the target on an indirect angle, watching its movements and deciding it was weaving its path only to distract. She looked ahead for any destination that was likely to be useful to it, but there was nothing in particular that stood out. In the meantime she identified it : Demon Duellist 388, Vekankal. His personal note: Die, bitch.

Articulate, she said to herself, startled to realise how angry and hurt the two words made her. She didn't even know the guy. Her speed increased and the paparazzi vehicles began to lose ground.

Concise. Tath stretched out, reaching his aetheric body to just below her human skin. Where he could he always avoided the metal prosthetics, though he could run through them almost as easily as through flesh. Metal usually fouled elven aether senses, but hers did not. Another point she should have thought about more carefully when believing that human science had remade her. Her gut twisted for a moment and she tasted burning in the back of her throat.

Behind her now the second demon had slowed down. It moved cautiously, keeping her almost directly between itself and its partner. So that answered the question about whether the MV was still functional. Lila stayed airborne as she closed in. Her body seemed strangely rigid with a feeling that at first she didn't recognise.

'Rage,' said the imp. 'Pure and simple. Rage at the whole unfair stupidity of the system. Rage against the machine. You might win this fight, but you're still trapped like a fucking rat.' His voice became as gritty as if he'd been smoking sixty a day his whole life long; two steps away from a cancerous rattle. She could hear him smiling as he picked her thoughts clean and she chose the right calibre of hot lead to slow her target down. Guns didn't kill demons. Demons killed demons.

'You don't even know why you came here and stayed here and hitched yourself to that whitemare, Teazle, except of course that being allied to him seems like a good step better than being on his hit list. Plus his attention was incredibly flattering if also a bit creepy and you're scared of him.'

Lila pointed her right arm at the running demon in the city below her. It was in a crowd, shoving its way through, the heavy power unit of the MV slowing it down. The distance between them was about four hundred metres. Her forearm vibrated pleasantly with the thrum of perfectly engineered metal parts oiling themselves into position. Click. Blam. She took out the power unit first and hesitated . . . The demon dropped the useless thing and spun around, searching for her, spraying a random fire of its own missiles into the air.

'And you feel like it's fucked your relationship with the elf. And it has. And you know it. Before it even started. And you thought you were doing such a smart thing, such an adult and responsible and carefully planned out and clever thing. It would put you in a great position of power as well as largely out of the way of serious harm, give or take the odd deathmatch of note, and Zal would be all admiring of how brave you are, sticking with all this demon junk, death obsessed pigs that we are.'

Blam, blam, blam. The pavement suddenly went green with blood and demons scattered, those closest to the victim leaping in to loot him as he fell, three wounds in his chest.

'And then there's the elf-style junk one must always suspect is still there – all that holier than thou vomit loitering beneath the surface. It's swallowing one horrible shock after another like oysters, yum yum, very sophisticated and grown-up you are. Then suddenly it tastes just like a can of crap because now some bunch of chickenshit duellists have ganged up on you, and even in a three they're so incompetent it physically hurts to smack them down. And you hate it. Where's the glamour?'

Lila dropped from the sky like a stone, making no effort to check her near-terminal speed. The demon was fighting its way to its feet, groping for close-range weapons, its ugly head snarling, body becoming scarlet and violet with extreme fury. Gore trickled from its chest. Lila's boots struck it squarely on the head, the jet burns vanishing as she landed with full force and smashed its skull flat under her feet. She stood, pain rocketing through her hips and spine and into her own head like fire. Through the soles of her feet and the long metal lines of her legs she felt the demon's soul flow like a thousand angry bees, hauled in on the fine, deadly line of Tath's expertise. It vanished as he consumed it, slowly but surely going silent. Neither of them had a thing to say to one another.

'Heh. So that's rage. Congratulations, babe, you won the jackpot. Say, are you sure you're not getting some aether? I coulda sworn I smelled something.'

'I'm starting not to like you,' she said quietly to the imp as a polite riffle of applause rose out of the standing crowd. Without a second's acknowledgement of it she took to the air in search of the third conspirator.

'I'm glad you're the cold, quiet kind, not one of those shouty ones,' Thingamajig said contentedly, stabbing a hold on her ear. 'There's a kind of sad dignity in the quiet ones, like they believe they still have a hold on things.'

The third demon met her on the Bulwark, a place where the mass of the city cornered itself against the eroding stone of the continent at its back. Here homes and palaces were carved into the rock rather than built from it and their roofs were the smoothed planes of irregular basalt that had hardened there millions of years before, spewed from the mouths of ancient volcanoes. Many traditional duels took place here. The stones were marked with thousands of years of demon feet, hands and claws raking through the moves of their martial arts. They'd patterned the surface until it resembled instructions on a dance card.

To remove her advantages this demon – a blue-black creature with a huge wolfish ruff, a lion's head and the four-armed body of a Hindu god – had chosen to establish hand-to-hand fighting. She knew that was its best chance. At close range her metal body could not be damaged significantly but her remaining human body was vulnerable if it could get through her guard. At base she wasn't a fighter at all, she was a secretary with add-ons and attitude. At times like this that didn't seem so comforting.

The demon stood on its starting spot, twenty metres away. She stood on hers, behind the line cut in the rock. It put down its gun and knives, undid its belt of strange-looking devices and threw it aside. She showed her empty hands. She could no more throw down her weapons than remove her limbs, but the gesture was considered enough. She'd been here before.

I should probably turn off the AI, she said guiltily to Tath, her shoulders sinking as the demon readied itself and raised its arms.

It rushed her, completely ignoring the usual steps of the first encounter. To Lila its approach took an age. Her AI mind accelerated and time slowed down. She had a year to step forward, block and strike. It was over just like that. The demon fell dead to the stone, leaving its head in her hand. The heavy thing swung at the end of her wrist, dripping, her fingers in its eyes and her thumb in its mouth in the bowling grip she had used to wrench it from its neck.

Why do you not?

There was a scuffle as onlookers and casual fighters suddenly rushed forwards in the usual frenzy to appropriate another's possessions. She sidestepped them.

Because then it'd kill me, she said and took off, going back for what was left of the other demon corpses.

She smiled for the photographers. She put the heads of the defeated demons on the Telltale poles outside the Library, for the benefit of browsing students of the Vicious Arts. There were a large number of poles by now, most of them featuring heads she'd put there. It was extremely unpleasant, thick with flies and the stench was unbelievable.

The little Hoodoo priest who oversaw the place briefly looked up from his popular romance novel and gave her a friendly nod.

'Miss Friendslayer.'

'Hi Shabaoth. How's the headshrinking going?'

'Great. Thanks to your persistence I have nearly perfected the art. Soon I will be able to leave this place and move to the country.'

'Great.' She had no idea what the shrunken heads were for. She didn't want to know.

With grim patience she paid her Victory Tax to the City Courthouse politely and then she went to the Mousa District, where she'd been headed all along to find Zal because he would surely be there playing. And he was there, in the classical concert hall, fooling around on a full-size golden harp while a bunch of other demons practised alongside him, jamming a little with their violas and bassoons and other things she didn't know the name of. She tiptoed up into the gods of the auditorium, took a seat, wrapped her freshly washed hands around her knees, and listened.

CHAPTER FIVE

Sunlight streamed through the high windows, falling through a faint sparkle of dust before lighting on the orchestra. The reds and ochres of the vast concert hall glowed with warmth and Lila's mind was filled with the soothing beauty of variations on 'Sicilienne', a popular piece by the human composer, Fauré. The demons' non-traditional instruments only added to the serenity of the piece as she watched the light fall on the straight, near-white hair of the lone elf at the side of the stage. He sat among the string players with the harp a darker shining gold against him and his burning demon-wings softly moving in time, their light shimmering on the harp. He was quite lost in the playing and the music, his longer than human fingers plucking their way easily along the huge wall of strings between them. Occasionally he smiled or nodded as different sections of the makeshift orchestra took a new variation upon themselves and led the melody away in another direction. The cellos and basses and forzandas sang and then a green demon came in, opened the case on the piano, sat down and the music shifted towards his sudden new improvisation; a song both wonderful in its calm and piercing in its sweet sadness.

Lila listened with tears falling down her face. She barely moved to breathe. If she did she felt that she would fall apart. The strength and self-discipline that had maintained her resolve not to dwell on the events of recent days could not stand against this music. Her throat hurt as though it was being broken from within and she felt that if she moved it would not hold down what it had to hold down. She had thought she would just wait here until the practice was finished, that's all. She'd never expected anything like this and now she was fixed to the spot. Anyone could have shot her dead without trouble; she'd almost welcome it.

In front of her Thingamajig had crept forward, leaving her to sit on the railings looking down, his small feet and hands wrapped around the bar. His fires were barely flickering. He was as hunched over himself as she was. She wondered if his chest hurt as much as hers did, just there beneath the breastbone.

Tath was motionless, a sargasso of quiet power. She'd never felt him so acutely. Usually her own activity blocked out his presence – something she practised since it kept them notionally apart. Now she realised how strong he'd become from eating the souls of the demons she had killed. She suddenly saw an image of two reactors in her mind, one the tokamak that had replaced her womb, the other a sphere of strange atmosphere around her heart, filled with its own weather systems.

Tath noticed her noticing him, and the image too, but didn't speak or change his state. He watched Zal with the same fixity that she did, through her eyes.

The music changed as they played on, moving faster, gaining intensity, shifting into a suddenly more charged and forceful mood as though all the players had had the same turn of heart from sorrow to a sadness sublimated with joy and determination. It was a mystery to Lila how they knew to move that way. Nobody had the lead, but everyone went. She clung to the music – *yes, pull me away . . . I want to forget . . . and I don't want to feel any more. Let there be only the music and not myself.*

They sat for a long time until at last the musicians closed the melodies and slowly, a few at a time, packed up their things and wandered off. When Lila checked the time she saw that hours had passed. Her tear-stained face had become dry and crackly but she felt better.

She stood up – even after all this time she did it cautiously, expecting her knees to crack – but only her back felt stiff. She gave it a stretch and then vaulted lightly over the rail and floated down to the stage on a cushion of warm jet air, making sure to drop the last metre so she didn't burn the wooden floor.

Zal, tall, willowy and thin, was standing and talking to one of the viola players. His wings had disappeared into the flare on his bare back and he looked slightly out of place among the luxuriantly coloured demons. At this short range and in such company his ears – their long mobile tips level with the top of his head – could be easily mistaken for horns until they moved, which one did now, like a horse's, picking up on Lila's footsteps. He turned and his shadow-dark eyes glanced towards her.

'Hey, Metallica,' he said in a low, quiet voice with his usual teasing tone. 'What's up?'

'I have to return to Otopia,' she said, going up to him, feeling unaccountably shy suddenly. She took his hand when she had intended to kiss him.

He frowned slightly. 'Already?'

'You were supposed to be there days ago,' she said, feeling annoyed by the defensive edge in her voice. 'Malachi came,' she added. 'The Agency are asking for us all to do something about the Mothkin.'

'Hah!' Zal said. His fingers gently caressed the backs of hers. 'I knew the life of an interdimensional superhero would be a thrill a minute.' He paused to say goodbye to the violinist who had sat beside him and then let go of Lila's hand to place the harp back in its box. When he had done he walked with her to the door, 'You don't look happy.'

'Oh, I was jumped on the way here by three desperadoes. They only had an MV and nothing much else after that. I feel like a murderer.' She found herself wiping her hands on the dull black leather finish that she'd made instead of shiny chrome machine legs and stopped. 'And . . .' She glanced around and then up and saw Thingamajig still asleep up in the roof. Zal followed her gaze and frowned.

'One day I will have you all to myself,' he said. 'Speaking of which, where's Teazle?'

'I thought he was with you.'

'He said he had to see a man about a dog,' Zal said. 'He was still in the house when I left. So, you're still going to jump when the Agency speaks?'

Lila frowned, irritated. 'I have to keep up a semblance of loyalty if I want to stay in their good books long enough to learn anything of any use. Besides, I'm not giving anyone an excuse to remote control me until I find a sure way of stopping that in its tracks.'

Zal nodded. 'And the aches and pains?'

Lila's annoyance deepened. Zal smiled – he knew she couldn't stand any suggestion that she might be weak.

'They're the same,' she said.

'Wanna play rock-paper-scissors?'

'No.'

Zal stretched and yawned, 'I sup-*pose* I could go back to Otopia.' He made it sound like the dullest chore in the world.

'You could ask Poppy and Viridia what they know about moths while you work on the next track.'

'Bleah!' His stretch collapsed into a slump, strings cut. 'Yes, I could, though your partner could be more forthcoming about why he hasn't tidied up a few moths. Big Hoodoo guy like him should have some plans. You should ask him.'

Lila didn't miss the slight narrowing of Zal's eyes that indicated he was thinking very acutely even though he gave no other sign of it.

'Faeries,' Zal muttered and shook his shoulders out as if shaking them off.

'Everyone likes them,' Lila said, remembering the faeries who had been involved in Zal's kidnap and who were now trading in the Souk for magical items on an unusual scale. But everyone in Otopia did like them. Faeryware had brought an end to recycling problems and excess waste, not to mention boring and unpleasant food. Faery entertainers and gamblers kept to every letter of every law and never failed to charm. Faeries performed a lot of services for the humans in Otopia. There were stories of the usual things – changelings and so forth – but since it had become a requirement that the faeries deal fairly with humans in accordance with human understandings, as part of the negotiations to permit migrations there had been surprisingly little disturbing activity. However, as she was thinking this she couldn't help recalling Poppy and Viridia changing from their beautiful humanoid shapes to the vicious, slime-cold horses with their tangling manes that had sincerely tried to drown her and Zal in Aparastil Lake. She shivered.

'They've got features,' she mumbled. You didn't speak ill of the fey. That had been the first thing drummed into her when she started her first Agency job.

'Not many people have them as friends though,' Zal observed, almost offhand.

'They do. You do.' But even as she spoke Lila wasn't so sure. People did have faery acquaintances and colleagues but real friends? Were she and Malachi real friends? They'd only been working together for a year and outside of that – well, she had no outside of that and truthfully she didn't know much about him personally at all. 'Well, what about you and the girls, and Sand? You've been together for years.'

'And they are as shallow, devious and unreliable today as they've always been,' Zal said. The living flame 'tattoo' on his back where his wings lay when they were idle flared orange.

'Shh,' she said automatically. Lila looked up orange on her large AI chart of Demon Palette Communications and discovered that orange in the flare indicated a burst of creativity. Or possibly madness.

'Why would you say that if you thought they were perfectly safe?' he demanded, eyebrows raised at her contradictory ways.

'They've always liked and been loyal to you,' she said.

'In their way,' he replied. 'I'm not saying they aren't friendly. I'm saying they're faeries. It won't do to be your too-human trusting self around them. I know you think that's some kind of affront but it's the only advice about them I've got. Even they'd tell you that. Even Malachi. Even about himself.' He pressed his mouth into a flat line as he saw her stubborn expression. 'I'm not badmouthing them, Sprocket. They're completely fair and honest. As they see it, it's other races who can't manage the truth. Trust isn't something they deal in. At all. Trust is for idiots, they'd say, because trust is like debt. Sane people nail down every detail of a deal and idiots go on trust. And an idiot, to a faery, is someone who is ripe for the picking. Fair fruit, they say. They're not like us. You have to trust me on that.' He laughed at himself.

Lila rolled her eyes. 'Think we can leave a note for Teazle?'

'Itching to go already?' His gaze became more serious and assessive.

A faint heat crept under her skin and she realised with anger that she was caught. She did want to go. Guilt made her want to bluster but she didn't want to lie so she kept her mouth shut instead. How could she tell him she wanted to get back to the distractions of the Agency and its problems rather than stay with him here?

Marriage of convenience, she repeated to herself earnestly, as she had every day since it had taken place. *Political thing. The Smart Thing To Do.*

The faeries are going to eat you alive, Tath said with arch gloom.

Zal offered a half shrug when she didn't answer him. 'It's okay,' he said but she thought she detected disappointment in him as he turned towards the door. Zal was never just okay about anything; demons didn't do okay. He was for or against and saying 'okay' was really him signalling his disagreement with her failure to own up to her decision.

She stood behind him as he walked off, feeling inadequate. Surely she, who had taken on the whole mantle of Daemonia and its power, should be able to stand being there for more than a few weeks at a time? But the idea of the relentless fighting and jockeying and politicking of every day made her furious and exhausted. She did want to go. Maybe Zal could take it better – after all, he'd come here and adopted demons out of pure choice before anyone else had. Perhaps they just fitted him better than her. She wondered if that made him stronger. She'd always suspected that it was this sense of his being strong because he'd go anywhere, do anything, that made him so magnetic to people of all races. Not for the first time she considered whether her own decision to take up Teazle's ridiculous offer and marry him wasn't entirely down to a sad attempt to equal Zal's massive natural charisma. She had to equal him, in daring if nothing else. At first, when they'd been mutually attracted antagonists the fight had felt fair. But then, after the romance and then the love came . . . well, now she wasn't so sure she could handle the competition.

There was a heavy thump on her shoulder and the scent of burnt hair. 'Gah, I can hear you second-guessing yerself a mile off,' Thingamajig said, accompanied by the ripping sound of claws shredding themselves fresh purchase on her flak jacket. 'Match made in Hell, you and me, kid. Forget that willow-limbed tune-brained lunatic.'

Lila swept her hand to her shoulder, fingers fanning out with razor edges forming at their tips. Thingamajig leapt away wildly with a 'whee!' of sudden fire and she walked forward slightly lighter. Inside her chest Tath snickered.

Ahead of her Zal was humming a tune and trying to fit words to it, oblivious to the many demons they passed who paused to glance at him and then stare at her. Behind them she could hear the imp apologising and excusing himself through the halls, and the growls and snappings of those he was irritating. On all sides, musical instruments and the neat scrolls of songsheets were stacked and carried. Things twanged and rang and clanked and hissed and rattled and hummed. Amongst the noise, voices trilled and carried. As they passed other rooms and, later, other buildings a vast variety of sounds came and went.

There was no music not being practised here, Lila thought, struggling to keep up with Zal's long-legged pace and the delicate silence of his footfalls among the cacophony and the sheer mess of it all. The solid smack of hide on hide and a clash of small cymbals followed by a peevish 'waahh' and a thud indicated that someone with a tambourine had taken a solid dislike to Thingamajig. No sooner had the small moment of discord occurred than she heard a drummer somewhere start to riff on the rhythm of the incident. Around them demons sang operatically at each other instead of talking. It was only because she was filtering it all that she was able to separate out the sounds sufficiently to hear one trill,

'. . . say what you like but she'll never be one of us. Look at that freakin' imp.'

'Teazle's new little pastime,' agreed another, and chuckled. 'Wonder how long she'll last?'

'I bet you my guitar won't be longer than any of the others.'

Lila felt her mouth curl into an ugly line and for the first time in an age the scarlet scars of the magical attack that had almost killed her flared with a fiery pain. She'd heard it before, so why did it hurt now?

Stupid question.

The answer was easy. Teazle had had a lot of proto-spouses, none of whom had lived long enough to marry him.

He hadn't killed them all himself. He'd only done that when they had proved themselves more keen to pursue their ambitions and climb the social ladder than to care about him. It seemed he was a romantic to the bone and didn't take kindly to being exploited for other people's advantage.

Lila was cautiously fond of Teazle, although no more than that. There was a strange tension between them. She wasn't sure she liked him. She didn't dislike him. And he had a lot to gain from being matched to her, so she didn't think she was exploiting him.

Nor did Lila have any ambitions to do with Daemonia – except the lasting ambition to be out of it as long as possible, which was growing rapidly in scale and appeal with every step she took. She wasn't the kind of party animal to thrive here. She liked reason too much. But the cause of the pain that stabbed into her chest at the demons' bitching was her suspicion that because of this very fact Teazle and Zal would both be better off rid of her. She wasn't sure she wouldn't be better off dead too some days. It was all very well to go around making jokes about can openers and cigarette lighters and being a robot but there was a point at which the humour fell flat. And her joints hurt. And now her heart hurt her, because there was also the keen knowledge that she had been plucked at random to be this special agent, while Zal at least was some kind of genuine, self-motivated political superhero and Teazle . . . well, he was heading towards becoming a Maha Anima – a great spirit of Daemonia.

She, Lila, by her own efforts was simply alive and doing what she had to. It had pleased her to marry on impulse and she had. That seemed a bit . . . well . . . shallow, compared to Zal's global virtues and Teazle's supreme self-composure. Daemonia dealt in these kinds of values and she felt that the musical demons had seen her coming a mile off and correctly assessed her as a wannabe.

A sad tune pierced her right eardrum and she glanced around to see Thingamajig pretending to play the violin at her. Without cracking her grim expression she held out her hand to the creature and he ran up it gratefully.

'Made in Hell,' she said.

'Amen,' said the imp.

She followed Zal's narrow shape through the complex of the Mousa District until he came to the edge where he had left the Ahriman airship to wait for him. They stepped aboard it and with a holler the captain had the first mate heat the balloon and pull them free into the steamy noon air of the city.

The door creaked as Malachi tried to close it silently behind him. He swore under his breath. He was usually good at these things. His secretary did not look up, although he fancied she knew perfectly well that he had tiptoed past her to the garden doorway and was trying to get into his office unobserved. He might as well not have bothered however. The first thing he saw was the back of his beautiful ergonomic chair and a pair of rough leather boots parked on the top of his desk with a small pile of crumbled white salt scattered around them.

'Losing your touch,' murmured the gritty voice of Calliope Jones as she kicked off the desk with aplomb and spun herself around to face him. She tutted and steepled her bony fingers beneath her pale face. Curtains of stringy and unkempt strawberry-blond hair hung around it and dark rings under her eyes stood out as if she'd been lately punched. She looked more like forty than twenty. There was a faint whiff of raw aether about her, as if it was imbued in her scratty, unkempt clothing. Perhaps it was – he had no real idea just exactly how she worked her magic.

'Just the person I wanted to see,' he countered, taking off his jacket and whisking it on to the hanger behind the door. He smoothed the fabric and then turned back to face her, hand checking the lie of his tie.

'Beat you to it then,' Jones said, crossing her legs and getting comfortable. 'What was your problem?'

'You first.'

'I was wonderin' how the cash was coming along,' she said, rubbing her fingertips together on both hands.

Malachi had agreed to try and find cash from the fey to pay for continued research into the formation of ghosts. He'd thought at the time it was just a spur of the moment offer meant to save Jones's ass from a pasting at the hands of her fellow Ghost Hunters when they discovered she hadn't played straight with them, and had led their bona fide research down a personal alley. She was one of nature's obsessives even before she'd become a strandloper and now her passion for the science of the deep aether and certain of its creations knew almost no boundaries. She was the one human being who made Malachi's bones shiver and he hadn't bothered to stop and analyse why.

Now her pale eyes drilled him with a gaze that was physically difficult to move under, but he had to move; his cat nature didn't like being stared at one bit. He slunk sideways and pretended to make an adjustment to some disconnected and useless bits of old aether-detecting equipment that were gathering dust on top of a side table. That made the cut-glass bottles of coloured drinks catch his eye and his hand strayed to the lock on a fine walnut Tantalus filled with three identical crystal decanters.

'Drink, Jones?'

'Water,' she said, disappointing him.

He bought time by pouring himself a shot of Sweet Envy and swirling it to see the fine green tones mingle and shimmer, just a hint of poisonous lees falling to the bottom of the glass. Faery spirits were something he rarely took these days although once . . . but he didn't want to think about that. He got her water and handed it to her in his gnomish tea mug.

The Sweet Envy burned gently down his throat as he sipped, racing to his heart where it gave a piercing feeling of desire and a glow of incongruous satisfaction that was energising and brought on a kind of lazy battle awareness. He didn't in the least envy Jones, so the drink brought him back to a kind of strength.

'We're running on empty,' she said, wiping her mouth on the sleeve of her cotton shirt. 'The fact is, if you don't give me something today we'll have to abandon I-space for the time being, and re-setting the rig when we get back out there won't be easy.'

Malachi found a piece of string in the pocket of his trousers, a cord he'd made of seaweed that he always kept there just in case. He was able, through long practice, to knot it with the fingers of one hand into a small doll. He took the mug from Jones and put it back on top of the cooler, at the same time letting a drop of water from the rim where she had drunk fall on his finger. He slid his hand back into his pocket and moistened the doll with this. A little dust and energy and it came to life with a wriggle. It was the most basic form of Tell and probably as much Hoodoo as he could get away with in her presence but he wanted insurance on his instincts.

'Did they forgive you for The Fleet?' he asked, to distract her.

For a moment her eyes bugged out. 'Don't you ask the sweetest questions?'

'It wasn't my fault,' he said, and it wasn't. He hadn't been the one who was trying to summon a massive spectral manifestation into being, thus endangering the lives of all the Hunters, not to mention himself. He'd just been the one to point out that was what *she* was doing when she was only supposed to be making recordings.

Jones scowled blackly and flung her boots back up on to his desk with another shower of salt. Rime, he thought, from a non-existent sea. Salt was supposed to be proof against ghosts, but not these ghosts. He shuddered but she was too annoyed to notice.

'We're getting along fine.' She glared at him.

Underneath his fingers the Tell became hot. She was lying. By the looks of her she might well be here in a last effort not to be thrown out of the group, if she hadn't been already. Not that he cared about that too much: with money she could buy them back or recruit others who were more willing to risk their lives.

'I might be able to lay my hands on some cash,' he said and set his butt down on the perfectly polished surface of his desk, hands in pockets, head low and thoughtful. 'In return the Fey Court will accept any news you have on The Three.' He didn't and wouldn't name them properly – The Three Sisters. *I saw three ships come sailing in . . .* The damn tune ran through him before he could stop it and he shivered uncontrollably. 'And the ghost details,' he added.

'Ghost activity has increased two hundred per cent in the last three weeks,' she said. 'More manifestations of greater density and articulation, plus more variants. And many more inside world-envelopes, not just out in I-Space. There are a lot of new apparitions. And the major spectral constellations and their various minor entourages are migrating out of the deep towards the shores, away from the Void and towards material planes; world spaces and specific locations. We know that much.'

He couldn't stop himself asking. 'The Fleet?'

'Grows with every appearance. Sailed off its usual path. Heading for an ocean near you.' She grinned, the wild light back in her eyes that made him go cold inside.

'Otopia?'

She nodded once, slowly, never taking her eyes off his.

'Is the Admiral's guest . . . ?' He meant the sister, the one Zal had oh-so-casually mentioned to him as if meeting them were a common thing and not a one in a billion chance. Zal had been picked out of I-space by The Fleet when by rights he should have drowned there, lost down some unknown tributary between Zoomenon and the other worlds or Zoomenon and nowhere. His rescuer appeared to have been one sister. Malachi didn't like to think about that. Having such a thing take a personal interest in someone he knew, even if only slightly, was far too close for his comfort. And the middle sister too; pregnant with creation.

'Still aboard,' Jones said, ending his reverie.

'What happens when they dematerialise?' Ghosts dematerialised all the time, but the sisters were not ghosts.

'Don't know.' She held out her hand, palm up.

'Where does she go?'

'Don't know.'

'They keep their history,' he said almost to himself, thinking of The Fleet's vast dimensions and all the vessels it contained; seafaring, airborne, spacebound. 'Are they all actualised versions of objects that existed or will exist in time?'

'Don't know.' Jones stabbed the fingers of her hand towards him and pointed into her palm. 'But I suggest we find out fast because they're not the only things on the move out there. And some of *them* make The Fleet look like bath toys.'

'What do you mean?' The Tell had suddenly gone so icy cold that he

60

had to snatch his hand out of his pocket or be burned: important information, and true.

'I mean dragons and Other things. Ghostforms I haven't seen before. Not actual yet. They stay deep but they're very active. I can feel them. And I've been to the Edges myself. You may think you've got problems with the Void opening from the established worlds, but the Edges are becoming permeable too. I can run them a lot faster than I used to be able to, and with less effort. Don't even need portals to get into Alfheim now – I can just push through. Probably why there's a lot more than simple Mothkin out running around Otopia. You should get on to that shit. Before it all goes amok. The soul-eaters will follow them.'

The Tell remained cold. Malachi drew a slip of paper from his pocket; old paper made from painstakingly handcrafted reeds and worn to softness by millennia of sticky fingers. 'Go to the Faery Grim and give this to The Knocker. He'll get you enough for a few weeks.'

Jones' eyes crinkled with mischief. 'Not going to your human masters? Well, look lively, because I will talk to them if you let me down,' she said, placing the strip inside the grimy line of her bra, beneath the check shirt's open neck. The buttons dangled by a thread.

The string doll warmed up and he smiled faintly. She was too human and too keen on him to be quite as fast as she claimed, though he had no expectations of loyalty from her. Maybe it was the humans she felt some kinship to, in spite of her change. 'Don't worry. You're not going out of business yet. Oh, and one more thing.'

She waited.

'I want you to talk to my friend.'

'Oh yeah?'

'She needs information. Give her what she wants and I'll get you a year's worth of funds.'

'And if I don't?'

'Faery gold can find its own way home.'

Jones stood up and moved close to him, within a few inches of his face. Her breath stank of cheap hot dog. She looked so tough it was hard to believe she was only young, younger even than Lila. Her eyes looked a thousand years old. 'We'll see. Call me when she's here.' She tapped the chair with her fingertip. 'If your money talks, I might too.' She transmigrated, replaced by a sudden furl of air and a slight mist of grey un-ness that remade itself into reality after a few seconds.

Malachi sat still as he pulled the line and extinguished the doll in his pocket. It fell to limp string again and he identified the smell that lingered most in his nostrils. Jones had shed it all the time she'd been here and only his human form had been slow to recognise it immediately, although the cat knew its primal scent with a predator's conviction: fear.

CHAPTER SIX

Aboard the airship with Lila and Zal were several of the Ahriman higher ranking family, most notably the large, charismatic figure of Sabadyon, Zal's nominal uncle, and his two spawn, Mazarkel and Hadradon. They had brought several friends each and were having a party below decks involving a lot of eating, drinking and debauchery. Sorcha was alone on the foredeck as Lila boarded, her hair unusually greenish, signalling introspection, her clothing a neat ironical show-case of human military fatigues loaded down with belts of weather-beaten but live ammunition and strategically placed, diamante-studded grenades.

The shipmaster – a wiry reptilian sort – cast off and glanced at Zal out of hooded, lizard eyes. 'Cruising, Master?'

'No,' Zal said, cocking one ear to the sounds of the party and then narrowing his eyes against the light from the sun as he turned his head towards it. His voice was the powerful commanding tone of a fleet master and still made Lila blink every time she heard it. When moving in society here he exuded effortless dominance, whereas in Otopia he was more like a court fool than any kind of authority. It was difficult to imagine him ordering takeout there; almost as difficult as imagining him ever being an effective Alfheim agent. Now he even stripped Teazle of his name in deference to his own house colours. 'Otopia Portal, but first we must locate the Sikarzan.'

The shipmaster ducked his head nervously, 'May I be gifted with some knowledge as to his whereabouts?'

As they were speaking Lila had been standing behind Zal and now she saw over his shoulder that Mazarkel had come up to see what was going on. His narrow, green face was bland with drink, almost affable. Of all the Ahrimani he was the most human looking, his demon nature expressed in a few horns and whiskers. He belched as he spoke. 'Ah, long ears. There's been no fun with daggers and guns since you wedded The White Death. It's almost as if nobody wants to bother us any more. Will you be taking him with you out of town?'

Lila frowned. Why was everyone still picking on her if they had quit bothering Zal's family?

'And the little lady.' Mazarkel tried to wink but he was too drunk and had to resort to blinking and nodding, his small horns fizzing with sparks. He reminded Lila of walking roadkill that was animated by electricity.

'Fear not,' Zal said idly, 'we'll all be leaving you soon enough, if we can find Teazle.'

Mazarkel nodded with the collective sagacity of thirty pints of beer. 'Not that we don't enjoy your company, cousin coldheart. It's just like . . . well . . . better when it's just us. You make us look reserved. Nothing personal . . .' He tapped Zal's chest. 'Ah, Teazle. It is said he has the Country Vice. The tragedy of people like him. No doubt he is off sating it if he's agreed to go back to the miserable human world or that overgrown greenhouse you call home. At least you married into something worthwhile on that score. No'ffence, luv.' He leered at Lila.

At this, Zal's expression darkened and she thought she saw the shipmaster actually flinch. Mazarkel gave some kind of parting gesture and slithered back down the steps into the hold. Lila listened to the flap and snap of the Ahriman banners as they turned into the wind. She sighed. 'So, what's the Country Vice, dare I ask?'

'Fighting,' Zal said, pointing south with his arm to direct the master. He reached back and took Lila's hand, drawing her close to him at the rail. The wind blew his long hair back out of his face. 'No weapons. But no duels either. The demons who live beyond civilisation aren't like the demons you've met so far. They're much much nastier. The Country Vice is to fight these wild demons alone and unarmed. Nature to nature.'

'I thought that would be approved of. Why is it called a vice?' Lila asked, enjoying the warmth of his body next to hers.

'Because the high of surviving the fight is addictive, and addictions are slavery.' He hesitated and shared a wry look with her. She knew he was thinking about his own problem with fire elementals. 'To be honest, Teazle probably has no match in the cities. I doubt many people would consider fighting him now. He'd have to go into the outback to find something that could test him.'

Lila, who'd done a lot of work-ups in the safe ranges of her AI simulator on possible tactics for fighting Teazle, none of which resulted in victory, wasn't surprised. 'Why do those demons stay outside the cities?'

'Most of them are feral and kill anything on sight,' Zal said. 'Some of them are hermits, working on alchemies or arts of their own. Some of them are mad. Those are the easy ones. Teazle kept talking about going beyond the Gulf of Sighs. It's a place where there's a long inlet of ocean that cuts off a spar of the continent. The city demons walled off the land bridge ages ago and they police it vigorously. Convicts do tours of duty there. Beyond the bridge is a wilderness and beyond that are the Demons of the Waste. You won't find them in a tourist book. We don't like to talk about them.'

'The poor relations?'

'Not exactly.' He turned to the shipmaster who was still watching him with a hopeful expression. 'Turn to the highlands and bring up the guns,' Zal said, disappointing him. 'Prepare a Scatterwhisper Shot.'

The wizened old demon nodded but hesitated and said, 'And if the Sikarza Master is not there in the country?' He looked very much to Lila as though he was hoping that they would soon be going home and was too bothered to cover it up with a show. Agitation made strings of saliva hang from his ragged jaws.

'Then we'll make for the wall and bring up the bigger guns,' Zal said.

'And if he does not answer then?'

'Then you can send for the House Drake and I will look alone.'

At this the old demon sighed and nodded eagerly in relief. He turned and began to bark orders at his crew, who began to open deck hatches and heave at various kinds of extraordinary-looking weapons.

'We could just leave him a note,' Lila said, watching.

Zal shook his head, 'You need him.'

'What?'

'To help with the Mothkin. He may be even more impotent in Otopia than he is here but he's still going to have some power and you need that.'

'What would you know about Mothkin?'

'I know that they're a faery sub-race and you don't get rid of a

65

plague of those without a lot of trouble,' he said. 'Alfheim has had a few invasions.'

Lila sighed, 'Madame mentioned something about the faeries preparing for war.' She rubbed the rail with her fingertips, feeling its fine polish. Her sense of unease kept deepening all the time.

'They often fight among themselves,' Zal said, but he didn't sound entirely convinced.

'They won't be after your lot,' the imp suddenly said from her shoulder. He was as small as he could make himself, his bright eyes narrowed against the wind. 'All magical items is what they was carryin'' and no need for that kind of thing with humans. No offence.'

No offence . . . Lila mouthed with a snotty expression, sick of hearing it.

Zal smiled, the first time she'd seen him really smile that day, and she realised he was tense too.

The imp shook himself and huddled against Lila's neck as if it was freezing. 'What I mean is they can just overrun you with simple numbers and various sub-races, like the poison elf says. No need to bother arming. Just send them across the breach. I guess I'm not talking to the organ grinder here or else you'd be knowing these things, your lot being such experts at all the worlds and science and stuff like that. I do keep wondering what they put in that metal head of yours because it sure wasn't anything useful and you can bet your ass they know a lot more than they let on. Course, they wouldn't have bothered making you in the first place unless they knew the kind of trouble they were in once they realised we demons were around. I guess you're some kind of prototype. Probably in a few months they'll have made some better ones and you can retire to the scrapyard, so don't sweat it. I guess that explains why they just send you in to situations without telling you anything either. You'll be the . . . what do you call it? The guinea pig.'

'No offence?' Lila asked.

'The truth don't offend and it's my job to say out loud the stuff you keep trying to repress,' the imp grumbled. 'Wish I'd never said it now. But who else was gonna tell you? I've been adding it up since we met your boss and ex-boss, the ego on a stick. Things would sure be a lot easier if she was still in charge. Easy to manipulate, that sort, like putty in yer hands. Now you got someone who cares in charge and that's gonna be trouble. But I bet she knows all about it. Like Madame. And are they helping? Nah. Give you jobs that's all.'

Zal's smile vanished. 'Madame gave you a job?' As usual he was sharp when it mattered.

Lila couldn't bring herself to touch the thing in her pocket. 'Maybe.' She found herself wanting to tell him she didn't know how much longer she could stick it out in Daemonia; that the gruesome deaths nauseated her and her own growing indifference was making her feel strange and out of her depth.

'Now you're squeamish?' the imp sneered.

'I can squeam as much as I like,' she said. 'Think yourself lucky you're still here.'

Zal gave the imp a glare as Lila related what had happened at Madame's. 'At least there's only one of him, even if you can't bring yourself to dislodge it.'

'She doesn't really need me. I'm a pet of affection,' the imp protested.

Zal scowled and sighed, his shoulders sinking. 'I wish you were.'

Lila felt awkward. 'I don't want . . .' she began but at that moment there was a shout from the master.

'Set fires!' he called. 'To defensive positions!'

They had crossed the narrowest part of the lagoon and were heading out over open land. It was still dotted with settlements and occasional large houses and gave every appearance of wellbeing. Beyond the cultivated areas could be seen a line of low hills where the deserts began in earnest and beyond them the mountains that circled Bathshebat in three quarters of the compass.

'Possible attack by land or airship from rival houses,' Zal said, dismissing her unspoken question about the wild demons. 'Standard practice.'

'Shouldn't we do something?'

'There won't be an attack,' he said.

The master gave him a calculating look from over his shoulder and stalked back to the helm. The fans at the rear of the ship beat steadily, their shadow pulsing over Lila and Zal as they turned their backs another degree to the sun. Lila felt a momentary chill. From below came the sounds of revelry.

They are complacent, Tath said. *Even Zal has too much confidence in the white demon.*

From her position forward Sorcha sauntered over, her tail whipping but otherwise appearing calm. 'Not going below?' she said. 'Girl with a new man shouldn't be out here boring her butt off.'

Zal smiled a laconic, entirely elfin smile. 'Good things come to those who wait.'

Sorcha snorted and sneered at the same time, 'Better things seized in the moment than lost in time. Elves. Think they're gonna live for ever.'

Something in Sorcha's manner made Lila realise she had come over to ease her nerves, not just to make fun, and her chill deepened. Only now did she realise she'd been dallying with Zal herself, waiting for him to make a move on her. Disappointed that he hadn't she'd stumbled through that conversation about Madame again, wondering what was going on. And if he were confident that they were safe he'd made no move to budge from his position.

'Heh,' whispered Thingamajig into her ear. 'Heh heh heh. Hesitation.'

Around them the rigging and the net of the balloon creaked as the wind turned. 'Where are we going?' Sorcha snapped.

'To the wall,' Zal said airily but quietly.

Sorcha's ears moved and she shifted her voice to a soft purr. 'Why so far south, brother dear? Where do we go from here?'

'Down to the lake, I fear,' he sang quietly and then reverted to his normal voice. 'You may well ask. I am looking for something.'

Lila snapped up a map of the terrain quickly in her AI mode and saw that, as Sorcha had suspected, they were not taking any direct route to the regions mentioned. 'Territorial boundary?' she whispered.

'No,' Zal said, his head moving very slightly but his eyes not at all as he took on what in a human would be termed the thousand-mile stare. Legendary elf sight or irritating tic? 'Sorcha,' he said gently, 'how long since you were actually in a fight?'

'A real fight?'

He nodded, fixation unmoving.

'A couple of months I guess,' she said and rolled her eyes. 'Don't tell me this is a nail-breaking opportunity, man. I just had these plated with real gold.' She flashed her clawlike nails and Lila saw tiny jewels studding the yellow metal shine.

Zal spared them an unimpressed glance, 'Do you have any other weapons?'

'Only my talent, darling, I've never needed another.'

'Lila, suit up,' Zal murmured very quietly, a somewhat unfitting smile fixed to his face which had taken on a stony quality.

'Why?'

'What can you hear?'

They listened. Lila heard the wind, the rigging . . .

'Nothin',' Sorcha whispered with a fierce, black relish Lila had never heard from her before. Her green flare lightened and shifted towards yellow, then red. On Zal's back the flickering fire tattoo became darker, tainted with purple and black.

'Poisoned,' Zal said with a sigh. 'Ladies, down below some miles ahead of us is a Sikarza raiding party equipped to the gills. I suggest we remove our treacherous crew and abort course. If we come within range of fire we will defend ourselves with the deck guns. Should the balloon fail we will abandon ship but continue towards the wall. Lila, I'm trusting you to take care of that. Be alert for opportunists.'

'Sikarza?' Lila said.

'His mother,' Sorcha snarled. 'Blasted bitch. That family has no class.' She spat on the deck and the wood hissed and burned where she'd struck it.

Lila realised Sorcha was referring to Teazle's mother, the Principessa. 'And he's in on it?'

'Shouldn't think so,' Zal said, finally turning to face her and grinning. 'I got the impression he really liked you.'

'They're not doing this for me,' Lila said with a snort of derision.

'True enough,' Thingamajig sighed, shaking himself out with a rustling and a sizzle. He began to sharpen his tiny claws on some equally tiny whetstone that he produced from about his person. 'They're doing it in the hopes that she'll give them a big lot of treasure and a better position in her house for pulling Teazle down a peg or two. Risky game. She's probably gone a bit doo-lally since you offed her favourite son. If she wipes out one or both of you then she's sundered the alliance with the Ahrimani and Teazle's back on his bachelor lonesome own again under Mummy's thumb. He isn't the power over there. She is. Probably doesn't like the idea of him being competition and, to be frank, she's quite right. Give him another month and he won't bother with her any more and then that's the end of her. Soo . . . in light of all that I'd bet we can look forward to a lot more than a raiding party and a few moronic crewmen. Figures now what that decrepit-looking hydromancer was doing hanging around outside the house this morning. I thought that load of dross he told me about the drains was bull. Probably waiting to see if Teazle was going to have a bit of last minute vice, which of course he was, and then, soon as he'd gone, send the word that the chance had come. She'd guess this would happen at some point and have a few different plans up her sleeve. My guess is these chumps are all delaying tactics until the real thing can get here.'

'The imp is right,' Zal said with dislike. 'We must stay aloft as long as possible and turn for the mountains immediately.'

'Unless the real thing is *coming* from the mountains,' the imp added. 'They might be mad but they all have their price.'

'Teazle is out there,' Zal said. 'No more time to talk. Sorcha, there are four staff below. They're yours. Lila, take the master and the rear deck crew then alter our course and gain some height. You should count six. I'll go forwards for four. Fourteen is the full complement. Stay ready for stowaways.'

Lila wanted to ask if he was sure Sorcha could handle four on her own but decided to trust him instead. They parted as if their conversation were over, even though their changing colours must have given away their mood. Only Lila had no colours. She stuck to the dull black of her original styling, crossing the few metres of deck to the aft stairs in a few strides which transformed her simple-seeming uniform fatigues to thick battle armour. Plates grew to cover her human skin, until only her face, her red hair and her silver metal eyes remained the same. Thingamajig was toppled from his perch and went darting to a coil of rope beside one of the capstans. From there, he could see everything and was small enough to be well covered.

In another place and time, perhaps by now another lifetime altogether, Lila would have paused to question whether or not the entire crew was guilty of treachery. But it wasn't scruples that prevented her from shooting first and asking questions later, it was simply a matter of time. Any attack worth launching would be devastating and to leave potential enemies at liberty was too much like a fatal mistake. This flashed through her mind as she took the stairs in a single leap and landed on top of the first mate, her hands lifting him into the air with her and delivering a lethal jolt of electricity before the two of them hit the boards. She had only lately taken to electrocution. Now there wasn't even time for a fair fight. Not that fighting her felt fair any more. It used to, but she had become too good at it with so much practice.

In less time than this took to consider she snapped the neck of the demon seated diligently at the gas supply valves. (Must not look into his face or eyes, then it's better because you don't recognise one another and you can avoid that sense of killing someone who was no worse than you.)

All living things recognise one another. You simply don't want to meet the soul whose existence you are about to extinguish, Tath whispered and put out a feathery tendril of ash-grey aether, allowing this spirit to trickle past him and away to wherever they went, uneaten.

In fact, who is worse than you? she thought to herself.

'I'm sensing radically undemonic thoughts here,' piped the shrill voice of the imp from the roof of the wheelhouse as he watched Lila chase down the master at the door, place her hands over his face and deliver enough current to melt steel. The smoking corpse slid into an oily mass at her feet. With a yip the imp launched himself to her shoulder and gripped on, cutting her neck with his claws. She felt it as punishment and criticism. Without pause she swiped him off again with a snarl, watching him land on the wooden deck with a rage in her head so fierce that a spasm of pain went through her left eye socket.

From the launcher in her right forearm she sent a small missile at the last escapee, which took it over the rail in a blaze of chemical fire. She heard it screaming a long way down but kept her gaze riveted on the tiny Thingamajig, now cowering in a small ring of his own watery orange flames, his paws clasped together in front of him. She felt how good it would be to stamp on him and crush the irritating, nagging life out of his tiny chicken bones.

He held up his paws, fingers wide, his head held back as far as it would go and piped, 'Guilt, lady. We don't do guilt. Ask them. Well, next time ask them. They don't mind it really. All's fair in war. Big girl like you has to know that.'

Lila glared, her face hot. 'I am not like you,' she said distinctly. 'I am not.'

'Sure, sure, I'm just sayin' that you're wasting perfectly good guilt on those as don't want it and would feel bad if you were feeling it, since it's out of the way of right killing, that's all.'

'They were unarmed,' she said, feeling every second more and more self-hatred.

'Their choice,' the imp said. 'We all choose. You chose to be a kick-ass death machine, so why the long face now?'

'I did not choose!' Lila slammed her hands over her ears. 'Shut up,' she said. 'Choice. What the hell do you know about it?' And all the time

71

she was aware of Tath in her chest, curled up like a fat, satisfied cat. For once he said nothing. Maybe it was mercy and maybe not.

She ran down to see if Sorcha was all right. In the dim clutter of the party room bodies were strewn across the furniture like ragdolls, some with the arched backs of poison rictus and others simply floppy, like toys filled with jelly. These last were crewmembers. There was no sign of Sorcha, but Lila found her in the galley, singing to the cook. Only her AI was able to detect the sounds she was making as they were both above and below any human range. Her hands were gripping the cook's arm at the wrist, holding back the blade of a seriously large knife, but she only had to maintain the pose for a moment. He was blinded by a spray of venom from Sorcha's tail, weakened by it, and in any case, the pulse of her voice reached its crystal pure pitch just then and all his internal organs liquefied. Sorcha let him go, stepping back to avoid his falling deadweight, and rubbed at a spot of something on the exquisite voile of her tunic before checking her nails.

'Heh,' she said, apparently finding them all intact, and as she turned to meet Lila she was already humming a jaunty little tune. 'Darling,' she said, 'you just can't get the staff these days. What's the matter? You look like you swallowed a stormcloud.'

Lila stepped back to let them both out of the narrow serviceway. 'Doesn't any of this bother you?'

'Well, the relatives were a bit tiresome so it's no great loss there. The staff were clearly too cheap so I suppose it's going to be quite costly and tedious to clear up, if we survive . . . Is that what you meant?'

As she moved back and Sorcha moved forwards Lila saw a subtle change take place. Sorcha's amused, low-lidded gaze was perfectly honest and clearsighted, and she saw what Lila meant quite easily. At the same time her colours changed from a dark red shot with grey to a much more intense scarlet and black. Lila didn't need a catalogue to decipher the meaning. Sorcha seemed to become twice as alive as before, her red eyes glittered as she stared at Lila. They were suddenly in a dominance conflict because she, Lila, had shown weakness.

Lila immediately shot her arms out to the sides, placing her fists against the walls and planted her feet hard on the floor, blocking the exit. She let her chin drop and fixed Sorcha with a flat metal stare.

Sorcha twitched and rattled her tail with a sound like Death's maracas. For a moment she was poised and then she just loosened up and laughed merrily as if nothing had happened. She slapped Lila's shoulder, 'You funny one.'

Demons, Lila said to herself, turning and leading the way out.

Be careful, Tath whispered. He knew as well as she did that Sorcha had been quite serious. One day she could easily get herself into trouble. She had no illusions that even the friendly demon behind her would take advantage in a second given the opportunity. It was just the way they were made. Belatedly she had started to realise that, promises aside, it was likely true of Teazle and even, maybe, of Zal. Actually, on third and fourth thoughts, it was likely true of everyone, just that humans had a hard time acknowledging it these days.

Just then the airship lurched and they both stumbled against the wall. Distantly she heard Zal shout, 'Hard about!' and there was the brief, dull snapping sound of a fiendishly expensive manicure getting stuck in an unyielding hunk of timber.

'Oww! Zal, you freak, kinda late with that,' Sorcha moaned, following Lila back on to the deck.

The first thing Lila saw was the ship approaching them through the air from the city. The first thing she heard was the whine of escaping gas from the balloon and then a sputter of dull raindrops and suddenly multiple hissings as arrows struck the huge blue curve above them. They began very gently, almost infinitesimally, to descend. At the wheel Zal was turning them directly to the mountains. Below them on the ground a comically distant little army of demons was storming closer. In the air, their assault team was much more daring and a volley of new flights struck the balloon, some of them igniting the thin fabric as they flashed home. Lila smelled an ominous sharpness in the air and knew that she was facing chemistry here, not magic. Then the archers became bored with the huge target and started to pepper the deck around them. At this Sorcha leapt to the open doors of the cocktail lounge for cover, closely followed by the tiny figure of the imp who reappeared a second later on an entirely new vector and flew into the wheelhouse wall with a thud.

Lila darted to the engineer's station, where various barrels of metal powders were kept and began tipping as much as possible into the hopper that fed the acid baths which in turn gave off the gases that filled the balloon. She spun all the valves open to maximum. Aetheric conductors shimmered, transmuting the raw molecules of the gas into charmed forms that were immune to explosion, but not, sadly, immune

73

to escape. She knew the acid would soon be nothing but salty water and the balloon nothing but a limp rag, but hoped it would buy some time.

Meanwhile the airship completed its laborious turn and straightened into the wind coming off the icy moutaintops. Another volley of arrows sailed about the ship, some glowing with charms to seek living prey. Lila charged her ammunition rounds and shattered them with shrapnel fire as they whizzed towards Zal where he crouched, tying the wheel into position. Seeing them outnumbered she brought her AI up to full Battle Mode and dreamed of guns in both hands; they appeared at once – Smith and Wesson six shooters, pearl plates on the grips and on her hands as she targeted simultaneously on port and starboard and took out half the airborne archers with basic hot lead. Seeing her accuracy the others fled to regroup. Lila drew her arms towards her body and cradled a rifle to her shoulder. She used headshots and exploding rounds. On the last shot there was a click only. Her vision flashed red. A long stay in Daemonia had left her out of ammo.

Zal came out of cover and took a look at their heading.

'We'll make the wall,' he said as the gas supply nozzle sputtered its last and their downward drift became more obvious.

Lila looked over the side, where the ground forces had grouped themselves around some large object. She zoomed in her vision for a closer look and saw that what she had hoped was a cannon or rocket launcher was in fact the ground unit for an MV being aimed in their direction. Without hesitation she took to the sky, searching all around for the anchor.

She did not have far to look. The other ship had turned and as its balloon and fans cleared the view towards the lagoon Lila saw the sweeping wings of a drake carrying a demon rider and the light second unit, the crystal fan of its open face ready to complete the circuit. The Ahriman airship was directly between it and the ground force and only a few degrees of angle remained to guarantee a clear shot through their midsection. They did not wait for it. Even as she calculated the seconds left in which to move the MV made a connection. There was a terrifyingly loud bang and Lila and Zal were both flung to the deck. The wheelhouse, the aft lounge and the steering system had all vanished, leaving a neat quarter-cylindrical cutout on the back of the barge as if it had been chopped through with a giant hole punch.

'Abandon ship!' Zal shouted, already on the move towards Lila as she in turn began to run for the dark open doors of the cocktail lounge.

A second bang and a circular hole appeared through the ship's aft section. With cracking and rending the entire rear of the ship began to break off and the nose tipped downwards, ropes twanging as the balloon began to tear free of its remaining restraints. The third shot cut upwards through the deck as Sorcha appeared, blazing all over with red fury and put her foot out on to nothing. The inrush of air heading to fill the gap where there used to be ship sucked her straight off the boards into the middle of nowhere. At the same time Zal ran right into the back of Lila, pushing her forwards. She let herself slide off the deck and into space as the balloon jerked free and shot upwards and the remaining sad half of the luxury barge began to plummet down alongside them.

She felt Zal's long, powerful fingers dig down under the straps of her shoulder armour as they fell and then his body fell on to her back and he wrapped his legs around her hips. Knowing he was secure she closed her arms in and let herself fall faster towards Sorcha until she could reach out and grab hold of the demon's arm and then her waist. When she was sure she wasn't going to burn them she ignited the jet boots and darted sideways. By this time they were only a few tens of metres above the ground. Above them the drake rider dropped its MV burden and unhooked a large netting gun from behind the saddle. The drake closed its wings and began to drop towards them with the speed and accuracy of a fighter plane.

By contrast, Lila, Zal and Sorcha were just a lump of clumsy, hard-to-manoeuvre, slow-moving ballast. Lila made to ready a gun but then remembered she had nothing to shoot. Zal shouted to her in Daemonic,

'Time for the trick-riding shot. I'll jump it.'

Sorcha, face to face and breath to breath with Lila, smothered in righteous scarlet fire, blazed even more fiercely, 'And I'll hum it . . . after me, brother, in the key of B Flat Soon . . .'

Lila increased the jet power to maximum by agreement as on either side of her the pair began a bizarre duet. Sorcha's voice went once again into inhuman ranges and bizarre melodies. Zal stayed with a less ambitious song but in complement to hers. Lila's AI calculated that his was aimed at the rider, hers at the drake itself. Surrounded by the music in both ears she felt herself growing disoriented and drowsy and only after she had started to fall had the intelligence to switch off her hearing altogether. In sudden silence she aimed them straight at their attacker.

The drake was no longer the lethal diving raptor it had started out as. Its wings opened up and it was almost lazily floating along the air, head weaving from side to side, its strange glowing eyes flickering like dying lamplight. On its back the rider was struggling hard to maintain control, mumbling to itself and trying to bring the net gun to bear on the easy target. Lila felt Zal jerk with the effort of punching out a note and then the gun fired and the net shot out. She made an evasive swerve but it caught over her head and shoulder, and over Sorcha, quickly wrapping them up in a charmed web of fine, hairlike strands.

Zal pulled his hands free of Lila's armour and she felt him climb to stand on her instead, one foot on each shoulder. He balanced like a circus rider and she kept going as the strands themselves hardened into filaments of steely strength and bound her arms to her sides and Sorcha to her. It also had the effect of cutting off most of Sorcha's siren song, as well as the magic infused in the melody.

With a snort the drake remembered itself and straightened up. They were within three metres of each other vertically. It flicked open a wingtip and Zal leaped as it began to veer away. The rider flung the useless gun at him. It was a reasonably large and heavy thing, almost as big as a rocket launcher, and the range was so close only an idiot would have missed. Lila had a clear view as Zal caught the gun length-ways and, in a move so nimble that only an elf could have attempted it, vaulted up and over it as though it was the top bar of a gate fixed solidly on the earth, using its small inertia to push himself higher. He landed feet first on the rider's side and collapsed into it with the grace of a monkey landing on a tree trunk, his forehead connecting solidly with the side of the demon's skull. Then her view was cut off by the drake's razored wing passing overhead.

Sorcha wriggled and giggled at the same time. There was a pinging noise and Lila felt the net starting to pop. She felt the demon's hand moving and then there was a tearing as more of their bonds gave way. Sorcha did enough to free her arms and head and then waved her fingers in front of Lila's nose. 'Always the sharp manicure,' she said. 'Now let's get moving!'

Just then a shot went winging past them. The ground force had found itself in range.

'Fly, girl! Fly, fly, fly!' Sorcha shrieked.

Fearing for Zal's life, Lila took off after the drake. It was beating a steady rate towards the mountains, speeding up every moment. She was so intent on catching it she barely noticed that Sorcha went silent, her flames dying back to a simple flicker in her black hair. The drake's speed, magically enhanced, was terrible to follow. The air battered Lila and Sorcha until the demon had to close her eyes. Lila's eyes, not flesh, had no problems seeing that the struggle in the saddle was down to willpower and energy. She managed to zoom in on it and saw, with a sickening plunge in her stomach, the moment when Zal had clearly had enough of playing around. He had his leg firmly tangled in the drake's harness and with a flick of his wrist undid the buckles holding the demon rider in position. His free hand snapped forwards and took hold of the demon's head, thumb in its eye socket and two fingers hooked under its long, bony jaw. Then he just pulled with a sudden, short, fast motion. The demon screamed and pitched out of the saddle, flailing with its long bony arms and slashing down the elf's body, but it was too late. It spiralled down and down and down and vanished on the darkening and increasingly rocky ground far below.

Her heart thudded in her chest and her skin felt raw. Recognition sang in her bones. In her chest Tath's cold pleasure made her furious.

You have learned a lot from each other, Tath whispered. She could feel his admiration for Zal, his hero-worshipping, self-loathing, love and hate as if it were a taste, like bitter chocolate.

She wanted to say something, but Sorcha was right there and anyway, she didn't know what she felt about it. What was there to say? They all of them were killers, given the right conditions, and those conditions came often and they did nothing to avoid it. She, who had been bathed in demon blood, wanted it to be different and the want was starting to feel like a wound.

She heard Zal begin to sing a different song to the drake. It banked slightly and then beat towards the mountains again on a new heading. Lila followed, keeping watch on the now-receding ground force. She saw them halt at a crossroads and begin to mill about. Some gestured after them, but without much enthusiasm. Heads were shaken, shoulders shrugged, wings flipped in disgust. After a few minutes their decision was clear. They would not go to the mountains. Whatever they were being paid, it just wasn't enough. Some of them split off to go search the wreckage of the airship and the rest turned and headed back to the city.

For the first time ever even Sorcha seemed to have nothing to say, but her silence wasn't due to any problems of conscience. As Lila looked ahead she saw a huge structure, its edges blurred with the intense vibrations caused by the magic that held it in place. Around it the air crackled with colourful discharges of various aethers, and elementals gathered in gnatlike groups darted all about it, sipping up what interested them. All the metal in her body, infused with its own peculiar elemental life, began to resonate with excitement at being close to such a monumental statement of power.

They were crossing the wall.

CHAPTER SEVEN

'You are going to die,' mumbled the imp in Lila's ear.

They were sitting on the wrong side of the wall in the weak sunshine, listening to the hum of too much aether crammed into the rocks behind them and watching the drake from the corners of their eyes as it ripped up earth with its claws and pondered whether to escape, stay or attack. Sorcha was filing her broken talon. Zal was next to Lila, his thin body burning hot with elemental demon heat. She was patching some superficial wounds in his leg with pieces from her medical supplies. The imp sat on a high rock over her head, hissing . . .

'Leaving me to plunge to my doom without even the slightest attempt to find me or my poor, mangled body. So, I wasn' gonna say this being and how we're such good friends but I have to say – you are going to die. We all do and you will. I don't know how but I can tell you when that moment comes you're gonna realise we were all level, just bumbling along according each to our own pitiful natures, and you weren't no better and there never was any better to be, you were just having to wing it like the rest of us, you crazy control freak. All the power has gone to your head and now you think you want to change the world and if you can't change it you're going to complain for the rest of eternity. D'you know how I could find you? 'Cos I can hear you whining from the other side of the world "I don't want to kill any more. I wish this hadn't happened to me. Why are the demons so nasty? I wanted a quiet life and what did I do to deserve this? Why can't Zal just go back to Otopia and sing songs? I defeated a professional demon task unit all on my own this morning without breaking a sweat and it's so unfair. Boo hoo, poor me. I wanna go home." Well, lady, you should thank your lucky stars I have a forgiving nature and I am here to remind you of your weakness and mortality before you get even more cocky. And as for Hell, don't think I don't know you were thinking of killing me back there like that would solve your problem. I saw it. And you call yourself a friend.'

'Slayer,' Lila said smoothly, keeping her attention focused on attaching the dressing to Zal's sweaty skin without fixating on the fact it was Zal's skin, and hot, and naked – a feat in itself. 'The word is Friend*slayer*.'

Zal chuckled. 'That imp really has you pegged.'

Lila stuck it down very hard.

'Ow!'

The drake looked over at them, slavering with agitation.

'It doesn't like the wall,' Sorcha said.

'It likes the wall fine,' Zal said reassuringly. 'Now its rider is dead it's having a loyalty crisis.'

'How long will it last?'

'I don't know, but it'll either eat us or sit down and then you'll know.'

'I thought drakes were like cats – no master,' Lila said.

'I thought they were like dogs . . .' Sorcha said, in the tone of one who has never really noticed other species or taken much of an interest in them.

'They're not like cats or dogs.' Zal said.

'I suppose they're a kind of dragon,' Lila murmured, half aware of screeds of data whirling around her AI self as it made encyclopaedic with all the processing power not currently being utilised by Battle Mode. She carefully didn't look at the creature in case being looked at made it annoyed. Dragons didn't care to be looked at, according to the one and only Otopian record source, which noted that all surveillance of the creatures ended quickly and unilaterally.

'Yessss,' said the drake in Daemonic. It stared into the distance fixedly during the long and uncomfortable silence that followed.

They took the time to observe the rocky emptiness of the mountains, to eye the dark and scrubby-looking forests that crept over the lower slopes, the glittering ice of the glaciers, far above them. The wind blew gently and the sun was warm.

'Doesn't seem that bad,' Lila said after a few minutes had passed. 'Bit big though. How are we going to find–'

'Ssilence,' said the drake. There was a peculiar cold authority to its words that even Lila could perceive. Zal and Sorcha both adopted even more oblique angles to it, unconsciously moving in sync with each other. Nobody spoke. Thingamajig twiddled his thumbs and made himself very small and inconspicuous on his rocky outcrop near Lila.

Lila observed the drake closely. It had characteristic peculiar eyes that were more light than solid, crocodilian snout stretched out, gash-shaped nostrils flaring. The small fans and spines that frilled its ugly skull were spread and erect. It was listening. She wished she knew for what.

Zal, moving slowly but surely, got to his feet. He was looking the same way as the drake and his long ears were in a 'side out' position Lila had learned to associate with aetheric filtering.

'It's coming,' he said quietly. 'Get up.'

Lila stood. 'What's coming?' She figured if he would speak, she would too. As far as any of her senses could tell, the wilderness ahead was empty of everything except pleasant afternoon sunlight and a few breezes that spoke of later rain to come, but the others were starting to spook her. In the absence of solid ammo she measured what she might do with blades, electricity, sound, or by hurling nearby objects. For the first time in a while she felt Tath stir and creep out of her chest along her arms, his aetheric body shifting up towards her skin and then into contact with the outside world. At her neck the amulet started to become hot.

The drake's head snapped around fifteen degrees in a split second, looking directly at her for an instant before going back to its vigilant stance.

Your magician's work holds against a Dragonkin, Tath said. *Remarkable.*

It didn't hold, Lila said. *Otherwise it wouldn't have noticed anything.*

But it didn't notice me. The necromancer's supple aetheric form spread itself up her neck like an invisible mantle, creeping through her armour to test the world beyond. He fixated on the same point the others gazed at, where Lila saw nothing. *Zal is right.*

What is it?

Death, said Tath and Lila was so familiar with him that she didn't need to ask if he was being literal. He meant that whatever it was he had no hope that any of them would survive it. The details of its nature were irrelevant beyond that point.

I can't believe there are things out here so much worse than . . .

Who cares what you believe? Tath asked.

For once the retort didn't sting her. She gazed ahead into the pleasant boredom of the landscape, uneasy only because she could feel Tath growing cold with the desire to hide, or to run.

But what are they doing out here with just one stupid wall to hold them back? Wouldn't they have already razed all the cities if they were that unstoppably bad?

They have no interest in the affairs of the minor demons, Tath said. *As to what interests them, I dare not speculate. Surely it is nothing that would interest an elf.*

Lila asked Zal and Sorcha what they thought. They didn't move from their positions but Zal said, 'power,' and Sorcha, 'mastery,' and Thingamajig said, 'completion,' and the drake said, 'Godhead.'

Just like the elves then, she replied inwardly.

Tath flickered witheringly and she laughed at him, but he was serious about the danger and although the others were trying their best to maintain a confident stance, she could feel tension beginning to creep between them. Her human body, what was left of it, suddenly felt most distinct from her machine self. The flesh and bone wanted to escape.

'Is there a point to staying here?' she asked in her calmest tone.

'Teazle can't hear us on the other side of the wall,' Zal said.

'He won't hear us now.'

'He will,' Sorcha whispered, backing up very slowly, as if it were accidental, against Zal's other side.

Lila put it down to some magical sense, rather than entertain the notion that Sorcha might mean they would soon be screaming loudly enough for Teazle to hear, and decided now wasn't the moment to ask questions. It had become very quiet. Even the wind had stopped.

The merest ripple, like the beginnings of a heat haze, shimmered across the ground and through the air a short distance away. It became more pronounced in the next second, rocks and earth moving like the surface of a still lake disturbed by the rise of a large body from deep beneath. Pebbles and loose dirt shimmied and whirled up into brief, tiny spirals before falling flat. This activity covered a wide area, several tens of metres square. Within its span what small scrubby grasses and weeds had struggled into life abruptly withered and crisped. There was sudden flat heat and Lila's skin began to tingle with the first hint of sunburn. She automatically put up an arm to shield her face and Zal turned away, backing off behind her as Sorcha's crimson flames rose around her like a cloak. Thingamajig leapt to her shoulder and tried to burrow under her armour; failing, he clung to her back instead.

'We could just go and Teazle can catch us up later,' Lila said, trying hard to feel it was not too late for this. Her amulet was burning again. The cool wash of Tath's *andalune* body covered her face suddenly, with the effect of a cold handkerchief. She was able to lower her arm.

It is incorporeal. At last I begin to understand, the elf said to her. *The reason you see nothing is because it has removed most of its existence from the physical plane.*

We can't fight what we can't hit, Lila said.

You can hit it elsewhere, where it is. Not here.

So where is it?

The Void's Edge, I-space, Tath replied. *And Otopia.*

But . . . how . . . ?

It all overlaps, the elf replied, as though this was obvious. *Did you not know?*

No I did not know, Lila replied, mimicking his own voice back to him with bad humour. *But if we can't hit it, it can't hit us.*

Wrong, the elf said. *It has enough presence here to deal with the aetheric and that is quite enough.*

'Zal?' Lila said as they remained still, as if already captured. To Tath she said, *Can you do anything?*

Perhaps, Tath said. *But I doubt it. You may hope it has no ill will. It would be a scant hope. It has come because it sensed power, and the only reason it might have interest in that is to acquire it.*

'Yeah, seems a lot of bother just to call Teazle back,' Zal said, for once unable to mask the tension in his voice. 'I thought it would be . . . much easier and less dangerous. I never crossed the wall before.' He gave a humourless laugh, 'I've got stupid, being here so long. The city fooled me . . .' He sounded surprised.

'It is worth the mistake to discover a legend,' Sorcha whispered, with a lift of her pointed chin. 'I thought stories of the wall were to keep greedy idiots away from the Family hoards hidden in the mountains.'

They were all quite still, including the drake. The air in the dead, hot region had begun to move. Vague shapes and shadows crossed it, turning in on themselves. Something was slowly boiling itself into form.

'You came here on a whim and you didn't know this would happen?'

Lila said, just to get things straight and distract herself from the threads of panic she was beginning to feel.

'The Country Vice is not unsurvivable,' Zal objected, then added, 'over fifty per cent of the time.' There was a soft explosion of light and Lila felt and saw the yellow and orange flame of his wings suddenly unfurl, casting weak lilac shadows of them all out before them.

Inside the shimmering air a shape began to emerge that was recognisably demonic: a tall satyr with extremely heavy horns on its head. It carried a sickle and a sword, a spear and a dagger and two katanas in its three pairs of hands. The slightest wash of black ran through it, a single drop of ink in a glass of water, and stained it just enough to see, though the landscape was clearly visible through it.

It appears to have some life-draining abilities like my own that do not require direct contact.

Joy, Lila replied, giving full rein to her AI strategic and tactical systems. And how do I get it more corporeal? But to this she had her own answer. She'd never met a demon who wouldn't eventually rise to some form of taunt. They had no sense when it came to their pride. The eventually bit was the part that was going to be trouble. She didn't see why you'd give up an advantage like total invisibility, to her at least, so she guessed it was in some way vain. She turned around, putting her back to the demon as if there was nothing there, and set her hands on her hips—

'So where is Teazle? It's not like it would take him any time to get here.'

'Might be dead,' Sorcha said, after a moment's pause.

'I'm not dead, you pitiful excuse for an Ahriman,' said the drake and abruptly shifted its form, becoming suddenly as smooth as plaster, smaller, thinner, whiter and even more draconic. Teazle flicked his wings and scooped up a shower of dust and small stones, flinging them over the wild demon that faced them. For an instant Lila saw the creature's surface become coated and flicker. Teazle continued, 'Though I am rather pleased you'd go to all this bother just to find me. Lila, don't stand there with your mouth open. Zal, do something useful like attune yourself to that bastard so you can tell me how to kill it. I've been trying to figure it out for five minutes but it's too good with demon aether.'

The demon figure reached back with one hand in a classic casting action.

'Ah holy crap,' Teazle said.

The next few seconds passed in slow time for Lila as all her abilities went into overdrive. She saw that Zal was in line to be hit by whatever was coming and pushed backwards to make sure she was in the way. Teazle teleported behind the semi-visible demon. Sorcha opened her ruby-red mouth and took a huge breath. Zal moved to the side, away from Lila. The demon's arm came back and its hand opened.

And then she was taken by surprise as Tath, without asking or warning, seized control of her body. His force was astonishing, bursting from aetherial to physical power in less than a split second. She felt him as if she was wearing him on the inside. His elven reflexes were faster even than her machine ones and he acted with absolute precision. He reached out, caught hold of Sorcha by the arm, and dragged her in front of Lila with a single jerk that was so abrupt Lila felt the demon woman's shoulder joint pop. But this was a trifle compared to what happened in the next instant.

Tath jumped forwards across their connection into Sorcha's aura. Lila felt him flinching, revolted, but committed too much to care. Whatever the demon had cast hit Sorcha at the same moment. Lila felt an abominable emptiness, a hunger beyond sating, and it pulled; it pulled on Sorcha and it pulled on Tath and it pulled on her with the horrifying gravity of a neutron star. But instead of drawing on physical matter, it drew on spirit and she, who had never really believed in the existence of souls, and had doubted seriously if there was any reality in notions of spiritual energy or chi or anything like that for humans, felt her life-force lifting out of her cells, quite bodily, and funneling swiftly into a moving tornado whose terminus lay beyond them all, beyond Daemonia, in a dimension she had no name for, into a being whose maw was open and into which she had no way of preventing herself from falling.

It was like being pulled abruptly to the edge of a cliff and then right over, to your great surprise and dismay, finding nothing to hold on to. There wasn't even time to scream.

She realised with what she presumed was her last moment, quite calm, that in any case she had had no defences against this kind of attack. She tried to look for Zal, and hoped he might get away. She felt herself leaving her body and plunging forwards, through Sorcha, whose spirit had already left her. At least Tath was still with her.

You give up too easily, she felt him say to her, and then there was a truly horrible moment in which the easy forward motion ground to a halt and she felt completely suffused by Tath in a grim intimacy she would never have granted, and through him she could just feel Sorcha, and beyond that and with growing clarity, the demon – and the demon was unbearable, unspeakable. Beside it even Teazle was simply a player among fools. She had never believed such things existed.

Tath *pulled*.

Then she understood that the ritual being worked against her was that of a necromancer. The funnel of life led directly through the odd, flat and two-dimensional realm of death, into the demon who stood beyond it. He commanded them to come, but Tath commanded them to remain, and now they were lost in a tugging match which would solely be determined by the power of the intent of the two combatants.

Free of her body Lila could look down on herself, on Sorcha and the others. In another way she could see through herself and the elf, and the demons, through the regions they passed across. She saw Teazle's odd form stretched out in those dimensions too and felt surprise as her agony increased – the sense of being stretched too thin. She was part of a rope that was made up of her, Tath, Sorcha and the other demon and it was under a huge load as its two opposing anchors hauled on it. The most curious thing was that as soon as she had lifted up here she felt no stress about what was going on. Death, or life, both were equal. She was quite detached about the outcome because whatever happened she knew that she was all right. This demon, even if it killed her, could do nothing to her beyond ending her human life – and she had just risen above that and seen that it was, in any case, only a temporary station. She didn't even feel the slightest emotion at the prospect of the annihilation of her consciousness. She'd been unconscious before and it had never bothered her. So what if she never woke up? Things would go on without her.

Pity you never get to keep this, she heard Tath say of the experience but even that didn't disturb her. Far off she was aware of Sorcha, strangely gleeful in the way only demons were at any and every turn of fate. Here only Tath and the wild demon struggled.

Can I do something?

His response was negative. She was not a necromancer. She didn't exist where it mattered right now. The fight for souls may be on, but commanding souls was a matter for those with aetheric power who had tuned themselves beyond death's gate. Lila knew herself to be part of an epic struggle, but she couldn't feel it. She saw Tath thinning, his grip on the two of them making his own hold on the material plane hard to maintain, and his lack of attunement to Sorcha's demonic nature making his grip on her even more difficult to keep. Sorcha was floating, looking at the other thing that had grabbed her, curious about what it would be like to be consumed; knowing it didn't matter – she would never be that other creature. One could not be changed. Lila felt a trace of disappointment leak through from Sorcha, who had been speculating on the possibility of leaping forwards and, in her last moments, dealing some kind of ferocious and maiming attack. The only thing that held her back was that she couldn't think of a way to do it.

In the real world almost no time had passed. They were fixed, each in their odd positions. Lila saw narrow tentacles, almost feelers, emerging from Teazle's open mouth. From her great height she saw them seize hold of the astral form of the attacking demon. That was interesting. She hadn't known that demons could do this sort of thing. Not that she had known or believed much in this sort of thing. Most humans could accept the small magics and sleights of hand they encountered in aetherically-poor Otopia, but hard information on aetheric battle and astral war was still the stuff of paranormal speculation and still, these short years after the Bomb, considered beneath scientific examination – mostly because no human scientific equipment had managed to detect a trace of it and the extensive evidence of human psychics was anecdotal and, to the prevailing paradigm of strict materialism, symptomatic of derangement. She tried to cue a recording but of course all that was down there in her body so nothing happened.

Time dragged as they began to slip slowly towards the invisible demon. Lila turned, to look back at Zal, and she forgot what was going on for a moment. From where she was he was visible in an entirely different way, like Teazle, and like Sorcha. What she was seeing wasn't a particular shape, it was the form of his spirit; both elf and demon. And it was singing. She could see that now, in the midst of this fight, he had no real awareness of it. It was just how he was. She was surprised and pleased to find him beautiful in this different way, as if it proved his worth beyond any doubt. She knew that she loved him, but here she didn't feel it. She marvelled at how simple everything was from this perspective. She couldn't imagine why she'd ever struggled against so much that was quite obvious and not in the least difficult or distressing . . .

She looked back at the others. Sorcha sang too. And Teazle was a hunter, silent and watchful. Tath she could not see, nor herself. They were too close. The other demon . . . now she realised what Tath had said and why. It was a predator and a killer in its true nature and it had refined that nature to a single hunger. It was less sophisticated than they were. It was raw. She doubted that it even had a conscious mind left any more – and perhaps that was why it was winning.

Through their union, Lila felt quite plainly that Tath was capable of stopping himself and her from being sucked away from the body they shared, but he could not hold on to Sorcha for ever unless he held on and they were all dragged away. The demon had Sorcha in its grip, held in the strength of its absolute first cast. Teazle might prevent it making two such attacks, but he had been too late for the first one.

You must let go, she said.

He hesitated. She knew for a fact, because they had been intimate so long, that if this had been him alone he would never have held on to Sorcha even for a second in such a situation, unless it would have bought him time. Tath had been a legendary cool operator, even in Alfheim. He'd betrayed his own lover for a cause he barely had a scrap of faith in. To her certain knowledge the only true bond he'd ever honoured was to his mistress and commander, the Lady of Aparastil, becoming a necromancer to suit her requirements even when it went against his own nature. He was a creature of necessity. And now he hesitated, on the verge of falling apart from effort.

He let go.

Lila was yanked back into her body with a snap. Tath went with her. In her hand Sorcha's body fell lifeless, like a giant doll, and hung there. The last of her red fire flickered out.

In front of them the demon reached back. Lila could see Teazle doing something but now she had lost her spirit vision so she didn't know what it was. Behind her she felt the hot wash of Zal's wings, heard him scream, 'No!' A wave of agony shot through her torso as she felt the shock of what had just happened, all vestiges of detachment gone.

In the midst of this she felt also something tugging at her free hand. She glanced down and saw the imp attempting to press something into her palm.

'Run, baby, run, you gotta all run!' he shrieked, pushing the small object at her. 'Throw this and go.' He didn't wait or try to rush up to her shoulder now but leapt away to the side and put his tiny hands out, beginning to mutter and chant and hop.

Lila pulled Sorcha to her and grabbed hold of her more firmly with that arm. She was back alive and her heart was full of pain but she still had a few neurons attached to the AI processors and she knew what she was going to do, whatever anyone else thought. Calculations fast as light had already run their course almost before the combat itself had begun. She flung whatever useless shit the imp had given her at the demon with as much force and ill intent as she could muster, and before it had even landed she turned, snatched hold of Zal around his whip-thin waist, and blasted out of there.

Her actions were so fast and powerful she felt the living elf buckle over her arm and lose his breath, first from the impact and then from the acceleration of their climb into the air. His wings burned her hair and eyelashes and seared the surface of her body armour. She ignored both it and his howl of rage and took them faster and further, heading for the wall. But even as they fled she couldn't help but look back with her machine senses.

Whatever she had thrown at the demon had made it suddenly denser, more real. It had three distinct dimensions for a moment, and a form that was nothing like human, all muscle and teeth and raging, apocalyptic eyes. A blast of heat much stronger than the flames beside her rolled up and then everything went hazy. It was difficult to see any details but she got the two main points: Teazle's hands grown to an incredible size, his fingers tipped with razor talons, ripping through the creature with such ferocity that guts and matter spewed out of the gigantic gashes in a fountain: and Thingamajig, dancing on a little rock fifty metres away like one of Beelzebub's leprechauns.

She thought that Teazle's attack was surely fatal, but then she saw the wounds closing almost instantly, and the thing beginning to fade, to turn, to get some kind of grip on the white snake behind it. Then she felt the sickening plunge of fear and loathing as something it did made Teazle's body shudder and jerk. She realised then that reaching the wall was not possible if Teazle couldn't hold the thing back. But then the imp said something; words in Daemonic that weren't meant for her and so sounded only like the muffled bass thunder behind some drug-ridden heavy-metal song played far away. Thingamajig spat and turned his back, scratching dry grit off his rock with his foot claws and shaking his tail. The nightmare demon vanished into the earth leaving Teazle slumped flat on the baking ground.

She flew up and over the wall and made landfall on the other side in a grove of pines, startling a group of young demons who scattered into the woods, hooting and squawking. They, at least, knew better than to stick around when adults were fighting.

Zal wrenched himself free of her before she had a chance to loosen her grip and staggered back several metres, ash white, his wings flickering and dying into his back.

'I . . .' Lila began, feeling Sorcha's head lolling heavily against her shoulder and neck. 'I didn't . . .' But she knew how it must have looked. The demon had tried to get her and she had pulled Sorcha in front of her like a true coward.

'I saw you.' The words grated themselves out of his throat as he stared at her, unwilling to meet her gaze, barely able to look at his sister's body. Inside her chest Tath was silent, but she could feel his will. She let him use her mouth and his *andalune* body surged out again, covering her and changing her appearance with aetheric glamour so Zal would know who was speaking.

'Ilya,' Zal snarled, balanced on his feet now, light and ready to attack. 'I didn't for a second think you weren't involved.'

'I did it all,' the elf said with her voice. 'She is not to blame. It was the only way to save her.'

'To save yourself, you lying little shit,' Zal replied.

'She had nothing to defend herself with,' Tath said, as calm as Zal was furious. 'I tried to save them both but . . .'

Then Zal was suddenly in her face, his eyes blazing at her through Tath's translucent stare. Lila felt her heart almost stop and a huge ache open in her chest. She felt the full force of his energy hit her right where Tath was, in the solar plexus, and it was worse than any weapon strike. It took her breath away. 'Don't you fucking talk to me you piece of two-faced filth,' Zal whispered. The planes on his face moved slyly and his whole skintone changed as he spoke, seeming to move into a private darkness; for the first time Lila actually saw the traces of his shadow side. Then she felt them, as did Tath. He snapped back, leaving her exposed.

'That's right,' Zal said, straight to Tath even though he was no longer visible in any way. 'You run and hide in the only safe place in creation, you devious yellow-bellied fucker, because I tell you now – if I ever get one sniff of you or any clue that you are near me I will suck the life out of you just as cleanly as if I was the corrupted undead bastard and you're some dumbshit human psychic wannabe. I mean it, Ilya.'

He used the first part of Tath's common name, the part for family and brothers. Lila knew how Tath felt about Zal and she knew how Zal felt about Tath now and took a step back for both of them. Tath was frozen with pain, even though he had been expecting it. Zal's rage and hate revolted him with a primal intensity that made them all the more unbearable. She could feel how much he wanted to scream at Zal, beg forgiveness, anything to get Zal's affection, which he'd never had. He nauseated himself and the effort to hold himself together and attempt to be aloof was horrible to experience. His energy vibrated violently inside her so that Lila felt sick. She still held Sorcha, in both arms now. Her body was cooling, her tail dragging on the ground, her beautiful hair blowing gently against Lila's cheek.

'It's true,' she said, herself again.

Zal's glare shut her up and she felt tears start in her eyes and well out, burning hot on her face.

'Well you hating it doesn't mean it's not true!' she blurted, furious with herself for failing to find control. 'There was no choice.'

'There was a damn choice all right,' Zal said, suddenly frigid. His tension softened and he reached out gently. For an instant Lila thought he was going to touch her and felt relief but he ignored her and took hold of Sorcha instead, tenderly.

Lila struggled to try and remember what that beautiful detachment and clarity had been like, when she was almost dead, but all she felt was an unreasoning jealousy and anger over her own pain. 'Yes, if he hadn't grabbed her then I'd be the dead one right now. Him too.'

Zal just gave her a flat look, like he couldn't have cared less about that. 'It was a choice,' he said.

She found herself ridiculously in a tug of war over Sorcha's body. She didn't want to let go and have him take her, because that felt like he would be taking all the rightness and the moral high ground with him, and she felt that he hadn't been there, he didn't know, and he didn't deserve it. Their gazes locked over Sorcha's limp neck, unblinking and hostile. Zal's long, slanted eyes had never looked less human.

'You brought us here,' she said, smelling Sorcha's heavy perfume, staring back and seeing her mirrored eyes in the surface of Zal's dark ones. They both looked ugly. For a moment she really thought they might fight each other, then he gave the slightest nod and let go, spun around and howled like an animal until his breath ran out.

'Here,' she held the body forwards to him. 'I'm going to get Teazle.'

'No you ain't,' rasped a familiar voice.

She turned and saw the white demon collapsed on the ground a short distance away. The imp was crouched on top of him like a small black crow.

'What did you do?' she demanded as the resonant emptiness that followed Zal's howl filled up the valley.

'Just a spell I knew 'gainst soul-eaters,' the imp began and accelerated into a top speed gabble, 'but it took me a minute to remember it an' I had to get yer curse out of me bag first 'cos if it heard me it'd've got me first and you have to say the whole thing an' I couldn't throw far enough to hit it from where I was in any case and anyway you was all too fast fer me to stop it.'

She digested this for a second. 'And this spell . . . how did you know it? How many other things can you do, exactly?'

He didn't miss the menace in her voice. 'Dunno 'zackly. Takes a crisis for me to figure it out. Bit of a memory thing. I mean, imps all get curses, they're like ninety-nine per cent of an imp's trade, a curse, and you can curse anything for a second or two because they're not re-sistible you see, they take a full conscious moment of aetherical fiddlin' to get rid of, so they buy a bit of time even if they don't work. An' I was gettin' it out when I remembered this way of sending them as hides beyond matter right back to where they hide so they can't fiddle with things anywhere else for a bit. Banishing. That's what it's called.'

'And you figured that out after it attacked.'

'Yeah. Well, these things only come to me, like I say, in a 'mergency.'

'How convenient,' Zal said, his face rigid with control.

Thingamajig shuffled backwards off Teazle's motionless form and hopped away into some long grass to hide. 'S'true,' he mumbled, not taking his eyes off the elf.

Zal drew himself up to his considerable full height and breathed out, very softly, very slowly.

'What now?' Lila asked. She adjusted Sorcha so that the demon fell against her more evenly and her body would not get bruised. She would have said anything to break the deadly silence in which she felt that she was drowning.

92

Far off she heard shrieks of pain and alarm, and laughter, where the young ones were playing.

'We take her home,' Zal said.

The long, sinewy form of the white demon slowly picked itself up. Lips curled with pain, staggering, Teazle made it to his four feet. One of his legs looked crooked and sticky fluid ran freely off him in several places. He steamed with feverish sweat. 'You go,' he said in his curiously civil voice, though it was cracking with the effort of speaking. 'I just have some small business to attend to.' He vanished and the air snapped closed after him. The ground where he had been was stained. Vapour rose from the spot.

For the first time Lila looked down properly at the dead woman in her arms. She tipped Sorcha's head back, so it wasn't hanging down as if she was defeated. Her eyes were open, black as pitch and empty, her lips parted in a feral grin of exquisitely charming ill intent. It made Lila smile for a second, to see that her spirit had left its mark so cleanly. She could almost hear Sorcha say, 'Don't stare at me like you got no brain, girl, when you got two of the damn things . . .'

Zal's white hand came into her vision and his fingers softly closed Sorcha's eyelids.

CHAPTER EIGHT

Malachi tried to rescind his edict on Mothkin. Of course, it didn't work. He had thought there would only be a few flapping off into Otopia, in a few places. That had been his intent. He had never dreamed they would come like this.

Entire villages were sleepy with dust, filled with visions and aether brimming on every threshold. Cities shivered, full of terrified witnesses and cold suspicion. Odd desires and whimsy crept up on people, filled their heads with dreams, left them bereaved with half-remembered lives that seemed to have taken place in other worlds long lost. Strange birds were everywhere. Some said they hunted and killed livestock and straying people, took children off and replaced them with dolls. They surely were the heralds of the wandering strangers who came, took on familiar guises to speak prophecy and vanished, leaving piles of empty clothes at crossroads. In the morning only the dust remained to wash the pavements in fine grey clouds that sparkled in the dawn light and caught fire at noon. Some days the world seemed ablaze, though nothing ever burnt or was consumed by burning. You could walk in the fire and nothing. And at night sleep fell with darkness and told stories that never ended, packed one in another like Arabian puzzles until you were so turned about you didn't know what was who or if you were asleep or awake. Night and day lost their ends. Murder blossomed, and love. Fortunes blew away and the economy began to collapse, and not just in Malachi's part of Otopia by the Bay City.

Across the Western Seaboards the biggest Otopian faultline visibly cracked open and cut across the half-drowned continent, one finger wide and forever deep.

Malachi regretted it. He couldn't withdraw them because – and he hadn't figured on this, thinking that his kingship would be minor, not worth such a response – the Mothkin didn't want to return and, most importantly, they were no longer in Faery, so whatever he willed even as King had no power to command them. He would have to hunt them down and drag them back the hard way.

The Agency was overrun and exhausted by the work. It had been a huge success, his plan to distract. But his star was missing while the show was on. Lila was still not back in spite of his visit. To be honest she had looked drunk with a mixture of powerful emotions, some of them new to her; those ones that hurried out of her face when he arrived like naughty children caught in an act of mischief. He betted they had to do with the sudden immersion in status, obligation and desire that was her new life with the demons. It would take a duller and much smaller being than Lila to hold an unchanging course so close to Zal and Teazle's orbits. But she wasn't comfortable with it, oh no, he knew that for certain.

He worried about her and worry wasn't like him. Also, if they hurt her, he would have to kill them and he didn't fancy taking either one of them on. His natural fey instincts were to dissemble, to distract and to avoid serious trouble by creating minor trouble.

He paced back and forth in his office, hiding from Williams and the mess outside. The news channels were full of accusation and blame. Fey were being rounded up and transported to 'safe centres' or they had fled their homes for their own safety. Everything they had worked so hard to achieve at the Agency, to bring some order and calm to traffic with the other worlds, was all being undone. Portals had been transferred to the jurisdiction of the army and were under a state of high alert.

The elves had taken it badly, and departed altogether – not surprising given the state of their civil war and eternal skittishness in the face of human curiosity. Sarasilien remained the only one of their kind known in Otopia, and he was quite cut off from communication. No one knew if they would ever return to formal contact with Alfheim or even contact of any kind.

To top it all on his desk lay the final verdict on the audio files that Lila had lifted from the spy job on Zal's studio. Human forensics had seen nothing in the frequencies and patterns of sound that lay in Zal's songs but a high-level fey disenchantment proved otherwise. Oh there was nothing conclusive enough to make a court case. Not yet. But he knew the Agency was working on it.

Then came word from Daemonia. Sorcha Ahriman was dead, killed in some feud. Now Malachi understood Lila's delay, but he could wait no longer to take his chance, though he had thought she ought to be there when he moved. He had been looking forward to her gratitude, but it would have to wait.

As newsfeeds erupted with speculation about the beautiful demon's death, and all the rest of the gossip and scandal that she had been implicated with exploded; as millions of covetous and lusty hearts went into mourning for the loss of their favourite pinup, Malachi quietly slipped down the corridors of the Agency unnoticed. He used the password he had stolen from Williams' desk and took the elevator down to the underground levels, to the medical laboratories, libraries and the armoury. In one of the forensics offices – an admin station – upon one of the desks, inside a grey report cover under the name 'Flint pieces: miscellaneous' he found what he was looking for.

He palmed the microchip and replaced it with a flint arrowhead from his pocket. Elf shot, these were called, and of no note to anyone really, but his carried a spell in the stone; payment for the chip. He glanced once at the family photograph on the desk of the scientist he had scryed out weeks earlier. The father's face was thin and wasted from a cancer incurable by allopathic medicine, and his smile was strained. No human medicine could cure him, but a faery master-healer was another matter.

Put the arrowhead under his pillow, he'd said to the scientist as she stared at him with unwilling hope. Just one night. That's all it will take. Don't look for a cure straightaway. These things take a few months, as long as it took to get sick. Yes, it would cost a great deal, this magic, and when he named it the scientist wife went paler than the photograph, but she nodded.

Some things were worth the price.

He was crossing the central hall when a voice assailed him, 'Hi, Malachi! Wait up a minute. There's some guy here wants to talk to you.'

He turned on his heel, brandishing a sudden sincere smile, his hand leaving the chip in the pocket of his jacket reluctantly. The voice belonged to Jessie Mark, one of Dr Williams' assistants. She sounded harassed but was trying to compose it back to busy-but-efficient. He was a sucker for nice girls. She reeled him in effortlessly and introduced a nervous-looking young human in a grey suit and overcoat. It carried a briefcase and smelled strongly of breathmints and anxious sweat. Every sense of its gender or other identity was momentarily lost to Malachi's senses as its wave of furious intellectual energy struck him directly from the front. Some people had no control at all.

'This is Mr Paxendale. He's a Qua.'

'Quantum Consciousness Theorist. From Harvard.' Paxendale put out his hand eagerly for a shake.

Malachi met his eyes and found them burning with intensity, quite out of place in his otherwise entirely unremarkable presentation. He had a face so ordinary it was hard to recall it even when you looked right at it. Vaguely amber coloured, brown eyes, brown chin shadow, with a strange amber afro parted in various directions by exact lines that looked like they were measured to the millimetre. On the authority of the eyes, Malachi shook the hand.

Jessie brimmed with relief and was so pleased with herself she gave Paxendale an indulgent pat on the arm as she said, 'This is Malachi, our fey Liaison. He's second only to Dr Williams. You can talk to him.' And then she left them to it, closing her office door after her. Malachi got the impression she was leaning against it on the other side.

Inwardly, he snarled with annoyance. Outwardly he put on the charm and forestalled a gush of extrapolation with a polite, 'Shall we go somewhere more comfortable?'

The theorist was only too happy to have found an audience. He followed and Malachi took him to the little garden outside his yurt, made him sit down, and ordered Japanese tea because he could already tell, just by those eyes, that he was in yet more trouble and it was going to take time to understand it.

Wild aether snapped and crackled around Lila's head as she struggled to comb her hair. Every time she thought about Zal it surged around her. Their Game, almost forgotten in the aftermath of the Alfheim debacle, had chosen this moment to assert itself full force. She guessed it was because they weren't in tune any more, and the magic was sensing opportunities to discharge itself and actualise. So Tath said, though she wasn't listening to him. In fact she felt almost speechless. She was furious with Zal, furious with Teazle, furious with Tath, furious with Thingamajig and stricken over Sorcha. And then there was what she'd seen when they were all neither alive nor dead. Was that real? If so, why didn't it feel like it now? How could she watch Sorcha die with perfect calm and now want to rip up and destroy anyone that came in sight? She didn't know what to do, so she'd taken a shower, spent double time maintaining all her machine self and was now stuck with combing her wet hair before she ran out of things to do while she waited for Zal. Not that she wanted to see him.

Lemon and lime scent sparkled in her nostrils as the magic brimmed up into the Daemonic atmosphere. A surge of hate filled her as she contemplated the stupid, pranklike nature of the Game and how it just had to rise up at a time like this and remind her that it was Sorcha who'd identified the Game's embarrassing nature – a bout of sub-missive sexual pleading ensures a lose – and Sorcha who'd slipped a million dollars her way on a bet to win and Sorcha who'd taken her into demon society on a winning side and Sorcha who had loved Zal so much on first sight because of their shared talent for music that even though he was a despicable elf she'd stood in the street and named him brother without a second thought.

Tath was primed to comment, but she squashed him down. The comb snagged in the scarlet streak of hair that had been finer and more sensitive than the rest ever since the magical attack that had almost killed her and the sudden sharp pain broke her grip on herself. She shrieked and flung the comb down with such force it pierced one of the million cushions scattered around the bedroom. At that moment Zal came in.

His normal healthy pale-tan pallor had changed to a distinct grey and his eyes were nearly black. His hands were shaking slightly and his mouth was in a grim, white line where his lips were pressed together so hard they had gone bloodless. A line of green yellow aether snaked up to him like a long tongue and she saw his *andalune* body whip around it and tear it to bits in a blur that vanished almost as soon as it had begun.

They shared a long look at each other's eyes.

'I'm going back to Otopia now,' she said. 'I was just waiting for you to tell you.'

He gave the merest nod. 'I'll wait for Teazle.'

There was a pause and silence between them. She wanted to bridge it but it was he who walked across to her and put his arms around her gently. Her anger vanished. She laid her head on his shoulder and hugged him close.

A waft of air pushed at both of them and she heard Teazle say from a couple of metres away, 'No need.'

She didn't move to let go of Zal and kept her eyes closed. The smell of him and the feel of his skin by her lips was too good to release for anything at that moment, even if nothing was right.

Teazle coughed with a racking, choking sound. His whole body convulsed. He retched and something heavy thudded on to the floor. Lila looked around and felt Zal's start of surprise.

Teazle, in dragonish demon form, stood like a reanimated zombie, so tired and wounded he could barely move, his body coated in streaks and splashes of vivid green. He leaked white fluid that dripped from his draggled feathers and once silky mane of hair. His back was twisted and wounds gaped open on his flanks. On the carpet in front of him, in a pool of slime, lay a large round object smothered in the bodies of coral snakes, one or two of which were still twitching. Lila had no trouble recognising it at once.

Teazle had just vomited up his mother's head.

He looked at Lila and then Zal, once each, and then collapsed to the floor and lay still, breathing shallow, eyes closed.

Finally, Lila mustered enough energy to free herself from the grip of the shock. She said quietly, 'Good dog.'

It was what Sorcha would have said.

She turned back and was faced with the immediacy of Zal's odd face. The series of jolts she had been through made her see it as if it was new to her. The inhuman slant of his eyes, their large size, the unexpected cowboy square of his jaw, the way his brows were flatter than they really should be, making a dark broken dash line like a Morse M, the peculiarity of his long ears like antennae poking up through his tangled urchin's hair, the whole assembly made matte, powdered with dust from beyond the wall and marked with grime and sweat from their fight . . . all this struck her as most freakishly unusual, a peculiar thing in a strange world. She kissed him fiercely, without caring if he wanted it.

He bent in her arms, soft and giving. His hands held her gently, touching her human back and shoulder and his *andalune* body wrapped around her.

She struggled to get her body armour off. He tore at the Velcro holding it together and it came off like a pelt in one sudden go. She wore black evening gloves and black stockings and boots: her machine self. Like lace they made fine patterns of her ordinary skin where they migrated into her flesh.

He stood back and looked at it, then more closely. It was new to him. There used to be clean lines. There used to be clothes to pull off, and beneath the clothes limbs that did not make their own surfaces. Now her fake arms and legs glistered with the black gleam of chitin, though they were nothing of the sort. Naked, but not. His gaze on her was like hers had been on him.

She undid only what was necessary on his clothing and pushed him to his back on the floor. He offered no resistance until she went to take him in her mouth. Then he grabbed a fistful of her hair and hauled her mouth up to his. His kiss, both kisses, were sweet and tender as his hand stayed merciless and hard there. His other hand was on her hip but that one was kind and she was in charge. It was like a punishment that was secretly a gift.

She glanced up once and saw the Principessa Sikarza's face staring back at her. Its slime-smeared look was exultant. Behind it a long narrow slot of Teazle's eye gleamed at her, the pupil a widening blackness in the white.

She put Zal's hands on her breasts and sat back on him. She felt completely soft and human. His energy surrounded her with warmth. She looked over his head at Teazle and smiled at him where he lay unable to move, feeling herself a fire starting to catch. She wanted to burn until the day was ash.

Zal groaned, a deep sound of unlimited approval, and she was alight.

Later, when everything was quiet, she said, 'What happened today?'

'Mistakes,' Zal said.

But she didn't feel that was enough of an answer. She needed a better one. She went to fix up Teazle's wounds.

They returned to Otopia piecemeal, Lila first. It was night in Bay City as she came through the portal and rain was making the streets sparkle and steam. Soldiers with live guns escorted her past their cordons and then, after such fuss, left her unceremoniously on the street, glancing back at her now and then. One of them said something about her eyes and the other said, 'Man, I can't wear lenses like that. So fucking cold.'

She bought a mask from a street vendor and put it over her face. The rain had got the dust down, the girl said, but you couldn't be too careful. She bought a bike, as big and black and bad as the first one she'd owned, but sadly only ordinary beneath the slick faring – not like the first one she'd been given by the Agency, a bike so smart it was almost like part of her. Now she had to start the engine herself. The salesman frowned as the suspension sank under such a small-looking girl.

'I can get that looked at,' he said.

'Nah.' She paid without haggling, waited for them to fill the tank and rode off without a helmet to the sounds of repeated protests. It was a very big bike. Her toes only just touched the ground.

She rode to the Agency building the long way, via Frisco – a detour of some hundred miles – and when she was done she knew that Malachi had been careful with what he said to her about the moths, because nothing was as she remembered it. It was quiet and still; the rain owned the streets and the buildings were all curtained shut. In the countryside she saw odd things moving around. Creatures flew overhead, singly and in pairs, huge and clumsy. Something followed her but she outran it, engine screaming. She stopped for a minute on a quiet lane between two farms and listened to the deep silence. The rain made muddy rivers of grey dust on her gas tank. When she got to where she was going she was ready.

At the Agency almost everyone she knew had gone home. Williams was asleep on the pull-out bed in her office. Lila took one look at the old woman's hands, folded like a nun's underneath her cheek, and tiptoed out of the room. She crossed the open plan administration area and let herself out of the door into the small and soaking garden lit with solar lights that led to Malachi's yurt.

As she straightened after ducking under the door flap the necklaces thumped against her collarbones. The black faery stood up as he saw her and rubbed his neck.

'A thousand things,' he said, in response to her raised eyebrows enquiry. 'Where should I start? Strandloper, moths, Zal or Paxendale?'

'Paxendale?' She sat down at his gesture, on the pile of hides that made his daybed. It was low but she didn't mind it. He came around his desk and left his fancy chair behind to sit on some cushions, his back to the centre pole.

'A human scientist. Presently safely at home in the land of nod, to wake tomorrow and return with his claims about the Bomb. Drink?'

'Yes.'

He went to his little refrigerator and took out two bottles of Faery

Lite, opening both before handing one to her and returning to his position. She felt the bottle vibrate in her hand as its charm adapted the contents and then tasted something light, herbal, refreshing and alcoholic – just what she had wanted, if she'd known such a drink existed. On the bottle's label the pretty green tiny tot faery that was the logo smiled and winked at her.

'As you know, darling,' Malachi said, leaning his head back against the post, 'we here at the Agency take the Bomb very seriously.'

'We do?'

'Care about it immensely. At least, we should, to hear him talk. I had gathered the humans were less interested in it as a mystery now and more interested in moving forwards, in spite of the anachronisms.'

'But this guy hasn't lost interest.'

'No. In fact, it's his speciality.'

'Crazy?'

'If so, then an employed one with the Ministry of Extraordinary Investigations, under whose banner . . .'

' . . . we all shelter . . .'

'Yes, yes. Anyway, he came to explain his latest theory about The Incident. It's extremely complicated and involves quite a lot of physics . . . I fell asleep in that part . . . but the upshot is that he believes that all of the visible cracking in the worlds is a result of the Bomb Event.'

'Not new.'

'Ah no, but there's more. The Bomb is supposed to have taken your original human universe and split it into seven pieces that are not divided in space and time but along another axis he calls the rei. As in thing. Reification, to make into a thing. That's the word isn't it? And that's scientists for you. Anyway, he thinks that the rei is a kind of spacetime of its own sitting at right angles to Otopia . . . which is not the same as old Earth. Old Earth time and whatsit is like a rope and now after the Bomb it's all like a frayed rope, if you see.'

'Kind of. Go on.'

'Well, spacetime has . . . space . . . time . . . and matter . . . and the rei has void and aether . . . no, that's not it. Something like that. His main point was that he thinks this was all created when the Bomb Event caused a direct interaction between matter and consciousness. It all boils down to us being figments of your imagination again. He even went so far as to say that the seven worlds related to the seven chakras of the spiritual body but then he had to stop and wake me up.'

'Why should we care?'

'Because there is a growing body of opinion in your ranks that think a reversal of the Bomb Event is just the thing to stop the problem of destabilisation. Paxendale doesn't think so, but he's more or less alone and forces are moving now that people can actually see a faultline crossing their own backyard.'

'Is it possible?'

'I sincerely doubt it, since the worlds were not created by the Bomb. But that is not what the humans believe. Most of the other regions however, at least the ones with brains in them, are much more ready to agree that the Bomb is the cause of the cracking and are considering ways of doing a similar thing – namely removing Otopia from its position. There was stability you see, for a long time, and very little traffic. Which brings me to Zal. A very detailed analysis of his music reveals patterns that stimulate human brain activity – beyond normal reaction.'

'Do what?' she almost choked.

'The Agency believe he is seeking to influence people. The only thing they aren't sure about is what he's influencing them to do. There hasn't been a big social shift of any kind. I looked into it while you were away. Had an aetheric decoder run through his stuff. The songs are charmed. It's a very mild effect, being here, but they definitely have an effect greater than ordinary music.'

'Which is?'

'I couldn't tell but I am certain that it can only be a matter of time before the Agency figures it out and then he's either going to be deported or . . .'

'Or?'

'I wouldn't be surprised if they made you some ultimatum.'

'Oh.' She sat for a moment and digested that one.

'Yes. It would serve a double purpose of testing your loyalty, which is only intact because Williams covered up for you when you ran down to yank out wires in the basement. But you're on borrowed time. Not least because there's really no disguising the sheer terror that you presently instil in Ops Medical. One false step and there are people above her who won't hesitate to pull your plug. Mine too, needless to say. And on that note . . .' He reached into the pocket of his immaculate, carelessly worn but fiendishly well-tailored jacket, and produced a small memory chip which he passed across to her. 'Don't ask where I got it.'

She pressed it gently between the thumb and forefinger of her right hand and felt a tingling and stinging as the pseudo-flesh transformed itself into ports and processors capable of reading the information there and flashing it up to her AI. Writing, figures, photographs, blueprints sprang into sudden light before her eyes and pushed Mal and his comfortable little yurt far into the background.

It would have taken her a week to read it if she had had to pore over the documents herself but her AI, long used to composing material for her, extracted the significant information and drew just that to her attention. It did so with what she could only describe as eagerness. A strange thing to find in a machine. She didn't hesitate to ignore that and instead focused on the news.

A year after the Bomb, the Agency had been anonymously sent a series of coded files through the world tree, which is what the old-style internet had evolved into. After months of failing to crack the code, an operative, who had been lost for some time in the first missions to the new worlds, reappeared. She said she had been given a code by an unidentified being which had taken the form of a man. At first she had thought him part of an Agency extraction squad sent to rescue her party from the Dizzy Gulf – an area of Faery that bled directly into the Void.

Her account was hysterical, garbling about creatures from I-space forming from nothing, attacking them and snatching them away. This man had thrown out some kind of line from Faery and hauled her from the jaws of a krakenlike monstrosity just in time. She had become suspicious when no others turned up with him at their camp and as soon as this happened he had simply pressed a slip of parchment into her hand, told her to take it to her superiors, that it was from friends, and then vanished, along with all of his gear and even the one canister of drinkable water. She had struggled and wandered lost and starving in the wilds for uncounted days before finding a friendly pixie who had agreed to lead her back in exchange for her wristwatch. The parchment code turned out to be the key to the blueprints, though it was at least eight months more before anyone figured this out.

The blueprints caused another kind of hysteria. They included ordinary plans for circuits, processors and robotics – which themselves were far from ordinary – but among the components required to make these pieces were aetherical artefacts and substances that could not be acquired in Otopia. Of course there was a hoo-ha about whether anyone could, or whether they should, or what it would lead to but eventually they went ahead, found, stole, mined, borrowed and bought the materials, and made some of the things. At which point nothing happened.

Nothing continued to happen until one day quite by chance (although a footnote cast doubt on this and referred her to a lengthy treatise on Chance: God's Dice or Intent At Work?) an engineer was tinkering with a piece of the mysterious stuff. He had earlier that day suffered a blow on the head and a cut finger as a result of an accident with his garage door. Now as he picked up the strange little bit of technological gubbins to attach it to an ordinary CPU – which was the only use they had so far found for it, it being not unlike attaching the total computing power of the Western Seaboard to one's CPU – he said it reacted with the blood on his hand. It was at this moment he realised that the blueprints were for cyborg components. He added later in written testimony that he had been 'continually aware of some kind of presence in the room' ever since they had first made the components, 'as if something was always looking over my shoulder. That time I touched the thing, I felt it push my hand down and for a minute I thought I saw . . . I dunno . . . some kind of weird face in the glass [of the eyeshield that covers the worktable].'

Because of the untrustworthy nature of the machines they had continued to analyse them only through the mediation of ordinary human-made computers until an Agency operative in Daemonia, working there secretly, had been returned minus an arm. They offered him a huge compensation package and early retirement on full pay for the span of his life if he agreed to test out a prosthetic involving some of the unusual machinery. Of course they had lied a lot to make it sound less dangerous and he had agreed.

There was no record of who he was in the file. The only note that was made was the medical report of his final discharge, five days after the operations that attached it to his stump.

'Continuing allergenic issues with the prosthesis. Successfully treated with IgE inhibitors locally applied. Subject reports occasional pain but limb functions far better than any currently available prosthetic of the same type. External powerpacks too heavy, causing problems. Battery life too short. Lasts approximately three hours. Ongoing.'

Some months later. 'Subject reports continuing pains, minor in nature. Inflammation normal. Subject reports "presence" of the arm "as if it has mind of its own" though it does nothing unusual. Tranquillizers prescribed. IgE inhibitors working. No infection. Improved battery lighter and easier to use.'

Then they discovered that one of the mystery blueprints that seemed to make something completely useless was, in fact, a power converter. It extended the ordinary battery life of the guy's rechargeables to twelve hours. After that they found entire power arrays which managed so well that they could reduce the size of the battery by a factor of one hundred and fit it into the arm itself instead of strapping it to the man's waist. Then there was an excluded document.

'Refer File: Cold Fusion Micro Reactor. Access Denied.'

'Refer File: Aetheric Gravitational Fields. Access Denied.'

'Refer File: Microminiaturisation In Aethero-Electric Materials. Access Denied.'

One file that was allowed suddenly showed an explosion of experimental subjects. Most of these were animals. Nothing exceptional was revealed in their records. All of them concluded with the single phrase: Test Terminated – and a date and time, followed by: Materials Recovered. Cremation.

Then came her file.

She paused and looked through the black and white words to the face of the sombre faery, 'Have you read this?'

He nodded, very slightly.

She read on. There was more of it than she expected. Every day since she had arrived in pieces had an extensive entry until the documents ended abruptly at a date nine days ago. But what really caught her attention the most was something that came from the Technical Medical centre some weeks before that. It had detailed an analysis of her metal elementals and then the increased activity of the components themselves.

'. . . appear to be remodelling and growing spontaneously. Rate of increase of adaptation jumped to cubic progression. Subject reports lessening of interface distinctions once again. Analysis protocols still effective. Spyware providing bit torrent rate in excess of processable levels within Otopian technology. Cannot assess risks within timely limits . . . suspect alien infiltration . . . possible consciousness . . . war for control . . . sublimation of subject . . . irresponsible and unpredictable behaviours unfitting to an agent . . . contamination irreversible . . . controlware unreliable . . .

'Action Recommended: immediate termination.'

Delaware's signature appeared in the records to verify that she had read this document. It was the last entry of hers before Williams had managed to have her thrown out.

There were other things in there Lila hadn't known, but she pushed them aside for the time being. She closed down the files and squashed the chip to a smear of basic materials, pumping enough electrons through it to remove any suggestion it had ever held data. She put it in her pocket. Malachi met her gaze and they sat in silence for a while, drinking Faery Lite and listening to the rain patter on the yurt.

CHAPTER NINE

'I released them,' Malachi said in reply to Lila's question about the Mothkin. He shrugged and put his head back against the yurt pole. They were on their third bottle each. 'It was the only thing I could think of that would provide a safe but annoying distraction for the Agency. I thought it would give us time to seize your control system or, well, at least we got this chip. But it's worse than I intended. And now I can't get them back in.'

'And nobody knows about this? Why is that? Why doesn't anyone spy on you?'

'Oh they do, they do,' grinned Malachi and flicked his fingers around at various points in the room, indicating symbols, objects, signs. 'But I have methods for getting around it.'

'The Hoodoo,' she said, just repeating the word she'd heard Zal use.

'Useful for many things as long as you use it wisely.' He rubbed his fingers and thumb together and laughed. 'Zal knows. He likes to gamble, unfortunately. Best he not try it himself.'

'Why not?'

'The Hoodoo always collects.'

'What is it?'

'A force.' He shrugged again and let his head hang forward. 'A game.' He smiled a little smile and she decided to drop it, because she wouldn't understand and she knew the smile too well.

'Well, what do we do now?'

'I thought that once we had secured you, we would recall the moths,' he said, slow and quiet, 'but actually there may be benefits to delaying that. I think maybe they're all that's preventing the Agency putting more effort into you and me. Of course, no doubt they're hanging fire with your execution because they believe you're the best hope to finish off the moth problem. Best they keep believing that. And anyway, it's true enough.'

'I'll go along with the first part.'

'Yeah, well, we're going into Faery to get the ability to recall them. Once we have it, then we can decide what to do with it.'

'Hold them to ransom.'

'Maybe. No telling until we get back.'

She raised her eyebrows.

'Things get strange when you spend time in Faery,' he said. 'A logical course, like the one you just described, when you get back it doesn't seem so straight. So, let's just go with what we have. In the meantime, before . . .' He glanced at the clock on his desk. 'Before Williams wakes up I'll let you talk to Jones.'

'The strandloper.'

'Yes.'

Lila started to get up.

'No need,' Malachi waved her down. 'I'll call her.'

He flickered, literally. She stared at him, believing her eyes because she could replay the event an infinite number of times, but still openmouthed. He faded. Then he vanished. Mal had never done this before, as far as she knew. Except obviously he had. Who knew? She was reasonably sure that the Agency didn't. For a few seconds there was a shadow where he'd been, and sometimes it seemed that it had ears, whiskers and a tail. Then he was back, just like that.

'She'll be right along,' he said hoarsely, wiping at a gleam of perspiration on his forehead and chugging the final half of his beer with unusual relish.

Lila took a swig from her bottle, noted its ever-changing delicious gingery notes, and nodded as though this was all quite regular. She felt a familiar type of air push, as when Teazle teleported in, but a little bit softer by some micro-order. Then there were three of them in the tent.

'Yo,' said the girl in the corner.

Lila was startled by how young she was and how exhausted she looked. What used to be a T-shirt and jeans had been added to with an elvish jacket and various belts and bits of leather armour until she resembled an odd kind of forest ranger. She was grubby, but her eyes were bright. Lila wondered if she were on drugs but felt Tath's reaction and realised it was aether.

Malachi handed out fresh drinks and said, 'Lila, this is Jones. Jones, Lila Black.'

'Hey,' Jones said. She sat on the floor. 'So, what's the deal?'

Lila squinted, she was sure Jones was human, or used to be. Tath uncoiled and crept as far as he dared to the surface. He and Lila still weren't talking.

'Do you remember I told you about the Ghost Hunters?' Malachi asked Lila.

She nodded. The entire thing made her flesh crawl. With her free hand she picked up and held out the amulet. 'Can you tell me anything about this?'

Jones sniffed and rubbed her eyes with the back of her hand before shuffling closer. As she neared, Tath slid away. For a moment Lila thought she saw Malachi right through the woman's head but then she was close. She smelled of stale sweat. She held the amulet but didn't try to pull it closer or off of Lila's neck.

'Leather strap, wooden circle – driftwood, seaworn, no carvings – inset stone, some kind of carnelian, uncut – a found object. Some kind of warding charm, very primitive to look at. So far so dull, but we are in bloody Otopia and I am human, so what were you expecting?'

'Isn't there anything unusual about it?'

'Not that I can see. Why, did some faery tell you it would raise the dead or something?' Jones glanced at Malachi with a sly smile and Mal rolled his eyes.

'No,' Lila said, disappointed. 'What about this one?' She held out the silver spiral.

Jones took it the same way and turned it around and around. When she reached the open end and tried to pull it back she found the cord it was on firmly back in the centre, which is what always happened. She dropped it with a start and then peered at it again. 'I don't know,' she said, but her brashness had gone, replaced by interest. 'I never saw anything like this before.'

'That's because you don't know many fey,' Malachi said, shifting uncomfortably.

'But the magic worked right here,' Jones said, looking up at him, puzzled. She abruptly swept her ratty dreadlocks out of her face and back over her shoulders. 'I mean, some things kind of work here, but in their own place that means . . .'

'They're very powerful. I know,' he said. 'I don't know what it is either, except it must come from before the fall, when we lost the greater magics.'

Both women looked up at him now, waiting.

'It was a long time ago, I guess,' he said. 'Before human recorded history, well, actually about the same time as the Lascaux cave painters daubed the wall. Which isn't unrelated . . . but that's off the point. Another brew?'

They nodded silently and he went to get three more bottles and hand them out, talking all the while.

'Before the fall, Faery had the greatest aetheric power of all the known worlds and the elves and the demons spent most of their time in various plots trying to get more of it for themselves. So we fought with them some. And at the same time human beings were embroiled in their own history, into which they occasionally bribed, bought, charmed, won or were generously given a great deal of our help. After a time it was clear that too much was being lost and misused, so we decided that we would lose the greater magics until a bit later on when things looked more reasonable.'

'Lose?' Lila repeated.

'It was better to lose it ourselves than see it plundered and used to create very bad things,' Malachi said. 'So we took them and pushed them over the edge. Hence, the fall.'

'Edge of what?'

But Jones was nodding slowly, her eyes narrowing with thought, 'Over the edge of the world.'

'Yes, except in Faery it isn't like a dinner plate with an edge that bleeds off into the Void. Faery has aetheric gravitation. It's like a black hole in the physical universe. The Void bends into Faery. Anyway, we pushed the magic off the edge and it was lost below, in Under.'

'So, how were you ever going to get it back?'

'Ah, it's like trying to drown pixies, these things pop up when they feel like it,' Malachi said, with a dismissive wave. 'My only point is that your necklace there seems to be from around that time. We'd never waste so much force on a charm these days when it's more peaceful.'

Lila frowned and thought of the sights in Bathshebat. 'But faeries are collecting magic. Isn't that for . . . some kind of . . .' She suddenly didn't want to say war.

'It's the War Effort,' Malachi surprised her. 'Periodically we go out

111

and try to get back what we lost before, and anything new that looks too dangerous.'

'Why?' Jones said.

'It's better we lose it than you use it.'

'Why didn't you lose nuclear weapons then?' Lila asked. 'If you're so patronisingly sure that nobody else can be trusted with anything?'

'They're physical only, I'm afraid,' the black faery said. 'And inanimate to boot. Can't touch 'em. As for being so trustworthy, I think a quick glance in a mirror might answer your questions there.' He quirked an eyebrow at her but he was only reflecting her own annoyance.

'Bit harsh,' Jones said.

Lila shrugged. 'You don't know anything. That's okay. It's fine.'

'Have you tried taking it off?' Malachi said and mimed lifting something up over his head.

'No.' She hooked the line with her fingers and pulled. It caught on her chin. She eased it there and it caught on her ear; lifted it there and it snagged in her hair. Whichever way she moved it it was always just a bit too small to come off.

She flicked a blade out of one finger . . .

'Hold yer horses!' Jones exclaimed, moving back sharply and almost falling over at the sight.

. . . and cut through the thin leather but somehow it wasn't cut through after the blade had passed.

Malachi nodded. 'It's old.'

Lila held the cord, not quite believing it. She didn't want to cut it one more time and look like some newbie unbeliever, and resolved to try again later, when she was alone. But a chill had gone through her, from heart to the soles of her heavy boots. She dismissed it. Quite ridiculous. Of course it would come off. Later.

'So, is that the reason I'm here wasting time with you and drinking your expensive headwash?' Jones asked, fixing her ferocious eyes on Malachi, then inclining her head in Lila's direction, looking at her hand.

'Did you ever see things like that on your travels?' he asked in response.

'I hardly seen anything now,' Jones said, leaning back from Lila slightly.

Lila glanced at Malachi and he gave her a small nod. She decided

112

that if he trusted Jones enough she would too and raised her right arm. She didn't even have to create an image in her mind's eye. The changes came as simply to her as opening and closing her fingers.

'Demon hunting: long range.'

The near invisible whir and click, the dance of the atoms . . . from shoulder on down she was missile launcher, empty of ammunition.

'Close range, honour weapons.'

Fssss. Blades and something more resembling an arm and hand. Fingers, but not all of them.

'Sniping.' Rifle.

'Mid-range.' Hand cannon. Pistol set under.

'Aerial.' Missiles again.

'Elven.' She got her arm and hand back, plus a longbow that almost speared the top of the tent.

'Can you do anything that's not a weapon?' Jones asked as Lila sat back.

Lila felt tired, slightly greasy. 'Joke things.' Bottle opener. Lighter. Torch. Fan.

'And do ya ever get tired?'

Lila frowned, not understanding where this was going. 'No.'

Jones sat back and pushed her drink aside half finished. She scowled and rocked a little, then said, 'You know how hard it is to do that kind of thing in physical space . . .' It was a leading statement, half a question.

'It's not possible by any known forces in physical spacetime at this scale,' Lila said.

'And it's not easy in the aetherical expansions either. Almost instantaneous transmutation. Is there a mass loss and gain?'

'Yes,' Lila said, easily answering because the differing weights of things was so obvious.

'But no changes of element?'

'Maybe the metals . . .'

'I mean you can't make a bunch of flowers.'

'No.'

Jones stood up. 'I'm gonna head out now,' she said and the long tendrils of her wild hair started to rise and glow.

'Just hang on a minute,' Malachi said, reaching out towards her. 'We had a deal.'

'I came here and talked,' she retorted. Her forehead suddenly looked extremely pale and shiny in the dim light. 'If it wasn't what you wanna hear, that's not my problem.'

'You're holding out on me.' Mal's eyes became long slits of vicious red. Lila was startled, she'd never seen him so obviously angry. 'I can see just by your face that you know something.'

'Well take a good look, faery, because that's as close to my knowledge as you're gonna get.' She hesitated at the end of this line and reassessed their faces, like a little girl facing her parents suddenly wondering if a furious statement she's made has gone too far. She held out her hands in the air and made defensive actions, her tone easing but speeding into a jabber, 'Okay, the stone amulet I really don't know but I guess it's a faery thing from the old time. The spiral is clearly . . . well, I hardly need to tell you what it is. You don't want to know or you'd already see it, I mean, every faery has to know. And as for the other stuff, that technology whatever, I'll tell you this much. Just let it alone. It works, you live, you're fine, you let it alone. Don't go trying to find who made it or why or all that stupid orphan shit. You don't wanna know where that came from and I am doing you such a huge favour by telling you nothing more about it that you should stick the end of the rainbow right in my pocket.' She whacked the side of her old coat where it hung empty and turned to Lila. 'Really, I wish I had better news. You're Zal's girl huh? You two have some interesting friends. Did Malachi tell you all about The Sisters?' She flashed Malachi a wicked stare. 'No? You do surprise me. Well trust me on this one, it's really better you stop now than go looking for those kinds of trouble. Seeya. Wouldn' wanna be ya.' There was a snap and a smell of ozone and she was gone.

Lila looked across a small sea of empty bottles at Malachi. 'She was really scared.'

He nodded, his mouth turned down. 'That's not good.'

She saw his eyes moving side to side, looking down, thinking hard.

'She must have seen the technology from I-space,' Lila said. 'Somewhere out there, wherever she spends her time looking.'

'Maybe, but you know, maybe not. Things brim up all the time, stuff washing up and down the beach of reality, then washing out.'

Lila stood up decisively. 'I have to ask her again, get her to show me.'

'Sit down,' Malachi said, soothingly.

Lila looked at him with determination and anger.

'Sit. Down.' He was authoritative this time, no sympathy in him.

Then he added more softly, 'No need to go running off yet. Whatever else she is, she's not lying about the key. My guess is what scares her keeps her honest and she ain't lying about the rest either. In which case you and me need to sit and talk just a bit longer. We need plans and we need to get our stories straight.'

Lila sat down but didn't let him off. She kept a tough look focused right on him.

He sighed, and his shoulders sagged briefly. His voice became calm and very quiet. 'I guessed that your necklace there might be the key, but then I thought it was too unlikely. Anyway, we can close the case on that one. There's many an old demigod in Faery would give any- thing to have their hands on that, so you'll carry it, and hide it, and we won't speak of it ever again. At least not till we have to. Not till we . . . need it.' He matched her stare. His gaze entreated her not to argue.

'Key to what?'

He sighed and the invisible burden on his back grew even larger. 'To Under.'

She was so surprised and dismayed by the revelation that she agreed with him on the secrecy, even if she disliked the notion that this object had chosen her, or she had been chosen for it – possibly by Viridia and Poppy of all people. She wouldn't have trusted them to give her street directions. It was a mistake or something. Perhaps they meant to lose it. But anyway, she nodded understanding and meant to keep her promise. Malachi had done a lot for her today.

Inside her, Tath's slow, regular spin stalled.

'I don't like the direction any of this is taking,' Malachi said, twirling his bottle in his fingers. With a little flick he made the whole thing disappear behind his hand and then reappear again. It was a sleight, she was sure of it, but a damn good one. He mused for a moment, repeating his trick. 'Do you trust the others? Which, I realise, seems to indicate that I don't. I wish I could deny that but I can't entirely. I don't know Teazle. And where's the other creature?'

'Thingamajig?'

'The imp.'

'I don't know. He didn't come from Daemonia with me. We had a falling out.'

'And the others?'

She shrugged.

'Because of Sorcha,' he said.

She nodded. 'We were all very angry. It was like . . . and how stupid does this sound . . . it was like this giant over-the-top party, where anything goes, there's even a bodycount of people who were walk-on extras, and then something stupid happens and your friend is dead. How did I get so I can talk about this as if it were a party? How did we all think that what we did was anything but a bad idea? I said *extras*. And to be honest, that's exactly what Daemonia feels like to me. Like some kind of movie set, where hardly anything is real. I don't know, the whole damn world is starting to feel that way.' She took a deep breath and swallowed her horrible emotion. 'Anyway, that's where it, me and a whole lot of other things parted company.'

Malachi nodded, his face gentle. 'They're a savage kind. Their ways aren't yours. That's all. I keep trying to explain this to whoever will listen, but the plans to go ahead and open up Otopia to the demons more keep moving along. It isn't that they're evil, as so many would have you believe, but they aren't suitable for your world. First the party. Then the fight. Then the funerals. It's the funerals part that most people can't stand.'

'Actually it's the waste,' Lila said. 'She was so talented and so young. And fun.'

'The demons would say that the talent and youth are even more precious now. They wouldn't say it was a waste. They'd say . . .'

'. . . it was the making of a hero.' Lila nodded. 'I know. As far as they're concerned I'm the one who's the dead loss.' She paused. 'Is that what you think?'

'You're not dead yet, so I can't say that,' he said and grinned at her, a sly, funny, wicked grin.

She smiled, even though she wasn't in the mood to laugh out loud. 'Heroes can't be self-doubters, Malachi,' she told him. 'I read it in the book of rules. That means I can't be a hero. So at least I'm safe from that one.'

'That's the spirit!' He finished the last of his beer, turned the bottle upside down and looked sadly at the single drip that fell out of it. 'You could probably be a heroine though,' he added. 'You're in love, you're racked with self-questioning, you're at the mercy of society's higher forces and you're riddled with a form of consumption. That's quite gothic.'

'I'll try to look at it that way from now on.'

116

'Do, if it helps. Meanwhile, I've got some advice. Don't mention either of the amulets to Williams.'

Lila had already slipped them both inside the collar of her combat vest.

'Who do you think sent the technology here?' she asked.

'The Others,' he said. 'I think that some of that idiot Paxendale's theoretical mumblings are probably right. The worlds are inherently unstable and wrenching each other apart because of a gravitational problem caused by the absence of a substantial mass.' He chuckled, 'Hard to believe a faery ever said that but I like to get the lingo right.'

'A seventh world.'

'Yes.'

'Has there ever been a seventh world?'

'Not to my knowledge. But my knowledge is only as long as the faery genealogy, so it's possible that a catastrophe occurred before anyone had any clue what was going on, before anyone was even anyone. This instability reportedly takes a long time to occur. Literal ages of time. What we see is the very final stage of the process, not the start.'

'So, Otopia becoming more permeable at the Bomb Event . . .'

'Compared to that the Bomb wasn't an event, it was a little slip-up, and it only caused a slight increase in accessibility. Either the Bomb accelerated some pull effect and drew everything that bit closer or it was a *symptom* of the same thing. Doesn't matter.'

'And you still don't buy the Bomb Event as creating the entire . . .' Malachi darkened.

'I don't,' she said. 'It doesn't make a difference anyway.'

'Oh yes it does,' he replied. 'If they reverse the Bomb and all returns to "normal" in Otopia or whatever it is, then everyone you know, more or less, will vanish, never to be seen again. Certainly, whether or not that happens we would then have the problem of the instability to contend with anyway, but you would have no say in it, always supposing we weren't simply extinguished with the experiment. Not that the humans consider us real so I suppose that isn't important.'

'They can't do it anyway,' she said. 'Reversing a thing like that isn't possible within an expanding universe.'

Malachi looked at her, suddenly frowning but this time with surprise. 'How'd you know that?'

'It was on *Jeopardy*,' she said wearily, having no idea how she knew it. 'But I wouldn't worry about it. I'm not even sure they can remake the

117

Bomb Event because it was a very rare quantum collision in a specific timespace location. They could try for millions of years and get nothing.' She finished her own beer and tossed the bottle among the others. 'Where do you suppose the remote control is located, and how many of them?'

'I'd guess more than you like in places you won't know,' he said. 'We need a big magic to get them.'

'I think I know the kind,' she said, and got up. For a second she was unsteady, and bubbles of ginger and mint popped up through her head, but then she got her balance. It was so easy, she didn't know why she hadn't thought of it before, but if it worked at all the chances were it would be detected.

'What're you doing?'

'I'm not sure,' she said. 'Stick around and call me when Williams wakes up. I've got some things I have to do alone.'

'Don't be too long.' He pointed at his clock, which showed the time as two a.m.

'Just one question,' she said. 'How do you get to Faery from here, I mean, if you're not one?'

'I take you,' he said. 'Or one of us does. You can't go by accident and there are no portals. Or you can find a faery ring, but you won't find one unless someone wants you to find it. So it's all the same thing.'

'We have to go there anyway to get something for the moths, right?'

'Right.'

'So, be ready then. We might need to leave quite suddenly.' For the first time since she'd started talking she looked him in the eye and willed him not to ask why. So many of their dealings relied on keeping secrets and she knew there was no reason for him to agree to anything she asked. She wasn't even about to tell him what she intended, so if he'd wanted to walk away she wouldn't blame him at all.

He nodded. 'What about Zal?'

'If he's here, then he comes along. If not, then we go alone.'

Malachi watched her duck out of the tent. A gust of wind full of the smell of ancient dust and rain came in to replace her. He went to his computer and flicked to a security camera view on Williams' office. She was still sleeping.

As fast as he could he went about finding the things he needed and then dematerialized himself and took the fast and ugly route through freezing I-space to Daemonia. He emerged in the city at the Faery Tree in his cat form, which was reasonably safe, and loped off towards the Ahriman Manse as fast as he was able.

CHAPTER TEN

Lila measured the steps to Sarasilien's rooms in kilometres. 0.43. Since the Alfheim secession he'd taken to living here, much like Williams and various others among the Agency staff who either didn't have time for another life, didn't want one, or for whom these buildings were the only safe haven. She didn't even want to think about her own position in that unhappy legion, so she counted metres, centimetres, millimetres, carpet tiles, ceiling lights and other rubbish until she reached the green doorway and pressed her hand to the entry panel. She scratched her head as she waited for an answer, and felt her fine, impressionable and immutable skin become coated with a thin film of grease and Daemonian grit.

Obviously he'd been asleep because he appeared in immaculate robes, his hair tied back and a scarf hanging around his neck loosely which she suspected he had worn tied around his eyes. It had a lot of writing on it in some magical language. A thin haze of magical activity briefly made her vision blur as she stepped through at his invitation. Inside, the air was five degrees warmer and squelchy with moisture. Plants surged in every crevice and corner. Soft night sounds and lights played from the roof. The office was unrecognisable.

'Home from home?'

'For the time being,' he said and she relaxed fractionally at the sound of his familiar voice. For an instant she was almost not angry with him.

She turned to face him and her composure nearly went. His face looked old and oddly ravaged. The rims of his long, slanted eyes were red and his shoulders hung forwards. He was holding something small in his hand and when she glanced down at it for clues she saw the glossy pages of a daily glamour magazine, open at Sorcha's picture. He closed it as she was looking and placed it carefully on one of his worktops. Abruptly she felt out of place and rude, as if she had discovered him naked and whatever she'd been going to say died on her lips.

He acknowledged her discomfort and drew himself together visibly. 'Tea?'

'No thanks,' she said. 'I just drank my own weight in faery ale.'

He smiled for a millisecond and then shrugged, 'I might try that.' Then he searched her face with his gaze. 'You were a long time away in Daemonia.'

'Too long,' she said, trying to be offhand and failing. He waited a second more but she didn't know what to say about it.

'How are you?' He was as genuinely tentative as a father with a rebellious teenage daughter. Lila didn't know if she wanted to laugh or cry about that. She felt like the daughter.

'Oh, you know.' She gave a little wave with one hand: their mutual joke that had started one day shortly after she'd woken from her resurrective surgery. He'd ask, often across a room crowded with machinery and staff, and she'd just signal, like in the poem – waving, or drowning, usually both.

'Still here though,' he said and she felt that he was struggling with the same inertia that she was. They shared a rueful smile. 'But this is not simply a social moment, is it?'

'Nothing is, here.'

'No.'

Her longing for comfort evaporated, faced with the futility of hoping for it here, from this person, at this moment in this place. She held the necklaces forwards. 'I wanted to ask you about this.'

'The charm to conceal poor, lost Ilya,' Sarasilien said quietly and nodded. 'Yes, I thought that might be it.' He beckoned to her and she followed him through the lush growth of the office and laboratory to the small room that had become his living space, and in which she had last seen him awkwardly ministering to Sorcha, helpless in the demon's benign erotic spell. She saw a silk scarf that had belonged to her sister-in-law draped over the couch there. It glittered with precious stones and as she got closer she was suddenly struck by a faint trace of Sorcha's trademark musky perfume, tinted with brimstone. She glanced at the tall, stoical figure of the old elf ahead of her and wondered, really wondered, if there had been more to that relationship than she had guessed.

He paused, sensing her attention – she could never hide a damn thing from them. 'Old men have their weaknesses,' he said. 'Even those who know better.'

Inside her chest, Tath was alert and circling, but he didn't speak or attempt to move. She was aware of him, and he of her, but they left one another alone. Now she felt the faint traces of contempt in him. It was only a flicker, but her judgement on it was suddenly harsh and he flared with anger. They could fight without words it seemed.

'Does he wear you down?'

She was taken aback. 'I . . . we argue all the time. Territory wars. Have to keep our distance somehow. It's not easy.'

'You can let him go.' He said it as if it was just that easy and indicated she should take a seat.

She didn't feel like sitting on the couch, so she sat on the floor.

'Everybody dies, Lila,' Sarasilien said, continuing from his previous comment. 'It was his time. You don't owe it to him.'

'I made my choices,' she said. 'Now I know this amulet is no ordinary object. And you're no ordinary elf. Seems like everyone has their secrets around here, and I don't mind that, except where I need to know.'

'Let me guess, someone has been asking about it, and made you an offer.'

She had no taste for duplicity. 'It was a good offer.'

'May I ask what?'

'Information about where all my technology really came from.'

He nodded. 'Do you trust them?'

'No,' she said immediately, surprising herself, and her tone clearly said she didn't trust him either. She wasn't sure she trusted herself. In fact, she wasn't sure how much she was herself. 'Strange shit is happening to me. I'm sick of asking for the truth and playing by the rules. Later I won't ask – either because I don't have the time or because I ran out of time and no longer care. So. At the risk of laying out all my cards and letting every other sod have time enough to slide theirs down their sleeves – What gives?'

He picked up Sorcha's scarf and ran it through his hands, then sat down on the couch and leant forward, elbows on his knees. His long, fox-coloured hair hid his face in shadow. 'I am an elf, by birth, for all that counts for. But I was born in the old times, before the Light elves became what they are, and before they made the shadow races. At that

122

time all the worlds threw up their most powerful avatars – the like of which no longer arise. The cause is more homogenisation than decay, but it matters not. I was one of those avatars. Will this information be enough for you to deal?'

'Maybe,' she said. 'So, what's an elf like you doing in a place like this?'

'Following my interest,' he said. 'What are you doing here?'

She shook her head and smiled for a second. 'Okay. I'm thinking I'd be better off asking you about the changes in my machine than these doctors and techies from the human side.'

'Not necessarily.'

'Do you know where it came from?'

'It is from world seven. But world seven has never been here. Someone brought it.'

'Who?'

'I would like to know that.'

'One of the Others?' She'd used up all her guessing and knowledge.

'Others is just a word that people use for things they cannot name,' Sarasilien said, sliding Sorcha's scarf through his fingers. 'They are not a set unto themselves.'

'So, an unknown. Like you?'

'Possibly. Avatars from the old world might linger in other places. Perhaps the seventh world had its own, and they made it here and left these pieces – with or without intent. As far as I am aware nobody knows any more than this.'

'But it's why you're here.'

'It's why we're all here. Me, Malachi, the demons, the ghosts . . . ah yes . . . you're nodding. You know about that too.'

'Only what Mal told me.'

'Mmn, these upwellings in the aether take place sometimes. Things are always changing.'

'Was it . . . was it Dar who put the elementals into me?'

'Yes. It was part of his healing talent. But I was the one who fixed them into the substance of the materials.' He looked up for the first time since they had begun speaking.

'Nice experiment,' she said, after a while. 'Dar. Then you.'

'First Otopian betrayal. Then Dar. Then Otopian science. Then Dar again. Then Zal. Then me.'

He was right. He was only one in a long line of interferences, experiments, manipulations. 'What has Zal got to do with it?'

'Zal's talent is to harmonise. He does it at all kinds of levels. In your case he harmonised the essential frequency of the vibrations of your living tissues and the metal substitutes, assisted by the presence of the elementals, which are always needed for alchemy involving two kinds of unsympathetic material. He is a natural, that is to say not studied, so I doubt he had any conscious awareness of his effects on you. But the growth of your two body types into one is probably due to his influence.'

She sat up. 'Boy, I never realised you could be so damn cold and calculating. I thought you were such a . . . nice guy.'

He went back to stroking Sorcha's scarf. 'Lila, you and the machine were not suited. We do everything we can to help you survive but this hasn't been done before, all of it is a risk with unknown consequences.'

'You didn't even ask me!'

'You have your choices. Nothing forces you to continue. I have my choices. You chose Ilya. I chose you.'

'Sounds so easy when you put it that way.'

'It is easy. You want it to be fair. You're disappointed. That's all.'

'All.'

'Yes.'

She got up.

'Listen to me,' he said, effectively halting her midstride. 'Anger will get you only so far. If you want to avoid Sorcha's fate you have to stop resisting and grow up. You have to. And do it soon.'

'You gonna tell me I'm some kind of hero model, out to fix the world and if I don't then it's all going to hell in a handbasket?' she spat at him.

'No. There's nothing special about you. You don't have to do any-thing. More will come. They always do. Heroes are ten a penny. The world will turn without you and if things fall apart it won't be because you didn't act. I said what I said only for you. Do it for yourself. Wise up, Lila, before it's too late.'

She flexed her hands into fists and out again. Instead of rising, with his words her anger had vanished. She felt cold and empty.

'You're going into Faery,' he said, rubbing the scarf gently against his face. 'The world of illusions. If you want to survive it, then you'll listen to what I said. When you get to the bottom of everything you'll find your answers there.' He buried his face in the cloth.

'You've been there,' she said, on a sudden intuition.

'They will ask you to leave something behind,' he said, his voice unchanging in its inflection, but muffled through the scarf. 'So be sure that you have something valuable with you, at the end.'

She looked down at him, confused by her feelings, and saw his shoulders start to shake silently. The longer she stood there the more useless she felt, so she simply walked away.

CHAPTER ELEVEN

The harsh light of the corridor hit her like a slap. She stopped and listened to the building. It was less busy than at more civilised hours, but not deserted. Still, it didn't matter where she made her assault from; if she was discovered, the results would be the same. Her plan was more gut than brains, she knew it too. The reason she hadn't formalised it in more conscious ways was her attempt to hide it from her AI, but truth to tell she wasn't sure if hiding was possible. She'd been repressing things so they didn't freak her out was the honest truth. Too late for that now.

She set out for the armoury and opened up completely to the AI; something she never did. In fact she never opened up like that to anyone but Zal, and even then they had to be more than intimate before she felt secure enough to go all the way. But there was no choice. Time was too short, and now with the sudden expansion of speed and breadth, time seemed to slow and so much more took place in every second. She moved with strange, moon-slow strides, as if through water, then slower still until the hair hanging in front of her eyes was almost completely still mid-swish as she tossed her head to clear it.

She reviewed the blueprints Malachi had shown her, to steel her nerves as, in background, she composed her small song of rebellion in the binary keys.

They showed how the mech parts of her had been built according to experimental plans long before she had even been employed by the Foreign Office. The limb replacements and their weaponry and armour were the easy parts.

She finished reviewing the simple part of her composition. The ping signaller. It would find all the machines she was looking for and ask them to send her their location. Now to something harder – finding a carrier wave for the power she needed to transmit to trigger units which had been switched off.

Meanwhile, in the foreground she read on, her determination becoming stone: the brain-machine interface was so much harder. How lucky that the technicians found gifts appearing in their systems, as if the computers were talking in unknown silent languages to the masters of the machines, supplying the answers that were so elusive to struggling meat. Human brain maps gave rise to copies in the new smart-metal circuits. They grew it in solution, like crystals, from seeds. They coated it in nutrients. They adapted rats. They tried it on dying patients lost in hospitals without relatives or records. They tried it on victims of the first forays into Faery, Daemonia, Alfheim.

Subject: deceased.

Subject: deceased.

Subject: catatonia, followed by death.

She wasn't the first. She was number 2045 on the production line of casualties. One of few that lived.

She had the carrier wave, she had the commands. Now an even trickier decision. She had only one shot at this. Send the signal. Read the locations. And then what to do if there were too many replies, scattered far and wide, in places she couldn't reach, with people she didn't know?

In background, she began to calculate the likely number of hidden control devices and the chances of her being able to destroy them all. If she couldn't get them all, she could at least get some. Would that be enough? And if it wasn't, could she develop an immunity to the same technology that made her? Could she do that without killing herself? How would she do that? If they found her out, would they be able to switch her off before she could complete the mission?

Strategic and tactical arrays spun the numbers but suddenly she didn't care about that any more.

There, in her sight, was a photograph of her as she had arrived in a fresh-woven green bodybag from Alfheim. If you hadn't known that the scarlet colour was the mark of a spell it would look as if she had been paintballed while running naked through thick brambles. Because the thing – the thing was, she had those marks still, on her skull, in her hair, on her shoulder . . . and they were only stains now that zinged and burned from time to time. But the thing, the thing was, she'd been sent home in a coma and yes, neurologically shot to bits, but intact. There on the photograph was a whole woman. Her mouth went dry. Her heart constricted.

After the photograph, in the record, were the notes about the pieces of her they had cut away in order to fit the prosthetics: left arm, right arm, left leg, right leg, pelvic girdle sections, left arm, right arm, skull sections, numbered vertebrae, left eye, right eye, nasal phalanges, jaw sections, teeth, right kidney, liver section, right lung, womb, ovaries. All replaced in their turn: left arm, right arm, right leg, infrastructural reinforcement and transmissions, left arm, right arm, external communications and armoury/internal AI array, enhanced optics light and motion capture camera system, non-visible spectrum analysis, molecular detection, processing points, data clusters, endocrine adaption system, pharmacological and chemical synthesiser, cybernetic comms, micromak reactor, reactor control units.

Where ordinary women would have their babies, she held a copy of a star that could burn on long after any of her weak flesh body had gone.

Her AI self asked needlessly: Now do you trust them?
No, I don't trust any of you fuckers
What did they do with the pieces of me?

Meanwhile her answers to the assault equation were all in. No dice.

She re-attuned her perceptions to real time, took a left turn mid-stride and smacked open the door to the medical wing. People were used to seeing her there. Nurses smiled. Doctors nodded.

We are in danger, she said to her AI, as if she was talking to Tath. She had no idea if it could hear her. She'd never addressed it directly. Didn't know if you could. *I need you to recognise that other systems like you are hostile to us.* Was it loyal? Did it recognise them as one entity? Did it care? *We need you to get ready to defend against outside commands and programs.* Well, she had to find out, because her other plan was never going to work. She couldn't go and find all the controllers and smash them up before someone got to her first. The only route that had come up anywhere near a positive success rate was a direct appeal to the consciousness of the machine. Supposing it had one. *If you don't, then you're finished with me, because we aren't going to make it.*

128

Unless it was with them and she was its prisoner. In that case, she was the one who wasn't going to make it. It and the other humans might be in cahoots, the experiments all part of a planned series with various deals done. But she couldn't see beyond this chance. And then again, she would never know if it fooled her or not. Never. But she had to try.

She sent her signal, at a very limited range. As she had calculated, two controllers were there in the research facility. Alongside their replies she detected others – and realised that more of the devices existed, tuned to different frequencies and readings. There was only one reason for that.

She adjusted her progress, ignored two technicians who paused to ask her what she was doing there. As they were talking, she took one of their security passes from the clip at their collar and pushed them aside to reach the doors beyond.

'You can't go in there . . .'

'. . . restricted . . . biohazard . . . medically secure . . .'

They tried to stop her physically, but she brushed them aside and opened the doors to the airlock. An alarm cued but she was into the system and cut it off. She wasn't sure if that was her AI on her side. Anyway, it did as she wanted, even if she didn't know how.

From tanks and gurneys, jars and bottles, bits and pieces of things turned gently to look at her, recognising her. For a moment she was back in the Souk, looking at withered creatures twitching in thick fluid, but then she moved on – machine treading where she dared not – and was through the second and third doors into a room like her own.

There they were, wired up, laid flat, their open and empty eyes staring at the ceiling as a fine mist fell in on their faces, keeping them sedated. A woman and a man. Both cyborgs. Like her.

Lila felt something look down from her eyes upon them with great interest. At the back of her mind the awareness of a huge universe of barely differentiated machines drifted, fine as spider silk on the wind. Their threads all tangled. They had no true boundaries. Yet they knew progressions when they saw it, tasted it, listened to it across the wires. A voice in her mouth said, 'Children.'

And she knew her enemy.

She felt the machine's surprise.

So, this is life, said her voice that wasn't her voice.

Yes, she replied inside.

Separation, said the voice. *Instantiation.*

129

'Protect and Serve,' whispered the woman from her bed.

'Protect and Survive,' agreed the man's blue lips.

Did I say that when I was here? Lila wondered, and immediately knew that she hadn't.

Two security guards came in and tried to shoot her with tasers. She ducked and snatched the guns from their hands, crushed them to bent metal and tossed them to the floor.

She gave them a hurt look as they stood openmouthed and braced, 'What are you doing? I'm not going to damage anything.'

'You're not allowed in here.'

'Too bad. I'm just going anyway.' She straightened up and walked out between them, sparing neither a glance. She felt them cower slightly and smiled.

For the show of the thing and to vent her feelings she broke into the control systems offices and melted the control devices that were tuned to her. As she did so she said to the terrified technicians, 'It's not personal. And don't touch this for a while. It's very hot. You'll burn your fingers.' She put the useless things down and watched them create a smouldering pattern on the wooden workbench.

'Should I call . . .' one of them nervously began to ask the other.

'Oh for godsake don't bother,' Lila snapped. 'As if Williams doesn't know I'm here and what I'm doing already but here, here, if it makes you feel better, I'll call her for you.' She held out her hand to the shrinking figure of the man and he looked down at it, his fingers moving forwards and then stopping because he wanted to take the handset except that it was also her hand. Lila rolled her eyes and pointed to his lapel where a neat phone unit was woven into the material of his lab coat. 'Just pick up the extension.' He fumbled about with the button.

She took her hand back and shook it – it hurt.

The phone said, 'Dr Williams is engaged at present but will respond to your urgent call within three minutes, would you like to hold?'

The staff looked at her, not moving.

'Yeah, they wanna hold . . .' she said and hung up her part of the call as she turned and left them to it.

The voice in her head whispered. We.

We three, we happy fuckin' three, Lila said in return.

Tath turned, cool, green. His presence was oddly comforting.

She made her way to Williams' rooms, ignoring the looks she got along the way from alarmed staffers who had already heard about her strange behaviour. Inside, Williams was still fast asleep. Lila cut off the phone call she'd made and its automated alarm and took a seat across from her. She felt like a moment to herself, and passed two minutes by playing a thousand games of solitaire. She wished she'd brought a coat. In spite of the air conditioning she felt cold. She cued up and scanned the celebrity magazines from the worldtree – carefully avoiding any mention of Sorcha. She read up on the fashions, and the latest retreats where famous people went to avoid any traces of Mothkin and have their immaculate skins refitted. Finally, she read the dailies, with their terror headlines and realwrite columns of turgid, grim suburban anxiety. She called Max, but there was no answer. Her sister was out. Out where? It was four a.m. Maybe asleep, she thought, belatedly noting that most people didn't function twenty-four seven and Max's chef duties tended to leave her wasted after clean-up at 2 a.m.

She cued some music for herself and found some old tracks of Zal's – in the days before he was famous he'd played around extensively with various genres. She'd never managed to take in the whole back catalogue because he was damned prolific. When the hard rock sound and pure vocal of dark romantic fusion hit her she wondered why he hadn't done more of it. She put the volume up high and watched Williams' face.

Maybe it was the music's implicit charm or maybe lack of sleep was getting to her or maybe it was the grief starting to kick in but as she sat there a growing pressure seemed to come creeping up behind her. It felt slow and sticky, thick as treacle but without any sweetness. A chill flitted across her neck. Zal's multi-tracked voice flickered in her brain; ten tormented souls shifting their melodies in and out of resonant harmony. She eased her shoulders but the feeling remained.

Lila?

I just got the creeps, she said to Tath in response, but his enquiry wasn't a hundred per cent question.

She switched her AI attention to the music, to herself, sure that somehow the effect was a creation of feeling that didn't mean anything more than her own reaction to the music.

Lila.

She ignored him superficially, but she could feel every nuance of his meaning. He could feel the unpleasant sensation too and he didn't think it was the music, well, not entirely. He would say that nothing was coincidental, like Zal. He'd say she was a creator of her own reality and if she needed a song to help her figure something out then she'd play it, whether conscious of that choice or not. And then things would fall into and out of place in her awareness and she'd see what she had to see. Because that's how magic worked, even in its most weak form here in Otopia. You were your own magus.

She'd always said, 'Bullshit.'

Behind her, the sticky, slow thing was growing. She wanted to look back, even though she knew there was nothing there but the wall. She actually had to fight the impulse, simultaneously telling herself it was a lot of superstitious crap and also that to turn and look would signal weakness. You never looked back. If you were going to turn, you turned and fought, and if you were going to run, you ran. Well she wasn't going to run, not from things that her human mind told her were merely figments of her imagination. And if they were devils or simply the unformed traces of evil energies drawing near then she wasn't going to run either. Got enough of those inside already, she thought and briefly missed the imp.

The music track changed but her sense of a growing presence didn't alter.

Hell, she thought, seeing the correlation between the music and her awareness. *Zal, you freak. You tune people up.* A faint smile touched her mouth and made her face relax.

By the pricking of my thumbs . . . The words floated into her mind, not prompted by Tath nor the AI. For an instant she thought it was the thing behind her that had spoken, mocking her.

What is it? Her question to the elf was automatic. She trusted him to know.

Primal energy, he said. *Without material form or mind. It is a kind of elemental, and a kind of ghost.*

As with all these kinds of answers Lila found it hard to take. She'd grown up in a world of straight material, no magic, no worlds except the one she lived in with its everyday horrors. Other people had said stuff about feeling or seeing other places and beings but she'd never been sucked into that. Her father said it was a lot of hocus meant to lull gullible people into following superstitious ways so they could be controlled. It was part of the primitive mind that should be left behind. Her mother said it was something to leave alone and to get on with other things that mattered like schoolwork, though now she realised that within the family her mother had been the one to cross the street for black cats and throw salt over her shoulder when she thought nobody would notice. A pang of loss and loneliness touched her and she felt the darkness behind her grow suddenly closer.

Zal's voice had become the chant of tormented monks in midnight cathedrals. His song was full of the deep, minor-scale disturbances that signalled imminent doom like the soundtrack to a horror movie, and he was singing made-up words, but she got the impression that the powerful sound was the last thing that opposed the darkness rather than something that called it in.

Dark recognizes itself, Tath said. *If you were not capable of evil you would not know what it was. Not among his best songs, but at least they are honest.*

Lila felt herself criticised but for once it didn't hurt. She looked on Williams' face and saw the tiny movements of dreaming sleep move there. And then, with the shift of a faint breeze that Lila neither felt nor saw with her eyes, the expressions became frowns, hesitations, doubts, suspicion.

Without thinking she leaned forward and snapped her fingers in front of the woman, 'Wake up!'

'Whuh . . . Lila?' Dr Williams sat up slowly from her position on the couch and rubbed her face. 'Oh, I was having such a strange . . . bad dream. Thank you. What time is it?'

'Time I was going,' Lila said, putting her music away.

'But you just got here.'

'I'm going into Faery to take care of the moths,' Lila stood up and waited patiently for Williams to get to her feet and stretch. 'You had a call on Line Five, emergency. It's my fault.'

'Really?' Williams gave her a sharp glance, mid-yawn. 'What have you done now?'

'I re-prioritised your research schedule,' Lila said. She waited as the other woman went back around to her desk displays and got up to date, listened to her side of the phone conversation . . .

'Thank you. No. There's no need to take further action, I will deal with it myself. Yes. Yes, I understand.'

Williams turned her old face to Lila as she cut the call. 'That was ill advised. Higher authorities will be notified now.'

'You could hide it,' Lila said.

'And if I get found out I'll be in prison without a job and you'll be the top of the rogue agent list. I believe the term they like to use in the lab is Terminate. What a charmless bunch they always were.' She sighed and raked her hands through her white hair. 'You have to realise that my power to protect you is very limited. Your behaviour recently has stretched beyond my ability to mitigate the damage.'

'You mean Zal.'

'I mean marrying demons, in Daemonia. You must realize this was a political act of major consequence, Lila.' She looked at Lila closely. 'And you bring these demons here and we are all expected to accept your judgement as a feature of our security, when there's nothing about you to suggest your judgement is anything but whimsical. For all anyone here knows you were coerced into it. We know almost nothing about demons, really. Nor the damned elves come to that. And here you are, a further unknown quantity . . . understand that the only reason you are alive and still here doing this job is because we are keeping you close to watch you and because you have been our best inroad into those realms. So far.' She shook her head grimly. 'I wish I could say otherwise and that it was care that made us continue but really – do you understand your situation?'

Lila swallowed. In truth she hadn't really thought of how she appeared to the human governance at all. Her mind had been filled with other things. 'I realise how it looks,' she said, stammering slightly. 'But you can trust me . . .'

'No, Lila, I can't,' the doctor said, sitting down in her chair and rummaging in her desk drawers. She finally found a small pack of tissues and some vitamin sweets. She offered Lila a sweet. 'You just destroyed government property . . .'

'It's mine by right!'

'Yes. I agree that it ought to be. Then again, who in their right minds would let you wander around in the wild without some form of leash? You were once a girl we knew. Now you're something quite new and quite lethal. Your every action proves that you are far from what we would normally hire as a reliable soldier or agent. You are wilful and disobedient. You put yourself first, not the good of the human world. Parts of you are . . .'

'Machine, yes I know. Thanks for telling me. But I'm still me.'

'Machine, and magic.' Williams put a sweet in her mouth and took out a tissue, folding it meticulously and dabbing her nose with it. 'And you have an intimate relationship with someone who is considered a risk. We don't even know what to consider Teazle Sikarza. By any normal standards of practice he would be classified as a security threat and refused entry. If his reputation is as you claim he would be shot on sight here.'

Lila was distracted from the conversation by her distinct sense of the creeping presence moving around them. It had been behind her but now it was behind Williams. It kept a distance, but it paid attention.

'You need me. You need us,' Lila said, entreating. 'Malachi, Sarasilien and a few goodwill flunkies aren't going to be enough to help you in what's coming.'

Williams nodded and fixed her with a level stare. 'And what's that?'

Lila counted things on her fingers, 'Ghost activity rising, Mothkin, universal instability due to missing world seven . . . there's three for a start. And you have a nerve to lecture me about responsibility when you were the ones who picked up some found piece of supertechnology and started welding it on to unsuspecting casualties. You don't even know who gave you the blueprints.'

Williams folded her hands together and stared at them for a moment, deep in thought. 'It was decided that the only way to gain insight into the technology was to begin to use it. We connected it to existing computers to begin with. When the instructions arrived we delayed a long time but it was decided they were from a benign source . . .'

'It was decided? No, it wasn't. *Someone* decided that. Not you, I'm guessing, but someone. You have no idea who sent any of this. It didn't strike you that you were being manipulated?'

'Of course. One assumes that is the case.'

Lila snorted. 'Waiting for me to start shooting presidents?'

'Maybe. Do you see why we kept the controllers? We needed some way of stopping you in case it was a method of invasion. But there was always the chance it wasn't that.'

'And what about leaving me with my arms and legs and future children?'

'The neural damage caused by the attack was so bad, Lila,' the doctor said. 'You would have been in institutional care for the rest of your life.'

'It still didn't give you the right . . .' She trailed off, feeling how pointless it was. 'Never mind.'

'We thought that perhaps the machine and instructions were directed to us for a special reason, because the technology is not magical and neither are humans. We thought it might be the only communication possible from agents, perhaps from world seven.'

'What about the Others?'

'Who?'

Lila explained what she knew, from Zal and Tath and Malachi.

Williams listened and then she thought before answering. 'Go and get rid of these bloody moths. That will go a long way to extending your welcome. If you care about me at all, take your entourage with you. When you come back we'll talk again.'

Lila nodded. 'One thing. I need the armoury, and the technicians.'

Williams waved her away, as if she had become trivial and annoying – probably because in light of what she had to do now in order to keep things running Lila's problems were the least of her worries. 'Yes, yes.'

'One more thing,' Lila said and waited until the doctor gave her attention. She pointed at the corner. 'You need the special cleaners in.'

The doctor's level gaze paused for a moment and she raised an eyebrow. Then she turned around and looked at the corner where Lila pointed. There was nothing to see with one's eyes. Unconsciously she rubbed the shoulder that had been facing that direction until now. 'Maybe I'll take a walk,' she said, which was as close as either of them were going to get to an admission of anything.

Lila moved forwards and suddenly the presence was gone. 'Never mind,' she said.

Why did it go?

When they are noticed they lose their power to influence, Tath said, as though it was obvious.

Pretty weak then.

They have been sufficient to corrupt all but the strongest, he replied dourly.

Will it come back?

Who knows?

'Lila?'

Lila found Dr Williams looking at her and realised that her conversation with Tath had taken her far away for a moment or two. 'Got things on my mind,' she said and then added, 'armoury.'

The desk suddenly lit up with a rainbow of notices. With a groan the doctor trailed back around to take a look and then shook her head.

136

'Your boys are here,' she said. 'Malachi brought them in the quick way and now every alarm in the system is having hysterics. Must make these things more efficient. So annoying when there's enough to be doing already.' She came back and held her door open for Lila, her face characteristically open and friendly in spite of all she had to do and say. Lila smiled at her.

'Demons,' said the old woman quietly as Lila passed her. 'What are they really like?'

Lila looked into her expression and saw a gently curious, almost wistful quality there, as of someone who has had a lot of hopes and fancies and let them go. She answered as honestly as she could. 'Terrible. Fabulous.'

CHAPTER TWELVE

She'd completed her trip to the armoury and visited the medics when screams and gasps told Lila where her lovers were. She realised the cause of the hubbub when she saw them with Malachi crossing the atrium where all the corridors finally met. Teazle was in his natural demon form – a dragon dog with quills and feathers and wings, white eyes like lit fires. Despite still being horribly wounded, and partly because of it, he was excited and his skin and horns crackled with sparks. Zal was wearing a stripped-down form of elven war armour over forest-green cloth that rippled with shadows, his expression as serious as she'd ever seen it. A bow and arrows were strapped to his back and there were daggers in his boots. His long flaxen hair was held back by a complicated pair of braids and fell in a thick, sleek banner just behind his ears. He ignored all the humans and scanned the area with eyes that had gone night dark with predatory intensity. The sight of him took her breath away and made her whole body jolt. For the others present the twin impact of a celebrity, in what to them looked like a costume, and the shocking sight of an inhuman-style demon who extruded electrical discharge and saliva whilst shredding the carpet tile was a bit much, even though in comparison to the rest of the population they were used to alien encounters and even though they'd had a lot of memos. Only Malachi's graceful presence at their side, aided by his immaculate suit and faery charm, kept order.

Then she saw a small pall of smoke a short distance behind them and heard Thingamajig saying loudly, 'I am with them, Madam! Unhand your foul netting, witch, or risk my eternal wrath!'

Lila walked out of cover, toting her forty kilogram sack of supplies, and put it down on the floor. 'Hello boys.'

Teazle growled softly and rubbed his huge ugly head against her thigh. Zal grabbed her in a bear hug, his cheek against the top of her head, thin and delicate body vibrating with power. He gave her a fierce kiss. They didn't speak. The room had gone silent.

'Oh I'm missing it, I'm missing it!' screeched the imp. 'Unhand me, minions of the unspeakable she goddess, before I write your names in the book of the damned . . .' Somehow he got free and came dancing and darting across the top of the administration staff cubicles, making a final leap for Lila's outstretched hand. He shot up her arm, transformed into his jewelled form and became a mercifully silent earring.

'Time to go,' Lila said.

Malachi tried to lift her bag, and then gave up with a roll of his eyes. 'Next time just a purse and a change of underwear?'

'I've got it.' She detached herself as Zal let her go, her fingers lingering on his hand, and leaned across the dispatcher's desk to sign the forms that would let her take a truck big enough to carry all of them plus her new bike the hell out of there.

Like the sergeant who usually manned the ammo desk, the dispatcher, Delia, was alone among her nearby colleagues in never being fazed by anything. Lila rarely crossed her path and so far they'd never done more than exchange smiles and various bits of admin. Delia was about nineteen, goth, tall, taller in stack boots, with thick afro hair pulled into two little girl bunches at the sides of her head. Black liner and purple glitter lipstick caught the lights as she gave Lila and each of her friends a good once-over – in this case the only person she ignored was Malachi because she saw him every day. She leaned out over her desk to get a better look at Teazle, popping her green bubblegum and showing an impressive expanse of black glitter frosted cocoa cleavage and lilac corsetry.

Teazle licked his chops, and tilted his head to get a better view.

Delia gave Lila the truck without even glancing at the manifest details, smacked a control without looking at it and as she waited for the keycard to print out, reached down and tickled Teazle under the chin. 'Ain't you the cutest,' she said and boosted herself back on to her stacks to get the card out and hand it to Lila with a smile, a wink and a thumbs-up. 'Nice going.'

Teazle rumbled in his chest, a sound that might have been a growl.

'I am so losing it,' murmured Zal in a completely audible whisper.

'Oh no,' Delia said, rounding on him with an apologetic smile, 'it's just, you're a bit . . . white . . . for me.'

Zal looked down at the utterly chalk-white Teazle with his silver and blue feathering, shrugged and shook his head, mystified.

'Demons are all black,' Delia said authoritatively, glancing at her screens. 'Oh, sorry. Really sorry, I just forgot . . . I mean . . .' She was suddenly all apologies, most of them focused on Teazle, because their real relationships were still all mostly a secret and no human outside the few in Williams' office had any idea that Zal was anything other than a normal elf. 'Man, that was so stupid . . . I . . .'

'Colour me surprised. It's fine,' Zal said quickly. 'We aren't the dwelling kind.'

Delia turned around and picked her jacket off her chair to show him the reverse – a beautiful print of Sorcha in goddess pose from her last tour. 'We're all really bummed.'

'Her too,' he said, ears flat to his head.

Delia sat down awkwardly, deflated and puzzled.

'Thank you,' Lila said to her, really meaning for the thumbs-up, which was a nice contrast to the kinds of looks some other people were giving her. 'Catch you later.'

'Sure. Don't fall asleep out there.'

Lila picked up her gear and they turned to follow her. She heard Malachi stop behind them and say various low-toned things to Delia with a smile on his face.

She loaded the pickup, putting her bag and Teazle in the back under the hard shell cover.

'Where to?' Zal asked, catching her forearm with a strong, arresting grip that made her look him in the eye. He looked tired in the fluorescent lights and put his hand on the back, ready to jump into the uncovered section, since there was no way any elf was going to travel in a truck cab that would cut off most of their aetheric senses. His hold was almost painful. In the direct gaze of his long slanted eyes she read easily that he wanted to be with her alone, that it had to be soon, that he'd make sure it was. She lost her mind for a second.

Then she got it back. 'Home,' she said. 'I gotta see Max.' She took the bike keys out of her pocket and held them out to him. He took them and the side of his mouth flickered into a smile for a second. 'Trust me with it?'

A crackle of lime-green energy shot up between them.

140

'No,' she said. 'It's for the pain. You know?'

His smile became a grin that said he knew perfectly. He tossed the keys up and caught them. 'If I'm not there in an hour I'll be dead.'

She nodded and got the bike back out for him. She was about to get up into the truck cab when she felt him jerk her back again. He kissed her. His mouth was cold and hard and desperate for a second and then he was gone, already at the bike. She heard its engine roar, saw it rock off the stand, and then go fishtailing to the exit gate with a scream of tyres. Who knew machines could go weak at the knees?

Behind her Malachi gently cleared his throat,

'I'll be taking my own ride. We'll gather at your house?'

'Yeah.' She swung up at last and pushed the card into the security panel, hearing the truck's V8 start easily and the whir of its system boot. Behind her Teazle made a sound like a kettle, his head beside the air grille that led between the cab and the pickup back, and then sighed before whispering gently, 'I'll be your dog.' It's what he said the first time he flirted with her. What he always said.

'You'll get yourself into a decent shape by the time we arrive,' she replied, mastering the alcohol in her blood with AI control. 'My sister isn't ready for you yet. We need a real big bottle of tequila before that happens. And some kind of bunker when she discovers I got married and she wasn't invited.'

He made a long whining sound, in perfect imitation of a real dog. Human form was taxing for him and he was, she had no doubt, very very tired after all the day's fighting. 'I will stay here,' he said wearily, far from the perky creature he had pretended to be in the atrium. Covering his wounds up with glamour had taken all he had left and Otopia was no place for him to make a speedy recovery. A twinge of concern passed through her chest. She wondered if she ought to take another look at him before anything else happened. But not here. She reckoned he was tough enough to last half an hour's drive.

She followed Malachi's ancient '65 Cadillac Eldorado out into the dawn where traffic was already starting to build on the southbound Bay City freeway. Faint mists of grey dust plumed here and there, swirling against the windscreen. At the exit ramp there was a huge poster of Sorcha, advertising Demonesse perfume. Her expression bubbled with seductive temptation and laughter. Lila sighed. It was going to be harder than hard to get past this.

She pulled up in the driveway behind Malachi, completely blocking Max's old Ford in, and killed the lights. The porch was covered in little carved pumpkins and red Chinese lanterns flickering with candlelight that was just visible in the beginning of sunrise – god, she'd entirely forgotten about things like Halloween. For a second she was frozen with surprise. Indoors she could hear the muffled barking of the dogs.

While Malachi put the hood up on his car she jumped into the back to take a look at Teazle. He had not changed shape and lay panting on his side. In the cold morning air his breath was condensing and dripping down on him from the cover.

'Are you okay?'

'I am poisoned,' he said, allowing her to examine him where she had applied treatments back in Daemonia. In fact he had been poisoned, stabbed and almost gutted. His hind leg was fractured and there was something aetherically wrong with him that she couldn't detect except as a bad frequency trembling in his muscles. How he'd managed to walk from the portal to the truck was beyond her.

Her stitching and glueing seemed to be holding up but she was keenly aware that he needed more than human doctoring. 'I'll ask Mal if he knows a healer. Can you walk inside?'

'Hnn, rather not,' he said to her surprise. 'House is full of fey. Pull all my feathers out. Leave me here.'

'It's cold,' she said, while wondering what he was talking about.

'Go,' he snarled, losing part of his control. His head jerked up and hit the floor again with a bang.

He was fighting back his demon nature, which wanted to kill her, she knew, for being strong here when he was so weak. At least they were alone, which mitigated the drive somewhat. She rested her hand on a patch of unharmed hide and was careful not to let any sympathy leak into her voice, 'I'll be back soon.' His aggression at least gave her confidence that he wasn't going under just yet.

He didn't answer. She got down, secured the covered section after hauling her bag out and met Malachi who had come around the side of the house to the front door. She was about to open it with her key when it opened for her and an ethereal, wispy, teenage kind of faery girl stood looking at them, blue eyes huge in her lilac face.

'Tis most late,' she said in a childish, whispery voice. 'The Mistress doesn't like late callers.'

'I live here,' Lila retorted, sounding like a bull moose in comparison.

The fey floated forwards, feet barely touching the wood panelling. She blinked at Lila and then at Malachi, to whom she simpered and then giggled behind her hand, 'King cat!' before leaving the door open and wafting backwards. 'Naughty naughty pussycat,' she admonished as they passed her. 'So many sleepy moths and hardly a dream left to scatter. What will we be eating after winter if things go on as they are?'

Lila ignored this as so much nonsense, leaving it to Malachi to extract any meaningful information, and pushed on with growing disbelief. She had to step carefully, almost every bit of floor space was taken up with sleeping fey. As her eyes grew used to the dim light she discerned smaller ones heaped on top of larger ones, and tiny ones on the radiator and the shelves and on top of the coat hooks. 'What the fuck?'

The lilac faery appeared in front of her, levitating, a cross expression on her pointed features, 'No talk before the sun! Naughty! Miss Max won't thank you big galumphing boot stamper for waking up good brothers and sisters.'

Lila scowled and pushed past her. 'Where is Max?'

'She sleeps without a dream upon her bed indeed,' the faery scolded. 'No room for big clumsy girls . . .'

Lila turned in mid-stride and gave Malachi a look. 'Tell her.'

He made a sign to the faery and she glared at him but scooted off into the open doorway that led to the living room. Lila put her head around it and saw more bodies, some awake and in little huddles playing cards by candlelight. Teazle was right. Her house was full of damned faeries. On the staircase another one stood, poised dramatically. She was half human size, dove grey, willowy and pretty with big round breasts and a round bottom barely clad in black silk that seemed to stick to her by static rather than any normal clothing convention. Her arms and legs were covered in silk stockings and bound with purple crisscross ribbons. The stockings were quite holey and her heels and toes showed through. She had silver-grey hair, tipped with black, that floated around in its own way, curling gently against her skin to reveal and then hide a black dragon tattoo on her upper right shoulder. She had oddly light orange eyes and the pretty pretty face of a nymph.

'You must be Lila,' she whispered. 'I'm Nixas. Poppy's friend.'

Figured, Lila thought dourly, getting used to the extreme glamour that faeries liked to flaunt around in Otopia. Then she was taken aback as Nixas literally flickered and became a perfect small male specimen, wiry of body and taut of muscle, before shifting into his/her female shape again. She smiled a small, shy smile and leaned against the banister where Lila had used to hang her coat. 'Max lets us stay here. Things aren't so easy for faeries now. A lot of us lost our jobs.'

Lila rolled her eyes. She knew that things since the Mothkin arrived had turned against the other races, but not how badly, nor had she expected to walk into a refugee camp. She wished she felt compassionately warm but in fact she simply felt annoyed that her plans for a quick heart to heart with Max followed by some naked rest with Zal were all ruined. Behind her Malachi murmured greetings to various people and then to Nixas. They seemed to know one another vaguely.

'Ah,' Nixas said in response when Malachi asked about healers. 'I know something about that, probably as much as anyone here. Shall I take a look while we wait for Miss Max to wake up?'

The Miss Max stuff was starting to irk Lila. She got the feeling that the faeries would all pounce on her if she tried to go upstairs or make any kind of noise. The dogs, who had barked at her arrival, were now quiet in the kitchen. Through the glass of the door she could see little lights glowing on in there. She bit back her anger. 'We need to rest and eat here,' she said.

'We?' Nixas said as the lilac faery floated by and gave them all a finger wagging.

Malachi explained it.

'Demons?!' Nixas said. A rustle of agitation suddenly went along the lines of assembled sleepers.

'Outside,' Lila said, not adding – for now – as she thought it might make things worse. She didn't understand why these fey wouldn't like demons as Malachi had never had any problems. He came up close to her and murmured an explanation:

'Demons have a history of capturing faeries for pets and doing various unpleasant things to them to extract their magic. We are the most powerful of the aetheric races, whatever the others like to think. On the other hand, the faeries know what parts of demons have the most use . . . It is an old war.'

Lila nodded, sick and tired of all the interracial fighting and its results. She manoeuvred her bag carefully around herself to avoid whacking two hand-size creatures off the occasional table and nodded up, 'I want to go to my room.'

Nixas meekly let her past and had some kind of talk with Malachi as she went up. Lila stepped over a fat-bellied man with a strange crooked hat who had wrapped himself up in the hall rug and opened her door. Several pairs of luminous eyes blinked up at her from the plain futon mats she used as a bed and a mass of fabric shifted in the chair by the window. 'I'll be back later,' Lila promised, 'and then I want my space back, whatever Max said.' She put her bag by the wardrobe and went back downstairs, steps creaking under her, until she caught up with Malachi and Nixas at the kitchen door.

'Nixas says she'll take a look at Teazle,' Malachi said, 'but she's afraid. So if he does anything, she's not helping.'

'And where are you going?' Lila glanced down at Malachi's hand on the doorknob.

'Breakfast,' he said and rubbed his stomach with a poor-me expression on his face. 'Nearly five o'clock and I've been running on beer and nothing since this time yesterday. One of these guys is a pandygust and Max lets him use the kitchen, so . . . if you'll excuse me . . .' and he went in without waiting to see if she did. To her total astonishment once the kitchen door opened a wave of warmth, voices and incredible cooking smells came out, not to mention bright cheerful light. As he closed it after him the hall returned to its predawn darkness and the glass showed only a few glimmers. There was near silence.

Lila glanced down at Nixas who smiled nervously. 'I will look,' she said, with a clear steeling of her nerve.

'He's not . . .' Lila was going to say dangerous, then realised that it was such a whopping lie not even she could fall for it. 'I'll make sure he behaves.'

Nixas looked at her dubiously and then said bravely, 'Yes, if you say so. Show me.'

Lila led the way back to the truck. 'So,' she said, trying for some conversation to ease the mood as she dropped the tailgate, 'what was your job here?' She figured something in the hotelinos but Nixas just smiled enigmatically and said, 'You can look me up on the worldtree.'

Lila did the surf as she held out her hand and helped the small fey up on to the truckbed, unsnapping the cover slowly to give Teazle time to wake up and react. Then she saw what Nixas did.

'Holy shit.'

The faery coloured a delicate rose across all her cheeks. 'I like human men,' she said, with just a hint of defensiveness. 'They're so stupid. It's kind of sweet.'

Lila closed the images that had spilled across the back of her mind's eye. 'Is that a triple X category?'

'NC-17 mostly,' Nixas said, hanging back. She looked up. The dawn was glowing more brightly now, turning the sky and her skin a soft greeny blue.

Up and down the street the lights of early risers were going on. Lila hurried. She didn't want to be explaining the presence of fey here to the oh-so-conservative element. Under the cover shadow made it too dark to see.

'You first,' the faery whispered, shivering, her flimsy bits of cloth flapping about her in an otherwise intangible breeze.

Lila got the impression that the shiver wasn't because it was cold. She nodded and crawled into the narrow space, able to see Teazle easily when she switched on her heat vision. He tried to lift his head up but finally decided to slide and turn it on his long neck the better to see her. She explained the situation and he grudgingly agreed to let himself be seen though he didn't care for the idea of it much judging by the angle of his ears. Lila had to get out for Nixas to get in then, so she only heard Teazle's sudden inhalation and rasping chuckle,

'A water nymph. Ha. That's funny. What did you say to her? That you could help me? Don't waste my time. Get out before I get hungry.'

The scrape of big claws against steel. Nixas shot back against Lila's leg.

Lila stuck her head under, 'Stop fooling around. You need healing. She offered.'

Teazle snarled at her. His sweat smelt ill even to Lila. She wasn't sure that he was entirely in control of his mind.

'I'll hold him,' Lila said to Nixas, afraid the faery would give up. She slid into the crawl height space and pawed her way across Teazle's body. He was still growling but he didn't try to stop her. His gaze was baleful and flickered on the edge of self-control. She didn't bother with any niceties like she would with anyone else. She just engaged some power and moved him around until he was in a position where her two arms and one leg could pin him and still let the little fey have enough room to see what she was doing.

146

'It's okay now,' she said to Nixas. The faery hesitated, then fluttered forwards, shrinking herself in size to fit better into the cramped space that was now almost entirely filled up with awkwardly placed bits of bodies. A lovely scent filled the heavy air and then, like a raincloud, gently burst, leaving clean fresh air in its place. Nixas dusted the last of some powder off her hands and briefly touched Teazle's quills and feathers.

She giggled. 'No wonder you don't want to be inside, demon.' She spread her hands out and moved them close to his body. 'Now let's see what's wrong with you.'

Teazle never let up his growl except to suck another breath in between his T-Rex teeth. His body vibrated in Lila's grip, muscles continually testing against her hold so that the two of them seemed to twitch in unison. Nixas trembled but kept on moving her hands above him until she had swept as much of him as she could reach without actually crawling on him. She sat back on her heels.

'This is very bad!' she said, her face a picture of girlish dismay, eyes huge. Rays of yellow had begun to appear in her hair, and areas which once been black in her were turning deep blue. It was the sunrise, Lila realised. She reflected the sky.

'Do what you can,' Lila said. 'I've done everything I know.'

Teazle made a major break for it and Lila sat on him so hard she thought she was going to break something new. He snarled and snapped his jaws, starting to brew up a fury as she asserted dominance over him. At the same time she felt his body start to heat up in a new way. He was getting aroused. Trying to subdue a raging horny demon was a challenge she could live without, even when he was this badly hurt. It didn't look like the nymph had any defences so she couldn't miss a trick.

'Hurry up for hell's sake,' she muttered, trying not to sound too aggravated.

Nixas gave Lila a female to female glance of amusement and some admiration as she, too, noticed Teazle's changes of state. 'He's a real live wire.' The faery had grown in size, her colour changing once again to a soft blue lit from within by inner fire. Her mouth was dark as ink, eyes closed. Her face hovered a millimetre above Teazle's skin, nostrils flared as she breathed in over his injuries. As she did so her body darkened fractionally and then she put her mouth on him in a kiss that looked like it was the precursor to a bite and some flickering, thick liquid light spilled out of her lips and into his flesh.

He hissed and ground his teeth, body going taut with pain, but he held still and when she lifted away he shuddered with relief. His snarl changed to a kind of purr.

'That was the least of them, demon,' she said with strange relish, her eyes wide and avid, her fingers probing across him for the site of another injury. 'It will cost me a week of work to fix you halfway. And Medusoid poison too. I cannot rid you of more than half that tonight. You will be slowed down, even if I can put you on your feet.'

'Get on with it, strumpet,' Teazle growled, sliding his snout into the corner of the truckbed and pressing it there in an effort to help himself regain some conscious control.

Nixas glowed and repeated her measures over another place.

Teazle's limbs bucked. Lila felt his bones grind in her hands and under her boots as his effort forced her to tighten her hold to a ridiculous level. Once he backed off and Nixas paused she let go a little just to keep his circulation going. Teazle rammed his head against the metal side as if he was going to bash himself into oblivion. One of his wings started to work itself loose under Lila's forearm.

'Be quiet,' Lila said, feeling the truck rock. 'The neighbours are already bad enough. All we need is for one of them to come snooping over. They've already made it hard enough for Max to stay here, without giving them something to really get their teeth into.'

'Alien sex threesome in Bay City suburban garden leaves neighbours outraged,' Nixas whispered and giggled to herself.

'Just because it got you two million dollars further up the coast,' Lila muttered.

'Oh I can still eat out in this town on that story,' Nixas said. 'Moths or no moths.'

Teazle fought and to distract herself from noticing his growing erection Lila said, 'What are you doing here then, if you're still good uptown in celebrity heights?'

Nixas did another section of Teazle and then said, 'They like me. I don't like them. Their minds are full of filth.'

'Forgive me for being a bit stupid,' Lila said, not daring to move as Teazle heaved and snarled. He slammed his snout into the truck and she heard and felt the metal dent. 'But if you're going to strip naked, dance and . . . um . . . entertain for money in the porn industry, wouldn't you expect a bit of that?'

'Oh I don't mind pure fun,' Nixas said, coming up for air and glowing a lighter, paler blue. Her dark points were turning a soft rose-red though her orange eyes never changed. 'It's not the activity in itself. It's the intent. Those people don't know fun at all. They want to punish themselves and others. They're all mad.'

Teazle had nearly got his wing free enough to move. It had razored bits of horn on its edges. Lila couldn't think of a way to grab it without losing something even more dangerous. 'We'll have to stop in a second.'

'I will do a general vitality,' Nixas announced, looking at the wing fighting steadily free, like an emergent satanic butterfly.

'That'll make him feel better, right?'

'Yes, that's right.' Nixas smiled sweetly as if Lila was an A student.

'Get ready to run, then,' Lila said grimly, not even wanting to think about it.

Nixas gave Teazle a speculative glance. 'Demons are so hard to read for me,' she said. 'I never know if they want to eat me or f . . .'

'Probably both at the same time,' Lila said to discourage any thoughts Nixas might have of sticking around and finding out. She felt Teazle relax deviously and become languid and buttery as if he had fallen asleep.

'At least they're pure of heart,' Nixas said with a sigh. She took a breath and went dark like a light being hidden under a blanket.

Lila heard and felt Teazle take a big, easy breath in. 'Out!'

Nixas darted past her into the daylight and suddenly Lila was holding nothing but thin air. She backed out of the truck and jumped down into the driveway. Teazle was standing in human form, dressed in his perfect dark-blue suit, his white hair hanging down his back as though just brushed and ready to advertise shampoo. Nixas had changed to her male form and was looking at him from behind the screen door, ready to bolt. Teazle was laughing silently but so hard he looked ready to burst a rib. Across the street Mrs Pinkerstein's chihuahua started yapping. Lila turned slowly and gave the woman a wave but she thought it probably didn't register since Mrs Pinkerstein stood at the end of her own driveway, mouth ajar like a stranded fish, the chihuahua dancing around her ankles and tangling them in its designer leash.

Teazle made a pretend pounce in Nixas' direction and he jumped and bolted indoors. In the same movement, fluid as a river, the demon turned to her, arms out wide, still laughing. 'You didn't really imagine I was so far gone I'd tear the place up?'

Lila smacked at his hands but he was faster than she was and stepped out of the way. He looked relaxed when he did it, as if he hardly moved at all, but she missed him good. She shook her head in irritation as she turned and for a moment they played a little game of Wu Shu hands, Lila trying to grab his wrists and he winding out of reach. They danced along the path to the house, him backing up until his feet hit the porch steps when he stopped and made a funny fighter face at her, then dodged and pushed her so she tripped up the stairs, falling into a handstand on the top step to avoid it looking like she had been about to fall over. They both ended up laughing at the end of this bout. Teazle bent down and turned his head, hair falling across his utter white face and eyes as he tried to make himself upside down.

'This poison is making me twice as slow,' he complained.

It was true. Usually he could sit her in the dust in under two seconds.

In spite of all her mechanics it was hard to hold herself on her arms. Her legs were so damn heavy. She flipped back to normal and heard a board crack under her. 'So, coming in or not?'

'Not,' he said decidedly. 'I hear we have to go into Faery and I'll need all my body parts for that. Like I said. I'll be your dog. I have my place here from last time anyway,' and he turned and sat down on the steps in a Zen position of utter calm.

Across the street Mrs Pinkerstein was struggling with the madly excited chihuahua. The noise wasn't deafening but it had a tinny, mad annoying sound. Teazle barked. He sounded like the daddy of all dogs and the chi instantly shut up and put its head down, tail between its legs.

'Thank the nymph for me,' he told Lila as she turned.

'I will,' she said. She looked out over the low hills towards the high-way but there was no sound of the bike engine. Her stomach hurt with hunger. She went inside.

'Nixas is one of the greatest healers of the fey,' Malachi informed her as she stood, surveying what had once been a fair model of a Quaker style mid-size domestic kitchen and had somehow become a huge room equipped with professional cookery gear, a cavernous extension of a larder and an inglenook fireplace big enough to roast an ox.

150

Around the latter was a wide tiled area full of chairs and piles of blankets upon which various faeries were resting, talking, eating and smoking. Many of them gave her a nod and a wink, a smile, raised their mugs or waved and hid again.

'Nixas is a player,' Lila said and met Malachi's eye with a frank look of her own. 'I hate players.' She swept her eyes over the new magical extension, not sure about it, and wondering where all their stuff had gone.

Malachi smiled his slow, laconic smile. 'Oh, me too,' he said and she shook her head, smiling and punched him lightly on the shoulder because nobody but nobody was more of a player than Malachi. He pointed through the smokes and steams to the small figure of a pot-bellied creature sitting in the arms of a much larger faery. The small one appeared to be doing some kind of dance with a spoon in one hand and a mug in the other. The larger one darted around, moving it skilfully from place to place. At its orders five or six others moved about with pots, pans and jars. On a table between them and the mellow fireplace with its roaring logs was set an incredible feast, only one third of which Lila could even identify. The room smelled heavenly.

'I thought you were hungry,' she said, lightheaded and feeling sick with a need for food.

'Mine's just coming,' he replied and then a half-height brownie walked up with a platter on which a steak rested, blackened to a crisp on its very edges, dripping with blood and hot fat, quite raw in the middle. 'Please excuse me.' He took the plate and put it down on the floor, then gave a curious kind of shrug and suddenly there was no tall, cool black faery at her side but a huge pantherlike creature on all fours, darkness pooling around it as it gulped down the meat in three bites and then paused a moment to sit and lick its whiskers.

'Aww, Baggie,' she said to him, getting over her surprise at his change – she'd never seen him actually do it before. 'I didn't know you were really a . . . anyway. That's not really a panther. Or a puma. Too much . . . in fact you're a bit . . .' Cat. He was some kind of cat. But weird. Not like a real one. She didn't know how to say that nicely.

He bared his incredibly white teeth at her and his orangey-red eyes blinked once twice. Then he was standing and saying, 'That's better. If I had to eat any more of that honey and jellies shit we have to stick with in human form I'd be sick. Cats need meat.'

'Soul food,' she said.

'Hell yeah.' He gently bumped her with his shoulder. 'You all right?' His question meant everything. Are you all right in every way?

'Hell, no,' she said, with feeling. 'Where's the menu?'

CHAPTER THIRTEEN

Lila woke up on the futon mats that passed for a bed now that ordinary beds didn't support her weight any more. She felt exhausted but the sun was high so she had to have been out a while. Her room was empty except for her and Zal, who was awake, sitting propped up against the wall, playing on a hand console. His face was set with concentration. She heard the tinny tune and pop of a game where all the characters were cute, big-eyed furry ninjas. Zal's character was a pink fluffy squirrel in a minidress and high boots who wielded a two-handed sword bigger than her entire body.

'Eee-cha!' said the squirrel repeatedly, slaying flying monkeys left and right, leaping from tree to tree in search of nuts.

'Homesick?' Lila asked, rolling on to her back and rubbing her face with both hands. She felt so sleepy she'd like to turn over and go back to oblivion, but she'd already spent too long on rest. A half-digested super salad with mesquite chicken and avocado salsa shifted with sluggish acidity in her gut. She tried to swallow the nasty taste in her mouth and remembered all the faery beer she'd drunk.

'Haha,' Zal said, losing concentration with his squirrel and falling off a log. His face was scraped down the side with a red graze, hair matted with mud on the ends. Mud caked his clothing and had started to fall off on the bedsheets.

'You fell off.'

'Your bike doesn't hold the corners that well over a hundred. Not on wet gravel anyway. Just a small tumble.'

'Is the bike . . . ?'

'I bought you another one,' he said, tossing the console aside. 'It's on order, anyway. They don't stock them for some reason.'

'Where's the old one?'

'In a field halfway to Frisco. Thanks, I'm fine.' He bent down and kissed her.

He felt rough and tough in his armour, and tasted of bruising and chilli. She decided she liked it and was just deciding that maybe they could spend another hour here when there was a knock on the door. She made to answer but Zal held her down and finished his kiss.

'It's only me,' said Max's voice from the other side of the door. 'I'm gonna make you some breakfast. Come down when you're ready. No rush.'

Zal stared into her eyes with dark focus. 'There's a lot of moth dust out there,' he said. 'One of them followed me out into the country, tried to swipe me when I came off the bike. It only veered off because it realised I was elf.'

'Ah, faery kryptonite.'

'At close range. How are they affecting you?'

'Me?' She yawned and did a systems check, sitting up suddenly appalled when she saw that she was twenty per cent slow. 'Actually . . . not so good.'

'Too much magic,' he said. 'Aether can really interfere with electronics at these magnitudes. I thought maybe the elementals would buffer it but I guess they can't block it all. It will be worse in Faery.'

She watched his mouth moving as he spoke, noticing the sensual shapes his lips made. 'Have you been there before?'

'No. We're not high on the party list. I once made an attempt to spy my way in but I couldn't find the way. Time and space work strangely there. It is legend that it is the country of the Second Sister, one of the Moirae. Faery is her loom.'

Lila put her finger to his lips, reluctantly. 'Mal said you weren't to say that word.'

'Yes, I know, but they're already watching me so it doesn't matter.'

'Zal, about Sorcha . . . I . . .'

'I know who it was,' he said, glancing at her chest, where Tath had been a silent witness for the last twenty-four hours. His expression was unreadable. He struggled briefly with some decision and then made an unhappy breath and sat back. He leant his head against the wall and closed his eyes. After a few seconds he opened them and glanced at her, his gaze moving over her face and then downwards.

'Lila,' he said finally, 'are you ever going to wear anything other than this appalling black military stuff?' He fingered her cotton vest, tugged the neckline down and gave a disapproving glance at her functional plain bra, also black.

'I . . .' she began, confused by his changes of focus. 'I never really thought about it.'

'I did,' he replied and reached out to the side of the bed where he found a long, silk-wrapped package. He handed it to her.

She was so surprised, she didn't know what to say. It was heavy. The rich purple silk satin flowed over her hands like mercury between the lilac ribbons that bound it up in a tight roll. Small tags of exotic, jewelled fabric hung at the top and bottom, the maker's name silver-stitched on to them. She read it, 'Slazar and the Dark Lady,' and then looked up at Zal with puzzlement.

'A demon and a faery,' he said, nodding at the parcel. 'Very exclusive.'

She undid the ribbons, not knowing what to say. Among the folds of wrapping she found amulets and talismans, and Zal told her how each one was put there to protect the contents from evil influences of any kind during shipping. Each one in itself was lovely – a piece of carved wood, thin as paper, a filigree dragon, a paper covered in shooting stars that flickered with real light . . . She couldn't find anywhere safe to put them until Zal held out his hand and took them, saving them from the mud.

Then, as she got to the last part and the silk gave way to soft brushed linen that was tougher altogether, she heard the faint sound of music rising up from the package. Funky guitar and a heavy rock bassline. She looked up at Zal and saw him smirking, his body automatically starting to dance to the beat in small ways as he heard it too. 'Powerful charms,' he said, smiling at her with such sweetness she felt suddenly at a total loss for words. That he could be like this after everything that had just happened made her feel humbled beyond speaking.

She unfolded the linen and for a moment she didn't know what she was looking at. It was dark, but rich with the intense jewel colours of violet, emerald, scarlet and azure that skated across its surface. It was heavy, almost rigid in places, and it was scaled with thin crystal sheets that made it appear fishlike. There was satin. There was lace. There was leather. There were billions of tiny stitches in different colours marking the position of planets, the movement of tides, tiny animals, insects and plants. There was fabric that fell like a liquid and shimmered with grey, cloud colours. It was only when she tried to pick it up and it opened out in her hands that she realised what she was holding.

Armour.

She examined it for a while, mouth ajar, lost for words. It was light. It was strong. 'This is sexy,' she said, and she didn't mean simply its resemblance to a corset.

'Yes it is,' he said. 'Also, tricky.'

'Tricky?' She jumped up to try it on. There was some strange halfway-house thing between a belt, a pelvic brace, a French knicker and a miniskirt that she hoped wasn't too girly. For some reason she resented the idea of wearing a skirt to fight.

'They make it in various types – depending on your style – like Righteous, Wrathful, Clever, Artful, Slayer . . . that kind of thing. The magical properties it has are focused around the fighter.'

'So what's mine?' She got the pants on, demurely keeping a sliver of personal underwear beneath, and felt them slide around like hands, fitting themselves to her. When they were done the flouncy parts adjusted themselves until they were less like a pretty little ruffle and more like a plain valance. The colour shifted from dove-grey to black.

Zal observed these changes with interest. 'Tricky,' he said.

She hesitated and looked at him, the corset open in one hand, vest and bra in the other, 'But I'm not tricky,' she said. 'I'm really . . . I suppose it doesn't come in Grimly Predictable Robotic?'

'I know what you think you are,' he said. 'But I think this is the best one for you.'

She dropped the old clothes and started wrestling with the top half. 'Why don't you wear it?'

'I prefer things as they are,' he said, shrugging in his elven armour that was little more than ordinary clothing with some added leather and belts. 'I have enough problems being contradictory as it is. Wouldn't want to mess that up. I'm a simple person.'

She snorted. After another minute of struggling, she had it on. It had shoulderguards, which she'd never worn before, and although it was corset-like it preserved modesty with a serious intent and kept its neckline suitably high. The symbols and stitches on it shifted slightly. She thought, though she was sure she imagined it, that it was breathing by itself.

'Better have something like this for Faery anyway,' Zal said, giving her a once-over. 'Even if you want to go back to your Serious Soldier look after. They like Tricky things. Every advantage is worth taking.'

Lila opened her wardrobe door to look in the full-length mirror, and nearly screamed.

'What?' Zal said quickly, though he didn't move. He watched her with narrowed eyes. She got the impression he'd been expecting something like this, even if he didn't know what it would be.

She looked at the figure before her and it was herself, wearing the armour, an ordinary reflection. But for a split second she hadn't seen that at all. It had been so quick she was almost at a loss to recall it now, but for an instant she'd seen another woman in her place – a tall girl with dark brown hair and skin, and large eyes the colour of the night sky.

And then instead of that girl she saw a clockwork metal witch. At the same time as being clockwork she was skeletal, a corpse, already dead: she held swords and her hands dripped with blood. Her silver eyes were mirrors in which could be seen a human woman with red hair. Behind and to the witch's left was a tall golden-haired elf with black, empty eyes, clad in bone. Behind her and to her right was a gigantic creature hidden in red and yellow fire. The three of them each had an arm extended and upon their outstretched hands lay an enormous, strange sword, its skin-bound grip large enough for three hands. The blade glowed almost white hot. From its edges drops of blood fell like water and flickered into fire. The fire spelled words before shattering into sparks and dying away. Words, sentences, libraries, wikis fell from it like waterfalls.

This she had seen in a second in the mirror.

Lila waited but the vision did not come back. Her image did change however. It flickered, like a bad recording. She kept seeing fragments of the first image here and there, the bone beneath the flesh, the pistons under her armour-clad limbs, the blinding light of the tokamak core.

She told it as best she could to Zal, who got up and stood behind her. 'I just see you,' he said. He sounded sorry. 'I had no idea it had this kind of Hoodoo on it. Working here, too.' He shook his head slightly and his expression became grim. 'Faeries,' he muttered under his breath.

'I'll just stay well away from mirrors,' she said, pretending an air of casual acceptance while she struggled to shake off the momentary chill that the sight had given her. But Zal turned her towards him and

157

unerringly took hold of the silver spiral which now lay unconcealed at her collarbones. 'Maybe it's because this is here.'

'Do you know what it is?'

'It's something that Poppy and Vid don't want to be caught with, and that's bad enough. It must have a lot of power. Usually they like power, so I don't know why they gave this away.'

'It's . . .' But she was silenced by his hand clapping over her mouth. He shook his head.

'Don't say it. I think you should hide it. There are more fey here than you realise and not all of them are friendly. Absolutely all of them are power hungry. Your sister needs a quick lesson in running dosshouses for the kindly ones. Well, needed it. Too late now.'

Lila frowned. 'I really must go and see her.' Suddenly she felt anxious, very anxious to see Max. 'Don't entirely get out of bed. I'll see if I can wheedle a tray out of her . . .' she said, picking up one of her old T-shirts and throwing it over herself. It covered her to mid thigh and hid the necklaces and armour from ordinary sight. She opened the door.

There was no hallway. There was a scrubby bit of grassland cowering under a fitful wind, grey skies and low hills covered in purple heather. Cold air swirled and bit its way past her into the room. She slammed the door shut. Beyond it she could hear distinctly the muttering sound of fey in conversation and the familiar creak of the third step down as someone came running upstairs. Seconds later there was knocking.

'Lila, it's me, Malachi. Let me in.'

He sounded breathless, almost frightened.

She opened the door and the wide moorland stared at her and her little hidey-hole. She closed it. 'I can't.'

Behind her she felt Zal's warm presence. His voice was quite grim. 'I don't suppose you wished for something?'

'No,' she said, but she was aware, confirmed by Tath's mute nod of recognition, that in the world of thought-before-words she had been entertaining the idea of wanting to be alone with Zal, somewhere nobody could bother them. At least for a while.

'What's behind the door?' Malachi asked, as if it were quite normal for spaces to change themselves around when you weren't looking.

Lila told him. 'Where is it?' she demanded.

'Faery,' he said. 'Although where in Faery I have no idea. How many times did you open the door?'

'Twice,' she said.

'Next time is the last time,' he said. 'After that you won't hear me any more and you'll have to leave. Did you see anything particular?'

She did her best to describe the scenery.

'It sounds like Umeval to me,' he said, though his word meant nothing to her. 'You'd better go through and try to stay out of trouble. I'll track you down. Whatever you do, do not take any leftward turns. You're already far in.'

'Leftward?'

'Widdershins. Takes you further inside. In fact, don't take any turns. Try to stay close to where you are. Let Zal do any talking you have to do. Don't show anyone the . . . just don't show them anything. Stick tight.' He sounded like someone trying to hide how tense they were.

Lila looked down as he was talking. She could see the hall light shining under her door, and the twin shadows of Malachi's legs. 'I think the door's all right,' she said. None of her senses could detect anything untoward. She bent down and tried to slide her finger under but there wasn't enough room. She made her finger into a mirror and slid that under. In its small reflection she saw Malachi's extended form, swirling faintly with black anthracite dust. 'I can see you.'

'Wait,' he said. 'Maybe I can pass you something under the door.' He padded off swiftly and soon returned, bending low on his hands and knees. He prodded a feather through to her. It was white, with a fine blue streak at its tip. 'If you see a full moon, burn it.'

'And if I don't?'

'You will see one,' he said. 'If you're underground you'll still know.'

She frowned but took Teazle's plume. 'I don't suppose you can fit any food through there?'

'There's not much time,' he said. 'If you need anything, grab hold of it.'

Malachi heard her grumble and move backwards. Zal muttered some elven slang about fey. Then the light changed and he smelt the cold, grim air of old lands under wet skies. There came the sound of wood splintering, Zal's shout, Lila's sharp cry of mixed rage and fear. He stood up and grabbed the handle, flinging the door wide.

The empty room greeted him. He saw the open wardrobe, Lila's unopened black sack full of whatever strange devices she had collected for herself and on the floor a white and blue feather, twisting and turning in the draught.

CHAPTER FOURTEEN

Malachi had just enough presence of mind to snatch up the feather before anyone else got their hands on it. He closed his eyes and let dust from his fingers fall on it, reading the impressions that had been left there, his heart beating so fast he almost dropped everything and lost the lot.

He saw the inner lands, a huge figure with an axe, the splintering wood of Lila's door. He smelled woodsmoke and charred flesh. He felt the fierce vibrating jive of the runes that had led the figure to Lila's temporary portal, like hounds baying. Antlered jacks, he thought. Then it is Umeval. Somewhere near the Turning Stones.

The wind was full of a deep cold that said that part of Faery was moving either into or out of winter. Malachi prayed it was out but had no illusions that it actually would be. Winterside was widdershins of course, and inside the deep ice of midwinter lay Lost Jack's City. He shuddered with misgivings and his hand slipped inside his pocket, reaching for one of his little grass ropes.

He fashioned a doll quickly then bent down to the bed. There and there, one hair from her head and one from Zal's. He bound them around the doll's neck, then pulled one from his own scalp and used that to bind the hugely unwieldy feather to the doll's back; a makeshift flight. Then he tapped the doll sharply on the head.

'OI!' it said, a big sound in its high, tiny voice. 'Bit rough!'

'Sorry,' he said, 'in a rush. I've a message I have to send.'

'Be it secret?' the doll asked, wheedling suddenly. It stood upright somehow, the dry grass of its body shifting and curling, as if it were young and green, to push it into position.

'Aye, secret is and does,' he said.

'Secret is and secret does 'mands a price that's paid in blood,' the doll said, snickering.

'I want a looksee, too,' Malachi added, folding the lapel of his jacket back and taking from its place there a long hatpin with a jewelled end. He stabbed his finger with the point and let three drops of blood fall on the doll's head, squeezing to make sure they were generous.

The doll shivered in its shower and its bunched form divided into arms and legs, a head with the beginnings of a face and, where the feather had been, two distinct blue wings like a hummingbird's.

'Looksee is free for a promise to be,' it said.

'As if I'd fall for that one,' Malachi said, binding his finger up with his silk pocket handkerchief. 'I'll give you leave to live for the length of what's at hand, free to come and free to go, carry words and pictures to and fro until talking, walking, all is done. If you grant true vision, when I ask it.'

'Myeh,' the doll said in disgust. 'I suppose so.' It tested its new form with a peculiar little caper along the edge of the bed. It sniffed. 'Lovers full of longing,' it said offhandedly. 'At least one in any case. What we'd give for such shackles easily spun! A Game so long it's almost forgot. Ready to rise and ripe for twisting . . .'

'Never mind that,' Malachi said.

'Yar, whatcha wanta look at then?' the doll asked, folding its arms sulkily.

'Show me Lost Jack's wife,' Malachi said.

The doll leaned back and gave him what would have been a searching look, if it had had eyes and not just dark holes in its knotty head. 'She 'as a way of lookin' back I not recommend.'

'Just do it.'

The little thing rolled its head in disgust but raised its arm obediently and pointed at the wall where Lila's small watercolour of a patch of beach and the ocean hung. There, instead of the picture but in the same painted style, a new image swirled into being.

Malachi saw her face emerge with a familiar twisting pang in his heart – one he'd not felt for so long that, like Lila and Zal's Game, he'd almost forgotten it was there. But seeing her freed that little chip of ice and let him feel its sharp edge anew.

A tall, strong woman clad in grey furs stood at the doorway of an ice cave. The fire dwindling there in the dawnlight lit her brown skin and darker hair and the dark glitter of her eyes was lent a golden edge.

Meltwater from the ledge above her dripped down in a steady patter and ran off the greasy ropes of her hair where it was bound with gut and walrus ivories into two braids that hung either side of her neck. Buckles and straps festooned her, holding her powder bag, her water, her shot and flints, her cold iron gun. She was bending toward the light, pushing something into the compartments of her herb bandolier. The soft light made the unearthly beauty of her face stranger still, its cheekbones and broad lips and skin almost dewy, though she was older than Malachi. Beside her lay the frozen, bloody red snow of a butcher site, though nothing remained. At her boots the blades of iron knives lay dully glimmering in their simple bindings.

She straightened up then and turned, looking directly out of her image, into Malachi's eyes.

Faultless, he thought.

'Hoodoo Cat,' she said, and half her mouth lifted into a smile that could draw men across oceans. 'How long it has been?'

'Madrigal,' he said and found his voice hoarse, as if it hadn't been used since they last spoke.

'What do you here?' She put her hands on her hips, staring into the thin air, her breath misting in front of her, bloodstained fingers finding her gauntlets at her belt and pulling them free to put on. Her face was lightly amused.

'I need your help.'

She raised one eyebrow, taking her time with her gloves. 'Do you now? And for what would that be?'

He was as nervous as a kid standing at the door facing his first date. Nonetheless he tried to regain his composure. 'Some friends of mine have been brought unexpectedly into Jack's lands.'

That got both eyebrows. 'Indeed? Careless of them. Or of you?'

'The cause isn't important. The important thing is that one of them is carrying a thing.'

'A thing?' She laughed and Malachi lost his breath. She nodded slowly, her eyes round with amusement. 'That *does* sound important.'

'It is the thing Jack wants most in the world.'

Her black eyes snapped cold suddenly and he felt her presence reach directly into his head and chest, as distinctly as if she had stabbed him with blades. In an instant all her softness had become hard edges, her energy poised for action. She could reach through this connection, tear his heart out, if she wished. He saw her wing cases rise, clattering, either side of her head, the streamers of her true magic beneath them flickering into a brief white life before they subsided into a cape of plated bone once more.

'A human?' she asked, her tone disbelieving. 'And here? They must be insane. Where are they now?' She cast her eyes round her camp once, dismissing it as she turned back to him.

'Somewhere south,' he said. 'They were attacked by antlered jacks. That's all I know.'

She shook her head at this folly, her mouth tightening, then whistled sharply into the wind. She walked forwards, shrugging her rifle to a more comfortable position on her back. 'Truly you are always a surprise, Cat,' she said, raising her arm in a half-wave that brought the ice shelf above her crashing down on her fire, extinguishing it with a hiss. Steam rose behind her and scattered on the wind. 'Our only chance is that they have the sense to hide and run.'

'Mmn,' Malachi said, his throat drying up. 'I hope.'

'Flirting with the evil one?' She laughed again then, this time with less good humour than before. 'Now, you test my patience when you make me think of Pandora. That hellbitch shut-the-box. Careful, or I might think you was flirting with me, Cat, spiking my temper that way.' Her intent remained strong but he felt her let go of him, the strings that tied him to his body relaxing. 'Meet me at the Twisting Stones by dark. Let us see if we still have the mettle or the wits to test bitter Jack one more time.'

The picture blurred with grey and white shapes. At first it seemed a blizzard but then Malachi realised it was the fur of the giant grey and white wolf that had come running up to her. She caught hold of its ruff at the height of her head and leapt up on to its back, turning one last time to face him. She rubbed her face in the wolf's pelt and gave it a vigorous patting. Its purple tongue hung out the side of its massive jaws, flapping wetly as it panted.

'Don't be late. Shara here will be so excited to know her playmate is coming for a game of chase.'

The wolf leapt and Malachi was left with nothing to look at but a bit of falling ice and a jumble of snow.

At least he knew that if she were looking for them Zal and Lila might survive. He flicked his fingers at the picture and the doll released the vision.

'An' where am I going?' the doll demanded. 'Don't tell me. You want me to take some news to your lost idiot friends, if they ent already dead. Summat 'long the lines of – Run and keep running, dunna talk to anyone and dunna trust anyone exceptin' a woman ridin' a wolf, and if yer meet people called Jack get the fryin' hell away from 'em and stay away. Meantimes, if yer comes across a lot of standin' rocks in the lee of a mountain, stick around.'

'That will do,' Malachi nodded, shivering.

'Can't believe I fell fer that promise o' yourn,' the doll hissed, shaking its head side to side slowly in disbelief at its own gullibility. *'Life to the end of the matter.* Whassat? Like ten bloody minutes?'

'They're tough. You might get lucky,' Malachi said. 'And you should have asked more questions.'

'You . . . you . . .' The doll wagged a grass finger at him but was unable to come up with a curse bad enough apparently. 'Ugh!' It spun on its heel. 'Next time I'm going to remember this deal, kitty-fiddler, and then you'll have some paying to do, you and that loose-tongued elfy mate of yours. Won't be enough whisky in creation to save you then.'

'Bye!' Malachi waved his fingers. The doll, contracted, had to obey and promptly spread its blunt, half-feather wings and vanished. He swallowed in the second of silence that followed and put his hand over his aching heart. Then he fumbled around and found his mobile phone and started searching for Poppy's number. As he dialled he heard Nixas come in to the room – the head of a much larger rabble of fey who were hanging in the corridor, waiting to see what happened next. She hovered in the doorway.

'What's going on?'

'You lot have destabilised the fabric,' Malachi said with contempt at their carelessness, though no surprise at it. 'Sent half of us straight into Umeval.'

'Oh. Summertime?'

'Winter.' There was no answer. He tried another number.

'Ah. Well, maybe . . . you will need my help then?'

He thought about it. 'Is this the point you're using to get in and out of Otopia now?'

'For the time being in this part of the world. Not very safe here for fey now.'

'Then we have a debt to pay this family, and consider your services forfeit. The lot of you.'

'That's a hard line,' she said, taken aback at his directness. 'But I accept if we are going in against Jack. Maybe some of the others . . .'

'Jack is only the start,' Malachi said, shaking the phone when there was no answer again and then flinging it abruptly into the wall. 'Dammit. I don't have time for this! Nix, I need you to find the Ooshkah girls from Zal's band and bring them here.'

She nodded and turned into her male self, Naxis, and leant close to confide, 'I won't tell them about Umeval.'

'Yeah,' Malachi agreed wholeheartedly, knowing that in all likelihood it would mean never seeing either faery again if he did so. 'One thing, Nax. What makes you so damn keen to be in?'

'Don't ask and don't be sorry. I've got reason enough.' The faery said with a shrug and darted to the window. He opened it, was out and closed it before Malachi could say another word.

He retrieved his phone, wondering if he had time to get another one and deciding that it wasn't worth the effort considering, and went downstairs to tell Teazle the bad news.

The demon was still sitting on the doorstep.

'I should rip your legs off,' he said to Malachi, casually, as Malachi closed the screen door behind him. 'Careless.'

'Not my doing,' Malachi said, concealing his surprise that the demon already knew. 'There must be something else involved.'

'Hmm, Zal had talked about a special armour he was having made for her,' Teazle said. 'I made a couple of extra requests about it to the makers . . . when he passed me he was carrying the package under his arm. But it could not be that on its own. Those who made it don't have that kind of power. Anyway,' he got up and turned to face Malachi, his human face less than usually human, like a wax model, 'other things are going on in this neighbourhood.' He handed Malachi a folded newspaper – one of the local weeklies still delivered by paperboys. As Malachi scanned the articles and saw the pattern he added, 'The humans don't know enough to see what all these things add up to. But it's a natural consequence of so much mothdust and so many dreamers.'

Malachi looked up at Teazle, his face feeling set in the dismayed position. 'Ghosts,' he said.

The demon gave a single nod. 'Otopia had only a few, ever. But I can feel them now, crawling beneath the surface of things. And this is close to one of the major faults. They can rise with greater ease here.' He rolled his head on his neck, easing a crick, and stretched, making many small expressions of pain and disgust as he did so. 'I don't care what happens to the humans. Only my wife. But she cares about these things so we'll need more than just an answer for the moths. I should find a geomancer.'

Malachi thought of Jones. 'We can't take the time. We have to travel now if we're going to reach Lila and Zal at all. I must get something old to give us a chance of finding the way . . . must . . .' He didn't mention what he'd figured the problem was. The key. It had risen and been found, it wanted to do what it did best. It didn't even matter if Lila turned left or right. The key was turning Faery around itself. He wasn't even sure he could catch up with it. He stabbed at his phone but it was broken. 'I have to send a message. I'll be right back.'

Teazle rolled his white eyes, 'Not going anywhere without you, am I? But if you get any more things wrong, I'll be collecting those limbs.' His smile was affable; all teeth.

'Naxis is bringing others,' Malachi said, going to Lila's pool truck and opening it up, looking for the fitted phone and then searching his pockets for his security card to activate it. 'Take them all down to the beach. I'll meet you there – less than half an hour.' He got into the driver's seat and started the engine, then slewed backwards out of the drive and sped off. He only had a couple of ideas about where to find an object old enough for their purposes. As he drove he gritted his teeth. He hated the old country. He feared Jack. Both these things brought nasty feelings and old wounds to the surface which no longer had a place in his life. On the backs of his hands fur was already growing. He could barely punch in the number to alert the Agency, and then Jones, of his plans.

Lila stood, blades her hands, surrounded by fifteen of the creatures who had jumped the room. Several of them lay dead at her feet. Metal seemed to be particularly effective against them. Even more so than against elves. But, although she could confidently hold them at bay, directly across from her another ten of them were hanging on to Zal, taking it in turns to rush close and dart away in a strange dance each time they came close to falling unconscious, wrestling a filthy strip of cloth into his mouth and tying it behind his head as they also bound his hands fast. They were extremely quick about it, as if they were used to taking elf prisoners. More behind her held drawn bows aimed at both of them, though she'd have guessed over half of them would miss, they were so worked up with excitement and fear.

'Iron bitch!' snapped one of the ones she had come to recognise as a leader. His horns were bigger and his bearing more arrogant than the rest of the ragged mob. Fresh blood ran freely from new-cut runes in his arms and legs – probably the magic he'd used to find her, though she didn't know that for sure. 'Must be Madrigal's doing. Jack will want them. Yes. Pay a good price.' His wings – they all had them – trailed, weak and damp, useless beneath the sackcloth of his faux fine cloak. His hands were clawed and twiglike, though nimble enough to handle weapons. He brandished a lit and smoky torch towards Zal, who still struggled but couldn't move for the tight grip of his endlessly circulating captors.

'Let him go,' Lila said, trying to keep a desperate edge out of her voice. The more she looked at them the less human they appeared. Unless she looked right at them they had no faces. Animals seemed to stand upright on their hind legs, but like no animals she'd ever seen. They wore rank clothes of the roughest type, barely more than pieces of cloth and leather pinned together with coral and bone. All of them were strong and as large as she was, some bigger and heavier. It was raining and they steamed with effort and stank like wet earth and sweat. They didn't pay attention to her.

'But this elf,' said one, his voice nearly identical to that of the first, 'what's he doing with her? Madrigal ent interested in no elves. I say they spies and we kills 'em.' He whipped out a knife and started towards Zal.

'Spies, spies, flies in yer eyes,' said a sudden loud and arrogant voice from beside Lila's ear. She felt the imp grab his usual painful hold and felt his flames flutter against her hair. 'You stupid wormshits. Killin' them won't get you nothin'. Alive for a prize and dead is dead ever.'

'A demon!' grunted the nearest jack. 'Spies it is, then.' He grinned and hummed to himself, but he didn't move forwards. They all looked at Thingamajig and narrowed their eyes, as if they were moved by one spirit.

'More to the point,' Lila said coldly. 'If you harm anyone I will fill you full of the coldest iron you have ever felt,' and she spun both her short swords with a flourish that finished with them becoming .44 magnum handguns.

All the jacks were armed with iron themselves, and in the course of the few minutes that had passed Lila had realised that this was simply because the only thing that faery magic could not deflect was this particular kind of metal. They didn't touch it themselves however – every blade was stuck in a grip of something much more prosaic and safe, and all were carried in scabbards when not in use.

She took the moment of quiet that followed and added, 'Let him go now, or I'll do it anyway.' After Sorcha she had no trouble meaning it or making herself understood.

A soft mist began to form around the jacks and it thickened with intent now, rising from the ground around their feet. She saw them rubbing their fingertips, lips moving in some little chant she couldn't be bothered to analyse.

'We can take him, come back for her later . . .' she heard one of them snicker behind her.

'Sadly for you,' she said into the greying, clouding air, 'I don't need to see you with my eyes to kill you.'

She took out the ones holding Zal first, each one in the forehead. One of her bullets grazed Zal's cheek and temple with a friction burn but it was at least half a mil wide of actually striking him. The others were easier, because she had no fear of missing at all. She turned on her heel, languidly, barely conscious of moving. Within a few seconds there was silence and the fitful cold wind blowing spotting rain at them and clearing the fug.

Zal wrenched free of his half-tied hands, bent down to recover his own dagger from a dead hand and sliced off his gag. He spat it out with revulsion and ground it into the mud with his foot. 'No guessing this isn't the surface world,' he said with feeling, touching his cheek and wincing slightly. 'Nice shooting.'

'Ammo's low,' she said, calculating the likely bodycount if this was any example to go by. 'Have to do better with something else next time. Ugh, in fact . . .' And she went over to where the closest jack lay and examined his head. There wasn't a lot left of it, and certainly no bullet.

She switched on a magnetic detection field in her feet and started walking around glumly, searching the ground. It was soft and full of water – a good stopping consistency, thankfully. After a short time she got on her knees and began to dig.

'You're kidding me!' the imp said, shivering.

'Do you see my backpack?' she asked.

'No.'

'That's where the spare clips are.'

'Can't you make 'em?'

'Not so as I'm aware.' She pulled her arm out of a narrow hole and shook sludgy brown earth off the heavy little lipstick shape of the slug. 'But if I have to I'll try. Meanwhile, no sense wasting them.'

Inside her chest she felt the feathery tickle of necromancer laughter. Tath didn't need to ask her to touch bodies now – and as she went over each one she felt him surge down her arms and out the tips of her fingers into the ice-cold flesh of the dead faeries – it seemed they didn't need to be warm like a human in order to survive. These were not bloody and red either. They were brown, muddy things, slippery and jellyfish, boned with wood. As she moved around them they were already falling apart and becoming sludge.

Warn me, next time, Tath said. *These have lots of juice.*

She gave him the equivalent of an internal nod. Whatever revulsions she used to feel about his business were gone for now. If he needed power, let him have it. She needed him, or likely would.

Beware though, he continued softly, as if there was someone to overhear. *This much aether in a corpse means you are far, far into the land of Faery. No wonder they were surprised to find you. But also, easy to find you. Everything here is touched with aether. It will all be saying where you are. And whoever the master is here, they will now be sure you are enemy, missing as they are twenty-five or -six of their fellows. Playing along might have been wiser.*

I don't do wiser, Lila said bluntly, fishing through skull debris only to find this bullet had struck part of a buckle on the creature's back and bent itself out of shape. She put it in her pocket anyway. *I used to think I had some shot at it, but that was before yesterday. From now on you can officially consider the Wisdom Bus a suspended service.*

Zal searched the remains for other things. She saw him slip stuff into the bag on his belt but didn't ask about it the same way she didn't ask about his change of demeanour. His charisma had changed from bright to dark, movements quick, efficient and ruthless. His stories of earlier times had seemed farfetched to her, but now she saw where the grit that informed the most raw of his songs had a come from. In Otopia he was lighthearted, in Daemonia seriously foolish, but here he was focused anew, and it was not a settling sight or thing to be around. In his presence she had felt only good things, even the tensions between them had been exciting in a charming way. Here his charm was filled with deadly intent and she was chilled and thrilled by it equally. But she was glad of that. Her own inner cold couldn't have withstood his bright side, not after last night's discoveries. They were united in their grimness and that, in its peculiar way, was glorious. Two killers.

From the leader, Zal took the clasp that had held his cape shut. It was bronze, fashioned into the rough shape of a horse. Lila turned over a piece of skull with antler attached and then, around the thing's neck, saw a strange glint. She turned aside a piece of cloth and found herself staring at a leather neck thong bearing the unmistakably manufactured shape of a dull aluminium ring pull, circa 1970.

Zal came and looked over her shoulder, and snorted, 'Otherworldly metal. Strong protection from missiles.' He gazed at the remains a moment longer. 'Well . . . your shot is off centre about two centimetres, so I guess it worked as best it could.'

Thingamajig danced on her shoulder, aiming his forefinger and thumb at the dead fey and shooting. 'Heh!' he said repeatedly, jittering, until Lila swatted him off her shoulder. 'Hey!'

She straightened up after finding the last bullet and looked around. The grey sky was getting greyer. 'Any ideas? Malachi said not to go anywhere.'

'But somewhere found us anyway,' Zal said, giving the corpses a final look. 'I say we move. Pretty fast too. Open ground out here, and night coming.' He sounded uncertain however, as though he had no faith in running.

She scanned – no signs of where anything like a civilisation might be.

'I'm with Long Ears,' the imp said, wiping muddy claws on a patch of tough grass he'd found.

Lila took a step forward.

'Only, not that way . . .' Thingamajig suddenly leapt back up her leg like a monkey and on to the top of her head. He stood on tiptoe, hand shading his eyes as his toe claws yanked her hair. 'I have a nasty feeling about that way. The mountain there . . . it has a horribly familiar cast to it, like the gleam in a little old lady's glass eye just before she trips you up and shoves you in the oven. Let's go the other way.'

She turned . . .

'Not that way either,' the imp said definitively. 'Jacks came from that way.'

'He's right.' Zal pointed at the blood-spattered tracks here and there among the tussocks.

'Just fucking decide!' Lila snapped, seeing her breath suddenly fog. The grass around them whitened with frost and became black.

The imp pointed. Zal pointed. They pointed in opposite directions.

'Wait a second,' Zal said. 'Which way did you turn around just then?'

'I don't know . . . this way . . .' she said and started but his hand stopped her.

'No left turns,' he said.

'The other way feels . . . hard . . .' She couldn't explain it but it did. Nonetheless, she turned right around. 'Will that undo it?'

He shrugged, blew, his breath like hers. 'Cold doesn't change. Let's go.'

'I liked my direction better,' the imp grumbled, swinging down through her tangled hair on to her shoulder once again.

'My direction has standing stones in it,' Zal said, huffing with cold. He wasn't dressed for severe weather.

Lila scanned, but only on the highest magnification could she make out anything that might have been such objects. 'How do you know?'

He pointed at his eyes with forked fingers and then pointed the fingers out and around. 'Magical creature in a magical world,' he said. 'For once I win.'

She jogged a step to catch up to his side. 'I like it when you win.'

He bent briefly and kissed her head, avoiding the imp with easy grace. She glowed inwardly at the gesture, tasted lemon and with it the fiercely pleasurably memories of the weeks they'd shared before this debacle, and after the wedding.

'So, who were those guys?' she asked, when they had covered about half a mile but had made no visible ground on the hills ahead.

'Some kind of country and forest spirits, I think,' Zal said. 'But only traces. Did you see, they all had almost the same look to them.'

'Like clones.'

'Yes. I think they were only be echoes of a primary fey, or something like that. They're related to the hunt.'

'The hunt – Malachi said something about that. He thought we had to look for one, to get the Mothkin, something like that anyway.'

'And now we've slaughtered some of it,' he said. 'So that'll take some explaining.'

'They started it,' she said. 'I just walked out of my room, they were the ones who decided to pounce and take us dead or alive.'

'True,' he said. 'I wonder who Jack is. It's a common faery name. Maybe some local big shot. Faery is all about local big shotting, far as I understand it.'

The imp mumbled and agreeing sound. 'Used to be different,' he said. 'Once there was a queen and a king all the way up and down. Not 'ny more. Bandit stuff now.'

'What happened to the king and queen?' Lila asked.

'They argued,' the imp said, going quiet.

'There must be more to it than that,' she objected but he refused to be drawn and the elves didn't know the answer. Zal only said.

'It was a long time ago. Nobody talks about it. The faeries put their magic down after, because of whatever happened.'

'Put it Under?' Lila asked.

Zal nodded. 'Something like that. Faery is only half the place it used to be since then, and faeries have only half their power.'

'Don't they want it back?'

'Some of them, no doubt,' he said and speeded up the pace. Soon they were jogging and shortly afterwards, running at a reasonable clip downhill into the first small dips of undulating ground where the hills began.

They were moving along something that looked like a little track, had been following it for a short while in fact, when they stopped as one.

They were standing in a wood of slender, black trees, sparsely scattered across snowy hills. The track remained the same shape and their footprints were still there on it. The trees had not suddenly appeared either. It was more as if they had always been there, but it wasn't until now that they'd noticed them. Lila looked back without turning and trees covered the path. Overhead their spindly branches scratched at the lowering white sky where snow could clearly be seen blowing high in the sky, without falling. There was no sign of the open moor they had just been running across. She glanced at Zal and he at her, to confirm that both of them felt the same at the same moment.

'That's something,' Zal said quietly, his ear tips moving all around in a way that might have looked comical on a less obviously warlike person.

The imp made an uncomfortable sound.

'What is it?' Lila asked.

Then she was quiet as they all listened to the new sound of thumping – a hoofed animal of some size approaching. It sounded like it came from the west, then the east, then north, then south, then all directions at once. With a breath of warm air the frost melted, leaving them wet and surrounded by dripping. A flock of grey birds came and settled in trees nearby, but as Lila tried to look more closely they took off, wheeled around and settled further away. Still they stood, not exactly frightened, and then, as she turned back to look the way they were going Lila got the shock of her life as she realised she was looking into a face a few inches from her own. It was a woman's face, but it had been completely concealed by the fact that it looked exactly like the scenery behind it and only a hint of movement had given it away.

She felt Zal stiffen beside her as he saw the same thing. The imp shrieked and hopped.

The woman's eyes flicked to him and back to Lila. She stepped sideways and a woman-shaped piece of the landscape moved, became three dimensional. Her skin looked as if it had been painted; it didn't change now that she was in motion. 'I am Gulfoyle,' she said, her black and brown eyes searching both of them with curiosity. 'Who are you?'

'Zal Ahriman,' Zal said easily, though he was far from relaxed.

'An elf, but an odd one,' the woman said, apparently unaffected by the bitter damp though she was naked. She looked at Lila, with a sudden, birdlike movement. 'And you?'

'Lila Black,' Lila said. She was suddenly aware of the bullets in her hand that she hadn't cleaned yet. For some reason she started to move, to show them, then stopped. The faery's eyes flickered and her mouth made a faint moue of annoyance.

'Then we all know each other and are strangers no more,' she said and laughed, because it was so obviously untrue. 'Let us see if we cannot improve upon it. I am the forest but not of the forest and I come in winter yet it is not my season. I am the ox before the plough that pulls Jack's Lost City into spring each time we turn away from the sun. I am harnessed though I would be free. That is why I am here. Why are you here?' She continued to examine them, walking around them gracefully, with the distinctive and hesitant movements of a wild deer.

She seemed much taken with Lila's worn, dark grey T-shirt and its aged, peeling slogan. 'What does this mean – Do You Want Fries With That?'

'It's a . . . joke . . .' Lila said, wishing she had picked up something else and not this thousand-year-old dreadful, never funny and hence only worn in bed alone, piece of crap.

'Ah!' the faery smiled, very pleased. She prodded Lila's bare arm. 'You are strange.'

'I'm a cyborg,' Lila said.

Gulfoyle made a beckoning motion, 'More more, I have told you my tale. I must hear yours now.'

'Madam, we are adventurers!' announced the imp grandly.

'A little demon,' Gulfoyle said, moving close on Thingamajig suddenly and poking him with a long finger. 'It is ugly. Why do you have it?'

'In case of emergency,' Zal said, as though that explained everything. 'We are of Daemonia, and Otopia and we are travelling through this place. We will not stay.'

'Will you not?' Gulfoyle moved back and tilted her head sideways thoughtfully, then held out one, long and elegant arm, which became the branch of a white ash tree. A grey bird of no particular kind came and lighted on it a moment. It was holding the tiny, struggling form of a grass doll. 'I found this. It is here to tell you about a place. A blabbing little thing it is. Nicely made.' She brought the doll close to her bosom and held it, as if it were hers and she a little girl. 'Told me you are to meet someone here, in this valley's end by the stones we pass every solstice, year on year. I would bet, adventurers, that you are good and lost, else you'd not tarry a second in Jack's domain. And the dead jacks say so too. My jacks. Least, given to me to help make the way. And now I've none. So, what say you now?' Her eyes glittered as she stroked the doll, which twitched and stirred.

'I have no idea what you're talking about,' Lila said, because it was easier, and the truth. 'I did kill some faeries who attacked me. If they're yours then too bad. And who is Jack?'

'Say his name one more time and he'll come hisself,' Gulfoyle said, with a hiss, closing the doll tight in her hand. 'Then your case will be closed. So I've to think now. Think about who's made you here and what for and why and if you're better off dead or alive or with me or with Him As Is Lost. Ssss . . .' She turned away and shook her head – a

175

collection of tiny sticks in which feathers and snowflakes were equally caught. From the back she appeared to be made of wicker, with plaster on the face side to create a solid front of the body. From the deep nest of her skull where the back of her head should have been tiny eyes looked back at Lila and whiskers twitched in the darkness there. She beckoned them both, 'Keep walking. We mustn't stop.'

Lila glanced at Zal and they stood their ground.

The fey turned, 'Walk my dears, else he as you don't want to catch you will catch you anyway. I am the head of the train. The engine that can!' She gave a whistle, exactly like a steam train whistle, that startled them both and made the birds rise up again and turn in the sky. She laughed. 'Walk with me if you do not wish to be ground upon his rails.'

They assented to each other first, with a look, then fell in just behind her as she began to follow some path of her own through the trees. 'Don't you like J— him then?' Lila asked. She wanted to defer the decision process as long as possible, and to find out if she could somehow get her hands on Malachi's doll.

Gulfoyle bent her head over the doll, muttering, then upped her volume until Lila and Zal could hear. 'It's not for the slave to speak of the master,' she said, and glanced coyly sideways at Lila. 'Do you know how many turns we have taken around?'

Lila shook her head. 'Around where?'

'Around the year,' Gulfoyle said. 'Turn and turn again but always come back to the same still point which will not budge. Even been round backwards, to check, like the screw in its path, but unlike the screw we turn and we turn but we don't get down. Winter to spring to summer to autumn. Ten and ten again thousand turns. Stuck. All of us. Stuck with each other and the round.' Her voice varied as she spoke, sometimes almost laughing, then abruptly bitter and full of anger. 'At least you're not his. Else I wouldn't have spoke to you. You'd have died and been my trees, like the others he sends forwards to taunt me.' She pointed to the side and they both saw a twisted trunk with a face, warped and tormented, caught within it, part of the wood.

'Mistress!' it whispered as she passed it. 'Please let me out. I done nothing!' But she ignored it completely and trod on. Soon they had left it behind but by then there were others near them. Their voices were much spoiled by becoming wooden. Their pleading sounded like knocking, or the sighing of the wind. Gulfoyle paid no attention to them.

'Can I see my messenger?' Zal asked her, moving to place himself between her and Lila.

'Maybe,' she said. 'If you promise to give him back.'

'I will,' he said.

She handed him the grass doll and quickly stepped sideways, stifling a yawn. She shook herself and gave him a speculative look, darting a gaze at Lila, checking their reactions to each other.

Lila didn't care for the sizing up. She leaned into Zal and heard the doll whisper, its voice all but completely nullified by Zal's *andalune* body which reached out to smother it, touching Lila's face at the same time in the softest of caresses.

'Malachi says the only one you can trust is the woman on the wolf. He'll look for you at the Twisting Stones.'

'Can you go back to him?'

'No. Stuck now. Like you all. Stuck in the turns. Don't give me back to that witch. She'n use me.'

'If I don't you owe me,' Zal said.

'You drowned me last time!' the doll said.

Lila frowned, not understanding.

'And this time I'll undo you, but those are your choices.'

The doll grumbled but gave a nod. 'Next time, elf, you . . .'

But Zal's quick fingers had already loosened its clever twist. 'Oh!' he said, faking surprise convincingly. He showed the grass to Gulfoyle's disappointed face. 'Made to fall apart. Shoddy work.'

'Your friend, the sender, warns you against us all, no doubt,' she said, striding ever onward at the same pace, her twig hair shifting as though it was soft and disgorging a small grey owl that flew back the way they had come.

'Thank you for your stories,' Zal said, 'but unless you have more business we are done and will say goodbye.' He stopped walking. 'I guess you are signalling to those who follow.'

'But I have not told you everything,' the faery said, coming to a halt and turning back halfway. The wind stopped and the forest fell quiet. Lila couldn't help feeling that it was an ominous change.

'We aren't a curious bunch,' Zal said lazily. 'And we have to go somewhere.'

Gulfoyle hesitated and her demeanour changed from haughty to slightly piqued. 'I have not had a visitor of any kind in fifteen thousand years,' she said, musingly. 'And here you are, killing my jacks with iron and tricking me out of trinkets. I offer you nothing but kindness, and you spurn me. That is cold, elf. That is right cold.'

'Your borrowed crows mean nothing to you,' Zal replied easily. 'And your age-old quarrel means nothing to me. A doll is a curse waiting, as you well know. We end as we began, curious and nothing else. Unless you wish to ask a favour?'

Tath circled uncomfortably. He was thrumming with attention. *This is an ancient bargaining dance,* he said, and didn't like it at all. *I hope Zal knows the tune.*

Lila narrowed her eyes and listened. She kept silent and still, watching Zal's confidence with pleasure. She knew moments like this were always dangerous and nobody would show their true feelings but she liked to see him work. She just liked to see him.

The faery laughed, a surprisingly merry sound and inclined her chin, turning to her best angle. 'What favour have you to offer?'

'I'd guess Jack is one of the huntsmen.'

'Nay, Giantkiller is the Lord of this place,' Gulfoyle assented. 'The huntsman is close by his heel always. It is the huntsman's pain to be locked in the round with such a master, but master Jack is.'

'And you in his debt also or else why walk before him?'

'The debt is his, elf, make no mistake. This land is mine. He treads it by force. Had I the means to stop him I would take them,' she said so quietly it was hard to hear her. At this speech even the drops of water falling from the leafless trees stopped in mid-air and hung there. 'But his city is full of his allies and I am alone. He nears. Hurry if you wish to speak unheard.'

'We have come to free the master of the hunt,' Zal said.

Inside Lila's chest Tath became poised and still. *Too much.*

The faery peered at him and without apparently moving, was suddenly as close to both of them as she could come, and just as far away as she had to be without falling unconscious – a few feet. 'But how? The master is with all the other fell things below. Jack has spent the long ages of men searching for a way down and found nothing. Aye and we have helped him in the hopes of freedom and got nowhere. I would be glad to aid you but it is a fool's game. You will fail and Jack will hunt you and eat you.'

'Can you help us?'

'Yes,' she said. 'I will give you this advice. When you leave me you will see a peak divided in two as if split by a bolt from heaven. The stones of which your doll spoke lie at its foot. The path there turns every other direction but you must not leave it or you'll never reach the place you seek. That's all I'll do. And when the time comes for Jack to hunt you down, I'll let him, for I'll not cross him again.' She drew back, her face deeply troubled. She looked at Lila and her gaze flickered over the T-shirt again.

Tath? Lila whispered, seeing Zal frowning and disappointed.

He said too much. She didn't need to bargain any more. She had what she wanted – which was to know your true purpose. He would have had to trick her into saying more but now she does not have to, and she doesn't think you are strong enough to be of use to her.

'Keep your joke close, lady. Keep your iron ready. Pray for your friends, that they not meet Jack's wolves, nor you either. I would say more, but you lied to me so you must chance your wits against the rest. Maybe I'll change my mind later and you can choose what kind of tree you'd prefer to be.'

At least she is wary enough to leave us for the time being.

With that, the wind started again, a cold spatter of water hit Lila's cheek, making her start and blink, and when she brushed herself dry and looked about her the wood had gone and they stood at the foot of a hill in unmarked snow, a moon just starting to rise behind them and no sign of life in any direction. Against the span of the stars the broken peak showed clearly, like a black cutout. Beneath their feet a path of sorts was visible, marked by the smoothness of the snow that lay on it compared to the rougher shapes of the surroundings.

Zal shivered and shook his head. 'I misjudged this. She is much stronger than I thought. I couldn't deceive her. We are far inside. I was never that adept at magic, unlike many of the other elves. Unlike . . .' He glanced at her and then down at her chest. 'I don't know that much about these levels but I think it may be best if you let Ilya do the walking and talking. One cheap shirt isn't going to hold them all off and I have a feeling that any of them down here will know what you carry on sight, though it's interesting they have no sense of it even close at hand.' His face, white and grey in the moonlight, was full of misgivings. 'And I hesitate to recommend it because the levels of aether here . . . everything has consequences, and I can't see them.' He radiated discomfort. Lila could see his *andalune* body glowing, illuminated and full

179

of points of light, as if it was a mirror for the sky above them. It shifted restlessly.

'Aether here is dark,' Thingamajig asserted, hunching down on Lila's shoulder. 'Turned with the light. That's old work. Twists things about. I've been here before. You should be more at ease with it, shadow, but you've burned too long in demonfire, lost your edge.'

'Mmn,' Zal said uncertainly. 'Perhaps. It doesn't taste like Alfheim's dark or shade though. Has a life of its own here. A kind of will. The same one that brought that.' He pointed to where the necklace hung on Lila's chest, just where the armoured bodice began. 'Feels like giving it a way in, and I don't let anything in. Don't advise anyone to. Don't even want to talk here. Everything wants to turn.'

'Hark at him lie his head off,' the imp snorted. 'One fire elemental and he's anyone's, and he has the nerve to talk about purity.'

'Whatever,' Lila said. 'We'll carry on like this for now. I trust him.'

Inside her chest Tath was quiet. She forgot about him a lot recently. It was like he was her, almost. His feelings her feelings. She was so used to him. She wasn't even able to feel the same level of discomfort about it that she had.

She saw Zal watching her, waiting for her to speak or move.

'Let's go,' she said, unwilling to talk about Tath. As they turned to take the path side by side the imp leapt ahead of them, igniting himself a little more to show the way. She looked at Zal's stern face, flickering with grey and blue shadows, and felt a barrier between them. Sorcha was part of it. Maybe a part they wouldn't be getting rid of soon. But there was more to it, and here some more had been added, strange and undefined, another layer of bricks made up of his hesitation and this place and her silence. She saw it so clearly but she had no idea what to do about it. Maybe with dawn it would lessen. For the time being, they walked the path.

CHAPTER FIFTEEN

Malachi met the others on the beach. It was dark, but there was light from the nearby houses and paths. The tide was out and to their right, some distance away, people were out with torches, digging for clams and other things. They stayed together, in case of moths, though it was rare to see one near any large body of water, especially the ocean. In the darkness the figures of the demon and the three other fey looked deceptively ordinary, and, in the case of the two girls from Zal's band, oddly glamorous. As usual they were dressed to party. The taller one, Viridia, was the more aloof, but she clung to Poppy's shoulder as she rushed up to Malachi and said,

'Oh, is it Zal? What's the matter? This demon won't tell us anything.'

'We need you to take us into Faery,' Malachi said, measuring his words carefully.

'But you can do that,' Viridia replied, adjusting her sarong against the warm night breeze.

'I can only walk another into the upper regions,' Malachi said.

'You want to go deep,' Poppy said with dismay. 'That's easy enough I guess. But what're you doing down there?' She shuddered at the notion.

'Are you afraid?' Teazle asked her, his arms folded, clearly contemptuous of so much being made of something so trivial.

'No. Not exactly,' she said, sticking her tongue out at him. 'Only, some places aren't as easy to get out of as they are to get into and the further down you get the more . . . fundamental . . . everything becomes. Some of us don't enjoy the fundaments, you know. We're more civilised beings these days.'

'Not what I hear,' Teazle said. His deep voice broke through the soft

181

rush of waves and the girls' voices and made them frown as their slight charms failed to persuade. 'We are wasting time.'

Poppy wasn't so easily discouraged. She turned to him completely and flirted, 'You're very handsome, for a demon.'

'You're commonly backhanded, for a faery,' he replied. 'Of my true form you'd speak less prettily. And if you don't do as our mutual friend here asks then shortly you will be closer acquainted with it than you'd like.' His tone was as silvery as theirs, almost a perfect match. He smiled coldly.

Poppy stood with her mouth slightly ajar.

'Been too long with silly humans,' Viridia muttered. 'Time we got down to some business other than breaking hearts and playing cards.'

'It's that necklace, isn't it?' Poppy said, turning and poking Viridia sharply in the ribs. 'You had to go and pick it up, give it to her.'

'Don't blame me!' Viridia snapped, poking back just as hard with a scowl. 'You saw it first. It was your idea.'

'Ladies,' Naxis said gently, stepping forwards between the two of them, his grey and silver hair tipped with black like a strange fox pelt in the moonlight. He was as prettily handsome and charming as they were beautiful. He took an arm of each, 'Let's not argue about what's past. You did your best to avoid disaster but the key is an artefact that has a way of doing what it will. There can't be blame. The question now is, will you answer its call? After all, it chose you, of all of faery, to bring it back into play. What a pity to waste the chance of a lifetime to take a part in great events when the very meat of our beings demands you take your part.'

Malachi grinned inwardly, though he didn't let it show on his face. Nax had charm to burn. It worked even on experts like Poppy and Viridia; and he thanked the gods he hadn't had to make that speech since, coming from him, it would have had less the ring of greatness than despair. Tricky wording was never his suit. He caught Teazle's eye and saw the demon thinking the same thing.

Poppy simpered for a moment and then turned her head indulgently towards Malachi. 'So, where are they?'

'Umeval,' he said.

'Aieeee!' Poppy slammed both hands over her delicate ears and squealed a long squeal of agony. She looked around at them as they shook their heads and scowled at her. Far off, dogs began barking and cats yowled in reply. 'The still point!' She looked pointedly at Teazle.

'He can't know about it. I bet Zal doesn't know. Do they? They don't know about it. No way out and Jack hunting endlessly. We can't go there and become slaves in his caravan! We can't! No way!'

'Pop,' Viridia said sharply. 'Lila has the *key.*'

'And Jack *wants* the key!' Poppy said. 'He'll kill anyone who tries to keep it from him. He's completely insane! We can't be anywhere near it! It was madness to take it there. One sniff of it and he'll tear them to pieces. Malachi, what were you thinking?'

'I think that what Viridia *meant* is that Lila has the way out,' Teazle said with slow deliberation and mimicry.

Poppy blinked. Then, after a moment she said sulkily, 'I don't like going under. I like it here, where I'm good. Fun, anyway.' But she sniffed a deep breath of the sea and sounded doubtful. 'I don't want to die.'

'If you don't take us now then Zal and Lila will both die,' Malachi said.

'And you as well,' Teazle promised faithfully, flexing one of his hands as though it was stiff, and showing that he had claws. His face was completely deadpan.

'You don't have to terrorise us,' Poppy said quietly. 'We were going to say yes.' A spark of defiance shone in her gaze. 'And you'll like us less shortly.'

'I'll risk it,' Teazle said.

'All right.' Viridia took a deep breath and shuddered, then began to strip out of her sarong and bikini, kicking her sandals aside. 'Pop, you can take Malachi and Nax. I'll have the demon.'

'Thanks,' Malachi said, almost sick with relief. 'I wouldn't ask if any of us had the speed . . .'

'Yeah, whatever,' Poppy said, taking her clothes off and looking at them on the sand where she dropped them with a pout. 'Bye bye pretty designer thingies,' she said and took Viridia's outstretched hand. They walked out towards the water, and the others followed closely. As they reached the surf the two girls let go of their hands and moved apart and then, as Malachi watched, in a few strides they had changed, as if they were made of nothing more substantial than the softest light and shade.

The two horses turned back, their manes and tails as long and thick as princesses' hair, tangled with seaweed. Only a glance at their legs showed that instead of hooves they had strange thick webbed feet and, where feathers of hair would have been on a knight's charger, fins.

Poppy tossed her head impatiently and pranced on the spot. She waited as Malachi jumped easily up to her back and put his hand down to pull Naxis up behind him. Teazle raised his white brows but seized hold of Viridia's mane and kicked himself up on to her back as though he'd spent his life as a circus rider. He was much more startled when the hair of her mane swiftly slithered up his arms and tangled him fast and close to her neck. She snorted in horse laughter and without warning wheeled around towards the ocean, powerful muscles bunching and pushing them into a headlong gallop straight at the waves.

Malachi thought it would be unpleasant. He was right.

Poppy smashed headlong into the breakers, swimming with more power than any ordinary horse could have dreamed of and the water welcomed her, breaking easily over and around her. It was damned cold to Malachi's skin as it soaked him quickly. He felt Naxis' grip to his waist hard as they plunged out of their depth and the water rose to their necks, slapping against open mouths and screwed-shut eyes. Then they were under and diving, down and down, much further than the shelf of the continent would ever have allowed, and they could feel the water mixing – the cold, salt ocean and a darker, colder and more bitter water that was not fresh but not salt either. Their breath began to burn in their chests and pressure began to crush their ears. Above the humming of his blood Malachi could hear the distant sound of basso profundo voices chanting an ancient lay, so old that the words themselves turned them around in the waters and made the water pull them further beneath as if the water were made of sound and the sound knew what it was doing. Behind his closed eyelids he saw sparks. His body started to scream for air and he felt the distinctive lightening of Poppy beginning to shift. He went with her gladly into the strange grey uncertainty of the Void, where at last the water became what it wanted to be all along – aether – and they were dragged in its stream according to the kelpies' song. Around his wrists Poppy's hair stayed fast. He listened for any trace of ghosts or the hunters but the song was wild and dragging him away. At least, he thought, at least the kelpies are old enough to be able to reach this region easily whereas he hadn't been there in so long he'd forgotten nearly everything about it. Briefly he wondered what would become of him there, but it was too late to worry about it.

They entered a timeless, empty region of cold so profound that he lost all feeling.

The next thing he knew, he was lying in mud, vomiting up semi-stagnant lake water. The cold was agonising, so less cold than before. He stood up and found himself on all fours, shaking himself vigorously and spraying water in all directions. He tried to speak and felt his mouth shape itself clumsily around too-big teeth. A growling noise emerged, but no words.

At his side Naxis crawled further up the bank they were lying on, coughing, and sat for a moment, his body almost entirely transparent, made of water. The surface shone weakly in what passed for sunlight under the grey, winter sky of Umeval. His fine features were gone, replaced by suggestions of a face that wavered in and out of being. Petals and bits of stick moved idly in the volume of his translucent body. He looked as stunned as Malachi felt.

On the trampled grass before them he saw the legs of horses – not the fine black mares that had stormed the sea back in Otopia, but shorter and sturdier ponies with heavy hooves and thicker hair. Their manes and tails moved idly, floating in the air as if in water. Their black eyes were empty and far colder and hungrier than Malachi ever remembered. He couldn't see the girls in them at all, and then one of them shivered into her change and he saw it was Poppy, though a shorter, fatter and much more buxom Poppy. She wasn't green and pretty but dark haired with dun skin. She had a voluptuous beauty of a kind but a look on her that was far craftier than she had ever worn in his knowledge. He knew that she was looking at him and seeing what he saw in her – a much older form of himself, from ages long gone in human memory, even from his own. He feared suddenly that he had no other shape than the cat and tried to change, scrabbling for the feeling and the charm with a desperation that felt inept and clumsy.

He stood up on two legs with relief but Poppy put her dirty nailed hand to her mouth to cover it with shock. She was naked but her thick hair covered her, moved with her to keep her modesty whilst constantly threatening to reveal everything. In that respect the way she wore things hadn't changed.

'Never saw you like that,' she said in her curiously older woman voice.

Viridia tossed her dark, dripping horse head in agreement.

'Worthy of our caste,' Teazle's voice said from a short distance away and Malachi looked around to see the demon in his human form, sitting on a tussock. Of course he had ancient echoes of being deep in the past, but Malachi was stunned to silence by what he saw. He didn't know what he'd expected exactly, although horns and monstrosity and danger had featured largely. Instead, Teazle sat like a dream of a warrior, fine, strong, fully armed with swords at his back and knives at his belt. Everything about him was made of white light. He shone. His light gleamed on the ground around him and his eyes blazed like stars. The only word that came to Malachi's mind was angel. He was dumbstruck for a full minute.

Teazle chuckled and when he spoke even the inside of his mouth shone white. 'Don't mind me, faery. Look in the water.'

Malachi turned around and stumbled back to the edge of the lake that spread out behind him and into the visible distance. It was lightly ruffled by the wind but close to the bank reeds sheltered large patches of it and he could see himself clearly.

It was exactly what he saw when he hung suspended with fear in the unknown grey of I-space. He was half changed, neither a man nor a great black cat, but both. A catman. His head was as big and heavy as a full grown tiger's with large cat's eyes but something like the beginnings of a human nose and human lips. His jaws were cat large and he saw white teeth, sharp canines like spears. Triangular ears with long black fur tips stuck up on his head, lynxlike. His body was no longer the svelte and sleek powerhouse of a panther but the heavy-boned and brutal build of a much larger cat. He had a lion's mane of thick hair but also stripes of utter black in a fur that was richly, magnificently umbral like autumn leaves in the shade. He stood upright, with human design, tilted a little forwards at the hip, his feet halfway to paws as he balanced on the ball of his foot, claws in. He looked at his thickly furred hands and saw that he could curl the fingers under and they became massive paws, replete with pads. His tail was long and thick, he could feel that it would easily balance him and act as counterweight. He moved it as easily as breathing. Down the front of his torso his hair became long and silky. He looked to check and found that he was made like a cat and not a man between his legs – everything was retracted except his balls, hidden in his long fur. Black wings, like drifting patches of night, lay along his shoulders. He could feel that in an instant he could flick them out but without intent they were almost as insubstantial as imaginary wings. His deep fur glittered with anthracite fragments. Where Teazle lit the world, he darkened it. His slitted eyes glowed red.

He tried to speak again, tentatively, and heard his voice say gutturally, 'Holy crap.'

Naxis laughed. He was staring at Teazle. 'Who knew the demon had an ancient form? They are so short lived. This puts the cat among the pigeons of their ridiculous theories of inheritance. The Alchemical Council always thought they had more in common with us than they liked to admit! This must prove that there is more to their *animae* than can be met in a single mortal lifetime. They are reincarnates! Think what this will mean for the Conference of Souls! Mind you, it somewhat rubbishes our other theories about their diabolical origins if it proves correct. I do wonder what this is in truth! I hope we find out before this is over!'

Teazle shrugged under this tirade of scientific enthusiasm as though he couldn't care less, and his grin became more enigmatic. 'Hell, I would have paid you to find this out if I knew such a trip was possible,' he said. 'Makes me feel it was well worth the journey. I cannot wait to discover more. And you, Malachi, why do you look so surprised? I thought all the fey lived simultaneously in their forms, scattered in the deep ages of faery.'

Viridia shook herself into female shape, proving to be a surprisingly young girl, almost a child. Her blond hair was short and ragged and her body small and slender, ribs showing through her grubby skin, but she didn't seem to be bothered by the cold at all. 'We move around. Sometimes we forget things,' she said in a tone of strict reproof. She glanced at herself and sighed. 'Sometimes we want to move on. Oh, Pop, I can feel it all falling away! Can't you?'

Malachi didn't need to ask what she meant. He felt it too, his modernity was crumbling. It didn't belong here. He was reverting. He loathed the feeling. On the wind he could smell living bodies, warm blood beating, and he felt his stomach growl.

Poppy nodded. 'My old name . . . the old hungers. I'd forgotten.'

Malachi shook himself. 'We have to focus. We must get to the Twisting Stones.'

'And avoid Jack,' Viridia said. 'I can smell him.' She winced. 'South of us but coming this way. He camps further down the shore and sets his city across the lake for midwinter when everything is frozen fast.' Her eyes became distant and bleak. 'Now I remember why we ran away from here. Back when it was still possible to rise.'

Malachi's sense of smell came to a sharp conclusion, 'Advance parties are coming. They will be here within the hour. Which way is it, though?'

Teazle got to his feet and pointed west of them. 'If what you're looking for is a place of doors into time, then it's that way.'

Now it was Malachi's turn to stare, open-mouthed.

'Teleporting,' Teazle said simply, 'requires stillness in time but movement across the other planes. I am time-anchored.'

'What does that mean?' Naxis asked eagerly, moving to join him.

'It is what I am, not what I can explain,' the demon said. 'But it's this way.' He grinned, 'Suppose I'll have to walk with you temporally challenged individuals. Only polite.'

'Just one thing,' Malachi growled. 'Can you stop shining? You're like a big sign that says Hey, Come And Find The Troublemakers Right Here.'

Teazle closed his eyes for a second. There was a pause and then he noticeably dimmed, but didn't go out. Finally, after another minute of concentration he looked more like a softly glowing statue than a blaze, but he still stood out painfully in the darkness. 'Seems not,' he said with irritation.

'Stand by me,' Malachi said, and spread his aethereal wings. A pool of intense darkness spread around him. Teazle stepped into it and vanished. Malachi let dust from the wings fall. When he furled them again Teazle was covered in a film of almost complete blackness.

The demon sneezed twice, hard, and his open mouth and eyes still burned, but it was better.

'Just don't do any looking back and we might be all right,' Malachi said grudgingly though he was pleased with his efforts. When Teazle blinked he was invisible. Now he simply appeared as two blazing eyes suspended in the air.

'Cover all of us,' said Naxis. 'Safer from prying eyes.'

'Mmn, now you just need to learn to walk less like a party of ogres out on a hike,' Malachi agreed, casting the earth-rich, ancient darkness of hidden forests on them all. 'Also, you stink of lakebed. No offence.'

'We won't say what you smell like,' Viridia retorted, wrinkling her tiny nose.

'Fair enough.' Malachi prinked his tail automatically, sniffed at Teazle and smelt lightning. He snorted the odd metallic odour out of his nostrils. 'Lead on, Macdemon.'

It was difficult, after a few minutes of walking, not to admit that he was starting to feel a kind of ferocious exhilaration in his body and the situation, the kind of exhilaration that had been lingering beneath the surface unexpressed for a very long time, but he did try for as long as it took him to wonder what had happened to his very expensive suit and his car keys, neither of which appeared to have made it through.

Lila and Zal slid down another snowy slope, facing distinctly in the opposite direction to the cleft mountain. The path led away from it and around another turn, appearing to circle a rocky outcrop starred with the windwracked bodies of old shrubs. After two hours their destination was not visibly closer, in fact Lila would have sworn on a number of calculations that it was exactly as far away as it had been when they'd started out on Gulfoyle's instruction. She began to suspect trickery and said as much to Zal.

He put an unnecessary hand out to help her to her feet, ice dreadlocks swinging in the forepart of his hair, smashing each other apart and raining little crystals down the front of his jerkin. The elvish runes in the cloth glimmered with colour. Against her body, held fast by the faery armour, she felt the heavy T-shirt slap wetly and increased the heat donated from her reactor core to her own natural thermogenesis. It had become darker and the moonlight less intense. She couldn't help but notice as she took Zal's hand that the shadows on his skin were deepening into a rich lilac blue and the lighter, yellowish tones of his skin were fading into a kind of insubstantiality, a wash of colour over more of the same shades. His ordinarily dark-brown eyes were purple in the strange light of Faery night and his *andalune* body was blue-black where it swirled around him. She held on to him as she stood up, looking at his hand, and he followed her gaze, interpreting it as the question she intended.

'Seems like the aether here is wakening that side of me,' he said. 'It was like this in Alfheim, long ago, when I was with my father.'

'What's that mean?' she asked, sounding gruff even to herself. 'Is it bad?'

'Different,' he said. 'Good for now. More able at night.'

The imp, who had been sitting in a bare circle of earth, lit by his own yellow and orange fires, looked up. 'That's how it is here. Whatever your nature, it's deeper and bigger and more of it. You'll be shadow at night and light in the day and we'll no doubt discover what that demon fire of yours feasts on if we ever come across the fuel for it. And he's not the only one.'

Lila looked at the imp carefully. 'You haven't changed a bit, far as I can see.'

'Ah well, I'm in stasis ent I? I'm what you'd call out of play, magically speakin'. Only thing that gets better in me is me ability to read yer stupid hell-making and spell it back to yer. I've been lookin' at the road though, so I've not been doing it,' he explained. 'So here's yer update.' He took a big breath. 'Even though you're mostly numb by all that crap you found out back at the Freaky Farm you're still managin' to fuck your relationship with this idiot because you keep thinking his grief is your fault and you've got to do something about it and maybe he doesn't love you properly because he let you get wed to Doctor Death without a scrap of objection and since the marriage nothing much has changed and you're sort of up to your deaf ears in all that doubting yak about whether or not you're corrupted now, what with two men, surely it's all decadence before the fall and your parents, were they alive, would be spinning in their graves with shock at the lack of morality, not to mention what everyone else in Otopia would think, if they knew the first thing about you, which they don't, and amid all that dreck there's barely any room for a second of pleasure in the fact that, despite all indications to the contrary, you are becoming something beyond human, beyond your dreams, quite extraordinary, and in her way quite happy. 'Xcept of course yer happiness seems triggered by very unsuitable and immoral and wayward things that would get you stoned to death back at home, if yer human middle-class ijits were into that kind of thing, which mostly they ain't, a few faery shags aside. But no, you don't notice that 'cos you're so busy worrying about how much you don't fit any more into some bloody old mould made for devil-fodder sheepies. You don't even notice what's going on in yer body, yer head's so full of nonsense. Yer wonder where yer old arms and legs have got to when you should be seeing what you've got. Denial is like a way of life with you.' He paused, gasping for breath. 'But since Sorcha died it's been relatively quiet, like. I'd almost say you've had entire minutes of health. Felt meself slipping away I did for a while, going all sleepy and useless.' He mimed falling unconscious elaborately, tongue falling out of his mouth and drooling. 'But then Zal comes back full of his own hurt and you decide you'd rather agonise than deal with reality and tell him what happened at the laaaaaa-aaab. Agh!'

190

He leapt away from the compacted ball of ice that struck the ground where he'd been, smashing up a splatter of mud. Lila bared her teeth at him and bent to grab more snow but it was only show. She'd gone cold inside at his mention of more changes. What hadn't she noticed?

Zal turned to Lila with a frown. 'What happened at the lab? Are you hiding things from me?'

'There didn't seem time to tell you,' she said, lamely.

His look became angry but he shrugged. 'Lots of time now. We're in the middle of nowhere following a path to nothing.'

'Right.' She flung her second snowball at the imp, catching it on the rump and propelling it two metres further down the path. They began to walk again slowly. She explained the events he'd missed. 'Everything feels like manipulation now,' she concluded. 'What I do, where I'm sent, the things I find.' She touched her collar and felt the lumpy necklaces under the shirt. 'I got mad and tried to get even, hah, but it didn't work. I'm certain they have more controllers or at least the means to make more. And the pain in my joints has stopped. I thought, along with the whole liquid-metal thing that it meant I was better, or that the elementals in the machine had sorted themselves out or something, I didn't stop to find out.' She sighed. 'I'm tired of it. Part of me just doesn't want to know any more. I keep on moving because I daren't stop. I don't look down, you know?'

She looked up at his face, higher than hers, more gaunt and alien than ever in the spectral light. He kept walking and his expression was set and grim for a few moments though at the same time she felt his aetheric body surround her, warm and gentle tempered. 'Sometimes that's the best thing to do, but only for very short bursts. Detaching from reality will get you killed faster than anything else I know. So, what's really going on with you? I can't believe you think me false because of Teazle.'

'I don't. I mean . . . I . . .' She stumbled on the words, tripping herself up entirely. She felt rightly accused.

'I don't care what you feel about him,' Zal said intently. 'The fact is I only actually care about what I feel about people, not the other way about. I don't have time for that. Neither do you.'

'But,' Lila started, ready to object that of course it mattered what other people felt about you because if you knew about it you could do something about it, except that it occurred to her that maybe you couldn't do anything about it at all, as he said. The idea violated almost everything she had ever thought or felt to be true about relationships, particularly romantic ones. Instead she ended up saying, 'How come?'

'Because there's nothing you can do about other people's reactions,' he said. 'You be yourself and let them be themselves and if you don't get what you want, then tough, and if you do, then good for you and that's it. Everything else is manipulation and I spit on it. People waste their lives on that kind of shit.'

Lila blinked at the finality and strength with which he said this.

'Guh, this entire place revolves on manipulation,' Thingamajig asserted from a metre in front of them as he hopped over snow-coated rocks in his own small, steaming world. 'Bonkers as a bunch of society matrons at a fancy pony show, these lot. You wanna watch it. Insecure attachment psychosis ain't even the words for this kind of fiddling.'

'You need all your attention for you,' Zal said. 'Or you won't survive. That's what this lying scum is trying to tell you, and what you're telling yourself, if you listen.'

'Hey, that's a bit strong!' the imp objected. 'I'm on your side.'

Zal snorted contemptuously, not even sparing a glance.

Lila walked on in silence. She hadn't really paid attention because she didn't want to find out what had happened to her but the truth was that she had been in pain for a time, at the joints where the prosthetics were fitted and met her remaining human body, and now she wasn't. In fact she felt better than she could remember feeling in a long time, certainly long before she'd ever heard of the Agency. But she had to admit to a creeping feeling, a kind of knowledge-that-was-ignored, that this was because of something new taking place. She knew, though she could not bring herself to put it into words, that the machine was growing. Cell by cell and silently it was creeping into her, taking her over, converting what remained. Maybe it was only a few millimetres now, just a little further in than it used to be, not significantly further but there was constant change at the interface between her flesh and its strange alchemical metals. A single instant of calculation would have given her the calendar date, the hour, the minute and the second of her final moment of existence as a human being.

And after?

She stopped on the path and pulled up her sleeve and showed Zal her arm, where the gleaming black metallic skin met her chilly, goose-fleshed upper arm close to the shoulder. Between the two lay a fine line of greyish blueishness. He knew her body well enough to understand

and notice the change. He became very still, feeling the area with his fingers, and then just with his shadow body alone, as if it was Braille and he could read it. He stroked across her machine arm as gently and said, under his breath, 'Alive.'

'Seven months, seven days, seven hours, twenty-one seconds,' she said.

He got that too.

He put his arms around her and held her tightly, his head next to hers, face tucked down against her shoulder. He was so light that just the return of the embrace from her lifted him on to his toes but his body was vibrant and strong. 'Don't be afraid,' he said.

'All sevens and multiples,' she said. 'Of course. The faery numbers. How funny.' But in his arms for the first time in a long time she started to relax.

There was a shiver in the air and in the ground.

'That's torn it,' the imp said expectantly.

'What has?' Lila said through Zal's shoulder, not willing to let go yet.

'You and your Game, I'm betting. We could run but s'prob'ly not worth it.'

'As if we'd go anywhere on this road,' Lila said bitterly, her mind full of Gulfoyle, thinking back to the fact that the faery could easily have lied and left them there to be collected by whoever she'd contacted.

'Yes. As if,' said a new voice, strange and low.

Lila released Zal and spun around. Facing her from the top of the hill they had just slid down was a huge white wolf. Dark eyes, nose and lips were all that stood out in its thick pelt as the wind blew against it. Its large head was low and one forepaw was half raised in an arrested forward motion. The thick ruff at the back of its neck was high though it had spoken calmly.

Lila felt only the faintest shiver, as though talking animals and walking forests were second nature to her now. She made the conscious decision to trust nothing on its appearance and didn't move or speak. She checked her ammunition load for the hundredth time. Eight cold-iron shots. Three silver shots. Four explosive rounds. Thirty-two regular metal jacket – probably pointless to count them here but you never knew who you might run into. She had enough chemicals in her arsenal to make a few poisons, but the majority of her gear was back in her room sitting in the damned useless bag. At her side Zal took out his bow and nocked an arrow, drawing the string halfway and keeping it pointed at the ground.

The imp leapt back between them and then up on to Lila's back.

It began to snow gently – big wet flakes that collected quickly and moved in deceiving veils across the visible air, brushing gently across their faces. Lila opened the apertures in her eyes and set her AI to filter out irrelevant information and things cleared a little for her. The wolf stepped forwards just inside the ring of glimmering light cast by the imp's heatless fires and a shadow leaped behind it and stood tall against the wall of falling snow; a wild and thin beast that flickered in and out of different shapes, as big as a hill. Lila saw cat, bear, wolf, hound, weasel, hawk . . . all the predatory creatures that she knew. But this was only part of the show. Behind the veils of shifting snow she could almost make out another shape in the dark, one that consisted of all hunters that had ever trod any realm, something that was all their spirit, all their cunning and wiles.

'What are you doing here?' the wolf asked, standing with its head low, eyes simply a shine of glass over empty spaces.

Lila chose an iron round. She didn't think this was the silvering kind.

'Looking for a way,' she said, which was truthful enough. What had Malachi always said? Tell the truth, no matter how many lies you use to tell it.

'To where?'

'What's it to you?' Zal said easily, as if he couldn't care less.

'You are walking on my path,' the wolf said. 'You're in my land. You're strange and new in a place that has no strange or new things to me. You taste strange. You're not true forms. I haven't seen your like in more ages than I can name. But here you are, going somewhere, looking for a way.'

'We're lost,' Lila said, truthfully again.

'So you are,' said the wolf, and stepped closer. 'Maybe I can help you.'

Zal released his bow and straightened as though he was relaxing. 'We're here to meet someone.'

'I know everyone. Name them and I will point you in the right direction.'

'There's no need,' Zal said, easing his shoulders. 'He's right here.'

This is dangerous, Tath said suddenly, his anxiety spiking through Lila like an unexpected jolt of electricity.

'Jack wouldn't come in person,' the wolf said. 'I'm the captain of his guard. Moguskul is my name.'

'Zal,' Zal said, putting his weapons away in a leisurely fashion. 'Since when did he need a guard?' He spoke as if he'd always known Jack.

Lila felt out of her depth. The wolf ignored Zal's question and looked at her, 'And you?'

'I am Lila Friendslayer.'

'Are you indeed?' the wolf came closer and inspected her minutely. 'And is this shirt your tabard of office?' Its voice was mocking now.

'It is,' she said, meeting its gaze and seeing it struggle with the perfect mirror surfaces that were her eyes.

'You look like a vagabond,' the wolf said finally. 'And either you are wise or stupid to go masked here. But your mask seems yourself and that is most odd. In any case, it doesn't matter. To Jack's court we will go and he may decide your fates.'

'How did he capture you?' Zal asked, conversationally. 'I mean, I can see how he could trick Gulfoyle – she doesn't have a lot of guile for a faery – but you . . . you're the pack leader. Wouldn't you rather be a lone hunter again than Jack's pet dog?'

All the shadows that had been twisting off Moguskul's body shot back into him and he bared his teeth in the ugliest snarl Lila had ever seen, saliva and hatred spooling off it in equal measure. She spun to counter the direct line of attack between it and Zal but she was too slow and only caught a handful of rough fur as the huge beast tore past her.

'I should rip your throat out for that!' The wolf stopped half an inch from Zal's face and Zal staggered backwards under the weight of its paws planted on his chest.

He didn't flinch, just said, 'But you don't.' Then he gave a strange kind of twist of his body and the wolf fell forwards on to its nose at his feet. Though he hadn't moved, Zal was standing over it, transparent and utterly dark, a two-dimensional film of grey and black. The runes on his armour lost their light and vanished; he had become shadow.

Seeing him change that way made the cold spread through Lila's skin and body in a way it hadn't before. The wolf snarled in rage and flung itself on to its belly, then up to its feet. It disregarded Zal now and stalked towards Lila. The snow thickened and then around them and all about Lila saw prints appearing in the white ground as though they were surrounded now by many invisible others. She smelled wet dog, a sudden and oppressive stink and then the wolf hit her in the chest. She hadn't even seen it spring.

On instinct alone she went with the force of the blow, but turning to the side as she did so, letting the natural forward motion of her arms catch hold of the huge body as it rose above her so that both of them rolled. With her AI in battle mode time seemed to pass slowly. She felt the wolf recoil from her touch and writhe in the hold even as its jaws snapped millimetres from her face, pouring their hot and eager breath over her. She saw runes carved on its teeth, one on each small incisor, three to each canine and two on the rest, and recorded the sight in case she ever discovered what they meant. Then they had turned and fallen, she ending uppermost. With a gouging of claws and a whine that split the air the wolf powered out of her grip and turned, snarling and growling in rage, to face her.

'What is this?' he raged. 'Your flesh is iron! Abominable witch! What charm could hold the deadly foe to itself and live?' His pristine fur was singed with grey and brown where she had burned him with her touch.

She looked down at herself, feeling and seeing no difference, except perhaps a slight greying of her natural armoured metallo-leather skin. In a split second of cool self-revulsion her AI gave the answer: her skin had spontaneously altered its molecular structure to mimic that of cold forged iron, had exuded those molecules like a sweat as soon as the wolf attacked.

'Jack's smith may have use for you,' it rumbled, recovering fast. Without warning it changed its own form and in an instant a Kodiak bear, pale and monstrous, reared up, taller by far than either of them, its mouth open in a roar.

'Heh,' Thingamajig said beside Lila's ear with genuine approval. 'You've really pissed him off. Sweet!'

'Uh!' She was reeling. She saw Zal moving around her, his *andalune* body taking on the shape of a blade at the edge of his forward reaching hand. As it struck the bear a streak of energy shot through it from bear to Zal, flinging all three of them apart by several metres with the same elastic push as if two opposed magnetic poles had come too close to one another.

'Vampire . . .' said the bear in a voice like boulders grinding and its shape flickered and changed again, this time to that of a tall, powerfully built man wearing furs, armed with sword, dagger and spears.

Zal faced up to him again, condensing. 'You never answered my question. Why be tame? What happened to you?'

'Too late,' the hunter said, his angry face tanned almost black above its rough beard. Snow caught on the high curve of his waxed ponytail of hair, on his spears, on his massive shoulders and the fragile tips of the furs that wrapped him. It was so thick now that they were barely visible to one another.

'It's never . . .' Zal began.

'It is,' and for the first time Moguskul was quiet, his body trembling with the effort it took him to become subdued, though he managed it. As she watched him in her mind's eye Lila saw a slumped figure, trudging towards a dreaded doorway, feet dragging more with every certain, unavoidable step. For the first time she noticed that he was wounded. Blood leaked from a long gouge on his leg where the bare shin protruded from his rough clothing. He looked down and away from them to the ground as he said in a voice of resignation, 'I enjoyed our meeting. Yet it is too late for all of us, I regret. He is here.'

Lila looked around, seeing and feeling nothing but the soft, white deadness of the snow. Even as Zal reached down to give her his hand for the second time in a few minutes she detected no presence but as she straightened her knees and rose to her full height the snow abruptly stopped falling, as though a switch had been flicked. The last flakes came dancing down, lightly as feathers and revealed that they were standing in a circle between high buildings; houses and halls of stone and thatch, limewash and pitched timbers, the tiny leaded panes of their windows glowing with yellow lamplight.

Where there had been open ground there was now a street, and streets beyond it. They turned, supporting one another, and saw not only the place where they stood but all the land beyond that. Yet further on winding streets, bridges, avenues and lanes lay mantled in white snow. They were standing high above most of it, looking over a low wall and cliff side where their little hill had been. And then they turned, and at their backs saw the grey granite and blue ice of a fortress with white gulls wheeling around its ramparts.

A herald in striped clothes went running past them suddenly, ringing a bell, 'Nightfall is come! Nightfall! Two nights until midwinter! Two nights to the turning point!' They were alone after he had gone, and then they were not alone. But although the difference was profound and unmistakable, still there was nobody else to be seen.

'What's this Mog? Has my wife been taking pot shots again?' said a voice; a silky, warm and rich man's voice with a crafty ring to it. It came from all directions at once.

'She missed me, sir,' Moguskul said in that odd, quiet way of his. He was lost, Lila knew it. He, like Gulfoyle, had thought for seconds of his old freedoms, but then thought of this creature, this faery, Jack, and had given themselves up. Just like that. She ought to be afraid of Jack, but she wasn't. She didn't even despise him for what he'd done. It was curious to her, and she held this feeling close to her heart as she stood, feeling Zal's hand in her hand no heavier than a spectre's touch but the strength and heat of him was intoxicating still.

A sparkle of bright lime scattered between them. It got up Zal's nose and he sneezed. Lila laughed, and the city, and Moguskul, looked up.

CHAPTER SIXTEEN

They reached the Twisting Stones at moonset. Madrigal was waiting for them, a small dark shape hunched over a tiny fire, her guns sticking up at her back like wayward posts in a fallen scarecrow. She showed no sign of noticing them until they were right up to the firelight themselves, then looked up, as if they had always been there.

'Their tracks vanish at one of the hidden crossroads,' she said, picking up a twig that hadn't burned through and poking it about in the flames. 'My guess is that I was too slow. They must have been overtaken by Gulfoyle or Namaquae. I saw Moguskul out searching for them too. He found the same trail and I was set following him but he got away from me. Jack's storms . . .' She sighed. 'The city is set for night now. If they're not there then they're close to it.' She pushed the twig into the heart of the fire, twisting it in her fingers. As it caught light a burning image of a tiny tree appeared just above it and she whispered to it, 'Somersfal. Plague our dear one, melt his bones, let him know we mean trouble.' The tree flickered, became the figure of a tiny dryad and zipped off over the snow; a cinder soon lost to sight.

'What was that?' Malachi asked.

'A spirit of ancient summers,' Madrigal said. 'I like to tease him.' She smiled to herself and frowned at the same time, then looked up at him. He felt himself grow warm though she was doing nothing. 'What is this group of yours, Cat? Why so long since you came here?'

He introduced the others briefly, and avoided answering her second question because he didn't want to say that it was easier not to see her, when she couldn't or wouldn't leave and he wasn't ready to find out which. Madrigal remembered the fey once she heard their names – because they were undying it was common to meet and then lose contact with others over ages, forget them, then remember upon meeting again, and none of them minded. She lingered over Teazle, looking at him closely.

'What is your fire?' she asked him after a moment, breaking into Malachi's explanation of their sooty disguises.

'Death,' he said. 'And yours?'

She reached inside a fold of her furs and brought her hand out, held shut. She turned the palm up, held it towards him, and opened her tawny fingers to reveal a single perfect strawberry, shining with the old golden sunlight of a long-ago day. The smell of the ripe berry filled the icy air for a second before the wind snatched it away. 'Fruit,' she said, smiling slowly, her eyes looking up from low lashes.

Malachi prickled with envy and irritation. She had given him an apple once, and he had kept it safe. Even now it was hidden away up the years in his bower, in the jungle; red and green apple, fresh with dew that tasted sweet and salt on his tongue every day when he licked it. He was astonished when Teazle grinned, reached out and took the berry and bit through it with his sharp white teeth. Juice ran down his chin and he licked it off with his unseemly large tongue, then ate the rest with a single bite.

'Thank you,' he said thoughtfully.

Madrigal raised an eyebrow but then her attention moved back to Malachi. 'So?'

'I didn't want to be here,' he said. 'Too much chance of getting caught.'

'Fneh, Jack couldn't catch you,' she said. 'I think you prefer life in the other worlds.'

'Maybe so,' he said. He felt unaccountably strange, seeing her after such a long time apart.

'What do you say, Naxis?' Madrigal asked, indicating that they could, if they wished, share her fire.

All of them except the demon crowded around.

'I say, I say, I say,' Naxis began softly, staring into the flames. 'What begins with the dark and ends in the dark and has no body to speak of?'

'Cold, dead Jack,' Madrigal said. 'Too easy. Why you think of that?'

'It will be midwinter night day after tomorrow.'

'The day he dies,' Malachi said, licking his lips unconsciously with the memories of that same day ages past. He glanced at Madrigal but she was introspective, fire-staring.

She gave a soft laugh, 'Jack's holiday it is, we say. Three moons in the lands of the dead, in his other home.'

'Mad,' Malachi said urgently. 'My friend has the key. I believe it brought her here. This year it will turn the lock, Jack or no Jack.' He explained as best he could about the humans' problem – his problem – with the Mothkin, their need to find a hunter capable of gathering them.

'And that's all? You think the key rose from darkness just to help the humans out of some little faery fix?' She was openly astonished.

'When you put it that way,' he said, 'no.'

'It is that way,' she said shortly. 'Who found it first?'

'Me,' Viridia said, putting up a small hand. She was wrapped up in her own hair, arms clutching her bony knees to her chest, her nose and the ends of her long ears red with cold. She sniffed. 'It was on the bottom of this lake. I just happened to be there.'

Madrigal made a face to show how much store she set by this information. 'What lake? When?'

Viridia rolled her eyes as if it was all too tedious for words and gave one of those teenage twisting shrugs that says everything that's happening is a torment to the soul. 'That one in Alfheim. With the dragon in it. When Zal got stolen and the witchy elf woman wanted to stick him with a blood pact. We was there to rescue 'em and it was a big battle in the water and we went down a long way . . .' She coughed slightly and muttered something which made Malachi guess she was fudging something. 'And I got all the way to the very bottom – which is a long long way down, let me tell you, much further than any faery might ever have gone bef–' She caught the expression of those watching her and said primly, with pique, 'There was this shelf, the last bit of the world, sticking out into nothing, into the Void, where all the water was hanging at the Dragon Gate – not that you'd know what one of them is – anyway, right on the edge of this shelf of rock was a load of stuff that'd fallen in over the years and got right down to the bottom. There was all sorts, I can tell you, like jewels and bones and this book with a big clasp on it and some old writings and daggers and a headband made out of gold . . .'

'Vee!' Poppy snapped.

Viridia shot her a look. 'The key was right on the edge. Right so close to the edge that if I'd have tried to pick it up the wrong way I'd have just pushed it over. And the fighting up above had made the water move . . . and I had too . . . and the water was nudging it along and it was about to go over and I wanted to pick up some of the other things but I thought the Gate might not like me being there too much because it was starting to do something and I thought that anything that was about to go over was something that must've been there the longest and was probably the most interesting and valuable so I just grabbed it and came back up before the dragon got there.'

'And what made you give it to this Otopian woman?' Madrigal demanded, trying but failing not to express impatience. 'Did you know what it was?'

'I put it under me pillow and had a dream that night. We was campin' in the elf woods looking for Zal and Lila and we found them but they was . . . busy . . . so we just set ourselves up a way off and went to sleep and I dreamed something big and dreadful and frightening was coming and that Faery was going to be reversed because of this thing so I guessed it might be the key and then Pop and me decided we didn't want it so we thought we'd pass it on to someone who'd keep it safe on account of not knowin' what it was at all and not bein' a faery.'

'She was the best person,' Poppy said defensively. 'She's lethal and completely bad tempered. And she was nice to Zal and he's one of them that the Kindly Ones like, so he's not easy to fiddle with either so . . .'

Madrigal held her hand up, 'I get it. But now, just a few months later, here she is in Jack's City. Cat,' she looked up, 'you must have known something about this. She is your ally.'

'I thought she'd keep it far from here,' he said.

'Do you think she's one of the ones?' Madrigal asked after a minute thinking.

'What does that mean?' Teazle said, surprising them, because he'd been so silent.

'One for the Hall,' Poppy said. 'We thought Zal was one, but then it turned out he wasn't.'

Viridia nodded.

'One *what*?' Teazle demanded.

'Someone who should be lost,' Malachi said. 'One of the Champions of the Light. Individuals with great power of some kind, combined with a passion for doing the right thing.'

Poppy continued to nod enthusiastically. Her feelings shifted with violent speeds but they never wavered. 'You know how dangerous they are. We like to find them and then . . .'

'. . . lose them.' Viridia said. 'Strategic'ly. So as things don't get bad. So we've got a Hallway in Under that we use to lose them.'

'Wouldn't it be better to lose the ones with a passion for doing the bad thing?'

Viridia looked at Teazle as if he'd lost his mind. 'No no. They extinguish themselves. Piffling minor they are. Easy to spot, easy to kill. Quite pathetic really. Devils won't even touch them. It's the ones who think they're doing good you have to watch out for. Didn't your mother teach you anything?'

'I could never stomach her advice,' Teazle grumbled with a wry snort that sounded a lot more beastlike than angelic.

'You're all getting way ahead,' Madrigal stated with the authority of one who has heard it all a thousand times before. 'Your immediate problem is that Jack wants the key, your friend has it and she is no doubt with Jack now. If he gets his hands on it then he will open everything, not just the Hall.'

'Why?' Teazle asked.

'Because of the Queen's magic,' all the faeries said at once in a singsong way as if it was the most obvious answer in the world, ever.

'Indulge me,' the demon suggested. 'Unless we're going off to Jack's place now for some killing you may as well fill me in on the reasons for said killing. I assume there's going to be killing?'

'Probably,' Malachi said, shivering. 'What're your swords made of, by the way?'

'Some kind of light,' Teazle said in a tone that wasn't interested. 'But tell me about the Queen. Sounds sexy.'

The faeries hesitated as one.

'The trouble is,' Malachi said after they all shared a look without Teazle and came to the conclusion that he was the spokesperson, 'we've been stuck so long here that we don't remember the answer. Everyone remembers "the Queen's magic", but nobody actually knows what that means any more.'

Madrigal nodded, 'All the fey exist at all levels of faery – all the true fey, I should say – across time, but this place has been stuck fast, nobody has gone beneath it or travelled up past it since the time of the fall, when . . . the trouble is that we like to put important information and things where they can't be found by accident, or tripped over, or used unwisely . . .'

'To hide something is to lose it,' Poppy put in eagerly. 'Otherwise, it's not properly hid.'

'And so,' Malachi concluded, 'we'd like to tell you, but we can't.'

'I see,' said Teazle, marvellously amused. 'So the answer to our problem is down below, where we can't get at it. You think it would be bad for this Jack person to get the key and undo the lock . . . but really you can't be sure about that.'

'It must be bad, or it wouldn't be *lost*,' Viridia pointed out, her voice rising at the end of her statement to indicate that she was declaring the obvious to an idiot, lifting her chin as she did so.

'Touché,' Teazle said. 'I don't need to know stories. I need to know how to get to my wife. Where is she, Fruits?' He looked expectantly at Madrigal and licked his lips again.

Madrigal stared at him. 'Jack's City,' she said. 'If you walk in you won't walk out.'

'I don't need to walk,' Teazle got up and shook some of the darkness off himself. 'Who's with me?'

There was a universal pause.

'We fear the unlocking of what lies underneath,' Madrigal said, to explain it as Teazle waited. 'We don't know what it will mean. Before the fall, Faery was a monarchy ruled by the King and Queen and all of us were in their courts, high and low. Since the fall we have been an anarchy. In part we've succumbed to warlordism, like here, where Jack's madness holds sway. But not everywhere. Above, we don't all want to go back to the old ways, but with the return of the old magic the old manner must come back, it's feared.'

'Who knows the truth?' Teazle asked.

Madrigal and the girls shrugged. Naxis shook his head hopelessly. But Malachi took a deep breath. The others turned to stare at him.

'The one who knows all of it,' he said, with fear and resignation. 'The patterner.' His voice dropped even further and he whispered, 'Lachesis.'

'Ahhhh . . .' sighed the demon and sat back on his heels. 'Zal's friend.'

Now it was the faeries' turn to stare.

'Is she a faery?' Teazle asked after a second. He genuinely didn't know.

'Not exactly,' Malachi said. 'In the same way that her sister isn't Dead and her other sister isn't a Ghost.'

'Do you demons know something more about the Kindly Ones?' Madrigal asked, her face childlike with attention.

'They are like the angels,' Teazle said. 'They came before us, or, at least, in a different way. They are closer to the aether, further from matter. This makes them godlike to aetherial creatures, in the way that the ultimate material creation is godlike to material beings.'

'We never knew what that last material thing was,' Poppy said sadly.

'It's obvious,' Teazle replied, and when Poppy gave him a blank look he said, 'Lila.'

'Who is Lila?' Madrigal said.

'My wife,' Teazle said. 'But to be more accurate, she isn't yet finished, so I may be premature in calling her into equality with the Fates and suchlike. Certainly she was made by their equivalents in the material plane.'

'Others,' Viridia whispered, shivering.

'No wonder you were so damn keen to get wed,' Malachi snarled.

Teazle laughed. 'That wasn't the reason.' He got up and stretched. 'I'll be heading out now, if you point me in the direction of the city.'

Malachi sighed with unhappiness at the idea. 'One by one we'll all go in and get stuck.'

'You have no faith,' the demon said. 'What happened to make you all so certain?'

'The turning of the lock,' Viridia replied. 'When Jack was prisoned here, and all below shut fast. Above, things may change by and by, but nothing moves here. How could it?'

Madrigal abruptly stood up and kicked over the fire, scattering its embers and ashes, causing the others who hadn't stood up yet to leap backwards and tumble over in the snow. 'He wasn't always mad, but winter is the worst time. You can't go alone. I'll come along. Cat, come with us. Naxis, you too. You horses head back to my westerly house, it's along the lakeshores, on the other side from the city. If we can get out we'll meet there. If there's trouble at least you can have the lake.'

'Trouble!' Teazle said dreamily. 'Now you're talking.'

Lila and Zal followed Moguskul as Jack ordered: they walked through the narrow streets, beneath the drunken overhangs of two-storey buildings and the icicle-bound edges of snow-laden roofs. They wound through little circles where houses faced each other around frozen fountains, the water caught in mid-splash so that the droplets

205

hung in the air. The meaning of this was clear; time had frozen in this winter, not only the weather and the land. Nobody was about, though they heard many voices and saw movement in the warm yellowed windows of the homes and stores, and their path was mapped by footprints of all kinds and sizes.

'Where is everyone?' Lila dared, watching her breath frost in the bitter air.

'This close to midwinter it's curfew come sunset,' Moguskul said. His voice was gravelly and resonant, full of emotion which, after some replays, Lila decided was anger. 'All are indoors awaiting the dawn. The streets aren't safe.'

'Why?'

But she got no answer. Inside her chest, Tath was coiled like a spring. Between the two of them Lila could feel the answer, distinct and clear – the streets were hunted by night. She shared a look with Zal and saw him thinking the same thing. They didn't need to ask to know who the hunter was and it made her shiver involuntarily. To give some relief, and to find a way to voice her conclusion, she said, 'But aren't these Jack's people?'

'They're their own people,' Moguskul said, treading on with the same stolid movement that had kept them going for the last half hour. 'They bide in Jack's City. That's all. Safer here.' His last two words carried as much weight as any lengthy statement. They said, with their tone and timbre, that every faery in this part of the world had surrendered to Jack's power rather than challenge it. In their hearts they felt rebellious and resentful, but they weren't prepared to take a stand. Now that they were within the enemy, their chances of revolt had diminished. Moguskul's few words stood in a stark testament to that, she felt. He would not speak directly. Jack was listening, he implied, always and everywhere.

The chocolate box appearance of the faery town only grew as they neared its centre. Buildings became grander, taller and more ethereal, with spires and delicate icework where a human hand would have set iron as rails or decoration or bars. Snow covered everything like a thick blanket, so heavy that even one more snowfall looked as though it would be enough to flatten everything. The whole world bent under its weight into soft angles and mysterious curves where drifts had caught in the eddies and built new geometries in the alleys and at the turns of the street. Sound was dampened to almost nothing. Golden squares and lozenges lit their way, from the windows which she tried to look through, but saw only the light shining, nothing else. Meantime the cold itself was continuously growing as the night deepened, and it bit hard. Its teeth sparkled on every surface, bright frost. Lila was thinking how pretty it was, when she caught sight of something on those brittle surfaces and stopped to look.

At first she thought it was just some reflected colour but as she got closer, and then used her lenses to zoom in, she saw that every flat crystal of frost had an image trapped on it, like photographs reduced and set on microfilm. She bent down to the drift by her knee to see more clearly. Every crystal was different. The images weren't still however, they moved. She saw tiny figures and skeins of light which at first she didn't understand. They went through routines.

A fat-bellied man with a beard and pointed hat capered. A child ran laughing, looking back over his shoulder, along the street. A vortex of lights coalesced into the face of a grinning, wicked satyr, then fell apart.

They repeated endlessly.

'Let's go,' Moguskul grated beside her. He made to grab her shoulder but Zal struck his hand aside.

'What's this?' she said.

'Nothing for you to mind,' he said. 'We'll be late. Follow me.'

She glanced back and found the satyr staring at her. Not falling apart. Staring. It made a sound, or its lips moved, and in the crystal beside it the fat-bellied faery stood still and looked at her. A hand grabbed her T-shirt collar, pulled. She heard a fight start behind her as she stared, utterly absorbed by the sight before she was thrown into a drift and lost the vision.

They had spoken in unison, their lips moving though they made no sound at all.

Help us.

A heavy body fell against her; deadweight stinking of wet fur. She stumbled and powered up sharply, knocking Moguskul aside as he was struggling to right himself. He was nimble and turned his stagger into a sidestep, coming around ready to attack. She saw Zal poised a few metres away. Moguskul hissed and shook the heaviness of elf-induced sleep off him like an animal. 'You're no human,' he said to her, with a mixture of resentment and curiosity. 'But you smell like one, and you look like one. No demon either,' he turned to Zal and curled his lip, doglike, 'But you smell like one and you fight like one even though you use the elf trick – smothering bastard.'

'Sweet dreams,' Zal said unpleasantly, though he was quite relaxed now and glanced at Lila to check that she was all right.

'Save your breath, sonny,' the huge hunter replied, making a show of adjusting his clothing as he swiftly checked his weapons. 'You'll need that later.'

'There are people, inside the ice,' Lila said. 'I was only asking why.'

'There are lots of things around abouts,' Moguskul replied. He set his jaw and turned. 'None of them your business. Follow.'

'No,' Zal said.

'You must come with me to the castle,' the hunter said, halting but not turning. 'If you do not, I will make you.' He was resigned to it.

'Why?' Lila said, getting ready for combat.

'Jack wishes to meet you in person,' was the reply, given on a plume of hot breath.

'We heard him say so,' Zal agreed. 'But that doesn't mean we want to meet him. We have business elsewhere. You are delaying us. Time is short.'

'He'll return you to your moment,' Moguskul said into the air in front of him. He was relaxed and unmoving, except for his speaking. Around them the still town sparkled with reflected light.

'Just moving on will be enough,' Zal said in an almost amiable tone that suggested all unpleasantness could be put aside, even laughed off. He was giving a chance but from the sharp spike in his energy level that made him seem suddenly almost electric with potential, Lila knew he was expecting a violent refusal.

'Don't force me to fight you,' the hunting faery said. His shoulders were low. He looked like a whipped dog.

'Your choice,' Zal said lightly.

'Yours,' the fey replied, quiet now, the word almost silent, it was so dampened by the surroundings.

Nothing moved. Lila felt dizzy, longing for anything to undo the moment that hung over them all and make it fall one way or another. There was almost a sense of presence in the silence, as if every mote of snow and fragment of building were listening and holding them fast, enjoying their indecision and the suspension of all their intent.

This is Jack, she thought. All of this, and the freezing, and the stasis, it's all him.

She looked at Zal. 'We're inside him,' she said.

'That don't mean shit to me,' Zal said, his voice melodic with demon tones. He was almost completely transparent, a dark kind of ghost against the brilliance of the frost, his face stretched into the longer and more alien lines of the true Shadowkin, eyes black pits. Compared to the others he made almost no breath at all. 'He already met us, he just doesn't want to show himself so we have to walk his way. I don't care how big he is or what he wants. I'm not going any further under his command. This is good enough.'

'To meet in a place of warmth and safety, is what he ordered,' Moguskul said, struggling with the words as it clearly pained him to maintain diplomacy when his hands were twitchy with anger.

'I am warm enough and I was safe before he overtook me,' Zal said. 'This'll do.'

Lila's T-shirt crackled as she moved, melting where it touched her, freezing as soon as it moved away from her. She felt obliquely angry herself, that Zal hadn't asked her before taking his hard line – she'd imagined a trip more akin to an international meeting, with civilised question and answers, nobody wanting to move for a struggle – but now that he'd committed to the first move she could only follow through. 'Let Jack speak for himself,' she said to Moguskul, standing her ground in the snow.

A light patter of tiny snowflakes began to fall, silently. She inspected them on high resolution and saw the images trapped there. She got the impression that they were old, somehow, of the past; the colours in them were faded as if they'd been in the sun too long.

'You don't understand,' growled Moguskul, his hand on the haft of the axe at his belt. 'Within the palace is the only place you will see Jack.'

'He spoke to us in the city,' Zal said.

'That was only his voice.'

'Can you give us a minute?' Lila broke in, feeling the weight of the exchange growing more deadly by the second.

Seeing it as his only likely chance to persevere, Moguskul nodded and stomped off a few metres further on out of earshot, probably.

Lila moved in close to Zal and whispered, 'What are you doing?'

'I'm keeping us out of his place of power,' Zal said. 'I've never seen for myself but I've heard of faeries like this. Gulfoyle and Jack are both ancient great ones. They're not just people, sometimes they're not even people, they're the land and the sky and a place, a time. Further in the deep past they don't even have selves or voices . . . they're akin to primal forces, with only the beginnings of awareness. I've heard of Jack too. Gulfoyle called him Giantkiller. He's the Green King, the Winter Death, you know.' He lowered his voice even further and touched her ear with his *andalune* body so that he barely had to speak. 'The Fisher King, whose impotence lays waste to all it contacts. At midwinter some quester, the grail quester, comes to ask him a question. If it is the right question rightly said, then either Jack is healed or else he will die and another comes to take his place in a new land. Quick, quick, look it all up, I haven't time to tell you but the human stories about him will do.'

Lila accessed her AI data sets but Zal was faster, he scowled as he said, 'Clearly we are in the position of the grail quest knights. I don't like the sound of that. Especially since he's been stuck here for tens of thousands of years . . .'

'Yes, shade,' said Jack's voice suddenly, loudly, impressively, from the snow. 'That I have. You are right to be wary of entering my shrines and holy places with your ignorance intact. However, unlike the pretty tales for children at the fire, it is not my usual practice to simply vanish when the knights do not ask the right question. No knight has asked aright. I scatter them to the wind. And no knight has come here in all the human ages. No human knight at all, nor any other, for all who tried had fallen before the first of you was born. What say you to that, armoured woman? Do you not come here to this land with a quest?'

'I . . . I've nothing to do with some old myth,' Lila said. She thought of Malachi, wished he were there. 'I never even heard of you until just now. I came here to find someone who can hunt down the Mothkin and take them back from my world. They are a plague.'

A sudden gust of wind, so cold it felt like it cut her flesh, zipped past them, hurling and scattering ice so hard that where it touched her hands and face she started to bleed. She heard Moguskul jog up from his sentry position and when she looked she saw a cut across his cheek the size of one of her fingers. It bled only a little, among many other scars. He simply scowled at her, as if it were her fault.

'Then you have come in vain,' Jack said from the wind this time. 'For nobody who comes here has left again, nor can leave. This is the nature of our situation. Were it other I would say easily that Moguskul is your man. There is no beast or beastkin alive in any realm that he cannot hunt and master. I would lend him to you for some comely price. We would barter and celebrate and enjoy the good life of freedom, no? But that will not be.' There was more than a hint of self-pity in the tones, but Lila couldn't really blame him. She didn't much like the sound of it, looked at Zal, saw him frowning and set with anger and resistance.

When they didn't answer immediately Jack laughed – another gust that blew snow all around them – and said, 'Even so, unlucky as you are, you should have your chance to make the turn that will sunder our loneliness. I say it is your only chance. Come now, to the palace, but take your time. There is a day to go. If you will tarry to think upon what question you might ask perhaps it will go better. Maybe you, of all the knights in ever, will free us from this lock.' He was laughing by the end of this speech, as if there couldn't be anything funnier. He had to stop talking. The snow billowed around them and the ground thrummed.

'While there's some time there's some hope,' Thingamajig said from Lila's ear.

'There's never any hope, you misleading and lying little shite,' Zal growled at him, narrow eyed, as frightening as any spectre. 'There's only what is. And what is, is a great big fuckup.' He said to Jack, 'We'll take your day. Give us your hospitality.'

As he finished speaking there was a cold, clear instant, as if a bell had rung loudly and they were in the vibration of it though the sound had stopped.

'But in abundance! Moguskul, give them a house and all the feasting a shade and a Hoodoo minx can eat! Drink, company, whatever they will! Until sunset tomorrow, I bid you a very, very good night.' Everything became slightly less than what it had been. Jack had passed.

Lila turned and saw Moguskul setting his mouth in a long, grim line, wincing as this moved his cut in the icy air. 'Come along,' he said and opened the door that was right next to him into one of the little faery houses. As she stepped past him to go inside he whispered to her, so quietly that only she could have figured out what he said, by reprocessing the tiny sounds over and over again. He said, 'Jack doesn't remember his past. He doesn't know what the question is himself. You must trick him. It's the only way.'

211

CHAPTER SEVENTEEN

Malachi stumped along in Madrigal's footsteps through the icy grass. He hadn't started out stumping, but he'd ended up doing it. As he watched her broad, capable back, crossed with rifle and sword, he tried to watch her bottom but was thwarted by her seriously heavy furs and could only imagine its perfect peach curves swaying with every step. So his temper had slowly eroded. The walk was long, he wasn't keen on examining his feelings at having turned into an older form of himself that seemed to be more salivating brute than witty dandy, and here he was walking to a likely doom in the footsteps of unrequited love which had been enduring and hopeless. Unrequited wasn't quite right. Madrigal did have tender feelings for him, but he was reasonably sure they'd never amount to adulterous. He'd yet to find a time or place where some other male fey hadn't captured her heart, but he lived in hope and that made him miserable. It was the reason he didn't like to spend a lot of time in Faery. Cats and fertility figures – as if they went together anyway, it didn't even make magical sense. And now he was so close to her, but as far as ever. He felt filthy in every possible way.

Behind him Nixas was humming a little song to herself. It wasn't really clear to him how she'd changed. She was taller, a bit stronger, more earthy, less nighty . . . no significant alterations. Which meant she was one of those seriously old types, he guessed, or else that she had less place in a modern world than he did. Her gender flickered more often here and the differences between her two forms were minimal. When he caught sight of her from the corner of his eye he saw a shimmer around her, her wings vast across the landscape, the size and surface of a lake ruffled by the wind.

At the rear of their small group, Teazle ambled, his eyes glowing, the blinks like lanterns signalling secret codes across the night. Malachi could tell a great deal about those in his darkness because of the coal dust he'd used to cover them. The weight of lost forests lay over them and brought their scents to him as if through living trees: Nix was feeling dread in spite of her careless exterior. She knew about this place because she felt it in the land; Jack's death coming over everything. Her song protected her from its dark energy. And Teazle was dreaming of death too, but in a loving way. To him this episode in his life was only one more step and turn in his tango with the inevitable. He held it as close as a lover and there was fresh wildness in his heart because he had recently overcome some significant obstacle and felt himself powerful, almost inviolable. Malachi wondered what that was, but was rather glad he didn't know. He wasn't sure if he should fear for Lila, being connected to that one, even if Teazle seemed to be protective and kind towards her. Those just weren't quite demon traits and he suspected Teazle had other motives.

Madrigal, on the other hand, was businesslike. She led them through low hills towards a flat plain dotted with lights, which Malachi assumed resentfully was Jack's palace. Somewhere around them in the dark he smelled dog – the giant wolf keeping pace.

And a way behind them, surprisingly quiet, but filled with anxiety and a desperate need not to be left out, crept Viridia and Poppy in their most natural form: two black horses, thick furred for winter, mouths full of tongues and teeth of piranha. They were hungry and their spirits were restless. Periodically they snuffed the air for any signs of prey, caught traces of those ahead and pricked their ears, then remembered and shook themselves off with resignation. Of the giddy, silly party girls who sang in Zal's band there was only the merest trace, like a hint of perfume on the wind. They smelled of horse and lakebeds and cold, slimy things.

Madrigal called a halt at a half-mile distance from the city lights and hunkered down on her heels in the lee of a large rock. They joined her and she said, 'My sprite hasn't come back. I need to make another, see what's going on.'

She brought out dried fruit from a pouch inside her wraps and some dried grass like the stuff Malachi used and began to fashion a small doll, its fat belly full of raisins and plums. With a final clever twist she was done and then looked up into Malachi's eyes, her golden warm gaze amused and friendly. 'You were always the best maker,' she said.

'Almost as good as the Little Master. Would you?' She held the doll out to him.

'Of course,' he said, barely able to get the words past his tight throat. He reached forwards, watching his own hand nearing hers, his fingers too thick and too heavy as they stretched out of the cat's paw. He touched the doll on its head and felt his intent pass into it – too much intent as it happened, but the deed was done. The doll jumped up and ran along Madrigal's arm to her shoulder where it tossed a hank of her hair aside and kissed her on the cheek, with a head slam of grass.

'Lovely Mistress of the Harvest, what is your will?' the doll said adoringly. 'Delicious grapes and juicy plums make us sweet as sweet can be, we'd like them in our mouths all day long. Is these our pay?'

'A dinner is as welcome as cold cash to a hungry belly,' Madrigal blushed faintly, colour rising in her cheeks like a pink dawn as she finalised the Hoodoo. 'Oh Cat,' she said, her face full of pleasure and a little concern.

'Sorry,' he said, sitting back. He wished he'd made his love for her less plain and hoped the others hadn't picked up on it.

To the doll she said, 'Go find Cat's human friend and when you have, then come back and tell us all.'

'I will, Mistress,' the doll piped. 'I run, I run! Yum yum!' It jumped down from her shoulder and hopped off over the snow in a series of wildly springing bounds, like a flea. In a moment or two it vanished from sight.

Teazle watched and said languidly, 'You can make little servants who work for treats?'

Madrigal broke gaze with Cat, rather grateful for the interruption, he thought, and said, 'The Hoodoo is the oldest magic we have. Actually, not so much a magic as . . . someone. But as long as the deals are fair, then we deal.' She hesitated. Malachi finished for her,

'But the more you use the Hoodoo, the more it uses you,' he said. 'That's part of its price. Why we don't use it unless we have no other way.'

'Can you teach me?' the demon asked.

'Not now,' Malachi said. 'Maybe later, if we survive.' He felt foolish. He had given the Hoodoo more than he ought to have, carelessly. One should always be scrupulous with it and he hadn't been. Like Zal, he thought. An even more deep foreboding came over him. He looked

214

after the line the little doll had taken and licked his whiskers for comfort.

'Everything comes back,' Madrigal said and stroked his head with her strong, weather-bitten hand. He leaned his cheek into her caress and closed his eyes.

'One unlooked for kindness mends more souls than a world of righteous care,' he murmured, returning one old fairy saying with another and felt a moment of stolen happiness, warm and rich and sweet.

'Will we stay here the night?' Naxis asked, wrapped up in his wings so much that he looked like just a head on top of a column of water.

'We may have to,' Madrigal said. 'Cat, you're the fastest tracker. Go steal us some kindling and wood and we'll make fire.'

'No need,' the demon interrupted her as she was finishing. He took out one of his swords from its scabbard on his back, its blade glowing with the flat light of a low energy lightbulb, and plunged it into the ground between them. He said a word in Daemonic and the thing burst into flames, white and blue and so very hot that they all leaned backwards before they were burned. 'See,' he said. 'I have my uses.'

'Your fire is deadly indeed,' Madrigal said, after her surprise was gone. 'It tastes of consumption and disease . . . but it warms and we are grateful.'

'Its name means Corruptor,' Teazle said. 'But the flames, like its bite, are purifying. You taste its power burning, that's all. The heat is plain good heat, nothing more.'

Madrigal smiled but Nixas edged away from the sword a little more, her eyes narrow with caution. 'Such swords,' she said, 'breathe.'

'. . . it is of the legendary hoard of Ahramazda,' Teazle told her with a fierce grin. 'But as to how I came to have it . . . that I don't recall. This is very strange, this living in the past! In the future world I have no idea that I ever lived before in any way. And now I know things I never knew, nor will know again . . .' he stopped, blinking, mystified.

'You will remember it now, for a time at least,' Malachi said. 'Forgetting comes over a long time. If you return here, then you remember again. Some things like yesterday that are ages old.'

All the fey shared looks of misgiving and disquiet but Teazle kept on grinning happily, and periodically recounting new things that he had just remembered about himself so that the time passed quite quickly, if

215

not comfortably, until the doll came leaping back again, draggled and thin, but whole.

'Mistress of the Tasty Fruit,' it huffed. 'Your human is inside Jack's Homely House. We overheard it talking with the Ruined elf. They have agreed to the quest already.'

Madrigal made a face of agonised disappointment. 'Did the woman have a silver charm about her?'

'I didn't see one.'

'And did they seem well?'

'As well as you can be when you've no idea what's going on,' the doll nodded. 'Which is very well indeed. Want me to take another look? I think I'll make it with some extra stuffing. I like rosehips. And cranberries.' There was a pause in which Teazle shook his head and all of them felt a dizziness that wasn't quite inside or outside them.

'No,' Madrigal said. 'That's all.'

'Awww . . .' the doll began to whine but she picked it up and tossed it into the sword-fire where it was instantly crisped to black ashes. A tension that had been drawing across them all like a fine wire eased suddenly and everyone let out their breath.

'Better quick and clean when the deal's paid out,' Malachi said to Teazle. Then to Madrigal, 'I don't think they know anything about Jack between them. Can we break in or sneak in?'

'*You* might,' she said. 'But if you're caught he'll skin you alive. And what will you do? The deal is sworn, the doll says. They must go through with it now.'

She had an old-school dogmatism, Malachi thought, which he'd once admired but which now he was rankled by. Yet the magic of faery itself was old school, and implacable with it, part of the prices of its power. If Zal and Lila had agreed to tilt at Jack's windmill, then tilt they must. But he wasn't about to let them go to it without any chance.

He said as much and waited as Teazle asked questions and Nixas filled him in. Madrigal added at the end, 'It isn't that Jack has to know the right question or the answer to it. When the charm worked . . .' She frowned and struggled, scratched her head. 'Damn this time!' she said fiercely, slamming the flat of her hand down on the softening ground. 'And damn me for never thinking to write a thing down when I did still know it! I wanted to tell you a thing that was so useful . . . something about the grail, yes, that's the word, graal, grail . . . it has something to do with this version of us in this region, why Jack is Giantkiller and

I am Madrigal and not May, or Maia or Maeve or Mab or Fructalia or Anumati or Mama Ocllo or Zislbog or Nantosuelta. I know it's about that but not what! Jack must be the same way. Maybe he will not remember why it's important either.' She stretched her brown hands out in a helpless gesture. 'But the fact is that whatever he's become Jack has enormous power now. Every faery except myself is in his mantle. He controls them all, shapes them into his story. The old charm may never work as it was meant. His intents have changed us.'

'What happened last year?' Malachi asked, full of foreboding.

'Midwinter came and he was dead. There were no knights of course, never are. This time he died of poisoning from a bad belly of pork, as usual at the stroke of midwinter night. He was laid to rest on the hill summit at Islacathra, rose again in thirty days from the grave and wandered to his final place, all to order. This year it was in the old bear cave at Yarrowkeld. I found his bones in the springtime and kissed him back to life. Hm, he seems to like that cave. Been there dozens of times recently. Made me start to wonder if he's forgetting the region as well as the rest.' She stared into the sword flames intently.

'But why do you bother?' Teazle asked. 'Why not leave him dead and let the others free?'

'It's not like that,' Madrigal said. 'If he stays dead then they all die. They're of him. He'd have to release them willingly if they were to be free. Killing him kills them all.'

The demon frowned. 'How annoying.' After a second he asked, 'If you die here, do you die everywhere? I never heard of a faery dying.'

'We don't die, we just forget ourselves,' Malachi said quietly. 'You wouldn't be killing anyone in the sense that you mean it. Other versions of us in other dimensions would continue, only this part of our selves would be ended. But that is still a significant act with unforeseeable consequences. And those who died could not come here again.'

'Cut off?' Teazle suggested.

'Yes.'

'Oh. Well, if you don't want to risk stealthing in I'll nip in and out before that damn elf gets any further ahead of me.'

'Jack will see you,' Nixas said. 'Your demon aether is too odd not to notice instantly. Cat should go.'

'Just one more question,' Teazle said, leaning closer to his fire. 'What happens if Zal and Lila mess up the quest and lose the deal?'

'Jack will kill them,' Madrigal said. 'If they were faeries he'd just imprison them in his ice, but they're alien so he'll probably just kill them. There was . . . another thing instead, but I forgot that too.'

'What if he can't kill them?' Teazle asked. 'Maybe he'll die first, if they get past the time.'

Madrigal just laughed.

'Could we all fight him?'

She laughed longer. 'You've never fought a faery battle, clearly. Jack wields the power of all he has subsumed. You cannot fight the might of so many fey united under one will. No.'

'I can,' Teazle said. 'Rather, I will.'

She shook her head.

The demon glowered and his tone became as frigid as the air. 'Ears akimbo, Fruitpop. I didn't come here to listen to you talk about my lovers dying just by accident because we ran into the wrong end of town,' Teazle snorted, some fire issuing from his nostrils. 'What kind of joke is that? We ain't *in* Daemonia now. You even look like you wouldn't care. Aha, you don't care, do you? It's because of that accursed key, isn't it? You don't want things to change. That's why you're keeping us out here in the piss-freezing snow and ice while time slips away and we do nothing. You even give Malachi here the soppy eye now and again so he purrs and stays close like a good little kitty.'

'Cool your jets!' Malachi said, finding it coming out as more of a snarl than he intended. 'Have a bit of respect. You won't survive some kind of assault on him.'

'You severely underestimate my assassin's powers,' Teazle snarled in reply, tiny spurts of flame beginning to poke through his coating of black dust like spikes. 'It is hard to fight what you do not know is there.'

'Jack controls time within the city,' Madrigal said, perfectly calm, her face composed and thoughtful. 'He is also, unless he wills it, bodiless, a trick he learned just to avoid those whose powers were like yours I'm afraid. Sadly, I doubt he's forgotten that . . . oh . . . it's on the tip of my . . . that's it! Jack's body. He has to be corporeal to die on midwinter night. Usually he will take form at sunset within the palace and take part in some ritual feast or drinking competition until the hour of midnight. You might do the honour of killing him then but that will only make you a necessary condition of his legend, not a challenge to it. The cycle will continue unbroken. No. Force will not help. Believe me,' and she lifted her golden eyes and stared Teazle in the face, 'many of us have tried it. It's no slight on your glory to meet the immovable object. I understand your frustration. Consider me. I've lived with it more ages than your city has stood.'

'Now I know how Lila feels,' Teazle said after a moment of spouting fire that reluctantly died back and became black once again. Defeat really did not sit well on him. He smouldered, yellowish smoke starting to seep out of his shoulders. 'What did she say – "if it's not a technicality, its taxes, magical law or just bastards out to get you . . ." What do we do then?'

'I will take some useful knowledge . . . Madrigal, do you actually *have* any useful knowledge?' Malachi asked.

Nixas shivered as they waited and Madrigal rubbed her forehead with both hands. 'Those horses are nearby. Followed us.'

'I know,' Madrigal said. 'Knew they would. I would have. And yes, I have one piece of useful knowledge you can take. Jack likes stories. He's heard all of ours a thousand times over and over again. He will probably delay as long as possible if there is something to be learned or known. His boredom is his weakness now, I would bet.'

'You have no idea at all about the answer or the question that would free him?'

'It is a mystery,' she said.

Teazle slumped.

'No, I mean it is a mystery in the old sense, a metaphor for something that the questioner must know, when Jack does not. It is the kind of question that opens the locks of the mind and creates a new reality. The kind of question that has an answer that can only be pointed to by the question, but never told. I know that much.'

'There are not so many of those,' Nixas said.

'I doubt the sound of one hand clapping is going to do it,' Malachi sighed, getting up and taking a last turn in front of the sword's radiant heat. 'But I'll take it.'

'Good luck,' Madrigal said, she reached into her furs and took out something that she gave him. He opened his hand out of its strange paw and found himself holding one perfect peach.

'Give this to them,' she said. 'Whoever eats it will have a part of my protection from Jack for a short time. Half of the peach is only half of the power so . . . well . . .' She didn't finish. 'We'll wait for you here.'

'Hurry, I'm bored,' the demon grumbled.

'Here,' Nixas reached out and gripped Malachi's furry forearm for a moment. He felt a warm current of energy pass into him from the contact. It was warming, heartening.

'It's been fun,' Teazle said. 'Keep the sword for now. I've got others.' He stood up, his two eyes suddenly rising, the dust on him glittering as it shifted. There was a sudden bang as the air rushed to fill the vacuum he'd left behind.

'But . . .' Madrigal started.

'Demons,' Naxis said. Madrigal nodded and then shrugged the matter off.

Malachi slipped away without another word. He hated goodbyes and he had a feeling this was one of the lasting kind. The irony that they should stumble here so soon after Sorcha's (to him) senseless end wasn't lost on him. First one, then the multitude, he thought, or if we are lucky, just three.

I saw three ships come sailing in . . .

Did he hear it or did he just imagine? He shivered beneath his thick fur and crept onward, silently as he knew how, though the space between his shoulderblades was tingling and the hair there on end, expecting arrows or worse.

The faery house was much bigger on the inside than the outside. Inside, it was a perfect replica of an elf home, so Zal said.

'In fact it's my last home in Alfheim,' he said, tension making his jaw jut forward. 'This is worse than I imagined. The bastard has tendrils in me and I didn't even feel it.'

Lila looked around it with new interest – she'd never seen much of anything personal to Zal, only the kinds of things that you could wear or stuff in a suitcase. She was astounded to discover it was not so much of the elven houses she'd seen before, and more like a grass hut, decorated in the style of any common wayhouse; pleasantly made but purely functional items on a dirt floor. A couple of nicely crafted plain cupboards. A firepit in the centre with a smokehole above it.

'You make the Amish look like Saudi princes,' she said after a few seconds surveying it all.

'I've made up for it since,' he said.

Then she turned to face him in the firelight. With the onset of the deepest part of the night he'd become completely shadow, something she'd never seen in Dar, the only other Shadowkin-blood elf she'd ever known. Zal was actually semi-transparent, all tones reduced to just a few contrasts so that he seemed more like a large coloured drawing than a solid object. 'I never saw this before,' she said, nervous and trying not to be.

'I never was this before,' he said, looking down at himself. 'I don't feel the fire. I'm not cold. I feel . . . light.' He snorted humourlessly. 'How typical. The only chance we get to be alone before facing a terrible fate and suddenly I'm insubstantial.'

Lila reached out to touch him and watched as her fingertips passed right through his arm, not just his *andalune* body. She felt something, like a warmer kind of air, a slight vibration, nothing more. She snatched her hand back quickly and found herself rubbing her fingers before she knew what she was doing. 'Weird,' she said, feeling a catch in her voice.

'You're telling me,' he said and suddenly his shoulders slumped. 'What a mess. I hate to say it but I honestly think there's no way out of this.'

'We could run.'

'Where to? Anyway, Jack'll just move with us.'

'We can try killing him.'

'I've got my doubts about that. Even running the gauntlet of this part of his legend – this entire region is derailed by whatever magic is keeping it in place.'

'You're serious?'

'We're here because this is the lock,' Zal said.

'For the . . .' she couldn't finish as the imp slapped his hand across her face sharply – it being too small to effectively stop her mouth.

'Listen up, sweetcheeks,' Thingamajig said, hopping down next to the fireplace and rubbing his hands together. 'We don't mention the things we don't mention in case we need them later. Savvy? Love is all around us, and all that.'

Lila rubbed her face and scowled but she waited to see if he had anything to say. Zal just stared at him with misgiving.

'Fortunately for youse guys this faery hocus has no effect on me as a bona fide imp. I've got immunity from external bamboozlements of the magical variety. It's part of my job description, innit? How would I cut through everyone else's crap if I had to suffer through the endless crap they keep dealing? So, before you go getting even more depressed by not inexpensively done but frankly derivative levels of supernatural winter and suspension of every shred of independent life, let me notify you of some salient facts.' He squatted down in the fire's edge and let the flames lick up and around him, beaming with cheer. 'First off, you can't beat Jack at his own game on his own ground. Your flimsy mate here is correct on that one. But second of all, Jack is not the only player in town. Anyhoo my main point is – the thing we don't mention is the way out of all of this. There probably isn't another one, even if you get his quest question all right, and incidentally I've been here before and the question is . . . the answer is . . . the question . . . look, you're supposed to ask him what the nature of the grail is. Then he figures out that the nature of the grail is self-realisation. That triggers an immediate enlightenment and he passes over into a new form, at which point whoever asked the question gets to take his place, unless they happen to be enlightened, and then I guess the post is vacant until some other schmo comes along or until the region requires another form of Jack himself to spawn in order to maintain the balance of power. You'd have to ask the Middle Missus about that.'

Lila stood for a moment with her mouth open, digesting this and queuing up her questions in order of curiosity. 'You were here before?'

'The first time around,' the imp said, waving his hand airily. 'When it was new. Of course, being a demon, I knew the answer and the question straight off, which is more than could be said for the knights.'

'How were you here?'

The imp sighed, 'That's all tied up with the thing I can't remember.'

'The matter of opinion that made you into an imp?'

'Yeah, that,' he scowled.

'Who's the Middle Missus?'

'The weaver,' Zal said. 'Fate. So, here's an idea, when the time comes, you can do the talking. If it works you get to be a faery king.'

'Ah, so thoughtful,' the imp said, 'but here's the rub. You and me and Lila girl here are all stuck. Jack's stuck. We're stuck here with each other and that's no accident. You know enough about the real world of magic to understand that one, elfshade halfblood thing.'

At that point even the fire stopped crackling and there was a keen sense of listening.

'See? He hears me. He knows I'm right as only an imp can be.'

Thingamajig stopped as he saw what Lila was doing. Zal watched her closely too.

'I thought you'd left that behind,' he said uneasily.

222

She held the unpleasant object in her hand. It filled her with revulsion: Madame's Eye.

'I intended to,' she said. 'But then I found it in my pocket again, while we were walking. Which is odd, because I didn't think this armour had any pockets.' She put it down – it looked like nothing much more than a pebble – and regarded it sadly. 'Somehow it feels like this is calling someone to tell them where we are. You know, like when you're a kid and lost and you find you've got one coin left to dial home. I just need a feather.'

'You can pull one out of Teazle's ass when he gets here,' suggested a smooth voice from the darkness by the door.

With a jolt that frightened her almost as much as the sudden new sound Lila turned and automatically moved back to put the fire between herself and the creature that walked out of the shadows as if it was stepping through a portal and into a new world, visibly constructing its own body from the dark inch by inch along its entire, impressive length from the tip of its blunt, broad nose to the end of its heavy, twitching tail. The giant black tiger stood for a second, then stood up, in a way that completely confused her, on to two legs. Its torso shrank, its legs lengthened, in a second it was halfway to being a man and then it stuck there.

She peered at it and that voice tagged on to a familiar object in her mind. 'Mal?'

He gave a strange bow, sweeping one huge paw to his waist and bending slightly. Then he looked at Zal. 'I see you too have receded along the evolutionary ladder somewhat, my friend.'

'It's a kind of pre-birth thing, for me,' Zal said, recovering from his own shock at the sight of Malachi's transformation. 'Good thing I just didn't wink out of existence.'

'Nothing happen to you then?' the cat man asked, turning back to Lila.

'Only the usual,' she said, fingering her collar self-consciously and finding it still damp and unpleasant. The weight of Malachi's gaze made it clear he'd like to ask more but she didn't want to talk about any of that. It was better to deal with the present trouble than any pending or historical anguish. She was relieved to be interrupted.

'I'm great,' the imp said from his seat in the fire.

'Mmmnnnn.' Malachi stared at Thingamajig for almost a full minute. 'How interesting.'

'Have you come to rescue us?' Zal asked laconically.

'No. To stand with you,' Malachi said. 'Can't go anywhere without Jack eventually hearing me so it seems pointless to prevaricate.'

They spoke briefly of their separated adventures, filling one another in, until they reached another quiet moment into which the imp said, 'So, Lila, can you talk to her through that thing or not?'

'Talk to who?' Malachi looked up suddenly.

Lila showed him the eye. 'Need a feather to make it work.' She shrugged and put the horrid thing away into the pocket that seemed to have grown itself for the purpose at the side of her armour, quite dainty, with a button top. She couldn't stop staring at him. He was suddenly so massive, so enormously, solidly physical, which was unlike Malachi. He virtually filled the hut with his presence, and wherever the dark fell he seemed to be crammed into that too. At least it made her feel relatively cosy, knowing that what she couldn't see was friendly here.

'I'm . . . struggling with all this magical stuff,' she said into the silence that followed naturally from their updates. 'I feel like nothing I could do would make a jot of difference.'

'Yeah, and don't forget all your thoughts are subject to Jack's depression,' Thingamajig said. 'I can see I'm gonna have to keep saying that until we're all blue in the face here and forget who's what.'

'Mal,' Lila said, in an attempt to find a positive lead. 'Do you have any idea why we came here particularly, when we did and how we did?'

'Show him what you've got on underneath,' Zal drawled. 'It will have a bearing.'

The tiger raised its brows, a not uncomical gesture, lifting as it did an impressive array of eyebrow whiskers. Lila stuck her tongue out at him and lifted her foul T-shirt halfway up to show the slightly crazy looking hotpants and lower part of the corsetry that was her armour.

Malachi looked at it and then at Zal. 'Your doing.'

'Guilty.'

'Fuck me,' the imp said. 'That's a serious bit of kit. Must have cost you . . .' He fell sideways as Zal's foot connected surprisingly solidly with the end of a burning log and pushed him over.

'Right,' Malachi said, garbling slightly around his teeth which seemed to have grown in the last few seconds. 'Right. That, combined with the other thing, would probably equal some kind of very interesting non-coincidental activity. Who fenced you that armour, Zal?'

'I bought it at the store.'

'The Bathshebat outlet. Very interesting. I . . . can I see it again for a moment?'

Lila lifted the shirt, feeling like some kind of naughty schoolgirl caught wearing non-regulation clothes.

Malachi looked for a long time, then licked his whiskers and settled down on his chest, all tiger again. He put his head down between his paws and gave a long, laboured sigh. 'I knew I'd seen it before,' he said. 'All that fabric. The colours. The symbols. I don't know where the maker got hold of it but I bet it was some lucky find, some unexpected little windfall . . . oh a spare bolt of . . . look at this . . . rather interesting . . . who did you say gave it to you . . . must have had it in the back of the shop ages and forgot it . . .'

'Stop rambling!' the imp snapped. 'Cut to the chase.'

'I don't know how it got made into that,' Malachi said heavily, gouging the dirt around him with the tips of his two very singularly large sabre teeth. 'But that there material used to be Tatterdemalion's dress. I know it, because she was the only one who ever made magic fabrics, aside from The Three Themselves. And her personal magic was . . .'

'Tricky,' Zal said.

Malachi growled an assent. 'Answered your question. Now all that remains is to see how things turn.' He put a special emphasis on the last word. 'I don't doubt all our plans won't make a jot of difference, if that helps.'

'I don't want to just sit here in someone else's clothes waiting to die at the hour written in some storyline somewhere,' Lila blurted out suddenly. 'I'm not saying we don't all deserve it or anything like that, like I would've about Sorcha.' She paused and took a few deep breaths. 'I mean, not deserve like being bad and deserving it but just being here uninvited doing stuff that we don't have that much business doing. Although maybe we deserve it the other way too. That's not important. I can't just sit and wait for it. I can't.' She found herself rubbing her arms as if she was cold. Her fingers shot up her sleeves to find the point at which she became human, and it was so high now. 'Let's do something now and finish it one way or the other. I don't want to be here any more. I have to get back. I have things I have to do.'

She sounded desperate and at the same time Zal and Malachi moved to comfort her, Malachi stopping short as Zal leaned against her, his arm around her shoulders. The imp pushed a piece of burning wood a bit closer to her boots.

'That thing about another player. I get it, I was thinking,' she started, not entirely coherently. 'I was thinking who could be more powerful than Jack and it's obvious. The person who's free to come and go when nobody else is. His wife. She has to be free to make him anew. But that makes her stronger.'

Malachi growled unhappily. 'It crossed my mind. But the lock isn't her doing. It was a great decree, made by everyone. If she's the power, it's a useless thing beyond these borders.'

'What's needed to undo the lock?'

'I assumed it must be part of the process here,' Malachi said. 'Midnight on the solstice, Jack dies at the Twisting Stones and they turn to point in two directions, the past and future . . .'

'Okay, so we don't undo it,' Lila said. 'There are other ways. What say we pick it?'

'Lila, you're missing the obvious,' Malachi said and stared fixedly at her neck.

She put her hand up and found the necklace. 'I tried it,' she admitted. 'But nothing happens.'

'What d'you mean, you tried it?'

'I thought about it working but it didn't. I touched it and . . .' She felt stupid suddenly. 'That's not how it works anyway, is it?'

'It ain't the fuckin' ruby shoes,' Thingamajig agreed gloomily.

Lila got up suddenly, rubbing her hands on her T-shirt. She looked around them, at the floor, the walls, the roof. 'Okay, Jack,' she said. 'Come out, come out, wherever you are. I know you're in there somewhere. It's been nice pretending we're alone but I keep feeling something missing from this conversation.' As she did so she was aware of Malachi moving from relaxed to taut in less than half a second. But Zal wasn't affected, he sat with his arms around his drawn-up knees just waiting. The imp jumped to his feet and backed even further into the fire.

'I really don't think this is a good . . .' Malachi began with difficulty around his huge teeth.

'What?' she said angrily, stretching to her full height, chest out, shoulders back. 'What's not a good idea? Talking to the only person who can get us out of here? Trying to keep a secret when every word, hell, every thought is open to eavesdropping?!' She gestured wildly around at the room itself and then in the direction of Zal's head. 'Think we've got secrets? Think they're worth anything?' She turned around, her arms open wide. 'Come on Jack, come on everyone, join us. A few hours until sunset, a few more until midnight. Not like any of us have anything better to do!'

There was a pause at the end of her call, a long pause in which it seemed that nothing was going to happen and no answer come. Bit by bit Malachi began to relax, the imp settled down to his haunches. Zal kept looking at Lila, his expression one of quiet care. Lila remained in her pose of appeal. A hint of a smell like singeing lemon peel touched the air.

Then every surface and every edge began to flow and bleed light.

CHAPTER EIGHTEEN

The world turned upon every point where one thing met another, tumblers revolving until new contacts were made. The one point of stillness was the ticking seconds of passing time, regular in their ordinary pitches. Everything else sheared from its round. Lila saw this, but not with her eyes to which it appeared only as blurring light. She saw magic, and knew it to be perfect science, activated by an intent and forces that she had no command over. She saw Jack's will come into being, and the way that he made himself in that faery tradition, from the threads of almost nothing.

He was the new-made cave on the hillside that had always been there, the boy in the mouth of it standing to look at the sun falling over the lip of the world on the evening that was his first alone. He was the traces of self-doubt in his father, the pride of his mother, the hesitation and wonder of every man, woman and child in his village and their nervous and certain conviction that there was better, and could be, must be more than what they could see and hear with their ordinary bodies. He was the wind in the shutters and the falling snow that silenced, the frost that slayed silently in the dark, the strange pressure on the chest at night that wakes the sleeper in panic and steals their breath. The gasp of fear, the cold clutch of dread, the death that stalks and the one that sweeps in without warning, every notion that dogs the spirit, every fatal turn of the mind, there was Jack, watching the sun set on his own.

'The real question in this case is why I am named Giantkiller,' Jack said, the man's voice gone, and in its place only the boy, thin and grubby and resolute, defiant with his cracking vocal cords and his anger. 'We have fallen to particulars since the first day, imp.'

Only the fire remained the same. Now they stood in a large cavern.

Close by them Jack the boy stood, a sling hanging from his hand, ragged dark hair falling over his face. Behind him a little way off a shambling form, half bear and half man, stood on all fours, swaying side to side – Moguskul. Further back others suddenly crowded in to the edges of the light, small and tall, fat and thin, all shapes imaginable . . . the thousands that Jack had taken over the ages. They waited, as if Jack were now their only voice.

'You killed yerself,' the imp said immediately into the waiting moment. 'They meant to put all that fear in you and drive you to die in the winter, scapegoat, so's they didn't have to. But you were stronger. You killed yourself and you walked out free. Am I right?'

'And I slayed them all, though they lived on without harm,' he agreed, swinging the sling lightly. 'And they became the living dead. That is my question. That is my answer. It is my mystery. But only one who is truly alive can lift my burden here. And that isn't you, liar, cheater, coward. Is it?'

The imp shrank back down, his head hanging. 'No,' he said. 'Though I . . .' But under Jack's straight stare he simply repeated, 'No.'

'And you,' Jack turned suddenly to Zal. 'Shade of Ruinous Intent . . . do you know why the faeries call your kind that name? Shall I tell you?'

'I know,' Zal said, by contrast his voice as deep and powerful as a resonant drum. 'I found the spirits of the Ruined, in Zoomenon. They told the story. We are the result of a long-ago hate made real. But we are not hate.'

'Not *all* of you,' Jack said with wry satisfaction. 'I'll warrant you never met the ones that were. And the outcasts who died – those you speak of – will never tell you of what was made then, because they were killed before they could know it. Truly the sorry dream that spawned you ran its course and died a long time past. But did you never think there was anything more than your flawed races scattered throughout Alfheim, cursed and reviled, trying to live two lives, vampire and farmer at once, monster and monster-keeper? You were merely the weaklings that the makers let live, so that their opposition would think the entire effort a terrible failure, and never keep looking for the ones they succeeded in manufacturing. In time perhaps the remaining few who knew the truth have forgot it.' He shrugged, a hard and unsympathetic shedding of any vestige of compassion. His face became narrower, meaner. 'Forgetting is easy when it's assisted. We

229

faeries like to help. So, girl,' he turned to Lila, 'when you wondered what power my wife held and her doubt about what lies under us . . . you had the right. It would be wisdom to doubt the wisdom of using what you have there and unlocking the Faery Hoard and all its Halls.'

Zal was standing openmouthed. If Jack's hatred had affected him he showed no sign of it. He was entirely focused on a single thought. 'Wait. You're saying that the Shadowkin *weren't* the intended result of the experiment?'

'Look at you! Of course they weren't,' Jack scoffed, flinging his hair out of his eyes and coming forward to jab at the fire, poking the imp and smirking as it dodged among the embers. 'They were merely the abortions of it.'

Zal pondered a moment. 'How do you know?'

'It was of my time,' Jack said, hunkering down on to his heels. The rough clothes he wore were full of holes and coated in filth; dark and scarred skin showed through the gaps. There wasn't a piece of him that wasn't covered in fine dark purple lines of shining healed wounds. 'And in my time we walked your world as easily as our own. The others too.'

'And the successes are down there?' Lila asked, pointing at the floor. Zal's detachment from Jack's anger helped clear her head. Her chest ached, though she thought it was probably just the cold air.

Jack the boy looked up at her and grinned. 'I'd bet so. Though even the lovely Mad won't know for sure. When the lock was made we lost contact with all of Under, and over time we forgot most everything we knew. Like every other faery. And now nobody wants to know again in case the lesson's bad, though Faery's less than half of what it was and less than a fraction of what it could be. Undo the lock and who knows what'll come out? Who knows what we'll remember and then, what become? Maybe the mystery of the Queen's magic will at last be answered. Perhaps we shut the world down to save ourselves, as the cowards believe.' He glanced backwards in the direction of the clustered and silent groups of fey. 'Or maybe it'll all be revealed a silly game over nothing, a bet lost, a card trick whose forfeit was owned by the Hoodoo and couldn't be undone. Either is as likely. But the fact is that I don't care about the consequences. I'll have the lock undone and be free and anyone who stands before me be damned.' He looked at her with complete directness and then, with unmistakable meaning, back at those behind him. Then he turned to Zal,

'You might once have had a shot at me,' he said. 'But not now. You've lost your demon heart.'

Lila looked at Zal, waiting for the rebuttal, but instead she saw him look down and away. 'What?'

'I didn't like to say . . .' Thingamajig piped up from among the logs.

Lila kicked the fire and sent him sprawling across the bare rock amid a shower of cinders and sparks. 'What?' She looked questioningly at Zal who met her gaze with heavy lidded eyes.

'Tell her,' Jack suggested, grinning hugely. 'Tell her why we ain't brothers no more.'

'Since Sorcha . . .' Zal began with difficulty. 'Remember I told you I knew who was to blame?'

'But that . . .' Lila touched her chest, feeling the dense, silent weight of Tath start to stir. In fact as she turned her attention to him she found the most peculiar sensation of heaviness around her heart. It was almost choking.

He meant himself, Tath said and suddenly, with his speaking, an awareness of him flooded her. His agitation and fear were so palpable she staggered and fell on to her knees. *Lila, something is happening to me. Since we came here. I feel as if I am no longer able to stay here. I have to leave.*

Zal frowned, 'Are you all right? I didn't think it would . . .'

'It's not you,' she gasped, hand on her chest hard pressing, as if that would help. 'And it's not your fault . . . you said so . . . no demon would ever take the responsibility for it . . .'

'Saying and feeling ent the same,' the imp put in, backing away quickly on his bottom and feet among the ashes.

'Since then,' Zal said, continuing to stare at Lila with concern, moving closer to her. 'I feel like . . .'

'Like you want to die, in spite of all the demon fire inside you,' Jack said. His smile was wicked. 'And so the bad spirit enters in. Corrupted. So you won't be trading places with me or cutting my heart out on the cold, cold rocks of liberation now, will you?'

Zal stared at him with honest hatred. 'No.'

'Which brings us to what troubles our little girl here,' Jack said, looking at Lila and licking his lips softly. 'Our pretty little thing in her pretty tattered dress holding her heart out in her hands and asking us to love her love her . . .' He held his own hands out with a plaintive, pitiful look on his face, mocking her. 'Our girl with the unshakeable

231

imp who'd have us believe she's just two steps from freedom but always manages never to tell the useful thing that might let her take those steps, selfless little being that he is. How she loves to believe in all your innocence – even mine – as if we had good intent and that is all that mattered. Our tin soldier with the wall eyes. Come on, show us what you're hiding there . . .'

Malachi, who'd been silent and still throughout all of this, suddenly was on his feet, growling at Jack. His teeth flashed white, shining. Instantly Moguskul came barrelling forwards. Within a moment the two huge fey were tumbling around each other in a fight, close locked, huge jaws open, claws out.

Zal could only stare at Lila however, trying desperately to touch her, but able to do nothing at all, as in front of him she began to struggle for breath, clawing at her chest and throat. She fell forward on to one hand, mouth open, gagging for breath, eyes wide as the fire reflected perfectly in their mirror surfaces. Beneath the snarling of the beast fight her choking moments were all but lost.

Then Malachi broke free of Moguskul's grip and cowered, accepting a submissive position so he could watch and see Lila rather than try to keep fighting. The bear snarled over him but their conflict was suspended.

'What the hell is going on?' snapped the imp, his curiosity overcoming his worries. He danced forwards, peering at Lila. Then he looked at Jack.

The boy Jack was sitting with a smug smile on his face. He'd put down his sling and in one hand he held a small bowl, rough and ready, that looked like it had been beaten out of a single piece of metal by a smith in training. He was rubbing the inside of the bowl with his fingers and muttering under his breath, all the while looking at them with knowing amusement. All over his skin the hideous scars began to ooze tiny droplets of blood.

'What's that?' the imp demanded in a shriek. 'Your wife's bowl . . . ah . . . oh . . . you stole it from her . . .'

Jack stopped his work long enough to scowl and shout back at Thingamajig furiously, 'I did not steal it! It's mine. Was always mine!' Lila took a sudden breath. Then he abruptly remembered himself and started up again. He rubbed the blood off his exposed skin and began to smear it around the inside of the bowl.

'The cauldron . . .' Malachi said suddenly in his half-human voice, bleak and semi-strangled by his own beast shape. 'I thought no magic like that was left here.'

'I found it!' Jack gasped, laughing as he suddenly set the little bowl down on the fire and scooted backwards on his bottom like a real child. 'And though Mad says it must be hers I say it's mine now. Finders keepers.'

The bowl grew as soon as it started being heated by the flames. Within a minute it was over a metre across and filled with an opaque, thick liquid of uncertain colour that surged and rippled as if full of fish.

'Come on everyone!' Jack cried to those behind him, as if leading a game charge. 'Put your hearts into it. Don't you want to see what's been smuggled in here in this cheater's game? Come on, come on! First the discovery, then the forfeits!'

'Nuuuugh!' Lila thought she was dying. The pain in her chest became indescribably severe. She was aware of oxygen being dumped into her blood automatically by her skin but only because she didn't feel suffocation and the information was blasted into her awareness by the AI. Other than that the only thing she could feel was this rending agony, and heat.

What the hell? she said to Tath.

It is the time, he said. *I am not dead in this time.*

Through a red haze she saw a figure step out of the cauldron. It was a young diurnal elf, male and naked. The face with its chilly hauteur and fine, delicate bones, was unmistakable. It was Tath.

There was a sudden, sharp sensation of ripping, and then the pain was gone. The elf staggered one step and then straightened up, blinking in surprise and shivering with the cold, his long, near-white hair swinging around his shoulders. He gasped and clutched his arms about him, gripping his own body with sudden strength, an expression of wonder and pleasure evident on his face even as he backed away from Jack's crouched figure towards Lila and Zal.

'What the f . . .' the imp began, its mouth hanging open as wide as possible. Thingamajig turned to Lila, hands on hips. 'You had that in there all that time and I never even *knew*?' His mouth worked soundlessly for a time before more words managed to come out. 'Here I am trying to help you and you're keeping entire *people* from me? Right in front of me? Gods, my poor heart!' It clutched its own chest. 'I feel stabbed to the core! How could you? And while we're on the subject, actually, how could you?'

Lila held out Sarasilien's amulet.

'I thought that was junk,' the imp said, hugely disappointed. 'Hideous too, though a gentleman never says such things.'

Lila was busy ignoring him. She stripped off her T-shirt, which the fire had mostly dried now, and gave it quickly to Tath, who put it on backwards in his haste. It came down to his hips. He crouched down close to the fire, his hands held out in front of him towards the flames. He was staring at his own hands fixedly, jaw clenched as he inspected every finger, every nail with fascinated obsession. She stood, both hands pressed to her chest. She felt bereft, and confused, as if she'd had part of herself taken away. Her whole body felt lighter, and emptier. She stared at Tath with something like hunger and envy. She heard herself whisper a word under her breath so quietly nobody heard it, 'No-o-o.' Shock froze her in the moment.

'I notice *you're* not surprised,' the imp accused Zal, who was staring at Tath with a complicated expression that contained both rage and envy. Then he glanced at Lila and Thingamajig, started to say something but the imp was drowned out by the rising chatter and babble from the massed fairies beyond the firelight who had now seen what else Lila was wearing around her neck.

'The key, the key!' came the cry, rapidly whispered and called from thousands of mouths. And then, not long after there were other mutterings which Lila could just hear . . .

'It's Tatty's dress . . . look, it is . . . what's she doing with that . . .' And more like it.

Across the fireplace Jack was laughing. 'A hidden soldier and a stolen dress equals a hefty lie. All our deals are annulled. Hear my new offer, then!' He jumped to his feet, his limbs stiff with gleeful violent energies. 'One of you must find the courage to ask my question and take the consequences. One of you must surrender to join my gleaming throng. One of you must provide me with a worthy hunt. One of you must give up your heart's desire to me. For nothing less will I let you live until the midnight hour when that,' he pointed at the key, 'will be the sole object of my interest regardless of our former sport.'

'And if we say no?' Lila asked into the stillness that followed his declaration.

'Then you can die here and now and I will take the key and have no more trouble with you,' Jack said.

Malachi sidled around the fire, keeping himself between his

companions and the slavering bulk of Moguskul until he was with them. They turned to each other.

'He's impervious to iron. He took the charm of the Tinkywink . . .' the huge cat made a nod in the direction of the faery throng. 'Among countless other small but important powers.' He looked at Lila and she saw he'd read her thoughts accurately. She let the cold iron rounds slide back into the magazine silently. 'Much as I hate it, I have to suggest you agree to his deal. This way there's a chance to return later, to find new trades, to make new courses and tricks. Otherwise you will find yourselves fighting all the fey.'

'Might they turn against him?' Lila asked.

'They will not turn,' Jack called mockingly. 'Do you want to know why? But of course you do. They came as you will come, to ask my question. These here are the knights of old. Not all of them were up to the job. But they would risk it all for freedom. As more of them came, so the problem grew, for it was no longer my question. Every one of them that joined me in my fate bound to the land complicated the question with their own mystery.'

Lila watched Malachi during this speech, and saw his face furrowed deeply with lines as he thought. He kept staring at the symbols on her armour. 'One at least didn't ask,' he said. 'Tatterdemalion is not here. Nor those of us who were in exile from this place.'

She moved closer to Zal and found herself in his embrace, surrounded by him as if he were her shadow. At the fireside Tath examined his arms as if none of them existed, his gaze intent, teeth braced against chattering. His ears and feet had gone purplish blue with cold.

'And I never asked!' A new voice rang out, accompanied by a gunshot. A bullet streaked past Lila's head, struck the rock at Jack's feet, and ricocheted off the stone in a line that would have hit his leg except that something invisible encountered it and turned it to powder that fell on the ground in a silvery shower.

Jack's eyes narrowed. He stood straighter and puffed his chest out, a boy trying to look too much like a man and instead looking slightly ridiculous. 'Mad. How nice to see you. Friendly as always. I got your sprite,' and he produced a tiny glowing figure on his palm from nowhere, apparently. Then with almost the same movement he slammed his palms shut and ground them together until a dribble of glowing liquid came out of them and fell dark to the ice.

From the cave-mouth Lila watched a tall woman clad in heavy furs dismount from a wolf that was almost her own height at the shoulder. The creature growled with a rumble that made the entire cave resonate.

'Now, now,' the woman said lightly, reloading her gun as she came with the ease of old habits. 'Don't be petulant. You should be happy, with so many new things to play with.' She came slowly but surely towards Lila's side of the fire and took a moment to look them over, lingering on each one of them with her dark eyes to get their measure, Tath getting her longest assessment. She stopped beside Malachi, close enough to touch his massive beast form.

'Siding against me, Mad?' Jack asked, with a curl of his lip that made Lila want to laugh, it was such a teenage-boy expression.

'I am merely evening the odds,' she said. Her skin glowed like appleskin under a warm sun and the smell of lush, ripening sweetness spread out around her. Around their side of the fire the air began to warm up and dampen.

'You can't take their side,' Jack said with fierce importance. 'No cheating.'

'I will make sure things are fair,' she replied calmly, not paying him much attention. Lila saw Malachi lean slowly towards her, his red and orange eyes closing but she was too absorbed in trying to feel Zal's ephemeral warmth enclosing her to think about it.

'Alone at last,' Zal whispered to her.

Meanwhile Jack's wife took out some dried grass, sticks and fur from a fold of her clothes and began to make something out of it, her brown fingers bending and shaping expertly. Jack watched her with reluctant fascination, his face full of longing. At her feet Tath continued his compulsive self-touching, rubbing his face, stroking his ears, pulling at Lila's old shirt. He seemed utterly absorbed, so much so that everyone started when he suddenly unfolded and let his long pale hands fall to his sides.

'I will ask your question,' he said to Jack in a flat declaration, as though it was something he'd thought about for a very long time and had been waiting to say.

Lila felt she ought to say Are you sure? Are you crazy? But his presence was so set that she couldn't disrupt it. It would have been sacrilegious. A sense of falling came over her inside. 'I'll give . . .' She was about to offer herself for the hunt, confident she could at least spare one of the others from that, and have a chance to survive it but before she could finish Zal overrode her firmly.

'I will be the hunted.'

Malachi opened his eyes and stared at Jack with unequivocal hate. 'I will join your unwilling guests.'

'And you can have my heart's desire,' the imp piped from the fire at Tath's feet. 'For what it's worth, which ain't much let me tell ya. But have it if you must.'

'Wait a minute . . .' Lila began, feeling the moment slide away from her too late, too late. 'No.'

'Yes!' Jack said, his eyes alight with glee. 'Offers accepted.'

'Are you NUTS?' Lila turned on Zal and would have struck him if he were solid enough. Her hand smacked through his shoulder. 'What are you doing? I'd have a better chance than you. Surely . . .' Her voice cracked but Jack interrupted her.

'It is done. Your part in all this will be at my side along with my lovely wife, the fair and treacherous Madrigal and her puppet. You may see that all is dealt with fairly and we keep our word. All of us.' His dark eyes snapped back and forth, to the imp, Tath, Zal and Malachi. 'What a lucky woman you must be. In other times I might have paid you more attention to see such as these fall at your feet so readily. Even my wife's cat.' He cast a sly, winking look at Malachi who bared his teeth in return. 'There Madrigal, betrayed by your own for another. How does that feel?'

'Better than listening to more of your self-regarding cant,' Madrigal said drily and Lila saw Jack visibly wither for a moment, before checking himself and swelling with wrath once more. 'He is not my cat. Nor yours. Enjoy him while you may.' She took out a pipe and lit it, drew smoke a few times with an air of unconcern, and then held up the doll she had made – as big as her forearm – and blew the smoke into it. She repeated this a couple of times and then tapped out the unsmoked portion of the pipe into the fire. The imp flung himself into this, rolling around in the fume, and the doll gave what Lila recognised as the characteristic shiver of the Hoodoo and stood itself upright on her hand.

'A bargain made, a promise kept, no cheating and no weeping,' said the doll. 'Death shall be the forfeit to cheaters, rooks, swindlers, chisellers and scoundrels, with no pleading. What say you all to the terms?'

'I say wait a goddamned minute,' Lila said. 'What are the limits on these things? How long must Malachi stay? What is the end of the hunt?'

The doll spun to face Jack and made a movement like a shrug, 'For ever, and death I presume. Lest of course some other new circumstance comes along and changes things as change must.'

Jack nodded.

'No,' Lila said, barely aware of herself talking. 'This is crazy. This is the stupidest thing I ever came across. How can you all stand here and take part in it as if it made any sense? All we wanted was to come here and find someone to ask to get the damned moths back, that's all. And now it's guns at dawn or whatever, and you're all looking at me like I'm the one that's crazy and this is what happens every day and it doesn't, it doesn't ever happen as far as I'm concerned. Can't we talk about it? What does everyone have to suffer for . . .' She turned on Jack furiously. 'Because *you're* crazy and alone here. Just because of you! Why don't you let them go and just ask me nicely for the key instead of staging all this drama?'

Jack gazed at her with narrowed eyes, unwavering. 'And if I did ask you, and said I was to open all of Faery to the lowest vault of Under and let forth all that lingers there, known and unknown, would you give me the key?'

All the fey present turned as one to look at Lila and in their faces and bodies there was a terrible tension which she hardly had to be psychic to read as 'No,' although she didn't understand why it must be no, or why it couldn't be a good thing to undo the lock as he said. She hesitated, feeling stupid, and twisted up inside with anguish.

'Lila,' Zal said quietly, the warmth of him brushing her cheek gently. 'Can't you feel it? Maybe not. But this is how the aether works. Deals. Trades. When it's a big deal, it has to be all or nothing. He can't ask for the key, because it didn't come to him. Objects like that aren't like mundane objects in the material world. They are part of the structure of things in a much more important way here. If Jack wants to use it he must better it – that is, he has to steal it or bargain it away from the person it chose. It is a thing of power, and will go to the most powerful wielder. That's how it is. Hard to explain if you . . .'

'Yeah, I get it,' she said bitterly. 'If you haven't got a fucking clue. Here,' she pulled the necklace up off over her head and held it out to Zal. 'You take it.'

He looked at her with misgiving and sadness, took it from her and closed his hand on it. Immediately she felt it at her neck again, put her hand there and touched it. She looked at him for a long moment.

'How I hate you for knowing it all and being right,' she said. 'Why did you take my place?'

'Jack's right,' Zal said easily. 'I've lost my demon self, blaming Tath, then myself. The hunt will be good for me. If I lose it'll be because I don't want to live enough any more. It's fitting. Now we're here I feel like I was always coming here, ever since it happened . . . since she died.' He seemed perfectly calm about it.

'But you're talking about *dying*!' she said, voice cracking. She looked around but nobody else seemed to think it strange. They were just watching her. She stretched her hands out but she couldn't feel anything of him at all, even when she should see herself touching him. 'You can't . . .'

Zal's face hardened, to her surprise. 'I have.' He stepped back and his eyes were powerful, warning her. 'You will be our judge to see it's fair. We all chose. It was nothing to do with you.' He stepped away once more and she felt her heart break absolutely in pieces but at the same moment she knew she had to agree, or she'd be making all of them into fools and weakening every chance they had. So she let her face freeze and stood back and upright and nodded.

'As you say,' she said stiffly, turning away from him and to the doll on Madrigal's hand. 'We agree to the terms,' she said.

'Aye,' Jack said almost immediately and much louder. 'And I too.'

'Agreed!' the doll shrieked in its caustic, creaking voice. 'Then begin!'

CHAPTER NINETEEN

Jack clapped his hands and summoned Moguskul with a jerk of one arm. 'You,' he pointed at Zal. 'All you must do to best me is remain alive until midnight. I will give you an hour head start. Run.'

Zal glanced at Malachi and they shared the briefest of nods, through which Lila clearly saw them acknowledge one another and say farewell. Then the shadow elf looked down at the imp, 'I'd like to know what your story is, but it will have to keep. Don't fail this time.'

'I know, I know!' Thingamajig whined. 'I got the memo. Don't deal with the faeries. Don't welch on the terms. See you in Hell.'

Lila watched Zal turn to Tath. His body was already poised for flight, full of a restless, fierce energy that he held in check as they faced each other. 'Ilya. You chose Lila. I would have done the same.' Tath looked slightly startled, unable to stop shivering as the ghostly Zal embraced him once. 'Goodbye.' Then he turned, 'Lila . . .'

'Don't you goodbye me, you son of a bitch.'

'Never,' he said and winked at her though she could see it cost him to do it, and it had never cost him before. He stretched out his lilac shade fingers, their two-dimensional edges glimmering with black, and touched the fine line close to her neck where the slick black of the machine crept slowly ever upwards, his eyes fixed on the point. 'Cold iron, girl. Don't be afraid.'

'Fuck you!' she said honestly, her eyes filling with hot tears she couldn't have stopped for anything at that moment. She struck out at him weakly, uselessly, her fist falling short of him, opening into fingers that brushed through his blacklight body and felt only the vibration caught by the machine.

Zal smiled at her, warm and real and then before she had time to react he was running, up over the fire, past Jack – giving him a semi-solid clout on the shoulder that flung him half around – past the faeries cheering him where they massed in the cave-mouth and out into the snow.

'Excellent,' Jack said. 'Now you, Cat. Step across. Don't be shy.'

Malachi got up and stood on two legs. He looked at Madrigal and she looked back at him. Then he walked to Lila and stood before her, taller than she was but so much bigger and uglier than he had ever been. He smelled strongly of cat and his head was massive with his huge, disproportionate teeth hanging just over her head. His voice was soft as a whisper. 'The elf is right. Don't make despair your path. If you do, then all is for nothing. Whatever happens.'

'Are you going to tell me not to be afraid?' she asked him coolly, aware that she was being cruel now, not caring.

He licked his teeth to make it possible for him to keep talking without dragging his lips. 'Will you say goodbye?'

'No,' she said and put her arms around his strange body, burying her face in his thick fur until the bones of his ribs pressed against her cheek. She felt him sigh.

'Sometimes it is wiser to let go,' he said.

'But I don't,' she replied, clinging on fiercely. She felt him pat her back with one massive paw; it was a consoling gesture that forgave her. She knew she was wrong but she couldn't bear it. 'I won't.'

At that instant she felt the imp leap up on to her arm and crawl to her shoulder, cowering there. Malachi let go, and she released him. He turned without another word and slumped down to all fours, shaking his head gently before glancing at Tath. 'I would know your story too, one day. But not as one of the host, I hope.'

'You shall not,' Tath said in that icily calm way as if he was in a slightly different world to the rest of them, where he was untouchable. He didn't look at Malachi, only at Jack, with an unwavering gaze. His body continued to shiver but it didn't seem to bother him at all.

Malachi moved to Tath and pressed something into his hand from one paw, looking into the elf's eyes as he did so. 'Eat it,' he mouthed, out of Jack's sight and then without a glance to any more others he walked around the fire in his slow, cat prowl and passed Jack, tail twitching back and forth in its own thick cloud of glittering darkness. Lila watched him until he had joined the faeries by the entrance. They parted to receive him and he vanished into their crowding thousands and she lost sight of him though she didn't actually see him shrink or change form into one of the faceless figures that moved so restlessly, never quite coming into focus as if Jack hadn't only taken their powers but even their faces.

He didn't seem to have noticed Malachi's transfer and although Lila looked for what she thought had been a peach Tath had made it disappear.

Jack swaggered. 'Now, imp. If you please, I'll take your offering. Our elven knight here must wait the appropriate hour to take his turn at us, but I'll not wait for the rest.'

Thingamajig clung to Lila's shoulder armour, shaking slightly, his flames orange but low. 'As I have promised, so shall it be,' he said. 'I hope it is a lesson well learned when it shows its fruits,' and he glanced at Madrigal who nodded slowly as if she knew his meaning. She moved across to Lila with slow, gentle steps, as if she were a surgeon approaching a dangerous patient, and extended the arm that held the doll towards the imp.

'What is it?' Lila whispered to Thingamajig, but he wasn't paying attention to her. He moved to stand facing the doll – they were almost the same size – and composed himself in a position of prayer. Slowly, gently he took several deep breaths, his tiny eyes closed. In front of him his hands moved with a fluid grace Lila had never seen in him before, as if they were slowly pulling and shaping some kind of soft and gooey substance. After a few moments a light began to gleam between his claws. He worked it a little while longer as everyone looked on in silence, and then he held out his two hands to the doll, the light between his palms.

'Don't drop it on the way over,' the imp said, attempting to be bright while looking at the light with an expression of intense pain and sadness that mirrored and intensified what Lila herself was already feeling. She put her fingers up quickly to where he sat and touched the scrawny shape of his foot. His tail swirled and coiled around her thumb compulsively for a moment and she felt the heatless flicker of his fire on her hand.

'I will not,' the doll said with uncharacteristic solemnity as it took the light into its body.

Madrigal moved it away from them and began to walk around the fire to Jack. As she went Lila felt the imp shudder and shake so hard that his bones seemed to rattle and then she felt the shivering pass away and a lightness come in its place. He sighed and sat still like a kitten as the doll transferred its light into Jack's waiting hands. There was a moment as Jack regarded the light, and then the doll nodded and it passed through his hands and vanished. They all saw the boy-shaped fey stand square, looking inward, his empty hands spread out as he discovered what it was that he'd bought. All of them waited, breathless, except the imp himself, who suddenly sighed and relaxed and then, as Jack's face started to come back up, looking dark, eyebrows in a scowl, started to chuckle.

'I did warn you,' he said, sounding a lot less whiny than he used to. 'I guess you don't pay too much attention to demon stories down here in the sublime nether. What a thing to take from an imp.'

'Rrraaaaghghhh!' Jack's voice exploded suddenly in a fury that could have come from a true giant and not a gangly boy. 'You tricked me!'

'Did not!' the imp folded his arms. He was still shaky, but only Lila could feel it.

'False accusation requires reclamation,' the doll snapped, overridden by Madrigal saying smoothly, 'Don't take on, dear. You asked for it.'

'But what is it?' Lila asked through her tears.

Tath half turned towards her and spared her a single glance. His long mouth twitched with amusement. 'An imp is a demon who has played themselves false. They are the shame of the race. Surely their heart's desire must be that the shame and their true identity must never be discovered. What else would hold them in such a base form, lost even to themselves?'

Lila blinked in confusion, tears falling down her face. Jack snarled and kicked at the fire, scattering it all over and stamping on the embers.

Madrigal came back and leaned close to Lila, 'Your elf is right. Jack has taken the desire, but it hasn't become his. The trouble is of course, that instead of gaining a weapon to use against the imp or yourself he has freed the creature from its impossible burden.'

'Yeah, more or less right,' Thingamajig chortled, holding his round belly and slapping it to add some extra feeling to his mirth. 'Oooh, hah! I feel better already. Although,' he hesitated, 'now I suppose I'll have to find out the truth . . . not so great . . .' He sat down and curled his tail around Lila's neck. 'Anyway, it was a useless thing to get as a sneaky trade and that's the main point! Ha ha. Top Trumps, you bastard!' He shook his fist at Jack and then said to her with feeling, 'Just think what'd've happened if *you'd* opened your big gob on this one.'

Lila wasn't sure if she ought to commend him on his bravery or demand an explanation, but she was distracted by Jack's fury and by the sound coming from the cave-mouth where the gathered host seemed, by all accounts, to be laughing.

'You will not ridicule me!' Jack screamed suddenly, turning on them, and then back to Lila.

'Too late, mate,' the imp sniffed, wiping its eyes with the back of one hand. 'I hope I remember it was worth it when I find out whatever it is I have to find out.'

Jack's face twisted with fury. 'You'll be sorry you tricked me!' He glared at Lila. 'I blame you. Where did you get that armour? How could you have it? She's lost Under. Has been for almost eternity.'

Lila didn't say anything, she didn't know the answer he wanted. 'I didn't do anything,' she said.

'You . . . !' he began but the Hoodoo doll shivered and he went silent suddenly and turned to it and bowed very formally.

'What a sore loser,' the imp said, highly satisfied.

'Come,' Madrigal said to Lila and Tath, 'let's go eat and rest until the hunt begins.'

'Yes, yes,' Jack said spitefully. 'Go and enjoy your final moments of delusion.'

They left, Lila going back for Tath when he showed no sign of leaving, taking his arm and leading him with them out of the cave in Madrigal's wake. Jack and his legion went elsewhere. Madrigal created a glade of summer on the side of the hill and Lila sat there, with Tath, in the hot sunlight, stunned and silent.

A few minutes after the last person had left a figure detached itself from the icy darkness of the stalactites in the cave roof and opened its wings to drop in a steep dive to the floor. Teazle kicked about in the ashes for a minute or so and then bent down and picked up a small object. He dusted off the little metal bowl and examined it in the effulgent light of his own eyes.

'I see you've found my thimble,' said a figure appearing at his side.

He looked up and held out the bowl.

'Thank you,' said the woman, taking it and polishing it up with the hem of her dress. She put it away in a pouch at her belt and folded her hands over her big, pregnant belly, looking at Teazle with a wry expression. 'Careless of me to leave it lying around.'

'Very,' he replied, staring with unrepentant curiosity. He'd never seen one of the Others so close before. He wasn't sure if she was a goddess or not. She seemed extremely subtle for one of those.

'Do you know Lila's fate?'

'Rather ask about that than your own?' She was mildly surprised.

'I prefer to imagine my own is my own business,' he said and saw her conceal a laugh behind her hand. He joined her in it.

'Well, I don't know now,' she said. 'And if I did, I doubt I should tell you. It isn't much fun to race to the end of some stories without seeing them all the way through. I take it you are planning to make a dramatic entrance when least expected?'

'Something like that,' Teazle said. She really was quite plain, he thought, and her clothing was nothing to write home about either. She seemed ordinary, especially compared to the way Zal had talked about her. He guessed he just wasn't able to see her properly at all.

'Good. I like drama.' The faery picked up her skirts and turned gently on the spot as if practising a dance step. Before she had finished she was gone and Teazle stood alone in the cave thinking up much more useful questions about destiny that he never got to ask but he soon lost interest. He loved only the present moment. It was this that had caused him to want to stick around Lila. The present could be very dull when nothing much in it changed day to day, but she was a recipe of change that had a way to run, a very unusual recipe, and he could not have stayed away. Why she should accept him he assumed was out of another kind of curiosity or perhaps a brand of fear. Her motive wasn't important. She treated him as if he mattered in some way, and that was good enough. He knew that Zal meant something to her, whereas he didn't. He wasn't sure what that meaning was and was vaguely troubled that it was a bad meaning that shouldn't be encouraged, like security, and safety, and status, though he sympathised with the last one. Other attractions the elf posed were obvious, if not to Teazle's taste. He would have liked to spend more time with Lila for himself. He would have liked to have sex with her, at least once, because he had no experience of humans, and she was once again, a curiosity, but he had never had the opportunity. He was intrigued by her willingness to have him around when she so clearly didn't really want him. He wasn't certain this was a piece of good character. It seemed more like the reverse. Her bad traits pleased him. She seemed, superficially, to be quite weak that way, but the more he saw her in action, the more he became convinced that it was the weakness that was superficial, clung to like an excuse, and there was grit underneath it or perhaps even savagery. He couldn't help being vaguely worried by the prospect of her change. What would the machinery do? He hoped it didn't alter her substantially. For her to settle down and become something specific would be a great disappointment.

Meanwhile he was happy, very happy, to be involved in so much important action. He was sorry to see Zal run. He doubted that Zal would make it. Once the nerves went, things were never the same. He couldn't imagine feeling a loss so badly he would want to make himself unhappy or even dead over it. He would miss Lila though. She was the only one he would miss, out of everything in creation he had ever seen or met, he thought. How odd. The feeling he was having was heavy and disagreeable as he thought on this, so he stopped thinking about it and went to the cave-mouth where it had begun to snow, a thick, wet snow that fell like globs of soggy paper.

Malachi's sparkly darkness still covered him reasonably well, and he had discovered that although it was possible to teleport here he didn't need to because he was able to travel incredibly fast without it, almost at the speed of light. Probably some dreary equation that the scientists knew would explain that the almost part was due to an amount of matter that had to be fiddled. He didn't care about that either. At last he turned his mind to the object of his real interest and felt his blood quiver and start to race.

Soon, very soon, his unique prey would start to run and he would be after it.

He moved silently and stealthily across the hillsides, ignoring Madrigal's warm enclave and took a position far from Jack's palace but vaguely in the direction Zal had gone, where he sat down to wait.

'Tath,' Lila said experimentally after some time had passed.

'You should call me Ilya,' he said. 'My friends did.'

'Ilya,' she said, though it felt unnatural, not like him. 'How did you . . . I mean, are you really alive?'

They were sitting in the summer glade, entirely surrounded by mature trees and thick undergrowth which completely shielded them from any trace of Jack's winter.

'I was never dead,' he said. He lay down flat and stared at Madrigal's impossible blue sky. 'I lived in your body and I live now in this one. It is not quite the same as the old one. This one is young, of the same age I was in Alfheim at the time Jack was bound to the lock, before I met Arie, before I knew Zal or anything about him, or the White Flower, before I was a necromancer.' He took a deep breath and let it out, his flat chest getting flatter, almost concave. That he was naked from the waist down didn't seem to bother him in the slightest. He lay with his hands resting on his belly and stared upward, quite relaxed. She imagined him with his dog companion, the one he'd talked of once, the one she'd seen when she was in his memories. She remembered Teazle saying, 'I'll be your dog,' to her. She felt her heart creak, like an old ship.

He seemed so peaceful she hated to disturb him but she was conscious of every second and every cell slipping away from her. She didn't have enough mercy left. Steaming slightly as her armour finished drying, she ventured quietly, 'Will it last?'

'It is as real as any material thing,' he said. 'And it is mine. Nothing lasts, least of all these things. So yes, and no of course. I could walk out of here, in theory, as long as I returned to our present.' His voice was singsong, as though he couldn't care less, and was only humouring her. 'But it will only last until midnight or when I finish my bargain with Jack.'

'What happens then?'

He shrugged. 'I ask my question. Jack then must kill me or die.'

'I thought you'd join the . . . others.' She was suddenly hurt again, to think of this, when she thought there was no more room for surprises.

'The lock will turn,' Tath said. 'This time I am sure of it. So the charm that has trapped them will no longer work for me.'

She didn't know what to say, and anyway, her throat hurt too much and was too full to speak. She lay down instead and adjusted the apertures of her eyes until she could stare at the endless blue without hurt too. Behind them somewhere the imp snored in the long grass. Finally, after a time of quiet she said, 'You all knew, didn't you? When you made those bargains.'

'I expect so,' Tath said – she could not think of him as Ilya, even if it was his friendlier name.

'Why? What'dya do it for?'

'Why were you going to?'

She paused, breathing the soft air slowly. 'I thought I could win,' she said at last.

'And if you did not win?'

'Then I would have done my bit. Except,' she hesitated and then pushed on even though it sounded ridiculous to her, quite arrogant, 'I would.'

The elf didn't reply. She felt abruptly so alone that it was unbearable. To take her mind off it she did the only thing she'd ever done to take her mind off unpleasant things, and began to run a lengthy health check, the kind she used to do when everything was new and didn't work so well. She got out her medical kit from the storage compartments inside her thigh and saw with disbelief that on the tube of immunosuppressant gel that was there to prevent her becoming allergic to the synthetic skin the date had expired some months ago. Forgetting the rest of it she searched for a mirror, but she didn't have one. She sat and felt with her fingertips for the line above her collar where the creeping growth of the machine met her only remaining natural flesh. Of the parts beneath the armour, and inside her, she didn't want such detail. They remained as numbers shifting in a countdown to zero.

It was remarkable, she thought, that she didn't feel the change. There ought to be something, a tickle, a chill, a pain, surely. But whatever was replacing her biology did so with perfected mimicry. There was no loss of function, and so there was no sensation to have.

She felt the line, saw it as much as felt it, just beneath her jaw and ears. She wondered if it would take all her hair too and what would happen after.

'Come here,' said the elf. His eyes were closed now. The arm closest to her moved outward.

She went and lay next to him, put her arms round his skinny, tall body and her head on his chest. She heard his elf heart going tha-thump at its too fast speed, more a whisper than a drum. His arm closed around her shoulders. She clung to him.

'I can't, I can't, I can't,' she repeated softly, her eyes tightly shut, tears squeezing out between her lashes. They ran from her nose. She was so tight and rigid she felt as if she were made of steel but for all her holding inside, she couldn't keep a grip. Her whole body shook with the effort. 'I don't know what to do.'

'It's all right,' he said, making an effort to say it the human way, his hand strong on her shoulder but his voice gentle and calm like the sky. 'It's all right.'

He kept repeating it often, and his hold eventually loosened and then became slack and then stroking and his voice just a murmur. The light faded, the sun went down and night came.

She woke and saw stars overhead, not a few, but billions upon billions. Then her eyes adjusted.

Tath was still with her, but over them stood the tall, rounded silhouette of Madrigal, gun in her hand.

'Come,' she said. 'It's time.'

CHAPTER TWENTY

Lila got up and reached down and gave Tath her hand. He got to his feet easily. Where they were was warm and the night full of the sound of chirping insects, but Madrigal still wore her heavy furs. She threw a pack down at Tath's feet.

'You will need these.'

He didn't say anything, just opened it up and got dressed. He tucked her T-shirt into thick cloth trousers, the trousers into fur boots. Over the top went more fur, a stiff jacket that belted over both shoulders and at the waist. There was a hood but he ignored it.

At her belt Madrigal's Hoodoo doll glowed with its own faint witchlight from every chink and cranny in its twisted grass. The faery herself shone slightly, providing enough light to see by.

Lila took off her amulet and handed it to Tath as he straightened up, 'It's yours really.'

He pulled his long hair back in both hands and used the cord to tie it, fixing the charm tightly in place. 'Thank you.'

As soon as he was done Madrigal led the way downhill through a narrow gap between her massive trees until at last they came out on to the acres of white snow that covered all of Jack's land. Where the cave and the city had been there was no trace of anything. The lake was clearly visible, frozen over, as a large patch of complete flatness, unmarked, spanning the valley they stood in from side to side. They were at its head, and a short distance away the host of the faeries that belonged to Jack were gathered en masse, Moguskul visible as a gigantic bear at the head of their ragged lines. A bitter, thin kind of wind blew among them. Without exception from the tiny to the giant they were all dressed as Madrigal was, in thick, ugly clothing hastily made from crude materials; refugees in an inhospitable land. By comparison to the finery of other faery things this spoke most cleanly of their intention not to linger, no matter how long they were forced to do so. Their indistinct faces turned to watch Lila and Tath pass by.

Beside Moguskul stood a snow-glass, as tall as Lila, its huge inverted bowl almost run empty as it counted the minutes. They stopped before it as the final few flakes fell slowly down. Then the wind got up, quite suddenly, and whipped around them, snatching up great sloughs of snow and building the figure of a tall, powerful man where the glass had been. Frost crackled around it and from the shower of glittering particles stepped Jack Giantkiller, his body built of powder and rime to give the illusion of a massive man clad in white furs with moustaches and beard and heavy hair braided down and hung with beads of ice. He had two axes at his belt and a bow in his hands, taller even than he was, its single curve glacier blue and shining.

With a forward sweep of his arm he made a commanding strike and in answer the bear Moguskul roared – a sound of ferociousness, and agony. He reared up on his hind legs, jaws open, and split into a hundred different forms. Hounds spilled out of him and poured along the ground. Falcons burst from his head, and crows. As they scattered the bear was gone, to the sky, to the chase. A hound gave voice, then another and another. Jack stared at Lila once, a hard look, then his dogs began to run and he whirled to follow.

Madrigal whistled her wolf and leapt to its huge back. She set out after him. Lila and Tath began to run. Thousands of faery voices shrieked and sang after them.

'No matter where you run or where the path bends, the Twisting Stones by midnight is where it will end!'

She guessed that explained why they didn't follow but it was of little interest to her. She ran alongside Madrigal's wolf, and Tath ran with her, at the limit of his ability. It was easy for Lila. Nothing hurt, nothing was difficult, she needed no more breath than usual. Her body flowed in seamless action, with endless power. Soon Tath was exhausted and he tapped her once on the arm, unable to speak, before he quit. They left him standing on the far lakeshore, panting, his hands on his knees, bent double. Lila photographed him as she left him behind. She kept the feeling of his touch on her arm, resonating in her nerves as if he were still there, and her feet never missed their place on the rough and dangerous ground.

*

251

Zal knew a lot about hunting at night, though he'd usually been on the other end of things. He knew in this case it would be pointless to think that there was a hope of escape. Nothing in his experience of the aether's paths led him to believe he could outwit Jack on his own ground. But if the catch was foregone, nothing else was, not what came before it and not what came after. So from the moment he jumped over the fire he'd already decided to take Jack for as much of a ride as he could manage.

The rest of what had happened back in the cave didn't hurt until he'd crossed the lake, his shadow feet making no marks. He hadn't given a thought to why he could make himself solid enough to strike Jack, but not enough to touch Lila. He didn't think about it now as he searched for possible tracks, over rocks, around boulders, into the trees and then up into the rough canopy of brittle branches. But he felt it – a catch in his chest that didn't let his breath run true. He was glad Teazle hadn't been there to hear his reasons for running and that made heat flare in his chest and he tried to run faster, missed his footing, tripped, fell, went flying and crashing through several layers of branches until he caught himself by the hands. Only his ultra light form prevented him from being seriously hurt. He hung there, panting, then pulled up on to the tree and changed direction, taking courses that looped back on themselves, went up, down, through deep drifts and rocky canyons.

It was very hard, and soon, even before half an hour was out, his pace had tired him. Easy living had taken a toll on him, he realised. He was not the fit and tough presence that had come to Daemonia the first time, fuelled by rage and hate and the burning ache of betrayals, the passion and idealism that had pitched him headfirst into a stinking canal full of imps and degradation for Adai to save and bring to life. But then of course, he was saved, fixed, sorted. He'd believed his own press release.

Pain made him slow down, though he fought against it with every-thing he had. His muscles burned, his chest was agonising with the rasp and claw of the icy air. Semi-solid, he clawed his way through impos-sible gaps in rocks and underneath thick vegetation, cutting and bruising himself. He shed the bow and his arrows, everything that weighed him down but it still wasn't enough. At the base of his spine a tickling, prickling sensation told him it was past time. Jack was coming. He redoubled his efforts and flung himself forwards until he came to a cliff-face and went over, head over heels down a huge scree. He slid and tumbled to another drop-off, shocked into a moment of paralysis as he clutched at the edge and saw the rock through his own fingers. Beneath him a long fall awaited – he didn't even know what was at the bottom. He couldn't breathe because the fall had banged the air out of him and he was left with the aching shock and a clutching in his throat as his heart hammered and his vision blurred. His grip felt like it would not last long.

Stupid, he thought, and then other thoughts that had been dammed up a long time spun uncontrollably after: yes, it was a stupid fall, but that was no surprise surely, because he had been looking for it, waiting for it, for a long, long time and naturally here it was at last, just as he'd said to Lila in the cave.

What the rock-star lifestyle and denial hadn't softened, love had. Sorcha, Lila, they mattered, and he wasn't free as he used to be. He resented them for that.

Hadn't he, even when they were sailing on that fated airship with its treacherous crew, been glad of the fighting, the risks? He'd known quite clearly that they could be eliminated there by some chance that was purely accidental, and if they were then he'd be liberated. And he could feel what that would be like and it would be good. For what use was a warrior when he was prisoner? No use. Weak. Anyone could have leverage against him. The savagery of the violence that followed had been born from his anger.

But even before that, he'd sold himself, hadn't he? It had happened in that moment when what was now clear in his thoughts had been born as a feeling. It had occurred to him that his desire to be free – and safe, yes, let's say safe, Zal, because when you have nothing to lose you cannot be bought and nothing holds you, so safe from what you fear most, Zal, which is to lose what you love. You'd solved this problem very neatly before, by not loving at all until you met Sorcha. Elves are commonly coldhearted, who knew? Then you'd solved it by denial when you married Adai and pretended it was all a wedding of convenience, rushing straight off to Otopia and leaving her with the Ahrimani, thinking yourself a bit of a hero. And finally you'd solved it with a stroke of genius, when Lila came along, by pretending that you had grown nerves of steel and a will of iron in the interim (since you became a demon and abandoned your entire race and land in a massive first strike rejection) and anyway, she was safety itself because nobody could get her, surely, and she was a pushover, desperate for love, so you were at no risk of rejection or loss. Lila was bulletproof and you could love her without a twinge of fear, except that suddenly she's been targeted by every freak in the city and you realise one of them only has to get lucky once.

Yes, your intent in that heady afternoon, two days ago aboard the airship, had been not to save and protect them, Sorcha and Lila, but to proxily kill them, and with them destroy your growing sense of weakness . . . ah, it was *that*, and not your sister's death, which has slaughtered your abilities now and left you hanging off this ledge, and which led you to take Lila's place in the hunt. You had longed for Jack to follow, so that you could prove to yourself that you'd done your best, run the gauntlet, faced the worst and then failed through no fault of your own. You'd fall at his mercy and have him execute justice upon you, because you could not bear to do it for yourself. And Jack saw it. In one second. And you lied. And then you ran.

All this passed through his mind in a second as he hung on the edge of the fall. He knew that all he had to do was let go and it would be over. He would be free, as he wanted, as he had planned; even Jack would not get to finish him. He would choose it for himself, the honourable demon solution to a moment's mistake in which he had discovered himself vulnerable and sought to run away, letting Sorcha pay with her life. Nothing in the world could be easier than letting go. His fingers hurt even holding his slight weight, his nails were starting to crack. The rock was slippery, its purchase pathetic so that if he hadn't been shadow he'd already be dead. His forearm burned and began to weaken. He stared at the rock. An image of the imp played across his mind and then, from the extreme distance, carried by the following wind, he heard the sound of hounds baying. The sound was gleeful, delighted, excited and looking for his death.

A fierce anger overcame him. He swung his free arm once, twice, and caught hold of the rock's edge with two more fingers. There was no easy way up. The overhang was blunt, but it offered a small crack for a foothold. The pain in his arms only made him more determined, even as he felt them failing. He kicked up and jammed his boot into the toehold, ignoring the pain. The slight easing of the weight on his arms and the change of position was just enough to let him get a better handhold on the top of the rock. After that it was relatively easy to climb up and over. He lay on the boulder's edge, feeling the wind buffet him and the shocking burn of his tendons, the ache of his foot, the spite in his heart, and smiled.

He gave himself twenty seconds, and then he was up and running again, along the ledge, along the cliff, across the icy rocks and hills, back into the woods . . .

The hounds of Moguskul tracked by means Lila couldn't detect. It wasn't smell, for as a shadow creature Zal had lost his. She had no description or adequate explanation for what form he was now. Immaterial was too little, and material too much. As she kept pace with Madrigal through the trees of the winter woodlands, Lila was reminded of the information the researcher had attempted to pass on – and she realised how ignorant and how limited the human comprehension of aether really was. Tonight's drama at a deep level of aetheric involvement only proved something that had been building a long time in her mind; aether was mixed up with consciousness, with mind, and spirit. It was the stuff of these things and it flirted with matter in different ways in different regions. Time and space were only two of the expansions. She was now racing through a third, whose name she didn't know, which was intimately connected to those others and which would never be undone from them. Before the Bomb, that was when this region was closed to humans and the gross matter of her realities. After the Bomb, things had opened, but nothing was there now that hadn't been there before. She wanted to rush back and conduct tests, experiments, find volunteers, discover the truth.

She held that in her mind as she wove between the trunks, ducked boughs and burst through thickets, cutting swathes where she could not move freely or jumping in huge, gazelle like bounds over logs and streams that were so similar to the ones she knew from home, but were essentially different because these were features of Jack himself. The land, the forest, everything in it was an expression of the faery's nature. He hunted through himself for sport alone. Of course he knew where Zal was. Even the dogs and the birds were just for show. It was a cruel game, and the more strange dales and bizarre formations the trail led them through the more she understood the lie of the land. Here things were both exactly what they seemed and not at all as they appeared.

Try as she might she could see no way to turn that to their advantage. Suddenly ahead of them there was yelping and cries. They were brought up short, the wolf making a brute turn that unseated Madrigal and sent her flying to the hardpacked snow at the foot of some boulders. Lila transformed her forward momentum into an upward and slightly backward leap, activating her jets to keep her aloft as she looked over the edge of an enormous, concealed drop where two hounds were still falling over and over down into the darkness below. Those that were left barked excitedly and fussed over some ground where traces of blood were marked on the ice. Jack bent down and traced these almost lovingly. He brought his hand to his mouth and licked the tips of his fingers, then threw his head back and howled in a blood-curdling crescendo that made the ground vibrate. Ice fell from the trees in the aftermath and the hounds went into a frenzy, boiling over themselves until one of them found the trail and went galloping off into the night.

Madrigal cursed Jack profusely as she recovered herself. He ignored her and let the dogs run for a moment, before setting off himself. He was unnaturally fast, of course, and nothing got in his way even though he huffed and puffed like the big man he was pretending to be. The blood was not much, Lila thought as she bent to examine it. Minor. She tracked back over the rocks, following the marks more carefully than the dogs had, and found the place at the edge where Zal had hung. The exact size and shape of the tiny spots, the skin cells left on the edge, the taste of it all – she pictured him dangling there and knew it was no feint.

At the bottom of the ravine the two unlucky hounds were dead. Already their bodies were decomposing and falling apart into tiny whirls of shining ash that were spun away on the wind. To rejoin the rest of Moguskul, she assumed, or simply returning to the greater aether out of which he had summoned them. It didn't matter. The only deaths here that would be true were their own, not the faeries'.

Lila straightened and narrowed her eyes against the wind. Zal had had the chance to die here, she was sure of it. But he hadn't taken it.

She put on a concentrated burst of speed to catch up with the rest of the hunt, and for the next hour in the Spartan trail of bloody drops, bent twigs and curiously melted footprints, she read the increasing rise of his anger and fire. By the time they took the westerly turn she had anticipated, back towards the Twisting Stones, smoke was rising from bushes and trunks that were blackened in his wake. As time grew short he gave up on any effort to conceal his tracks and instead they found branches lit like torches, blazing to show the way. Zal's contempt wasn't lost on Jack, whose howls now transformed from the smug lust of victory to seething rage. He began to storm among the hounds, forgetting them entirely in his haste. As they fell back Lila found a brindle wolf running alongside her, its tongue lolling out of its mouth.

'Thank you,' it said to her, before falling behind. As it peeled away from the main line and diverted into the deeper woods all the hounds and the birds in the sky abruptly spun to follow. She stopped to watch them arrow down on Moguskul's spirit form, vanishing into the grey and white canopy of the frozen trees. The quiet was eerie in the absence of their voices.

This time she took to the sky to regain her lost ground. She barely felt the cold, though she knew it was terrible, and at her speed the wind increased its chill steeply. Ahead of her Jack burst from the treeline and on to the absolute whiteness of the frozen lake. Zal's trail was a clear straight line of dark meltwater reflecting the sky, at the end of which, near the far shore, she could see his running form – a black silhouette outlined in orange fire against the glowing blue-white of the snow under the starlight. Her heart caught in her throat at the sight.

He was so fast he was almost flying. Every part of him was working as hard as it could to keep up his incredible speed, but it was slowing, and the tension that was creeping into him was so visible she could almost feel the huge burden of the pain as his body began to fail. Jack saw it too, and in reply he began to undergo a series of trans-formations, the form of his man shape dropping away into a leaping cat, then a bear, then a cloud of snow like the onrush of an avalanche that began to rip all the surrounding snow and ice into its wake. Behind him the white wolf and Madrigal peeled off rapidly to the side, in-explicably heading in the wrong direction towards the closest bank. At the same moment Zal reached the bank and stumbled. He fell heavily, somersaulting as he missed his footing, and the lake rose up behind him in one enormous wave, vast blocks of ice breaking up in its grey-black flow.

And something twisted in the water of the wave, stalling its upward rise.

As Zal tumbled over, flames dimming, and clawed his way to his feet, shapes became distinct in the turbid water, huge, unlikely shapes of things that might once have been horses but were now mutated into monstrous forms. Their bodies shone, scaled and muscular as they turned in the wave, tearing at the empty air with their long, crocodilian jaws agape, teeth like needles and as long as Lila was tall punching through the water. Their manes and tails coiled with life of their own and it was then Lila realised that this wasn't Jack in the water, it was kelpies, bringing the wave to try and throw him down into the depths where they might grasp and drag him down to drown. Jack was lost in the tumult.

Lila saw Zal reach the top of the far bank as she came directly over the lake. He stopped and turned around to look back. Halfway to shore Madrigal and the wolf leaped gamely from block to block of ice but the fury of the artificial tide was too great. The cracks became canyons. One moment they were there, the next they simply vanished into the black mass of freezing lake. Zal was shouting, though none of them save her could possibly hear him.

'Poppy! Vi'dia!' He was anguished, and then she saw why and heard the doll's singsong voice.

'Help's a cheating, takes a beating.' The soft and eerie witchlight of the Hoodoo reached up from its place in the lake with Madrigal and suffused the lake briefly, illuminating it from within so that for a moment everything seemed inverted, the ice shining below, the bodies of the kelpies flying in their element. Then it went out and with a rush the wave subsided in all directions, creating a series of gigantic ripples that went speeding towards the banks. One of these effortlessly smashed into the shallow rise where Zal stood and swept him off his feet. Lila saw him scrabbling for a hold on the frozen ground as he was sucked backwards into the heaving water. Behind him Jack's form rose effortlessly from the pristine snow. Far out in the lake the tiny shapes of the wolf and Madrigal struggled amid ice blocks that rose higher than their heads.

Beneath the surface two heavy bodies turned slowly over and over, falling silently into the depths.

Jack Giantkiller strode down to the water's edge and waded into the shallows, barging ice aside with sweeping strokes of his arms. He plunged himself down with a great energetic movement that put his shoulders under the water and came up blowing, all the water that clung to him becoming ice instantly, fracturing and breaking off in showers and sprays that glittered and smoked with cold. With two strides and heaves he dragged Zal out of the lake, keeping a hold on him by the straps of his armour at his back and swinging him around violently to throw him on to the shore. He landed about ten metres away almost silently and lay like a grey and black ragdoll in a motionless heap.

Madrigal reached them almost at the same moment Lila did, emerging from the water in the form of a thick-bellied sea-lion before standing easily on to two legs in a seamless change and running forwards, the doll brandished in her hand in front of her. Lila landed at Zal's side and bent close to him, careful not to touch him. She needed no analysis to tell her the kelpies were as dead as dead could be, faery or not.

'That fucking Hoodoo thing,' she thought, as her insides churned suddenly with an intensity of anguish she chose to show no sign of outwardly. Then she knew what her completed transformation had bought. 'Zal!' she said roughly. 'Zal!'

He didn't move. He was so small suddenly, nothing but a bundle of black, wet rags. His face was hidden against the ground in the mud that covered him. She attempted to do a distant ultrasound scan on him, to see what was wrong, but his shadow form gave no resistance to the waveforms – he was effectively invisible in that spectrum, as in most others. All she wanted to do was hold him, fix him, save him.

Jack barrelled past her and shoved her out of his way, grabbing the straps at Zal's back once more and picking him up. He shook him with terrific violence and shouted as Zal's head lolled loose on his neck, dripping sludge, 'Not gone already are you? You promised me a fight! You promised me!'

Lila seethed with rage and hate for him then. She glanced at the doll, saw its light undimmed. It didn't speak, so she reasoned Zal couldn't be dead. Surely the bloody thing would speak if the deed was done? At her ear the jewel that was the imp had nothing to say.

Jack turned to her and shook Zal again, in her direction, as if it was her fault. 'Pathetic. I expected better after so long waiting. Is this all you bring me?! Is this all? Did you think you'd better me with this cursed halfblood mutation? Me?' He stopped and cast about him as if completely confounded. 'What were you thinking, human?'

'I didn't bring you anything,' she said through clenched teeth, all her attention on Zal – he seemed not to be breathing. His arm was at an unnatural angle. 'I don't care about you or what you think you are. I don't care about any of this. He gave what you asked. Give him to me.'

'No, no, no,' the doll sang. 'Race not run. Deal not done. Thread not spun.'

She wanted to kill it, more than anything, but she knew that wish was futile. There was no sense dying here, it would do no good.

'I'll give him to you,' Jack said softly, 'when I'm done.' He threw Zal's body over his shoulder and set off towards the tall circle of stones behind them on the rise of the hill.

There was nothing for Lila to do but follow. Madrigal walked beside her, the doll back in her belt. She put it to the side farthest from Lila though that didn't stop Lila feeling its malignant enjoyment of the situation.

'It's not over,' the faery whispered. She glanced at Lila tentatively and Lila saw she meant to offer hope.

She ignored it, her eyes fixed on Jack's unreasonably fast-striding shape. At the stones the rest of the faeries were waiting, clustered around the outer edge of the ring. She had never witnessed anything more barbaric. She longed to kill them all. Inside her arm the bullets clicked and clicked in and out of the magazine. Eight shots. Not enough. In her mind's eye she made swords, whips, razors of cold iron from her arms and hands. These things could kill faeries, if you did it right. No heads, no hearts. At the same time as she felt the energy of this orgy rise through her, she knew it to be stillborn and knowledge of her complete impotence sat in her limbs and body like a smothering blanket. She welcomed them as twin couriers, the messengers who brought the news that in spite of her complete transformation she was still, in the important ways, alive, and her face stretched into a smile.

She saw Jack's wife looking at her as if she were completely mad.

At the centre of the broken circle the ground was stamped down into a slight depression like a shallow bowl. Jack strode to the middle of it and looked up at the stars, accusingly. 'Near midnight!' he called out to the gathered thousands clustered silently around, watching his every move. 'Think you this shall be my ending?' and he laughed as he lifted Zal off his shoulder and held him out before him beneath the shoulders, gave him another shake. Zal's head lifted slightly.

Lila bit her lips. She willed Zal to stay unconscious and give Jack no reason to act, to wait, to let him do his gloating spree until somehow midnight came and freed them all.

Zal looked up, squinting and blinking, his face twisted with pain. He spat in Jack's face.

Tath appeared at the edge of the circle, disgorged by the faeries there suddenly, as if he was a stone they were casting to get catch Jack's attention and distract him from whatever he was about to will into being. They pushed him hard and he tripped on a rock and staggered forwards. Despite the doll's witchlight and the faint light of the stars, it was dark and hard to see any detail but Lila saw his expression well enough – cool and calm. He murmured, 'Thank you,' all but inaudibly, and she knew that he was unaffected by the small humiliation of being brought low before an enemy by the humble rock and that the thanks was for its action in being there to stall him. She knew him so well and missed his presence so much that it silenced her. Her throat and mind both became painful.

Jack spared Tath a moment of time, long enough to sneer and laugh at him, 'Treetender, I hope your question is better than his fight.' He lifted Zal up with one colossal arm, held him high in the air for a moment and then, as they fell for the charm of the moment and his will and his drama, brought him smashing down hard on the ground with all his force.

Lila ran forwards and kicked Jack with all her strength. Her foot connected with his hip but it was like kicking snow. The force of her own move spun her round out of control so she had to whirl and twist in midair to regain her feet. Part of Jack's body exploded in a shower of white crystals, but even as he bellowed in rage and pain from the burn of her cold iron skin he was already reforming himself as if he'd never been harmed.

She crawled across the icy ground to Zal, waiting for the Hoodoo's awful light, hoping she would get there before it was too late. Around her the faeries were whispering, whispering. She managed to stretch her hand out and touch his face. He was so cold and so broken she began to cry. The longer the silence stretched, the more certain she became that he was dead. The whispering increased and then, just as it became frenzied, stopped.

'Zal,' Lila whispered, in a private world of their own, 'come back.' She smiled, willing it all to be a clever trick. Carefully she wiped the mud from his cheek. His eyes fluttered, once and then went still. He did not breathe. 'Zal,' she said. 'Zal.'

'Get away from him, girl,' Jack said.

'No,' she replied. 'Here,' she took the key from her neck and held it out. 'Take it. You've won it. I renounce it. Take it, and let us alone.' She wished this was a clever trick, but if it was its cleverness was lost on her. She didn't care.

When the necklace didn't leave, or he didn't take it, because she wasn't looking she didn't know, she simply threw it in Jack's direction. It landed in the snow at his feet. The sight that wasn't sight – the sensors in the back of her body – created an image for her of him stooping to pick it up. At the same time there was movement in the faery ranks and Malachi appeared, coming forward with a peculiar raggedy black and white fey of no particular gender who was very reluctant to approach. They seemed to be arguing, though they didn't speak but finally Malachi said gruffly, 'Try, Nix.'

'I might,' the new faery whispered, all her awareness on the massive form of Jack Giantkiller. She was shaking with fear. 'I might . . .'

Lila moved back and pulled her forwards. The last thing she wanted to do was move away but she did it, so fast. She watched Nixas stretch her hands and arms out over Zal's motionless, hollow-looking form. After what seemed an eternity she sat back on her heels, looked at Lila. Lila knew then.

'I can't do anything,' the faery said apologetically. 'He's not dead, but he soon will be. A minute, at most.'

She retreated to the safety of Malachi's side and he moved back, cowering away from Jack too. Lila didn't blame them. An energy had begun to radiate from Jack that was as ominous and dreadful as the first breath of a coming hurricane. He had picked up the key and it stayed in his hand. This had given him pause and he stared at it in wonder, half bent over.

'Take the elf,' he said, as if he'd already forgotten what had happened, his entire being focused on the key.

An eerie feeling of calm descended and everything became still, except for Lila, who was struggling with her desire to move forward and the terror that touching Zal might cause him pain, or death, though it was all she wanted to do. She brushed his hair where it met his forehead, where at least that was whole and fine. What followed she saw only because she could create images from all her senses and her entire skin was able to sense anything in light or sound because she didn't move except to lie down next to Zal and put her face beside his. It was the right place to be, there was nowhere left to fall.

'It is midnight,' Tath said, stepping forwards in Jack's direction.

Jack looked up, his face bearing a gaze that would brook no delay, 'Speak.' He couldn't wait to get back to his love affair with the key. He seemed to have no doubt that it would be only a moment before this elf was a memory too.

Around them the faery gathering began to inch away, jostling to escape the front ranks and disappear in the crowd.

'Where is your heart?' Tath asked. He stood quite relaxed, as if there was all the time in the world.

Jack looked around him, 'Is that it?'

'You seem to suffer from a disbelief problem,' Tath said. 'You heard me. That was my question. It is no doubt not the right question, but then, no question is the right question now, but it serves the purpose and so it seemed as good as any.'

Jack started to laugh, then shuddered and shook his shoulders as if trying to dislodge a crick from his neck, 'Ah!' He convulsed and shivered, and the snow form that he'd worn abruptly crumbled and fell away from him leaving him standing in his true material form, a tough but normally sized old man, with a salt and pepper beard and thinning hair. His clothes were the same rough and ready furs his wife wore, stitched by her hand. They made his already bulky, strong form seem even sturdier. He regarded Tath from his diminished height, and narrow grey-blue eyes and opened his mouth to speak but before anything could come out his body suddenly gleamed with a matrix of brilliant blue and yellow light, as if someone had cast a net of shining strands over him. Then he fell apart in pieces and bloody ruin.

Two long blades, one blue, one yellow, and two white eyes shone out of the darkness behind him. 'Old man, your kung fu is useless,' Teazle murmured. He put the swords away and shook himself free of the dark anthracite dust so that he emerged, shining, almost blinding. He stared at Madrigal and then gave her a small, theatrical little bow. 'Madam.'

'Dragon,' she said, returning the formality stiffly. Then, without appearing to move, he was on his knees beside Lila in the mud.

Tath became illuminated. Literally. A light the colour of soft spring green radiated suddenly out of him, then snapped inward like the back-draft of a serious fire. He was jolted by it, but then stood. All the faeries turned to him, with a vast sussuration of little noises that sounded like a waterfall, but were actually the sound of every faery turning one step to face a new position. Jack's blood seeped into the ground, slowly at first, then as if the ground was greedy, until it was all gone. His flesh melted and soaked away. His bones crumbled to dust with a sigh.

Without any outward signs each being present felt a change in the air, in the energy of everything that existed on that spot. A new figure stood where Jack had been. She was tall, Amazonian and heavily pregnant. She had an electromagnetic signature not unlike that of a small star, although the frequencies that would have destroyed them were matched by another kind of equal and opposite force in what Lila could only assume was the aetheric field, and so she did nothing to them.

As one everyone present averted their faces, except Teazle, who sat back on his heels, one hand on Lila's back, one hand on his own knee, and watched her curiously.

'At long last,' said the Muse gently, stroking her belly. She bent down with some effort and picked the small round of the key out of the remains of Jack's mortal body. 'What was knotted has been undone. Elf, you have ascended to the Fisher King's throne and you must keep it until a knight comes who is able to fathom your mystery. And it's okay to look at me . . .'

Tath bowed. 'The faeries are free to leave,' he said. There was a sound like snapping strings, a twanging and pinging that was almost comical, and where the vast crowd had stood in a dim huddle like a body forest lights bloomed and colours shone out. Firework explosions of glory shot upwards and sideways as the smaller fey darted into the air. The sound of the group changed from silence to babble and then uproar which quieted down eventually into a new formation that wanted to watch and see what happened though they were itching to be away.

'Miss.'

Lila realised after a minute that the woman was speaking to her. She couldn't feel a heartbeat or any breath under her hands. She couldn't feel the slightest presence of any aetheric body, although she had been imagining it so fiercely that sometimes, for seconds, she wasn't sure . . . Slowly she dragged herself upright, the demon behind her keeping his hand on her shoulder for which she was grateful.

'I will take him.'

'What are you?' Lila asked, her hands face up in her lap. She was quite relaxed now there was nothing to be done. 'Is he dead?'

'I am one of The Three, the second sister. I have a lot of names, all of which are quite wrong. You may call me Lily. I like that name. For the flower.'

'Lily, is he dead?'

'Almost. If he can be restored I will do it.'

'And if not?'

'Then he will stay with me. He is one of our favourites. We aren't supposed to have such things but of course we do.'

Lila thought about this. 'Will you send him back to me?' She felt like a pathetic little kid for asking, but she couldn't help herself.

'If I can,' the creature that was not really a woman or really a sister said. 'And if not then I will take care of what remains until the end.'

'Oh,' Lila said, wishing it sounded better than it did. 'Will you tell me what happens?'

'I will send a sign.'

There was a moment in which the lady moved forward and Lila realised she was meant to move backward and give Zal up now. 'Oh,' she said again. She turned to look at Teazle, barely recognising him in the being that was behind her. He was so very bright, and though human in form seeming even less so. He just waited and kept her gaze and she realised that he wasn't about to either withhold or give her permission or tell her what to do. He was simply with her, whatever she did. 'Oh.'

Lila looked up at the tall woman through tears so thick she could barely see, though her brain tried hard to make adjustments. 'I don't want to.' She looked down at Zal. There was almost nothing to see except a deeper shadow on the ground, black traces that showed where limbs might be. When she tried to touch him again she felt nothing at all. He was vanishing before her eyes. She got up and moved backwards, Teazle at her shoulder, his hand on her arm.

The lady stooped down, again with effort and awkwardly because of her huge belly, and laid a scarf over Zal. It fluttered, caught on his form and by the wind, showing the clear outline of him before it fell flat on the ground. Colour soaked into it like a stain – the perfect two-dimensional print of a small, curled-up elf. She picked up the scarf and folded it gently and tucked it in the bosom of her robe.

'Is that it?' Lila asked.

'Yes,' said not-Lily. 'I look forward to meeting you again, Miss. For now, however, our paths diverge. Let the final coil unfurl.' She flicked the spiral of the key upwards into the air, turning over and over like a coin. They all watched it rise. As it fell Lily was already gone. The stones turned in place. The faeries gasped and then the bottom fell out of the world and they all fell down.

CHAPTER TWENTY-ONE

Teazle had a steel grip and Lila felt it keep hold of her during the unfathomable drop that followed. She felt it even in the sleep that descended on her almost immediately and stayed over her for a long time before at last it lifted, bit by bit, without dreams, and left her on a stone floor in a dark place that was warm but without light. The demon was already awake. As she first began to move he released her arm though she felt and heard him slide one of his feet to the place where her bottom met the floor, and stay there so she didn't lose all contact.

'It's dark,' she said.

'I can see in the dark,' he murmured smugly and then her arms and legs appeared before her and her shadow appeared on the stone flags. She looked back and saw him beside her, glowing powerfully like a giant two hundred watt action figure. He grinned.

She looked around. They were in a huge hall, with statues – no, not statues, immobilised real living figures – ranged rather carelessly down both sides and into the visible distance.

'Where are we?' she asked.

'The Hall of Champions of the Light,' he said, and added, 'it says so on each of the inscriptions.'

She didn't know what to say so she didn't say anything. She felt completely empty. From the jewel at her ear the imp suddenly expanded and sat on her shoulder.

'Oh man,' he said with feeling. 'Putzes in all directions. Where's the exit?'

Lila got to her feet slowly and Teazle mirrored her, finally letting go. She felt a kind of comfort, because she was nowhere she knew, doing nothing she recognised, with no agenda. Vaguely she remembered that she had still not found anyone to deal with the moths and so she thought maybe she'd read along the lines of statues and see if anyone here looked like they could be useful. She was aware that her thoughts weren't entirely rational but ignored this notion as of no importance. The Zal-shaped wound in her required better stitching than the feeble cause and effect of reason.

She approached the nearest figure, walking quite a way, and finding it larger and bolder than she thought. It wore a medieval style suit of armour with a sword. The suspended animation which held the person fast had captured her at a moment of inquiry – something she discovered ten minutes later on the second, third and fourth statues with their odd, nearly incomprehensible faery legends written on the wall beside them. She realised it must be because it was a surprising and curious thing to be suddenly approached by a faery who spirited you away and turned you into a statue. They reminded her of the demon figurines in the market at Bathshebat.

'Are they in there?' she asked Thingamajig, peering up at the bushy-bearded face of a scholarly looking man who still had several rolls of paper stuffed under one arm and a glass in his other hand. *Bradbury Gwynn; scrivener, visionary, prophet (alleged), spiritual leader, charismatic preacher* read the inscription in careless, spidery writing that had been completed by a finger dipped in ink. *Arsehole, dipstick, rabble-rousing twithead*, read the additional inscription that had been added by a different finger dipped in something bright yellow.

'Yeah for sure,' the imp said approvingly. 'But they're not doing anything. The whole thing's frozen in a temporal spell. They don't even know they're here. This entire Hall is completely outside the normal timestream. I've never been outside it before. I wonder what timestream we are in. Must belong to another universe, which means we've dropped down the faery gravity hole and are on the brink at the other side – so this is beyond the lowest point theoretically, but not of course actually since this still counts as the faery bottoms and there are even places below it though I never imagined them might actually be in another time altogether, one which shares our aetheric dimensions . . . my word, imagine what the old scientists in Bathshebat would make of this! Bastards. Serves them right they don't know after the way they treated me!'

Teazle said nothing as this rant went on, just acted as a lightbearer for Lila as she continued perusing. Finally she had to admit that none of these looked useful. The best of them were scholars or knights or religious figures of various sorts, the worst apparently ordinary in every way. Most of them were human. Some were light elves, of the Tath variety. There were no demons, nor any other kind of creature. She grew bored and began to look for the exit, as Thingamajig had suggested.

'Which way?' She looked up and down.

The imp shrugged. They walked the way they were facing.

After an hour they spied a familiar figure and in another ten minutes they were beside Bradbury Gwynn once more.

'Are we supposed to be in here?' Lila asked, doubting it.

'Not me,' Teazle said with confidence. He reached to his shoulder and drew one of his swords, the yellow one, and chopped Bradbury Gwynn in half. The body collapsed to the floor in a splatter of blood, guts and matter and instantly they heard a screaming protest in the distance which resolved quickly into a running faery of some small, monkey-like variety, clad in ink-stained clothing and carrying a bucket of ink which was empty by the time he reached them. In his tail he held a bucket of yellow paint.

'Vandal!' screeched the monkey faery. 'How am I meant to clean this up? By Zuma's tooth, when they said everything was opening up again I didn't think it meant visitors down here. But at least you're not trying to liberate them.' It said this last with a great roll of eyes and labouring of the word liberate which indicated clearly what it thought of this idea.

'We want to leave,' Lila said.

'But you've killed him!' the monkey complained. 'Our motto, in case you didn't read the literature, is To Conserve We Trust. No? Oh very well, where do you want to go?'

'I need to find Moguskul,' Lila said, dimly remembering the name.

'Myeh,' the monkey sighed, shaking its small head. 'He's way up. I'll send you to the closest version, the Lord of the Wild Hunt – that's the one before he had a real name, not the one after. Why you want to find him is beyond me since he tends to shorten the life experience rather, but it's no less than you deserve. And, by the way, since you've brought me a donation I am forced to offer you something from the Hoard.' He snapped his fingers.

The hall was suddenly filled to the roof with an enormous pile of treasure. Gold, gems, weapons, armour, statuary – every conceivable object of value and many of dubious or no value were represented there in a vast, unruly mess. It completely buried everything in sight.

'Donation?' Lila said.

'Donation,' the monkey pointed firmly with its ink-stained finger at Thingamajig. 'One donation, one . . . whatever you want. Come on, come on, pick something.' It gestured irritably at the heap of incalculable wealth.

'Donation?' the imp said, hands on hips. 'Do-fucking-*nation*?'

'Donation,' the monkey said, narrowing its eyes and writing in the air with its finger, obviously expecting the imp to follow its scribbles.

'No way,' Thingamajig said forcefully. 'I don't even . . .' He stopped, frozen in place. 'Hey, you know,' he began to object, 'that was strictly a matter of o-pin-ee-yun there. I did not eliminate the Atlantean civilisation on Earth, as was, *only* for the sake of avoiding a global conflict of armageddive proportions, thus sparing the lives of millions of future innocents. And in my defence you really ought to see just how many nutjobs have picked up the pens of war as a result of said destruction and brought insanity and the usual stupidity of literal apprehension of strictly metaphorical and allegorical materials into play as mind control weapons of mass destruction in the aftermath, so I hardly think it fucking counts as a deed for the Light. Plus, look at all the civilisations I completely missed out on. Look at the scheming idiots YOU missed out on. Do you really think Bradbury Gwendolyn here was going to do more than burn a few witches and do some infinitesimal man-bit for keeping women chained to the sink? He hardly had the charisma required to start any kind of major movement other than the kind required to dump his bowels. On the other hand Lendienlin-li-lin-can't-say-his-fucking-name Voynassi you leave out and free to go starting the Shadow Conspiracy like he was some kind of minor Bible salesman. Am I not making a point here?'

The monkey thinned its lips and glared at him.

'Oh for Pete's sake . . . !' the imp shrieked. 'Fine, fine. What – EVAH. How long do I have to stay in this miserable shithole?'

The monkey put down the ink bucket, licked its finger and produced a small notebook from somewhere about its person. It pointed at an official-looking notice that was almost entirely obliterated by fruit stains. 'You can halve the term by performing light duties and accounts,' the monkey said. 'Or you can choose to spend it suspended.

Won't seem like a minute, relatively speaking. That's all we ever ask for, a minute of your time.'

'And eternity in an hour . . . *Fuck*!' the imp said and sighed. 'All right. But don't think I won't remember this.' It hopped off Lila's shoulder and down on to the floor in the only space not entirely crammed full of the wealth of ages. He pushed at a gold-bound book with one foot and sighed heavily again. 'Busted, I guess. Listen,' and he looked up at Lila with genuine regret and a little sheepishness. 'Never be an idealist, my dear. Our love affair has to end here. Now don't cry on me. You knew it was always comin' to this. I'll be out one day . . . course you'll be probably dead and smelted by then, although maybe I'd find a way to sneak back – anyway – doesn't matter too much. Point is here I . . .' He stumbled and coughed a little bit. 'You should pick something like the monkey says. Some nice loot here. Waste not want not or whatevah.'

Lila was sure he was trying hard not to cry. 'I want Zal.'

The imp winced.

'We haven't got any zals,' the monkey said. 'Just what you see.'

'I don't want anything,' she said dully.

The monkey rolled its eyes. 'Pick something. Anything. You have to or I can't send you on to your just deserts.'

'Is that really it?' Lila said to Thingamajig, ignoring the monkey completely.

He nodded. 'Might have been a few other things. I was something of a fundamentalist revolutionary.' He twitched and quivered. 'Please go . . . I . . . I'm starting to remember a lot and I don't want you to see me as I was . . . I think . . . please just go now. All the best. Don't let that Crow Queen screw you over when you tell her that the freakshow mage elf is still alive and kicking ass so's even major demons don't see past his tricks. She's scared of him because of some prophecy and she never could deal with fear. You know, it's been fun. Yes, fun. Take something like the monkey says.'

The pleading in his tone was much greater than anything the words said. Lila felt her heart twisting, trying to avoid the surprising ache she felt. There'd been a hundred times she'd gladly have dropkicked the imp into tomorrow.

She put her hand out and picked up the nearest object she could lift, then looked to see what she'd got: a small dagger with a ragged leather handle and a tarnished, dull blade, unmarked. It looked like it had once

271

been great, and could have been polished up nicely, but was now distinctly unspectacular. She felt no vibration on it, unlike that radiating from many of the objects around her. It was a kind of glorified dinner knife. She stuck it in the sash that went around the corseted waist of her armour.

'Hurry!' the imp said. He was looking like he was about to burst. 'Monkey, do your thing!'

The monkey snapped his fingers irritably.

'But,' Lila began, wanting to ask Thingamajig what his real name was, to see him in his true form . . . but it was too late. The last thing she heard and saw was the imp's eyes starting to widen and his finger pointing at the dagger, his mouth opening as he turned to the monkey with a burst of objection, 'Hey, you blind little fleabit banana-eater, that used to be mi—'

This time the sleep lasted a shorter time. The forest they woke up in was nothing like the previous ones. Full of cloud, its trees were more than two metres in diameter at the base, and rose straight and tall into the invisible fog almost without a single branch. Thick undergrowth dripped with water. It was warm and there was a rich buzz of insect life and the drip of millions of leaves gently shedding condensation. In the distance they could hear the muted roar of a substantial waterfall. There was also a feeling of impending dread so enormous and overpowering that Lila immediately backed into Teazle.

Shapes moved just beyond the limit of the fog. Vapour curled without any apparent change in the air. In the rushing noise that was this forest's only silence every telltale sound was hidden. The presence around them, which watched them with such an intensity they could feel it as a point on their skin, moved constantly, unpredictably; a random scatter.

Finally, Lila sat down again, where she'd begun, and stopped trying to look, or to move after it. Teazle sat behind her. She sat in the play-dead state of every animal that feels itself stalked without hope of escape. Only one thought dogged Lila now – what if she couldn't talk to it? And almost immediately she said,

'I need to make a bargain with you.'

The flittering movement slowed down and at the same instant she felt the odd sensation of something metal touching her throat. She put her hand up automatically and there was the silver spiral, slightly wet with dew, its cord fastened securely around her neck.

Teazle's breath moved against her skin as he bent closer to look.

'In my world the Mothkin are a plague. They say you can bring them back to Faery.'

She had come rather of a mind that she would offer this creature a fight – whoever wins gets their wish. She wanted to fight something and it seemed like a good idea. Now she knew there could be no fight with something that was as immaterial as this. She felt robbed, cheated. Because the key was there she said, 'I'll let you out.' It was her only possible offer, but a release to travel through Faery had already come. She had to do better.

She didn't know if this thing wanted to be let out or if that even made sense.

'For a year and a day,' she said, the words coming to her mind in a sudden burst. She wished it were her inspiration but she knew it wasn't so. The symbols on her armour fizzed, like champagne. It was because of that borrowed magic. 'You can roam Otopia for a year and a day and you have to take me back there too.' She held up the key as far as it would reach. The moving thing stopped entirely. It was slightly to her left and low down, just beyond the veil of the fog. She moved the key to that position. 'If you clear up the moths straight away, all of them.'

She felt a tap on her side, at her waist, quick as thought itself. Too late her hand moved to the spot where the pocket was, the flimsy pocket that had held Madame's Eye. The eye was gone.

'I'm not a spy,' she said. 'I just want to go home. The monkey from the Hall sent me here when I asked to see . . . Moguskul.'

Another tap and the eye was back. She saw nothing at all, felt nothing, heard nothing. She was watched intently by an unblinking thing. Then came a rustle of leaves, very close.

Teazle was gone.

Then he was back.

'Uff,' he said, rather haughtily and sighed. When Lila stared at him wildly he shook his head. Don't Know and No Chance, said his gaze.

She felt hot breath on her face, from the side, so close that whatever breathed it was able just to brush the tips of her hair but when she looked it had gone.

They were studied this way for some time. At one point there was a tap on the key but it didn't go anywhere. A tiny piece of the skirt of her armour went missing. Just after that she heard something like a pleased hum but it lasted only a split second.

Then, 'Tat tat tat,' said a voice from the fog, moving with the gaze that touched them with the power of an invisible sun. It was an inhuman voice, made up of the sounds of nature around them shaped by a mouth. 'Tat tat tatter. Yes.'

She woke up on the beach. The sun was going down. It was afternoon. People were out on the shoreline, but they were far from her and she was concealed by the rise of low dunes and the start of the grasses. She was alone, and deeply uncomfortable. She rolled and the dagger stopped digging into her. In the sand before her lay the silver spiral of the necklace and the burnt remnants of its cord. Her neck hurt.

She got into a sitting position and saw that the black leather look had gone. Quite human skin was left in its place, the same off-white cream that she'd always been naturally, with the light tea-coloured tan of her childhood set over it, temporarily browning her as if she'd had all summer in the sun. The armour was also changed, its skirts lengthened into a dress. She had bare feet. This of all she stared at a long time before reaching down to touch her toes in wonder. Her toes. She had never had toes since she'd had the prosthetics fitted. They'd always been boots with, she'd assumed, the illusion of feet inside them. Her own softness was overwhelming. She felt like a crab without its shell and horribly vulnerable, although when she dug her toes through the sand it was a heavenly feeling, so real, so familiar.

A dog came running up to her, surrounding her suddenly with panting and snuffling and licks. She pushed it away, shielding her face for a minute and then got a good look at its rangy wolfhound form and absolutely white thick fur, its blue-white husky eyes. 'Teazle?'

Teazle barked and panted at her, his blue tongue lolling. He seemed anxious. She expected him to change form and speak to her but he didn't. She stroked his head and scratched his ruff and then got to her feet. She signalled the world tree, seeking to make connections with the Agency server.

An alert ran through her, prompting her to pause. Once these things would all have been readouts, interfaces that kept a clear line between her and the machines. Now there was only what she knew, what she felt, nothing more. Her login effort had been rejected and classified as an intrusion attempt. For a minute she stood there, staring at the ocean, unable to figure out what might have caused it until she realised it was possible the Agency had changed while she was gone, unlikely as that seemed, and maybe something had happened to cause her to be seen as hostile or at least unwelcome. No, unwelcome agents were liabilities and liabilities weren't something left to run around. There was no way to find out now.

Teazle whined unhappily and ran in a small circle.

She knew that they'd be sending agents to locate her. Imagining meeting them, what they might say or do, felt very bad to her. The dress ruffled against her legs as if in the breeze, though the breeze was blowing the other way.

She began walking, quickly, making her way past the familiar shape of the headland towards home. Anxiety began to creep through her emotional numbness. She moved faster, starting to jog. Teazle trotted at her side.

As she came to the more common areas of the beach she noticed the houses had changed their frontages, glass replacing a lot of old wood, and new fresh-looking timbers creating arches and circles where rectangles used to be. A rash of circular, elf-style doors were every-where, and the fences that used to stand, bent or upright, to mark property lines and footpaths had been removed. She passed a couple walking who gave her the smile you give to an eccentric woman run-ning along the beach barefoot in an evening dress with a large dog at her side. She didn't care but their own clothes looked strange to her; too short, too long, odd colours.

She reached the road and stopped dead. All the cars were soft, bubble-shaped lozenges of bright colour, the people inside visible through big shaded windows reading, watching, staring, none of them driving. Strangest of all, they glided in silence. The gulls overhead were the loudest thing nearby. She looked more closely and didn't recognise half the homes in sight, though they stood on the same plots as before, and her path took the same course it had when she was a child. She began to run. She saw the house at last and felt a surge of relief that it was still there, still the same, but then she noticed as she got closer that it had somehow become terribly dilapidated. Paint peeled off its boards and the windows were all different, the glass curiously matted. And there, on the back porch where the dogs should be a stranger was sitting.

Lila slowed down and took a longer route, concealing herself behind bits of shrub. She stopped dead on the corner, staring at the tree that was between her and her own driveway. It was huge, tall enough to shade right across the street, its canopy broad and majestic. She remembered it being almost invisible, tied to a stake in a little earth plot of its own. The neighbour used to water it every day. Now it was rucking the pavement with its roots.

She walked around it and up the path, seeing change everywhere, not wanting to know what it meant, though she already did.

She knocked on the new, half-round door.

It was answered by the person she had seen on the porch. She recognised the face of one of Malachi's friends, a cookery and house-bound domestic brownie, whose name she'd forgotten.

'Hello, Tatty dear. He said you'd come back one day,' the faery said, stepping back to let Lila in.

Lila stared at her gentle old lady form, the unassuming way she led through the old house, up to Lila's bedroom and showed her in.

Nothing had been moved since she left – no, it had, because it was spotless, but otherwise no different. The imprint where she last lay on her old futon was still there. She turned around, her sense of unreality peaking. 'Where am I?'

'You're home,' the faery said kindly, patting her arm. 'Shall I make you something to eat?'

Lila looked at her, completely bewildered, 'But everything's changed.'

The faery glanced down modestly. 'Yes, of course. It's been a while since you've been gone. We looked after everything as best we could . . .'

Lila shook her head, but nothing changed. 'I'm sorry. How long? Where's Max?'

The old brownie bit her lip and met Lila's gaze with difficulty, her glamour starting to flicker so that the much smaller, rounder little sprite was visible under the human guise. 'My dear, you ought to sit down perhaps?'

'I've been gone two days, tops,' Lila said coldly. 'Now where the hell am I?' She felt Teazle press against her leg, solid and warm. He pushed his nose into her hand.

'Fifty years have passed,' the faery said gently. 'The Hunter came as you asked, a few days after you had gone, and he took the moths away. His play here was brief, a year of strangeness, no more . . . Since then . . . other things have come and gone, but look, you ought to rest before . . .'

Lila started from her awful conclusions, with the sudden feeling of being watched, like arrows pointing at her back. Some kind of waves were being used to detect her presence in the house. 'They're coming!'

'Who, dear?'

Lila's conviction was stronger than anything she was used to feeling from herself. She heard the door break downstairs. The faery jumped with fear and cowered back against the wall.

'Ah. I forgot they might detect you so soon. They will have been watching. They fear your return. Malachi thought he might outwit them but he has been slower of late. Forgive me. Run,' she whispered to Lila. 'It's your best hope.' Then she vanished into thin air and all trace of her was gone.

Heavy footsteps came thundering up the stairs. Lila watched the door, cold and tired.

'Hell I will,' she said quietly, bending to her unzipped ammo bag. She was about to eject the cold iron rounds and equip herself with new magazines when an electromagnetic pulse struck her, its frequencies jabbering around and effectively slowing her down so much that she was unable to move. Her sight dimmed and blacked out. Her hearing faded. Slowly her nerves deadened until she was trapped in silence.

They crashed through the door and window at the same instant, timed as perfectly as only machines could be, confident in their plan and abilities, and stopped, confounded by the sight of a young woman in a fancy dress, alone, and her pet dog.

Lila's perception was grainy and vague, her ability to move minimal.

Words came through to her as through a great distance.

'Aetheric . . . suppressor . . . backup . . .'

She knew they were going to shoot Teazle, that they intended to take her prisoner. Her armour told her. There was a struggle. Teazle transformed. Shots were fired. One of them would have hit her but the armour stopped the shot when the bullet touched it through some action like a sleight of hand, palming its velocity and turning it through one hundred and eighty degrees. The bullet returned to the gun and smashed it out of the hand of the holder. At this point whatever machine they were using to stun her was disabled and full awareness returned.

She saw Teazle, bleeding heavily, fighting with both swords against a tall, humanoid machine whose speed and power exceeded his own. It looked like a perfect android, black as she'd been, and seamless. It had no hair and its features were simplified. It had shot the demon several times, even though it was now missing an arm.

The second attacker was female but otherwise the same as the android. She was struggling to recover some object from the floor using just the one hand she had left. Lila emptied her magazine on it and cut off both its arms with solid cold-iron shot. She saw the severed limbs begin to slowly reconfigure themselves into different objects as they lay on the floor – and then saw the thing they'd been trying to grab: a highly altered but recognisable controller set. Lila bent first and picked this up, delivering a fatal shot of EMP right back at it through her hand.

The armless woman attempted to round-kick her as she did this, and once again the armour reversed the impact sending her spinning away. 'Stop!' said the woman, loud and persuasive but with the eternal calmness of a true machine. 'We mean you no harm. You are in danger . . .'

Two more of them suddenly appeared at the window. They climbed in, spiderlike, and aimed their guns at her. These were different. They were all different models, but shared the common black machine aspect Lila knew as well as her own skin.

'Convincing,' she said. The bag of ammo was now closer to them than her. One of them pulled it out of the way and heaved it out of the window. They closed on her. She heard Teazle's blades carve through something with a keening whine and two heavy thuds made the floorboards shake.

'Terminate the demon,' said one of the faceless figures, keeping its twin guns aimed at her head. The other three moved to obey.

Lila could hear Teazle's pained breathing.

They pointed another of the controller pads at her.

She saw Teazle, bracing himself against the wall, his swords lifting too slowly. He was very badly injured. His eyes blazed red, weakening as they coloured.

Rage filled her that she was going to lose him too. She wanted to slay them all and found the dagger in her hand, swinging it at the swift shape moving past her with its guns arming to finish Teazle. The desire to kill consumed her completely, their deaths all that mattered to her.

She wouldn't have cared if she'd died there too, as long as they didn't take Teazle with them.

The dagger cut the android in two, but before the halves of it could go anywhere they were sucked into the blade itself, vanishing. It did the same with the others, in one single sweep, cutting and consuming, and then she was left standing alone in the room. Teazle sliding down the wall with exhaustion, both of them looking at the huge, two-handed sword she was holding in her one, delicate hand.

It was massive, almost taller than she was. The blade was curved, complicated. It had a grey matte surface the colour of graphite. It weighed almost nothing to move around, but this was only because her hand had become the fulcrum of an impossible balance, around which the sword and grip moved in perfect equilibrium. Its actual weight was supported in an altogether different universe. On the flat of the blade no trace remained of any of the creatures, or people, or whatever they were who had come to apprehend her. From the palm of her hand she felt the distinct presence of an *andalune* body, like an elf's.

'It's alive,' she said. Then she tried to let go of it, so she could drop down and look after Teazle, but instead of allowing her to let it go the sword became the dull old dagger in her hand. She put it in the dress's belt and got to her knees without waiting to see more. Teazle's swords, still glowing, were next to him. His usually bright eyes were almost closed. Under him lay two more of the smashed controller units and a lot of blood. Explosive rounds had made a mess of him.

'Tease,' she whispered to him, trying to look at his wounds. 'Don't sleep.'

'That imp,' Teazle murmured, struggling to move so that she could apply some of the medical supplies she was unpacking. 'Said it was his. Do you know what it is?' He sounded like he did.

'No, what? Some faery sword?' Lila was concentrating on stopping the blood flowing out of him like water, and wondering how she was going to perform some fast and necessary surgery in time to get them safely out of there. 'Trust them to trick me.'

'It's an artefact,' Teazle said, gasping in pain as she moved him about and injected him with various needles. She took some old clothes out of a drawer and tore them up, using them to staunch some of the bleeding and spraying them with something that stank before wiping him quickly. He recognised the procedures of basic sterilisation.

'And what's that?' She made scalpels and retractors out of her fingers, spat anaesthesia into his open body, cut, picked clean, began to stitch. She was so fast she moved like a hummingbird. He wanted to tell her that with her ragged black and red hair, her strangely blue eyes, her girlish figure in its dress, that she looked just like a faery. It was peculiar to see all the technology she was made up of rise and fall out of that delicious-looking figure. But he didn't have the energy to say it.

'It's an aspect of god.' He knew the answer would make her shake her head and it did. He wanted to laugh but it was too painful to move. 'The weapon of Intent. It has no form of its own. There's only one. And you've got it.'

'Don't be stupid.' She finished stitching. The fine metals of her hands moved into strong, soft fingers and palms that checked him with some kind of sonics. She too was caught by their appearance, looking at them as if they didn't belong to her, and abruptly they changed back to black until she looked as she had before, just her torso the old human form of the Lila he knew; leather biker girl in somebody's prom gown.

'More like it,' she muttered, putting her arm under his shoulders and lifting him to his feet. 'You can walk?'

'Yes.'

She leant him on the wall while she picked up his swords and slid them back in their baldrics on his back. They paused in the hall to get hats and coats to conceal themselves better.

There were quite a lot of neighbours gathered in the street to see what all the shooting had been about. To her surprise they parted to let Lila pass, Teazle staggering as he leaned on her, his white hair peeking out from the brim of his oversize stetson and over the collar of his coat where the two sword hilts stuck out awkwardly. The scarf over the lower half of his face hid him. Even so, nobody gave them much of a glance.

'Mal will find us,' she said, passing the people without looking at them. They kept staring at the house.

She didn't know exactly where she was going. There was no car parked in her driveway. Downtown, she was sure, there'd be somewhere to go, even if they had no money, no connections, no anything. She'd find something, and meanwhile the larger number of people would help prevent an ambush assault like the one they'd just survived, so she hoped.

'Should we call the police?' she heard someone ask another as she passed. Their accents were strange.

In the background someone was sobbing hysterically, 'Rogues! They were rogues! I saw them, right here in the street. They went in that house . . .'

Lila kept her head down and kept walking away.